# PRAISE FOR
# THE HAUNTED YARN SHOP MYSTERIES

### *Spinning in Her Grave*

"MacRae does a superb job of coordinating her amateur sleuth ensemble cast . . . set in Tennessee. Snappy repartee and genuine warmth are both conducive to the best sort of cozy." — *Library Journal*

"A fun series and the latest book is a fantastic whodunit." — Cozy Mystery Book Reviews

"The mystery pleases with its plot and character development." — *Romantic Times*

### *Dyeing Wishes*

"A light paranormal cozy that will draw readers in with its small-town charm and hidden secrets." — Debbie's Book Bag

"[An] enjoyable mystery . . . filled with a cast of charming characters." — Lesa's Book Critiques

"[This] series is one that I've fast learned to enjoy for its cast of characters, its humor, and its primary setting of a yarn shop. . . . Oh, how MacRae's characters shine!" — Kittling: Books

"Molly MacRae writes with a wry wit." — MyShelf.com

*continued . . .*

"MacRae has the perfect setting and a wonderful cast for her new series . . . good setting, good characters, good food . . . and fiber and fabric, too. *Last Wool and Testament* is a wonderful beginning to a new series."

—Kittling: Books

## PRAISE FOR OTHER
## MYSTERIES BY MOLLY MᴀᴄRAE

"MacRae writes with familiarity, wit, and charm."

—*Alfred Hitchcock Mystery Magazine*

"An intriguing debut that holds the reader's interest from start to finish."

—*Kirkus Reviews*

"Witty . . . keeps the reader guessing."

—*Publishers Weekly*

"Engaging characters, fine local color, and good writing make *Wilder Rumors* a winner."

—Bill Crider, author of the
Sheriff Dan Rhodes Mysteries

"Murder with a dose of drollery . . . entertaining and suspenseful."

—*The Boston Globe*

Also by Molly MacRae

# PLAGUED BY QUILT

### A HAUNTED YARN SHOP MYSTERY

## Molly MacRae

AN OBSIDIAN MYSTERY

OBSIDIAN
Published by the Penguin Group
Penguin Group (USA) LLC, 375 Hudson Street,
New York, New York 10014

USA | Canada | UK | Ireland | Australia | New Zealand | India | South Africa | China
penguin.com
A Penguin Random House Company

First published by Obsidian, an imprint of New American Library,
a division of Penguin Group (USA) LLC

First Printing, November 2014

ISBN 978-0-451-47130-7

Printed in the United States of America
10  9  8  7  6  5  4  3  2  1

# ACKNOWLEDGMENTS

For tips on excavating nineteenth-century garbage dumps, thank you, Kristin Hedman and Sarah Wisseman. Any mistakes in technique, terminology, or condition of materials recovered are mine. For sharp ears and eyes and valuable editing pencils, thank you, Janice Harrington, Betsy Hearne, David Ingram, and again, Sarah Wisseman. Thank you to Libit Woodington for introducing me to fat quarters. For another charming pattern, thank you, Kate Winkler. For this opportunity, thank you, Cynthia Manson and Sandy Harding. More than anything, as always, thank you, Mike, Ross, Gordon, and Milka.

# Chapter 1

"**B**ut where will we find the *real* story? Where will we find the *dirt*? Where . . ." The end of Phillip Bell's question disappeared as he paced the stage in the small auditorium at the Holston Homeplace Living History Farm, hands behind his back. The two dozen high school students in the audience tracked his movements like metronomes. I watched from the door, where I could see their faces.

Phillip, who couldn't have been ten years older than the youngest student, screwed his face into a puzzle of concentration as he continued pacing. He brought one hand from behind his back to stroke the neat line of beard along his chin. If he hadn't been dressed in a mid-nineteenth-century farmer's heavy brogues, brown cotton trousers, linen shirt, and wide-brimmed felt hat, he would have looked like a freshly minted junior professor. The students' reactions to him were as entertaining as Phillip himself.

Without warning, Phillip jerked to a stop, swiveled to face the students, and flung his arms wide. *"Where?"* he asked. "Where are the *bodies* buried?"

Startled, the teens in the front row jumped back in their seats. The boy nearest me recovered first. He slouched down again, stretching his long legs out so his feet rested against the edge of the stage. He smirked at his neighbor, then turned the smirk to Phillip.

"In the cemet—" the boy started to say.

Phillip flicked the answer away. "No, no, no. Not the cemetery. Boring places. Completely predictable."

"Unlike Phillip Bell," a woman's voice said behind my left ear. "Full of himself, isn't he? What a showman."

I glanced over my shoulder to smile at Nadine Solberg. She'd crossed the carpeted hall from her office without my noticing. She didn't return my smile. She was watching Phillip as raptly as the students and gave no indication that she expected an answer to her comment. I turned back to watch, too.

"No," Phillip said to the students, "there's someplace better than cemeteries. That's besides the fact that no living Holston—or anyone else—is going to let us dig up his sainted Uncle Bob Holston or Aunt Millie Holston from the family plot. And you can bet *that* is chiseled in stone. Not chiseled on a gravestone, though." The students laughed until they realized Phillip wasn't laughing with them. When their laughter died, he turned and stared at the boy who'd brought up cemeteries. "You aren't a Holston, are you?"

The boy started to open his mouth, then opted for a head shake. Under Phillip's continued stare, the long legs retracted and the boy dropped his gaze to the open notebook in his lap.

Phillip looked around the room. "Are any of you Holstons? Last name? Unfortunate first name? Anyone with a suspicious *H* for a middle initial?"

Students shook their heads, looked at one another.

"Just as well," Phillip said. "The Holston clan might

not like what I'm about to tell you. Have you got your
pencils ready? Take this down. Two words. Two beautiful
words describing some of the most interesting places on
earth. Some of my favorite places. Much less predictable
than cemeteries." He turned a pitying look on the for-
merly smirking boy. "And that makes them so much *better* than cemeteries. Where are we going to find the *real*
stories? Two words. 'Garbage dump.' Yes sir, I love a
good old garbage dump. 'Old' being the operative word."

"Will your ladies and a crazy quilt be able to compete
with Phillip and his garbage dump?" Nadine asked in my
ear.

"I think we can hold our own, although 'crazy' might
be the operative word in our case. Is Phillip always 'on'
like this?" We watched as he described the contents of a
nineteenth-century household dump in loving detail.

"You should have seen him when he interviewed for
the assistant director position," Nadine said. "He wore a
purple frock coat. He looked like the Gene Wilder version of Willy Wonka, and he gave the search committee
a tour of the Homeplace like they'd never heard before.
As I said, quite the showman."

"And it worked. You hired him."

"Yes, I did."

There was something in her voice that made me turn
my back on Phillip Bell's theatrics and look at her more
closely. What I saw was the usual impeccable Nadine
Solberg, director of the state-owned historic farm—a site
people in Blue Plum liked to describe as Colonial Wil-
liamsburg on a personal scale, ignoring the fact that it
was a nineteenth-century farm instead of an eighteenth-
century town. *Slim, silver, successful, and sixty*, is how my
friend Ardis Buchanan described Nadine. *Sparkling*

would usually suit Nadine, too, but the sparkle was missing today.

"How's he working out?" I asked. "Are you happy with him?"

"*I* am," she said. "He's only been here six weeks, though, and the Holston jury is still out."

"Ah."

Nadine's unease was easy to understand. She was new at the site, too, though not as new as Phillip. She'd been the state's solution—plucked from a position with the Historical Commission in Nashville and dropped into this job in tiny Blue Plum—when the former director had resigned without notice four months earlier. Not only had Nadine taken over without benefit of a transition period, but she'd inherited a search already in progress for the site's first full-time professionally qualified assistant director. It was a search fueled by private money raised by well-heeled Holstons from Houston, Texas, who knew how to make things happen.

"They've been miracle workers," Nadine said. "They're kind and generous people."

"But that generosity comes with hidden costs?" I asked, thinking of the strings a powerful family might attach to the money they donated.

"You will never hear those words from my lips," she said.

"Ms. Solberg?" Phillip called. "Ms. Rutledge? Coming on the tour?"

Nadine stepped past me into the room. "Unfortunately for me, there's a meeting I can't miss. But I'll see you all back here in an hour or so. We'll have snacks and cold drinks in the education room, and then we'll get down to the nitty-gritty of Hands on History." She paused. "Unless by then you've buried yourselves in Mr. Bell's garbage dump and can't pull yourselves out."

The students laughed. Phillip didn't ask again if I planned to join the tour and didn't wait to see if I tagged along. Without looking back, he led the students out the door on the opposite side of the room. I turned to Nadine, but she'd already disappeared across the hall into her office and shut that door. I turned back to the auditorium in time to see the door closing there, too.

"Yes, thank you," I said, feeling grumpy, "I'd love to take your tour."

"That's not what I was going to ask you," a voice said from the stage. "But I'll be happy to show you around if you want."

I looked and saw a young woman standing in the middle of the stage, hands in the back pockets of her jeans, short dark hair pushed behind her ears.

"Are you one of the students with . . ." I pointed to the door Phillip and the students had gone through. But the room had been empty. I'd watched them leave.

"I'm a volunteer," the woman said. "You're Kath Rutledge, aren't you? I recognize you from your shop. I've been in a few times. I love the Weaver's Cat." She looked down at the front of her T-shirt. "And I forgot my name badge again. I'm Grace Estes."

"Where did you just come from?" I asked, ignoring her pleasant greeting and proving to myself, once again, how graceless my manners could be when something puzzled me.

Grace didn't seem to mind. She looked over her shoulder at the wall behind the stage, hands still in her back pockets. I followed her gaze. Of course. There was a discreet door in the wall for back-of-stage entrances and exits.

"The education room's through there," she said. "I was setting out the refreshments."

She hopped off the stage, and I made my way along a row of seats to meet her at the side door.

"Someday," she said, "if Nadine gets money for renovations, it would be great to bump this wall out, add seats, and improve the traffic flow in here." She grinned. "Do I sound like I'm doing a building usability study?"

"Are you?"

"Practicing, anyway. I took a class in building and design for historic sites last semester and I'm still psyched. Were you serious about taking a tour?"

"Believe it or not, I've never taken the official tour."

"Come on, then. We'll catch up with Phil."

She opened the door and we started through at the same time, shoulders and hips colliding. I reached out to steady her. Grace laughed, then caught at my elbow when she heard my sharp intake of breath.

"I'm so sorry," she said. "Are you okay?"

"Fine." I put a few steps between us. And tried to ignore the feeling of her shirtsleeve on my fingertips. Only a spark of emotion had passed through me—Longing? Loss? A stab of love and pain—it had been enough to startle me, not enough to make me stagger. Not enough to look her in the eye and know more about her than I should. I still didn't understand these occasional odd flashes. How was it possible that I could brush up against someone else's emotional state merely by brushing against a fabric they wore? I didn't like it, and I didn't know why it had been happening since Granny died and I'd moved here to run the Weaver's Cat—her shop that was now mine. It was crazy. *No*, not crazy; I was no crazier than Granny had been. And even if I didn't like the flashes, maybe I was getting used to them.

Grace still looked concerned.

"Really, I'm fine." I held out my hand and made myself smile. "It's nice to meet you, too, by the way."

Up close it was easy to see she was closer in age to Phillip than one of the high school students I'd mistaken her for. Her warm smile and the hands slipping into her back pockets again made her look confident and comfortable. I liked her. I liked the humor in her eyes.

We followed a brick path across an expanse of lawn toward the site's dozen or so historic buildings. The two-story antebellum clapboard house—the centerpiece of the Homeplace—sat on a rise to our left. I spotted Phillip and the students straight ahead of us, leaving the log corncrib and heading for the barn.

"So you're studying site management?"

"On again, off again," she said. "Small problem with cash flow, but I'll get there eventually."

"Stick with it. Of course, the cash-flow problems will stick with you, too, if you stay with the public-servant side of sites and preservation."

"Oh yeah," she said. "I've got firsthand experience with that. I worked part-time for a couple of years at a site in West Virginia. So, yeah, I've been there, but it's what I love, so I plan to keep doing it."

"Good. That's what it takes. Were you really looking for me earlier? You said you were going to ask me something."

"When I put the program handbooks together, I saw that you're talking about signature quilts."

"Signature quilts and crazy quilts. We'll work with the

students to piece a quilt combining both forms, although I don't know how far we'll get in two weeks." When Nadine had described her plans for Hands on History, an enrichment program for high school students, I'd told her it sounded ambitious but exciting. Then, when she'd asked me to be one of the volunteer instructors, and told me I could introduce the kids to nineteenth-century textiles—my professional area of expertise—I could hardly say no.

"I'd like to sit in on the quilt discussion, if you don't mind," Grace said. "Or if you have room for extra hands, I'll be happy to help with the quilting. I've done a few small pieces of my own. Nothing fancy, but if nothing else, I can thread a needle."

I laughed. "And that's not always a given. Sure, if you have the time, TGIF will be happy to have you."

"Teaching who?"

"Sorry. T-G-I-F—Thank Goodness It's Fiber. It's the needlework group that meets at the Weaver's Cat. Some of the members are quilters, and they're going to do most of the work with the students on the quilt. I'm just giving the kids historical background."

"Oh, right. *Just*," Grace said. "Nadine told me about your background in textiles and museums. It's very cool. Did you consider applying for the assistant director job here? I know you still get your hands on fibers and textiles at the Weaver's Cat, but they aren't historic. They don't have the *stories*."

"The timing wasn't really right."

Grace shook her head, maybe thinking I lacked drive or ambition. I could have told her about the personal and professional pain of losing my dream job at the Illinois State Museum because of massive state budget cuts.

But there wasn't time to tell that sad story—what I'd come to think of as my professional yarn—before we caught up to the tour. I didn't feel the need to justify my professional and personal decisions on such short acquaintance, anyway.

"I'll tell you what," she said. "You're a heck of a lot more unassuming than Phil's ever been. As soon as he saw the position posted, he *owned* it."

"How long have you known him?"

"You could say I've been there and done that, too. He's my ex-husband. Look, he sees me. See the look on his face? Now watch this." She waved her whole arm and called over to him. "Hey, Phil! Honey, I've got a straggler for your tour." She nudged me again with her elbow. "He hates that I'm volunteering here," she said, with a wicked chuckle. "And he hates being called Phil. See you later. Have fun."

# Chapter 2

"Limbs lost and battles won are of no particular consequence to Ms. Rutledge," Phillip said when I caught up with the group at the barn. "A textile conservator doesn't need to know that Carter Holston, patriarch of the esteemed family, fought in the Battle of Kings Mountain and left his left arm behind."

The students hung on Phillip's every macabre word. He sounded scolding, but then he raised his hat and smiled, and I decided his tone wasn't personal. It might be a lingering effect of seeing Grace.

"It's nice to have you with us, Ms. Rutledge." To the students, he said, "Don't let her mild manner fool you. Ms. Rutledge is a highly skilled professional when it comes to matters of life and death."

The teens turned to look at me, and I did my best to appear more impressive than the average, short, thirty-nine-year-old woman.

"That's the life and death of carpet beetles, clothes moths, and various fungi," Phillip explained. "But pest and mold control isn't a trivial issue for historic sites and museums. Ms. Rutledge will introduce you to quilting during Hands on History and, because you're very lucky, she'll let you in on the secrets of linen production."

"Which will introduce you to the smell of retting flax," I said. "That's something you'll never forget and kind of goes along with Mr. Bell's garbage-dump theme."

"Rancid and rotting," Phillip said. "Excellent. All right, time's wasting. Next stop *is* the garbage dump. We'll take a shortcut through the barn and stop to meet our heritage breed livestock."

The students crowded after Phillip, except for a tall, thin boy I recognized as the smirker who'd mentioned cemeteries. He'd stayed behind, looking toward the mountain ridges to our east. He wasn't wearing one of the lanyard name tags the students had been given, but the end of a lanyard stuck out of his pocket.

"I love that blue in the mountains," I said, "and the way it deepens with each receding ridge."

"I love the way this town recedes in my rearview mirror every chance I get." He kicked at a pinecone and trailed the group into the barn.

I followed, wondering about Nadine's assurance that the teens in Hands on History were avid, eager over-achievers looking forward to working alongside professionals. Maybe this guy was having a bad day. Or maybe an overeager parent had applied to the program for him. He did join the group, though, gathered around Phillip in the barn.

"Mules have a long and glorious history in Tennessee agriculture," Phillip said. "This is Alice." Alice pressed her long nose into Phillip's hand. "And Fred is standing over there in the corner with his back to us. He's jealous."

"What's the pig's name?" a sandy-haired boy at the front asked.

"The pig is a sow." Phillip shifted his attention and

ours to the pen where a large black pig suckled her piglets. "This is Portia. She's an elegant example of a Poland China, an American breed dating back possibly as far as 1816. The exact date is disputed and isn't important. More important is understanding that 'facts' sometimes change, and . . ." Phillip paused, and it was interesting to see that the students turned from watching the captivating pigs to look at him. "And more on facts later." He smiled, pleased with either the students' attention or his own magnetism. "And for a treat, if you come back during our fall harvest festival, you can have a portion of Portia's piglets. They'll be a good size then and delicious when roasted with sage and apples." There were a few gasps and a few squeals. "The Holstons living here in the 1850s didn't keep pigs as pets," Phillip said, "and neither do we. Shall we move on?"

The tall, thin boy lagged behind the others again, stopping at the barn door. I stopped beside him.

"Now you know the mules' names, the pig's name, and my name," I said, "but I still don't know yours."

With a toothy, insincere smile, he made a show of pulling the lanyard out of his pocket and dropping it around his neck.

I liked him for that smile. "Zach Aikens. Nice to meet you. Shall we join the others?"

Without so much as a grunt, he slouched after them.

Phillip was crouched, talking to a man who was standing chest deep in one of four squares laid out for excavation. Presumably this was the archaeologist Nadine had recruited for the garbage pit project. He would have been more obvious in an Indiana Jones-ish hat, but the hat he did wear looked well worn and often washed. Judging from the smear of dirt down his nose and the elbows of his shirt planted in the dirt at the edge of the square as he talked to Phillip, he was wise to go with washable. He didn't appear to feel at a disadvantage carrying on a conversation while standing in a hole up to his armpits.

To my textile-loving eyes, the symmetrical and crisply defined excavation squares looked like quilt blocks. They measured a good six feet by six feet each, and they were laid out to make a larger grid of two and two. The squares were separated from one another by a yard or so of untouched grass and soil—like borders of quilt sashing—and the squares' sides were outlined by wooden stakes at their corners with string wrapped around the stakes and pulled taut between them. One square—behind the currently occupied square—hadn't been dug yet; it was nothing more than an outline of stakes and string in the grass. The next square over had been stripped of sod, and the fourth square was dug evenly to a depth of about a foot and a half.

"I kind of thought it would smell," a boy said.

"Up to our waists in waste?" the man in the pit said. "Sometimes it works out that way. But you find that more often if you go rooting through a Dumpster or your neighbor's trash bags. Do you know what that field of study is called?"

"That's a study?" the student asked.

"It's garbology, dude," Zach said. "It's cool."

"A golden garbage bag to the dude on the end," the archaeologist said. "Nice job. So, what we have here, by contrast, is a good clean site." He stood up straight, spread his arms, and inhaled slowly and deeply through his nose, closing his eyes and expanding his chest. When he exhaled, he opened his eyes, the satisfied look of a connoisseur of soils on his face.

"Yup," he said, "a clean site. We do have a layer of clay over the original dump that's acted as a seal, of sorts, over what lies below. The clay might have been put down for that purpose when they quit using the dump. But it's been an imperfect seal, and we get a lot of precipitation in east Tennessee, and water takes a toll on organic matter. That means most of what you're going to find when you dig will be inorganic—ceramics, glass, metal. I'll show you examples, but first I want you to watch something very important. This is not optional."

He bent over, disappearing from view, and reappeared with a ladder that he leaned against the edge of the pit.

"When I climb out of this hole that I've dug myself into," he said, "I'm not going to do it by showing off my arm strength." He flexed an impressive set of biceps. "I'm not going to boost myself out of here like I'm in a swimming pool. I'm also not going to scramble up the wall by digging in with my fingers and knees and toes. I want to preserve the profile of each side in every square. And you do, too, as long as you're here digging for me. Has everyone got that?"

The students nodded. Despite the fact that I wasn't part of his new crew, I nodded, too.

"Climbing out of excavation pits is the whole reason ladders were invented," he said. He climbed out and used his hat to beat the worst of the dirt from the knees of his jeans. When he straightened to his full height, it was immediately clear that if he'd been chest deep in the hole, the hole was deeper than I'd thought. The students nearest him stepped back.

"Come on over here." He put his hat back on, tugging it low on his forehead, and headed toward the barn. Several long folding tables were set up against the wall, in the shade.

I fell in beside Phillip, walking behind the students. "That's an impressive amount of digging you guys have already done."

"Not me," Phillip said. "Hicks and a herd of Holstons." Then, in answer to my raised eyebrows, "Herd of Holsteins, herd of Holstons, get it?"

"I was wondering more about who you're calling hicks."

Phillip laughed. "The archaeologist. That's Jerry Hicks. He works for the state. He supervised a group of Holstons here for a reunion a couple of weeks ago, and they were ecstatic about digging up the family's petrified refuse . . ." His voice faded as something over my shoulder caught his attention, then it flared. "What's *he* doing?" he asked.

"He" was Zach Aikens. He'd stayed behind at the excavation—surprise, surprise. He was in the yard-wide grass strip between the pit Jerry Hicks had climbed out of and the undug square behind it. He was on his stomach, lying at the edge of the hole, worrying at something he could barely reach, even by stretching his arm as far as he could down the face of the wall.

"Blasted kid," Phillip said. "I don't care if he does know what garbology is—didn't he just hear Hicks telling everyone to leave the walls alone?" He shot a glance toward the barn. Hicks and the other students were engaged and apparently hadn't missed Zach or noticed what he was doing.

Phillip started back to the excavation. I followed—whether to act as Phillip's backup or as a buffer between the two, I didn't know.

"I knew this one was going to be trouble," Phillip said.

"If he falls in, he could break something."

"His neck would be good for starters."

Zach continued working intently at whatever he'd found in the wall. He didn't stop or look up as we approached.

"It's my fault," Phillip muttered. "I shouldn't have mocked him back there in the auditorium. He's obviously overly sensitive. Hey, Cemetery Dude."

Zach didn't answer. Delicately, deliberately, he continued scratching, scraping, and brushing at something in the earthen wall. Phillip and I stopped on the opposite side of the square.

"Can you see what it is?" I asked, craning forward and squinting.

"No."

I started around the square. Phillip took a shortcut. He climbed down the ladder, crossed the pit, and got to Zach first. The depth of the pit put them eye-to-eye.

"Hey, Dump Dude," Zach said. "Check it out. I think I've found where your bodies are buried."

# Chapter 3

"I'm thinking elbow joint," Zach said.

Phillip Bell snapped his mouth shut on whatever he'd been thinking and moved closer for a better look. Zach was still lying in the grass. I stepped around him and got down on my knees. A knobby tree root was a more likely discovery than an elbow, I thought. I'd seen plenty of eerily bonelike roots washed clean along creek banks. Given the number of trees surrounding the farmyard and the complete lack of gravestones, a root made more sense, too.

Zach had scraped a small concavity in the wall. He reached his hand toward it again.

"Stop." Phillip's own hand was fast, but he stopped short of grabbing Zach.

"But look," Zach said. "It's simple anatomy." He pointed without touching. "Ulna along here, ending in the olecranon." He tapped his own elbow, then pointed back at what he'd uncovered. "Radius here, and humerus. If we dig it out more, I bet we see the lateral epicondyle."

An ominous flush crept up Phillip's neck.

Zach, apparently a savant in anatomy but not in the warning signs for impending volcanic eruptions, kept talking. "It's an elbow joint, all right. Hey, maybe it's that

Holston dude's lost arm and I found it for him. You think?"

"Is it?" I looked more closely at the "elbow," an uncomfortable feeling oozing into the pit of my stomach.

"Carter Holston's arm?" Phillip scoffed. "Of course not."

"But is it an elbow?"

Phillip looked at the discovery more closely. "Yeah. I'd say it's an elbow at least. Maybe a whole arm."

"Told you," Zach said.

"And if it's an arm attached to a whole skeleton," Phillip said, "wouldn't *that* be a kick?" I'd been wrong about the flush on his neck. It wasn't a sign of ominous threat. It was excitement.

"Cool," said Zach. "So who is it?"

"At this depth and in this location," Phillip said, "it isn't going to be anybody who's supposed to be here, that's for sure. So, Cemetery Dude, that's the multimillion-dollar question—who is it?"

"Geneva?" Her name popped out of my mouth, and in that instant I wondered if this *could* be her and why I hadn't thought of that immediately. Or maybe I had and that was why I had the sick feeling in my stomach. But was this her elbow? Her body?

There was so much I didn't know about the ghost in my life, starting with why she *was* in my life. Mine and no one else's. But we'd met up here at the Homeplace, and she seemed to think she'd lived here. So, was she a ghost because she hadn't been properly *buried* here? Because she'd been . . .

I felt cold and short of breath. But if *I* felt that way, how on earth would Geneva feel when I told her what we'd found? How on earth or . . . or wherever. How strange my life had become. I was crouched next to a spotty teenager who'd just made a fairly major archaeological discovery where he shouldn't have been digging. I was thinking about the ghost whom only I saw, heard, or knew existed. And I was wondering how to tell that ghost—a scatty creature who wasn't entirely sure of her name or when she'd lived or died—that I might know where her body was buried. People who said life in a small town was simple and straightforward had no idea what they were talking about.

All of that zipped through my head faster than it took to sigh the words "Oh, Geneva." And those were two more words I wished I hadn't said out loud.

"Who's Geneva?" Zach asked. He and Phillip were looking at me.

I meant to say *"No one."* But too many other thoughts were still racing through my mind and different words came out. "Any idea how old the bones could be, Phillip, or how long they've been here? And they'll be able to tell if it's male or female, won't they? I mean, if there are enough bones left—" I stopped and shook my head.

"Hey." Zach shrank back. "You aren't going to hurl, are you? Because, you know, you can't do that here. We need to preserve the perimeter of the excavation."

He's right said Phillip.

I started to move away from the edge of the hole. And stopped. "Wait a second. That's all you're going to say? *He's right*? What about how *he* violated the perimeter of the excavation in the first place?"

"In light of his discovery, I think you're being a tad harsh," Phillip said. "Don't you? She has a point, though, kid. Whether or not there's more to this skeleton than meets the elbow, you've undoubtedly dug up a nest of red tape along with it. So let's go get Hicks. He needs to see this. And he's a stickler for people behaving, so you need to apologize for the trouble you've caused. Are you cool with that?"

"I'm cool."

Jerry Hicks was cool, too. After an intense minute of staring into Zach's eyes so that Zach couldn't have misinterpreted a single nuance of his feelings about people who messed with his site, Jerry climbed down into the pit to see the bones for himself. Then he pulled out his cell phone, made a call, and climbed back out.

"Here's the drill," he said. He'd rubbed a broader smear of dirt down his nose, but that didn't stop the rest of us from standing straighter at the authority in his voice. "The excavation is off-limits until further notice."

"But we can help dig it up," one of the students said.

"And you can teach us the proper methods, so we don't *screw* it up," another one said, aiming a pointed look at Zach. The look was wasted. Zach was still cool.

"Not an option," Hicks said. "There's legal procedure to follow anytime human skeletal remains are accidentally exposed. I've called the site director. She is placing the required calls to the medical examiner and the sheriff's department. This guy" — he pointed at Zach — "needs to stay here and answer questions when the authorities arrive. And you" — he pointed at me — "will take the rest of your students out of this area. Back to the visitors' center will do fine."

There were disappointed noises from most of the students, and I felt like adding my own. But Jerry was right. When the authorities arrived, they wouldn't want the site cluttered with two dozen curious teenage extras. Besides, a couple of the students had been looking peaky since hearing about the bones.

But I didn't want to go. Part of me was excited about the possibility of uncovering—literally—more about Geneva. The other part of me felt as though I'd be abandoning her if I left. That was a fairly off-the-wall reaction considering that even if these were her bones, *she* wasn't here. She was back at the Weaver's Cat, haunting it more or less happily. Even so, I could imagine the conversation we might have about the situation later, if she decided that I should have stayed to keep some kind of vigil. And because I had a decent imagination, I could imagine the volume of Geneva's end of that conversation as wide open and her tone as fully aggrieved. So much so that I cringed in real time.

Phillip saw and gave me an interesting look. I pretended not to notice.

"That's okay. The students are my responsibility," he said, to my relief. "We'll take a short break for refreshments, but then there's no reason we can't continue the tour and see the rest of the site. We have the house, the summer kitchen, and the outhouse all waiting for us. Plus the gardens. My friends, you have not lived until you've pulled weeds in a historically accurate herb garden or explored the charms of a nineteenth-century privy."

The students were back under Phillip's spell. He made gathering motions and they fell into a neat group, ready to follow him to an outhouse or to outer space. Before they left, he crooked a finger at me.

"I know the kid isn't your responsibility," he said, "but can you stay and keep an eye on him until Nadine gets here?"

I glanced at my phone. Still time before I needed to be back at the shop. "Sure. He isn't in any kind of trouble, is he?"

"Nah. Hicks is just crossing the *t*'s and dotting the *i*'s in his legal procedure. But they'll have to do a complete excavation to find out what we've got going on here. With luck, we can be part of that, so we'll be back in the digging business in a couple of days. And that's going to make it a much more interesting project than we planned. Oh—" He snapped his fingers. "That name."

"What name?"

"You mentioned her. Geneva, right? We need to talk."

Phillip swirled the students away, and after they were gone, I let myself blink. We needed to talk about Geneva? He knew about Geneva? What did he know? He couldn't know anything about her current nonexistence. But maybe he'd run across the name in site records. Maybe I would have, too, if I'd spent more time digging around. *Digging around.* Geneva would love that. Or be insulted—it was hard to say which.

"If someone's been found dead, could you be far behind?" Deputy Cole Dunbar was the first of the authorities to arrive, and his greeting illustrated why he would always be "Clod" Dunbar to me—although only in my mind. Besides carrying a gun, he was built like a bull and acted like a mule. He joined me where I'd moved into the shade of a poplar, his fists on his hips and his sunglasses shielding his eyes as effectively as blinders. He had enough starch in his uniform and in the lines of his face to meet the world at his own specified level of safety.

"Who's Hicks got in the hole?" he asked.

"We don't know. It's just arm bones so far."

He turned the sunglasses and a condescending nose toward me. Of course he hadn't meant the bones. Zach was in the pit watching Jerry Hicks take pictures of the wall.

"Sorry. Zach Aikens is one of the students. He found the bones."

"And what's your part in all this?" he asked. Annoying connotations dripped off his question onto my—admittedly—easy-to-push buttons. "Meddling civilian" was chief among them, followed by "little lady."

"Phillip Bell, the assistant director, asked me to stay with Zach until Nadine Solberg gets here," I said, proud of myself for letting his connotations roll off my buttons without causing a short circuit. "I'm a volunteer."

"Not if he told you to stay, you're not."

I should have known Clod would be the first to arrive, and knowing that, I should have apologized to Phillip and hightailed it back to the Weaver's Cat. That way I could have avoided annoying conversations like the one we were having.

"I'm a volunteer for the Hands on History program here at the site," I said as pleasantly as I could through clenched teeth. "Zach is one of our students. Phillip thought you might want to talk to him."

"Huh." Clod rocked on his heels a few times, but otherwise showed no inclination to move. I was tempted to ask him what his part in all this was, other than standing around, but my better judgment wasn't that foolhardy.

"Are you expecting the medical examiner anytime soon?" I asked.

"I thought I'd wait for him," Clod said unhelpfully. "This shouldn't take long, though. I'm hardly going out on a *limb* when I say ancient arm bones aren't going to be a front-burner case." He followed that with a stiff "heh-heh."

I was wondering where Nadine was and what the heck was taking her so long. What could possibly be more important than unexpected human bones? Or than letting me get away from Clod? I finally saw her coming across from the visitors' center with a man I didn't recognize. By the time they arrived, I must have been flushed from containing Clod-based irritation.

"Kath, you should go back inside and get a glass of lemonade or iced tea," Nadine said, putting her hand on my arm. "There's plenty. But before you go—" She moved her hand from my arm to the arm of the man with her. "I want you to meet Wes Treadwell. Wes is our newest board member."

Wes Treadwell looked as polished as Nadine, with the kind of shiny veneer that success and plenty of money provide. He wasn't as tall as Clod, and he was bulkier, but it looked like well-toned bulk. Interestingly, he and Clod wore similar sunglasses.

"Kath Rutledge," I said. "Nice to meet you." The hand I shook was softer than I expected.

"Kath who knows quilts and coverlets," he said. "I'm a complete idiot about that kind of thing." He dropped my hand and looked toward the excavation. "I am interested in these bones, though. I'd like to get over there, take a look."

"And this is Deputy Dunbar, Wes," Nadine said.

Clod and Wes nodded their sunglasses at each other, and then Wes turned his attention back to the excavation.

"What do you think, Deputy?" Nadine asked. "I told Wes that we should wait for the medical examiner to arrive before going closer. That's appropriate, isn't it? Do we have any better idea how old the remains are? And is it acceptable for the student to be down there with Jerry?" She smiled at Clod and it was his turn for her hand on his arm. "I'm sorry, I'm asking too many questions at once, but the situation is new for me and for the site. I can't help running worst-case scenarios through my head. Jerry said it doesn't look like a Native American burial, but we don't want to take any chance of stepping over a line, if that could possibly be the case."

"We'll be fine," Wes said, his eyes still on the excavation. Then, as though to soften what had sounded curt, he gave Nadine a quick smile over his shoulder. "Any problems that crop up, the board will handle."

If Wes' smile had come with more than a glance, he might have seen Nadine's frown. But the frown was quick, too. I got the feeling Clod caught that interplay. It was hard to tell, because of the sunglasses, but he stepped into the slightly awkward silence that followed, with an offering of stolid reassurance.

"The ME should be here any time, Ms. Solberg. In the meantime, the situation is under control. Hicks and I have worked together on previous recoveries of unexpected remains."

"Have you?" Nadine asked. "How interesting."

Clod showed the extent of his interest with a shrug. All in a day's work, apparently.

*Work. Oh no.* I pulled my phone out and looked at the time. Barely enough to make it back for a meeting I'd scheduled with a sales rep.

"Nadine, I'll see you tomorrow morning. The TGIF quilters are raring to go."

"Not sticking around to give a hand with the arm?" Clod asked.

"Sorry," I said. "Appointment. Already late. Must dash."

"Well, then, watch your speed," he shouted after me.

# Chapter 4

Clod Dunbar had issued my first — and only — speeding ticket six months earlier. That was also the first time we'd met. The ticket was humiliating, but really only a minor blip of an experience, and it would have been nice if Clod would let the memory of it slink away. He liked bringing it up, though, saying it was for my own safety, as well as the public's. Because I'd been brought up to be polite, I never told him what I thought every time he delivered his public service announcement.

I made it to the Weaver's Cat in good time, without going so much as a hair over the posted speeds. When I turned onto Main Street, I got stuck behind a tourist bus, so speeding wasn't an option, anyway. *Funny,* I thought, *if I still lived in the big city of Springfield, Illinois, poking along behind a bus would have had me fuming as much as the bus.* But this was a hybrid coach, clean and quiet, letting several dozen folks loose in town. And their pocketbooks would carry them in and out of the shops, including mine, and there wasn't much about that to make me fume

Ardis Buchanan, longtime friend and longer-time manager of the Weaver's Cat, made an art of our front window displays. She knew how to combine colors and textures that drew eyes and then feet through our front door. I enjoyed looking at her displays as much as our customers did, but recently I'd started bypassing them and taking the less scenic route down the alley behind the shop, to go in through the kitchen. It was all about the door. Our new electronic chime didn't ring—it bleated. "Baa" was what most people heard when they opened the door, but to me it sounded like "welcome home."

One of the reasons I loved that chime was the guy who made it for us—Joe Dunbar. Joe was something of a Renaissance Blue Plum man. He could paddle a canoe, knit a baby hat, and toss a pizza. He painted beautiful miniature watercolors, had an open and curious mind, enjoyed old movies, and read contemporary mysteries. Parts of his life were still a mystery to me, but I was working on that. One unfathomable mystery was how he could possibly be the brother of the lamentable Deputy Clod. That relationship wasn't something he could help, though, and it would have been unfair to hold it against him.

Ardis, Geneva, and Argyle, the cat who'd retired from a rough life to live at the shop, were waiting for me in the front room, each in her or his own way. Argyle made happy cat eyes, then curled into a skein of orange tabby fur near the cash register for another appointment in his never-ending schedule of naps. Ardis sat on the tall stool behind the sales counter folding a stack of fat quarters she'd cut from a new line of printed cottons. The fabrics reproduced 1920s patterns and were proving popular with quilters. Geneva perched on top of the button cabinet, watching Ardis and kicking her ghostly heels. There was no sign of the sales rep.

"Good, she's not here yet?" I gave Argyle a kiss between his ears, then moved around to the front of the counter so that I was more or less facing both Ardis and Geneva. Ardis might not know Geneva was there, but she was, and it seemed a simple courtesy to make her feel included. Especially because she didn't like being snubbed—*didn't like* being a euphemism for *became weepy, petulant, huffy, and louder than was necessary or pleasant.* "I didn't want to miss her."

"The rep?" Ardis asked. "She called. She had a flat on the way out of Asheville."

"Bummer."

"She said she'll try to reschedule in a week or two."

"Mm."

"It could've been worse. She could've had the flat up there on that bridge with the mile-high legs in Sams Gap."

While Ardis talked, Geneva floated over to sit on the shoulder of the mannequin to my right. I shifted around to keep her in the conversation, noting that Ardis had dressed the mannequin in the beautiful quilted jacket one of our customers had designed and brought in. Geneva's damp gray form did nothing for the jacket's predominant color scheme of watery oranges and green.

"That bridge used to give me the willies," Ardis was saying.

Geneva yawned with noisy exaggeration and rested her chin on the mannequin's head. Together they looked like a stumpy totem pole.

Ardis raised her voice. "But now I just close my eyes when I reach the crest, and I scream on the way down. Works every time."

"Sorry—what?"

"I knew you weren't listening," she said. "You're wearing your preoccupied and puzzling-something-out face. So tell me all about the bones."

"Bones?" Geneva sat up straighter.

"'The Bones in the Barnyard,'" Ardis mused. "It has a definite ring to it. And now you're wearing your *surprised* and puzzling-something-out face, and if you ask me, that's one of the reasons you're such a natural-born amateur sleuth. You're always puzzling things out. Even when you give me that less-than-attractive slitty-eyed look you're wearing now."

I kept the slitty-eyed look for Ardis' benefit and held up an index finger for Geneva's. In the human-to-haunt sign-language system Geneva and I were constantly working to refine, a raised index finger was supposed to mean *hold on* or *please be patient.*

"Are you scolding me?" Ardis drew back, looking and sounding hurt. "Why so touchy?"

At the same time, Geneva waved her arms wildly and shouted, "Read my arms! I want to hear about the bones!" Her contributions to our system sometimes gave me a headache.

"Sorry, sorry, there really isn't much to tell yet." I massaged my forehead.

"Oh, hon, no," Ardis said, picking up on that sign immediately. "There's nothing in the world to be sorry for. The heat of the day and unexpected human remains? They'd be enough to send anybody off-kilter."

"*Kilt* her?" Geneva said. "That does not sound like 'not much to tell.' Perhaps Ardis is right and the shock and the heat were too much for you." She left the mannequin and floated closer. "Would you like me to hold your hand?"

"Do you need to sit down?" Ardis asked.

I looked at Geneva, then at Ardis. Two unlikely peas in a pod, both sweetly concerned.

"I'm okay, but I've got three sleuth-type questions for you, Ardis. Who, when, and how?"

"Did I hear about the bones? Oh ye of little faith in the Blue Plum jungle drums and texting service. You had two dozen teenagers, on the spot, with phones and itchy fingers. By now it might be quicker to guess who *hasn't* heard about the bones."

"*I* haven't," Geneva said.

"Good point," I said, covering both of them, "and no telling what embellished information is flying around out there because of that. So here are the bare bones." I paused for Ardis to groan. She sounded uncannily like Geneva. "One of the students, Zach Aikens, found an elbow joint. It might be a whole arm. It might be a whole skeleton. They won't know until they excavate, but they can't do that until they get the okay from the medical examiner and the sheriff's department. That's according to the archaeologist, Jerry Hicks."

"How deep did he find it?" Ardis asked.

It was Geneva's turn to groan. "Please do not turn this into a philosophical discussion, deep or otherwise. Death and bones go together quite naturally, and that is the end of the story." She paused. "Although, as in my case, it is not always the end of the story, because here I am. Don't you find that fascinating and worth pondering at greater length? But here are my naturally occurring super-amateur-sleuth questions. Who is this Zach and where did he find these bones?"

"I'll run and get you a glass of water," Ardis said. "I don't like the way you're standing there staring at nothing."

"I am insulted," Geneva said with a huff.

I closed my eyes. "Thanks, Ardis." As soon as she was gone, I crooked a finger at Geneva.

"A secret confab?" she asked.

"Shh, yes. This might be hard, but I'd like you to be my ears and memory while I tell Ardis about the bones. Listen carefully and quietly. Think about it, and try to think back—"

"How quietly?"

I motioned zipping my lips.

"Sadly, I do not have a zipper and I am fairly certain that I have never had one."

"Silent."

"Really? Do you mean totally silent?"

"Yes." I heard Ardis coming back down the hall from the kitchen. "Silent. Please. Can you do that?"

"Watch me," she said with a ghastly wink. "I can be as silent as the grave."

I wasn't too sure about that, but she sat primly on the counter and clasped her hands in her lap. Her only other movement, after Ardis came in and handed me the glass of water, was to open her eyes wider and lean forward—an exaggerated look of earnest listening that made me suspicious, but she was as good as her word and she said nothing more.

Until I made a mistake.

# Chapter 5

"Not deep enough for a burial, then?" Ardis asked.

"Not if six feet really is standard. Besides, Phillip and Jerry wouldn't have been surprised by the bones if there'd been anything in the records about a family plot in that area." I finished the water she'd brought me and looked at the glass, turning it in my hands. Geneva hadn't interrupted. I glanced at her watery form. She hadn't moved, was still listening attentively. *What was the end of her story?* I wondered. *How easy was it for somebody to break a human body? To crack a bone the way I could shatter the water glass, and then toss it in the garbage?*

"I have an idea," I said. I put the glass on the counter and pushed it away from the edge. Ardis was a mirror of Geneva—both listening, neither speaking. At least one no longer breathing.

"What if we could figure out who it is? Whose bones they are?"

"The posse's first cold case? Oh, *hon*."

I could tell, then, that *she* was breathing. "The posse," as Ardis called it, was an unofficial subgroup of the TGIF knitting group called Friday's Fast and Furious. Together, we'd solved several local crimes, mostly murders. Ardis and Geneva were the posse's most ardent members, and one of Geneva's sorest grievances was that the other members were never aware of her contributions to our investigations. She considered herself second in command. I was the reluctant chief detective. But reluctant only up to a point. We *had* proved ourselves, and catching the bad guys turned out to be very satisfying.

"But do you think we *can* do it?" Ardis asked. "How cold is the case? Where would we start? Wait. Scratch that." She thumped a fist on the counter. "Of course we can do it. *You'll* tell us where to start."

"I have an idea about that, too."

"Of course you do. Go on," she urged. "This is very exciting."

Geneva was excited, too, and working hard to contain it. She looked as though she was simmering and about to bubble over. She clapped her hands over her mouth. Her eyes were huge. *Blue*, Geneva had told me once. She'd looked at me and told me that her eyes were blue like mine. I hadn't been able to picture it.

"Do you remember the night we opened the newel post in the caretaker's cottage at the Homeplace?"

"I'm not likely to forget anything about that night," Ardis said. "None of us will."

"No."

Geneva was still now and listening intently. The antebellum caretaker's cottage at the Homeplace was where she and I had met, both of us recently bereft of someone we'd loved. I'd only been staying there temporarily, but Geneva had existed in the cottage—no one had known she was there, so it wasn't really as though she'd haunted the place— for so long that she'd lost track of most of the details of her life. She hadn't even been able to tell me with any certainty that her name was Geneva, and it upset her now, if I pressed her to remember more. Her only connection to the outside world had been through the caretaker's television, which he'd apparently left on twenty-four hours a day to provide company for his own lonely life.

"We found a note in the bottom of the newel," I said.

"And we put it back. Joe resealed the newel cap."

"I memorized it. It said:

'Finished this house this day for this family

My dear wife and our dear children

Elihu Bowman

29th April 1853.'"

"A clue," Ardis said on a happy exhalation.

"It might be." I said that carefully, but *of course* it might be a clue. That was why I'd memorized the words. Someday I'd planned to search for Elihu Bowman or his descendants and to see if that path led me to Geneva. I'd met her in the cottage, so wasn't it likely that she'd lived there? Why else would she have haunted that house? I just hadn't imagined connecting Elihu's yellowed and fading note to a skeleton that might be a murder vic . . . I glanced at Geneva. She'd moved closer on the counter, settling next to Argyle. He shivered and curled into a tighter ball of fur. "I thought maybe we could look through records at the courthouse."

"Not 'could,'" Ardis said. "Pick that word 'could' right out of your pattern and toss it on the scrap heap. *'Can'* is what we are all about. We'll storm the courthouse and we'll get Thea to find out what other records are available in the archives at the library and wherever. But what are we looking for?"

"Names of children? Members of the household?" I hesitated. As usual, I was making the process up as I went along.

"His wife?" Ardis prompted. "You don't think it's his wife, do you? I have trouble thinking of anyone named Elihu as a low-down scoundrel. It's such an upright-sounding name. And this? Murder? Concealing a murder? Concealing a mutilation?" Ardis swallowed, looking sick. "This would be the worst kind of low-down."

Geneva looked as though she agreed, but not as though she felt a personal stake in Elihu's supposed villainy.

"I don't know," I said, "but we probably shouldn't start with any preconceived notions."

"Innocent until proven guilty—that's one way of doing things," Ardis said.

"Let's start out that way, anyway. I wonder how complete the local records are, going that far back?"

"No idea. That's not my area of expertise. I'll tell you what I do know, though. It is situations like this that call for Hansel and Gretel."

"Um . . ."

"Ivy never told you about Hansel and Gretel? It's her strategy, but I named it," Ardis said proudly. "Say a customer comes in with a vague memory of a pattern or of a book of designs that she only saw once and wished she'd splurged on when she had the chance. How are we going to find it if she doesn't know a name or title? With Hansel and Gretel, that's how. We ask for any information she *does* remember, no matter how small—even as small as a crumb."

"Okay, that works."

"For fairy tales," Geneva muttered. "And why do you keep sneaking looks at me? Stop with your once-upon-a-time stalling and tell us something useful."

Ardis was a close echo. "So, tell me, do you have any crumbs for us to work with?"

"Tell *us*," Geneva said.

"Elihu might be enough, but there is something else. I, uh, I did some poking around. After we found the note." I fiddled with Ardis' stack of pretty fabric fat quarters, smoothing and restacking them, telling myself I wasn't exactly lying. Telling myself that prodding at Geneva's misty memory was a legitimate form of poking around. Surely it was a form of oral history. Or was it spectral history?

Ardis moved the fat quarters out of my reach. Geneva drifted closer with an impatient hum growing in her throat.

"I came across—well, it's just a name. It really is only a crumb, but it's stayed with me, even though there isn't much to follow up on." I was putting it badly but decided to finish. "She kind of disappeared."

"From the records?" Ardis asked.

"I haven't done a thorough search."

"Or are you suggesting that she disappeared—as in, she might be the bones in the barnyard? Because I have to ask what makes you think that? It's not that I doubt you, but don't you need to have more than a name before you jump that far toward a conclusion?"

Geneva flew between us and flung her arms wide. "Do not listen to that kind of *twaddle*. This is too *exciting* to let rational thoughts intervene. Tell me, tell me, *tell* me. Who? Who *is* it?"

I saw Ardis as though through a film of water—through Geneva—and saw her batting at what she must have thought was an insect buzzing in front of her eyes.

"What *is* the name?" she asked.

"The *name*!" Geneva said.

"Geneva."

Geneva threw her hands in the air. "Yes, I am *Geneva*. Now throw me the *crumb*."

"I did. It's Geneva. The crumb is Geneva."

I wasn't sure I'd ever seen Geneva look so surprised. She froze, with her mouth open, in front of Ardis, who also had her mouth open. Geneva stayed there, staring at me. Ardis shivered and slid a few feet to her right.

"Hon?"

Then Geneva thawed, but in a more chilling way than I'd expected. Although, truth be told, I hadn't known what to expect. How could I? I'd been hauntless for all but the last few months of my life, and I had no idea where to find ghost guidelines to help me navigate these treacherous seas.

"I have never been so insulted in my life," Geneva said in a low, slow, unforgiving voice. That line, alone, would have been good for an exit. But never let it be said that Geneva lacked a keen sense of the overly melodramatic. In the same bleak tone she added, "You are dead to me."

"Maybe I should get you another glass of water."

That was Ardis. I heard her say that about water, but Geneva was taking my whole attention. Her nose was inches from my nose, and her hollow eyes stared into mine, so that all I could think was *bleak, bleak*. I cringed, forcing myself to meet her gaze and not shut my eyes. She didn't screech or scream. She didn't say anything more. She simply faded and was gone.

I heard a small, anguished wrench of noise. It came from somewhere deep inside me and scared poor Argyle. He backed away from me, low and hissing.

"It's okay, Argyle, sweetie," I said. He didn't think so. He slunk off the counter and ran from the room. I knew

I was probably alone, but I called softly anyway. "Geneva?"

Ardis came back with her cure-all of cold water and heard me call. "Where were you poking around when you found the name?" she asked. She held the water glass out to me. When I didn't take it, she took a sip herself.

"I honestly can't say."

She took another sip of water, and I went to straighten the other rooms so it was easier to avoid her eyes.

At the end of the afternoon, I climbed the two flights of stairs to the study—the room tucked under the eaves in a corner of the attic. That room had been Granny's retreat from the bustle of the shop, and now it was mine. It was a snug and private space, but it still contained so much of Granny, in her books and notebooks, and so much of Granddaddy's love for her in the shelves and cupboards he'd built, that I never felt alone.

"Geneva?" I called softly when I stood in the middle of the room. Another reason I never felt alone in the study was that Geneva and Argyle had also adopted it as their private space—"private" obviously having a different meaning to ghosts and cats. They spent many hours curled in the dormer window seat. Neither of them sat there now. Their absence wasn't so unusual, but Argyle hadn't ever run from me like that, and I wondered where he'd gone.

"Argyle?" I got down on my hands and knees and looked under the desk. "Kitty, kitty?" Not there, hiding or hissing. He wasn't the first cat to hiss at me. In fact, he was the only cat I'd known who hadn't. Every one of Granny's cats, over the years, had hissed and swatted at me. That made Argyle an altogether unusual cat, because he not only tolerated me, but he even seemed to like me. So where had my boy gone and what had gotten into him?

"Geneva?" I tapped on the door of her "room." It wasn't a room; it was a cupboard—tall, narrow, and painted indigo blue inside—that Granddaddy had built behind a panel in the wall. Granny had kept her private dye journals hidden there. I'd never asked Geneva if she noticed that her "room's" dimensions were similar to those of a coffin standing on end.

"Geneva? Come on, now. We need to talk." But she didn't answer. I tapped again and sighed. Ghosts and cats— would I ever know how they worked?

But saying "we need to talk" jogged my memory. Phillip had said the same thing to me before he'd taken the students back to the visitors' center. About the name Geneva.

The phone number for the Homeplace was in a packet of orientation materials Nadine had given to the Hands on History volunteers. My packet was buried in a stack of quilt and textile books on the desk. I excavated it and was happy to find individual numbers for Nadine and Phillip, too. By then it was late enough in the afternoon that the students should have gone home. I took a chance and called Phillip directly. The phone rang six or seven times. I hadn't really thought through a message to leave on voice mail, and was about to hang up when a woman answered.

"You rang?" she said with a sputter and a swallowed laugh. Then the laugh bubbled out of her throat. It was followed by muffled words, thumps, and something that sounded like a slap and a squeal.

Just before I jammed my thumb on the END CALL button, Phillip came on the line with a terse "hello."

"Hi," I said tentatively. "This is Kath Rutledge."

"Okay."

"It sounds like this is a bad time—"

"Only because we were having such a good time," Phillip said.

"I'll call back. But *not* tonight—"

"No, no, wait. I'm sorry. That was out of line. Was there something I can do for you?"

"You wanted to talk."

"I did? Why?"

"About a name. It's okay; it can wait." This could hardly get more awkward.

"Oh, right, *right.*" He suddenly sounded more engaged with our conversation—and less engaged otherwise. "Geneva? Yeah, definitely. What do you know about her?" Kissing noises somewhere near his phone broke his concentration. After a sharp intake of breath he said, "Look, this really isn't a good time. But I'm working on something you might be interested in, and you'll be out here tomorrow morning, anyway, right?"

"You're at the site now?" *With whom and where?* The italics of my subtext must have communicated themselves. Our awkward conversation became an awkward silence. Silence on his part and mine, anyway. There was an undercurrent of throaty chuckle in the background.

"I live here," Phillip finally said. "In the cottage near the entrance gate. A perk of the job. Convenient and cozy. I'd invite you for breakfast, but—"

I quickly agreed to meet him at the visitors' center at eight the next morning and was relieved to end the call. I'd planned to be at the Homeplace by eight thirty, anyway, to get materials set up for the first quilting session. Depending on what Phillip had to say or show me, there should still be plenty of time for that and to meet the

TGIF volunteers before our avid and eager overachieving students arrived at nine.

I called Geneva one more time before leaving. She didn't answer. I said good-bye anyway, gathered the books and notes I needed for the next day's program, and went back downstairs. In the front room, Argyle and Ardis were having a tête-à-tête. It was nice to see that he, at least, had returned to his senses. He sat on the counter looking entitled while Ardis asked his opinion of the orange-and-white-striped baby hat she was knitting.

"There's my handsome boy," I said. But I'd no sooner said it than he leapt from the counter and ran out of the room.

"What in heaven's name is that about?" Ardis asked. "I thought he liked my orange tabby hat."

"It's not the hat. It's me. The honeymoon is over."

"What are you talking about?"

"Facts are facts, Ardis. He's a cat, and he's finally caught on to the fact that I'm me. Cats don't like me. You know that. They never have. I'm going home now. I'll be in after the program tomorrow."

"But how did this happen?"

"Don't worry. He'll be back as soon as I'm gone."

I spent the evening going over my quilt notes and tried not to let the behavior of the ghost and the cat weigh on me. It was easier to deal with the patched-together facts about the quilts on display and in storage at the Homeplace. Facts were facts; sometimes they just weren't what we wanted to hear.

On my way out to the Homeplace the next morning, a small worry stitched itself into my thoughts. What if Phillip and his "you rang" friend had partied too hard and I had to call him and wake him up to come unlock the entry gate for me? But the gate was open, and I drove through and parked in the gravel area next to the visitors' center. I got out, glad I wasn't climbing out into the oppressive heat and humidity of an August morning back in central Illinois. Here the sky wasn't molten white, a mockingbird sang in place of the traffic noises I'd known in Springfield, and the air smelled of hay being mowed in a field across the road instead of like diesel and dust. But the visitors' center was locked and no one answered my knock.

I waited. I went to the barn and said good morning to Portia and her piglets. They grunted in return. I went back to the visitors' center. Heard and saw no one. I walked back down the drive toward Phillip's cottage— the caretaker's cottage. I wasn't sure I wanted to knock on that door. Somehow the cottage looked more lived in than it had when Geneva and I met there. Bees buzzed in the lavender on either side of the door. It was the end of the season and the lavender had seen better days. A breeze moved the curtain in the open kitchen window. There were no other movements or sounds.

By then I knew I didn't want to knock. I also knew that if Phillip took much longer to show up, he wouldn't have time to show or tell me what he was so excited about. I pulled out my phone and punched in his number. While I waited for him to pick up, I studied the cottage and pictured Geneva as I'd found her there— dismal, depressed, lonely. Where was she now? And where the heck was Phillip?

I thought about calling Nadine. But why? To tattle on Phillip? She would arrive before I needed to set up for the students, anyway. In the meantime, the morning was too beautiful to waste on sour thoughts or standing around. The pond, where Phillip had submerged the flax for retting, was a comfortable distance from the house. It lay beyond a wild growth of rhododendrons at the edge of the woods, but it wouldn't take long to stroll over and see how it was coming along—or to smell it.

I'd taken part in a retting project only once. The growing flax had appeared so innocent—stalks waving like a field of wheat, delicate flowers making it a sea of blue. But cut the flax and bundle it, lay the bundles in water to rot for a few days, weighed down with wooden planks and rocks, and the sweet, flowery story changes. I was pretty sure the students would be mightily impressed, if not completely overwhelmed, when we touched on the flax-processing part of the program.

Turning my back on Phillip's cottage proved easier than turning it on the nosy questions now pestering me. Especially the nosiest one—had that been *Grace* with him last night? Yow. And since when was I so easily scandalized? They'd been married, for heaven's sake. Maybe Geneva's prudishness was rubbing off on me. I followed the path into the gnarled rhododendrons—pushing past waxy leaves and twigs that caught at my sleeves like priggish fingers—annoyed at Phillip for being late and at myself for feeling so prissy. Maybe the smell of the rotting, retting flax would snap me out of it.

Or the sight of Phillip's crumpled body beside the pond.

# Chapter 6

The last time I'd smelled retting flax I'd been sure a sewer pipe had broken nearby—it was putrescence personified. And the smell rising off the pond now must have hit me with the same sledgehammer, but my other senses quit working as my field of vision contracted to the strip of ground occupied by Phillip's body. I had no doubt it *was* a body I was staring at. He was staring, too. But not at anything he'd ever see again. There was no movement. No breath. I made myself go to him to feel for a pulse. In his wrist. Not his neck. His neck—something had attacked him—bitten his neck? A dog? What else would make puncture wounds like that? I had to stop looking at it.

Sound returned to my universe with a rustle and the snap of a twig in the woods on the other side of the pond. I jumped back from Phillip. Looked around wildly. Saw nothing, heard nothing more than the whisper of leaves. Squeezed my eyes shut and touched his wrist. Searched for a pulse. Felt nothing except how cold he was.

Then, between the sight of Phillip and the retting stench that finally hit me, I lost it. I stumbled to my feet and ran—panicked that whatever had killed Phillip was going to burst out of the rhododendrons and catch me, too. I gasped and gulped most of the way back to the visitors' center, until I saw Nadine with a knot of women—my TGIF volunteers.

"She found him? Why am I not surprised?" That could only have been the voice of Deputy Clod Dunbar. Why was *I* not surprised?

I was sitting at a table in the education room of the visitors' center, a wet washcloth pressed to my forehead and eyes, courtesy of Nadine Solberg. I didn't take the washcloth from my eyes. Seeing Clod's mulish face wouldn't erase the image of Phillip's dead body from my mind's eye or improve this awful situation.

"Is she all right?" Clod asked.

I could have told him I was being self-indulgent and hiding from reality for a few minutes. He probably would have understood that. But I indulged myself further by pressing the washcloth more firmly to my forehead and letting Nadine or one of the TGIF volunteers answer. The problem with hiding behind a wet washcloth became obvious, though, when an annoying, familiar, but completely unexpected voice answered Clod.

"She's just unlucky."

"A regular Typhoid Mary," added another, equally annoying voice.

I couldn't help it; I groaned. When had Shirley and Mercy Spivey arrived? And *why*? The twins were, unfortunately, members of TGIF, but they hadn't signed up to work with Hands on History. I groaned again.

"I was going to compare her to Jessica Fletcher," the first twin's voice said. "Except that Jessica doesn't fall apart at the drop of a hat."

"Or the drop of a body," said the second twin.

At that point—and at practically no previous point in

the existence of our acquaintance—I was glad to have Clod intervene.

"Ms. Spivey and Ms. Spivey, I need you to step away from Ms. Rutledge. I need to speak to her alone. I'd appreciate it if you ladies will move your meeting to the auditorium. I thank you for your cooperation."

"Come along, ladies," one twin said.

"Chop-chop," said the other.

Chairs scraped and there was a buzz of whispers that reminded me of the bees in the lavender outside Phillip's cottage. I pictured the Spiveys, pleased with their new leadership roles, ushering the other TGIF volunteers into the auditorium.

"Deputy Dunbar"—Nadine's voice of reason cut in— "why don't you use my office across the hall?"

"I didn't want to presume," Clod said.

"Not at all. It makes sense. Although *I* presume you will also want to speak to me?"

"Yes ma'am."

"Whenever you're ready, then. In the meantime, we have our own work to do. There are people I need to contact. And the students. This is . . . we won't let this be a public disaster. But someone should meet the students as they arrive."

"I can do that."

I let my washcloth shift so I could see who'd spoken—it was the man Nadine had brought out to the excavation, the new Homeplace board member. Les something?

"Thank you, Wes," Nadine said. "Tell them we're meeting in the auditorium and let me know when they're all here, will you? I'll have to make an announcement—" She stopped and no one else said anything. I shifted the washcloth again so I could see her. She stood, head bowed. But only for the space of a few breaths, and then she was back in control.

"Deputy," she said, "I need information before I can make an announcement. Before I make decisions. Is this a situation where . . . what *is* the situation? Can I open the site for business today?"

"For the short term, until we have a better idea of what happened, no."

"I deal better with specifics, Deputy. When can I open the site? This afternoon? Tomorrow?"

"As soon as we have answers, I'll let you know."

"Then let's get going, shall we? Let me get my notes and laptop and then the office is all yours. Kath, how are you feeling?"

"She can't help it if she looks peaky," a Spivey said.

When had she popped back into the room?

"Redheads come by peaky naturally," the second Spivey said, thus proving a timeworn Blue Plum adage: *Wheresoever you find Mercy, Shirley, her sister, will not be far behind.*

"Ms. Rutledge is feeling fine," Clod said more loudly than necessary. "Unless she requires my assistance to walk across the hall . . . I didn't think so."

Nadine gathered her laptop and notes and gave my shoulder a squeeze in passing. Clod closed the office door behind her. I folded the washcloth—which I'd continued to hold against my brow to prove a point—and set it tidily on a coaster on the desk.

"This is so awful," I said. "Awful all the way around. For Phillip, for Nadine and the site. And with everything she needs to do now . . . well, it was nice of her to inconvenience herself and turn her office over to us."

The office was comfortable enough. Not cramped, as so many of the offices were in small museums I'd been in over the years. Nadine had room for a couple of bookshelves, the desk, and two easy chairs with a square red-lacquered Parsons table between them. But any small space with Clod standing in it was crowded.

"Not *us*," Clod said. He hadn't moved from the door and seemed to be practicing his "I am in command" stance, with his hands on his hips and his jaw set. Or maybe he was standing ready in case I tried to make a break for it. "Me. She turned her office over to me so that I can do my job with the fewest interruptions."

"You're right. Sorry." I went to look out the window behind the desk. It was a handsome desk. It looked like walnut, possibly an antique. "Oh." I gulped. "That might be another reason she didn't want to work in here." The window looked toward the woods and the pond. And several more lawmen walking toward the rhododendrons. "What did that to him? That injury?"

"Come away from the window. There's nothing to see."

"But did *you* see? Did you see his neck?" My hand found its way to my own neck and stayed there protectively.

"Kath, come on over here and sit down." He said that in his least cloddish tone, but then he blew it. "Unless you need your stage prop washcloth again."

I bared my teeth in a snarl, but only because I was still looking out the window and had my back to him. Before turning around, I took my hand from my neck and wiped the snarl away. Nadine's comfortable-looking desk chair caught my eye and tried to lure me into it and its power position. I patted the back of the chair and it swiveled seductively, but I made myself walk past it to one of the easy chairs Clod had asked me to sit in.

"Tell me how I can help, Deputy. I'll answer your questions as best I can, but then I should go see how Nadine is doing and find out how she plans to handle the program."

"What are you up to?"

"Sorry?"

He hadn't moved from in front of the door. He still had his hands on his hips, but now he also had an assessing look on his face.

"You're . . . different."

He'd noticed. I was pleased. But not in *that* way. I was pleased because I was working very hard to be "different." Clod and I shared the memory of that one speeding ticket. We'd also had one disastrous date. Ours was a history of butting heads. Although once it was my fist and his head. Actually, my fist and his nose. But now that Joe and I were dating, it seemed like a good idea to try to improve my interactions with Clod, starting with remaining calm and logical. And avoiding sarcasm. None of that should have been too hard. By nature, nurture, and professional training, I tended to be calm and logical

But sarcasm—that's what I had to fight against. *Sarcasm is the sign of a weak character,* Granny used to tell me. She was right, and I believed her. The joy of a good sarcastic zing fizzled in a nanosecond, and that fizzle always left me feeling less than minuscule. Before meeting Clod, I'd gone whole weeks, if not months, without being sarcastic. But since I'd known him, even my thoughts about not being sarcastic were sarcastic.

"I'm trying to do my bit," I said calmly.

"Huh."

"I'm at your disposal, although I have to tell you that I went, I saw, and I left, so I don't know how much help I'll be." And the longer he stood there suspecting my motives, the faster my character was heading downhill to its weakest point. I dug my fingernails into the palms of my hands, in hopes that the small pain would help me hold firm. "I didn't see any tracks, if that helps. It's been so dry lately, and there're weeds and rocks and not much mud near the pond. But what's your first question, Deputy?" Feeling civil. Holding my own in my skirmish against sarcasm.

"What is that god-awful smell at the pond?"

"Oh my gosh—the retting!" I told him what it was and gave him the gist of the process, and that was the first time I'd seen him show interest in, or be impressed by, anything to do with fibers or textiles. His hands even left his hips.

"Retting?" He held up his left index finger as if to keep that word pegged, then he held up his right index finger and asked with exaggerated enunciation, "Or rotting?"

"Both. It's retting, but retting really is rotting, possibly etymologically as well as physically, although I'm not sure the etymology's been proven."

"And it makes linen?" He mused over that, nose wrinkled. "Makes a pukey smell, too. It's so bad Shorty nearly lost his breakfast."

"Poor Shorty."

"Yeah. Heh. I could almost believe you needed that sham washcloth to help you recover from the stink. So why were you and Bell meeting this morning, and at what time? And why there? At least we know it wasn't for reasons of a romantic nature." He thought that was funny, too. While he laughed, I calmly thought about how it was only logical that I'd developed a low-grade headache to match his low-grade humor. "Did you see or hear anything before or after you found him?"

"Nothing unusual. A twig snap? That's what it sounded like. Across the pond in the woods. It spooked me. Well, not spooked; more like startled." Geneva took offense at the cavalier use of the word "spook."

"Nadine said you were running when she saw you. Getting out of there was smart. That's like leaving your house if you realize someone's been in it. Good. You're learning."

Should I burst his bubble? Logic told me yes. "But first I looked to see what might have made the noise. Only a quick look. And I didn't see anything. Then I checked for a pulse in his wrist . . . but I didn't think he was . . . and he wasn't. And *then* I ran. Do you think it might've been a dog? Or would a coyote do that? I remember reading about a bear down in the Smokies that killed a woman."

"It wasn't a bear," he said with clear derision. "Go back to why you were meeting him there."

"I wasn't. He was supposed to meet me here, at the visitors' center, to go over his research."

"Is that anything like being invited to look over his etchings?"

*Give me strength,* I prayed, *because the pressure of unzinged sarcasm is building.* But Granny would have been proud of me. Containment levels were maxing out, but a breach was not imminent. "He was researching local names," I said. "We were going to compare notes. He didn't show up. He didn't answer his phone. I was killing . . ." I stumbled and recovered. "I decided to go see how the retting was coming along."

"Given the stink, that was an odd choice."

"Given my professional background and interests, it wasn't." *Slipping, slipping.* I dug my nails harder into my palms and pasted on a smile.

"You're hiding something."

"What? No I'm not."

"In your hand, there. What's in your fist?"

*A knuckle sandwich.* Oops. Calm, calm. I opened my hands and laid them palms up, as nonthreateningly and non-sarcastically as possible, in my lap. And then I canceled the pretend smile. It was surely screaming "sarcasm" by then. But putting all that hard work into my sarcasm-prevention program had distracted me. I hadn't really been listening to the tenor of his questions. What was he getting at? Why did he care when or why I was meeting Phillip? Unless he was trying to pinpoint time of death . . . or didn't think it was an animal attack. So why had *I* thought it was an animal? Because what else could have caused that many puncture wounds? Because what kind of human being could inflict that kind of damage on another human being? And with what? And from what distance? How close? Arm's reach? Maybe I should have looked for defensive wounds . . .

"Two," Clod said, holding up both index fingers again. "Two bodies in two days."

I didn't see where he was going with that. And he was exaggerating. "One of them is only an elbow so far."

"Aha! *So far.*" He leveled his index fingers and stabbed them both at me. The stabbing fingers weren't particularly threatening. He'd probably read an article in a law enforcement magazine about useful unnerving gestures, but I'd seen him do it before and it didn't worry me. The slant of his eyebrows, though, made those fingers look *extremely* sarcastic, and that set my tit-for-tat reflex close to igniting.

"You can't tell me you aren't up to something," he said. "So there's nothing in your hands, but you are hiding something. I can see it in the way your eyes move when you're thinking."

*Calm breaths. In and out. In and out.* I made him wait while my sarcastic pressure came down. "Deputy Dunbar," I said then, my voice even. With an effort. "Truthfully, I'm not hiding anything. But I'd venture to say that you're hiding a *lot*." Voice not so even there. I smoothed a wrinkle in my pants leg before continuing. "What happened to Phillip Bell?"

"We're still in the information-gathering phase of the investigation."

"No. Don't hand me that."

He crossed his arms over his chest. "We are still gathering information."

"Hooey."

His eyebrows rose. *"Hooey?"*

"It's a perfectly good word, and I'm sure you know what it means."

"I do. For instance, your Ms. Oh-so-cooperative act isn't pulling the wool over my eyes. I saw what you were doing with that cold compress while you were recovering from your swoon—"

"I didn't 'swoon.'"

"Pardon me. While you were recovering from your near swoon. You couldn't help yourself, and you let your stage prop droop a time or two so you could see what was going on."

Our interaction was doing tremendous things for my character. So I told myself, as I bit the inside of my cheek and tried not to show I was in pain. To Clod I said, "And I probably looked silly."

"Nosy. You looked nosy."

"And we both know that I am, although 'curious' sounds more polite. So what's your point?"

He glanced toward the window, then at the clock on the wall, and back at me.

"Are you waiting for something?" I asked.

"No." He still stood at the door, arms crossed again. Like a sentry.

"But are you expecting something to happen? Outside the window—where you said there was nothing to see and so you had me sit over here?"

"No." He crossed his arms more firmly.

I debated getting up and looking out the window. Then someone knocked on the door and Clod gave a start—a suspiciously guilty start that he tried to cover with a harrumph as he turned and opened the door a crack. He only opened it a crack, though, as if he knew who would be there and didn't want me to see. Or was I being paranoid?

While Clod and his visitor communed in low, official-sounding grunts, I decided to go ahead and illustrate the point about how naturally curious I was by sidling over to the window. There really wasn't anything to see, though. Nothing obvious going on. How disappointing. I turned back to see if Clod had finished his conference.

He had. And he'd invited an unsmiling, uniformed friend to join us.

# Chapter 7

"**M**s. Rutledge," Clod said, "Deputy Munroe has one or two questions for you. Shorty, Ms. Rutledge has already told me that she had a meeting scheduled with the deceased this morning."

"Oh, hey, are you Shorty?"

"Ms. Rutledge," Clod said, at his most sententious, "I'd like to remind you that we are investigating a death."

"Sure. Sorry. Nice to finally meet you, though, Shorty. I mean Deputy Munroe. Sorry. Go ahead and ask your questions."

Shorty looked like an accountant. My idea of an accountant, anyway—slightly rumpled and soft around the middle, tired eyes behind round wire-rim glasses. His name hadn't taken any imagination; he was taller than me, but not by much. He looked like a short, pencil-pushing version of Henry Fonda.

"Ms. Rutledge, how well did you know Phillip Bell?" His voice was pure Willie Nelson.

"I met him yesterday for the first time. Are you from Texas? Sorry. It's just you remind me of—"

"Ms. Rutledge, how well do you know Fredda Oliver?"

"Who?" They both watched me so intently that I backed up against the windowsill. "What's this about?"

Neither answered me, but Clod turned to Shorty. "Told you," he said. "A built-in lie detector. I'd back her face against Fredda's for telling the truth any day."

"Who's Fredda Oliver?" I asked. They didn't answer.

"Heh," said Shorty. "And don't you wish we could get one of those genetically modified patents on an honest face like that?"

Clod slapped him on the back.

*"Hey!"* My shout didn't even make them blink.

Clod opened the door, and with a shooing motion said, "You're free to go now, Ms. Rutledge."

Shorty gave me a mock salute. "Nice to finally meet you, too, Ms. Rutledge."

They smiled and didn't wait to see if I returned the smiles—or even if I left the room—before falling into another grunt of private, exclusionary conversation. I thought about letting them know I was well aware that I didn't need their dismissal, and that I'd been free to leave all along. I also thought about *demanding* to know who Fredda Oliver was and what conclusion they'd just reached about her, me, or both of us. They were busy, though, and annoying. And there were other, more satisfying ways of finding answers. I left without a word, a wave, or the raspberry they deserved. I was the epitome of Zach Aikens cool.

Zach Aikens and Jerry Hicks sat several seats apart in the front row of the otherwise empty auditorium. They were mirror images, with legs extended, chins on chests, sunk in thought. Zach looked up when I stopped in front of him. Jerry Hicks snored. So much for being deep in thought.

"A couple of old ladies said you might be arrested," Zach said.

That could only be Shirley and Mercy Spivey. "Are you disappointed?" I asked. So much for giving up sarcasm.

"Nah. Some of the others believed it, but just because people are old doesn't make them right. Do you know those two have identical varicose veins on the backs of their calves?" He shuddered.

I liked this kid more and more. "What's up with Mr. Hicks?"

"Said he had a late night, not to bother him."

"And is everyone else in the education room? I thought Ms. Solberg was meeting with you in here."

He shrugged and let his chin sink back onto his chest. It suddenly occurred to me he might be having trouble with Phillip's death. Wasn't this the kind of situation where counselors would be called in if this were a school?

"Um, do you want to talk about what happened?"

"Do you *know* what happened?" With his chin still on his chest, he appeared to be looking at me over a pair of glasses—reprovingly—and that made me want to be accurate in my hedging.

"I know the end result," I said. "Mr. Bell died. I don't know everything that happened."

The twist of his lips didn't tell me if that answer disappointed him or confirmed something.

"What made you start digging in that spot yesterday?" I asked.

"Nothing *made* me. I saw an anomaly and made an educated guess."

"Sure, but didn't that anomaly beg you to come over for a look? Didn't it tease you to tickle the dirt away? And then, even if you'd tried, you couldn't have helped yourself? That's how I feel when something grabs my attention. And then it starts whole trains of thoughts, although my grandmother called them skeins."

Zach's cool shifted ever so slightly toward alarm.

"Anyway, has Mr. Hicks made any guesses about how long the bones have been there?"

A minimal head shake no.

"And this might be too much to hope for, but as you scraped the dirt away yesterday, did you see anything *other* than dirt? Anything indicating the presence of deteriorated textiles, for instance?"

"The old ladies also said you think you're a detective."

"Oh yeah? What else did they say?" And why hadn't Clod or somebody in less-irritating authority sent the twins home? Why hadn't Nadine?

"Everybody's a detective, kid," Jerry said, rousing and yawning. "We're all trying to figure something out and we're all following clues. Some people just wear badges to prove it to themselves. As for the bones, I haven't formed any opinions—none that I can share with the public at this time. Much as I appreciate the public's interest. Kid, have they got a pop machine around here somewhere? Never mind. I'll go see if I can detect one." He rose, stretched, scratched, and left.

"And I guess I'd better go find Ms. Solberg." Not that Zach cared. "No word yet on when excavation can start on the skeleton?"

"Jerry says he's giving it time, that archaeologists are born optimists."

"Huh. Does that make them excavation-pit-half-full kind of people, or half-empty?"

Zach repeated his reproving look.

"Sorry. Do you think Jerry will let you help dig?"

"I'm optimistic."

"Good answer. And if the others are in there"—I pointed at the door to the education room—"it's all right for you to be in here?"

"I'm cool."


But the education room was empty. Or so it appeared. The clever camouflaged connecting door between it and the auditorium opened in such a way that someone—or some two—wouldn't be seen, if they were standing behind it. As though standing in wait. As were Shirley and Mercy Spivey, the not-quite-enough-times-removed twin cousins of my late, much dearer grandmother. Shirley and Mercy had never broken the habit of dressing as twins. This time they wore almost identical knee-length muumuus, the likes of which I hadn't seen in real life since . . . ever. Dark puce predominated in the flowers of one muumuu and bilious chartreuse in the other. Catching sight of the identical varicose veins on their calves wasn't an immediate worry, because the twins faced me. Aggressively.

"Not arrested after all," the nearer one said before I had the wits to jump back through the door and slam it.

"A perk of dating the deputy," said the other.

"Only the one time, though," said the first. "Now she's dating his brother."

"Which amounts to the same thing."

"It does not," I said. "And it isn't."

"We're happy for you either way," said the nearer twin. "And happy you're still breathing free air. We have something to show you."

Free air, I might be breathing, but it was tainted by the awful cologne that only Mercy Spivey ever wore. She must be the nearer twin. I stepped back and made a show of looking at my wrist.

"Gosh, I'm not sure I have time right now."

But they weren't paying attention, and my wrist didn't have a watch on it, anyway. Mercy quickly turned around, and I realized they'd been standing so I couldn't see what was on the table behind them. She turned back holding a white muslin bag out on her arms, as though making an offering. *Don't fall for it* went through my mind. *That might be a quilt bag, or it might be a Spivey trick.* I took another step backward. But that just gave Shirley enough room to perform the sleight of hand they must have worked out between them. She slid her hands into the bag, under the contents. Mercy pulled the bag away with a flourish. Shirley laid a muslin-wrapped armful down on the table behind them, and the two of them hovered over it with their backs to me. They flipped and unfolded and then stood back to reveal a crazy quilt of vibrant velvets, silks, and embroidered embellishments.

*"Wow."*

"I told you she'd like it," Shirley said. Her breath caught when Mercy's elbow found her ribs.

"But the rest of it's my idea," said Mercy.

"Tell me about the quilt." Bravely, I stepped between them. I was in love, and neither Mercy's elbow nor her cologne was threat enough to stop me.

"It's family," Shirley said. "Yours and ours. Rebecca, as was our great-grandmother and Ivy's grandmother—"

"It's called the Plague Quilt," Mercy said, lopping off the family tree.

"Rebecca was your great-great-grandmother," Shirley said. "She made this. She must be where we all get our textile talents from. What do you think of it?"

"She's not listening," Mercy said. "She's hooked. She is in awe of the Plague Quilt's beauty and transfixed by the very wonder of it. She can't even bring herself to touch it."

"That's her training," Shirley said. "She's taken an oath not to touch or breathe on artifacts of a historical nature."

"*An* historical nature," Mercy said with an elbow that caught me instead of her sister. "Oh. I am so sorry, Kath. You can pass it along if you like."

I couldn't be bothered. The quilt was a gem. The colors glowed, and every eccentric piece of velvet and silk was a canvas for embroidered art—intricate flourishes grew into tiny flowers or delicate insects, and extravagant repetitions of looping and feathered stitches surrounded the pieces and drew them together into a carnival of colors. Best of all were whimsical touches such as a pink-and-gray mouse crouched at the edge of a mouse hole–shaped piece of black velvet, nibbling at an adjoining triangle of cheese-colored silk. The whole thing measured only about five feet square, typical of ornate crazy quilts made in the late nineteenth century, but I wished Great-Great-Grandmother Rebecca had let it go on and on.

"Why do you call it the Plague Quilt?" I asked.

"It's what Great-Granny Rebecca called it," Shirley said.

"Do you know why she did?"

"We do," Mercy said as she started to refold the quilt.

"Wait—"

"And we'll tell you why, and let you look at it again," Shirley said, holding the bag open as Mercy carefully slid the quilt inside, "for a small consideration."

"In exchange," said Mercy.

\*      \*      \*

I made my pact with the twin devils—they would be allowed to join the TGIF volunteers helping with the quilting portion of Hands on History, and I would be allowed to spend an equal number of hours alone with the quilt. They were right; it seemed a small enough consideration—the word "sacrifice" sprang more immediately to mind, but I wasn't going to quibble—if they were letting me get my hands on that beauty. I did ask if they would leave the quilt with me in the meantime.

"We'd better not," Shirley said after tut-tutting and shaking her head.

"We'll bring it back tomorrow," said Mercy.

I watched them go, and sent a silent plea to whatever entity watched over optimists that Zach would forgive me for ensuring a continuing plague of the twins in his life.

When I found Nadine, she was sitting at a desk in what must have been Phillip's office. Less generous than Nadine's, this was the kind of office I was more familiar with in small museums—uncanny in its resemblance to a glorified supply closet. At least the room had a window at the far end, with a view of the gravel parking lot. If Phillip had pressed one cheek to the window frame and squinted, he could have seen the mules or Portia and her piglets when they were outside in the pens on this side of the barn.

"I wondered how much longer Deputy Dunbar was going to keep you," Nadine said, looking and sounding relieved to see me.

A coat tree stood in one corner. Phillip's wide-brimmed felt hat hung on it. There was no sign of the purple frock coat Nadine had told me about. A bookcase with a few dozen reference books stood against one wall. A banjo leaned against a filing cabinet on the other. A copier or printer sat on top of the filing cabinet. Nadine had been leafing through a binder when I came in, but now she watched me as I looked over the room.

"I didn't even know he played the banjo," she said. "I wonder if he sang?"

"I'm sorry we won't get the chance to find out. Are you going to want help sorting through things here?" I hesitated, then added, "Or in the cottage? I'll be happy to do what I can."

"I'll let you know, Kath. Right now it's one more thing that has to wait until they tell us something. I hate waiting, but not knowing what's going on is even worse. Did Deputy Dunbar say anything useful?"

"Sorry, no. But I'm sure he didn't think I said anything useful, either." I hoped that would at least make her smile. It didn't.

"I sent the students home," she said. "I only told them there was an accident."

"That was probably best."

"And I probably came across as completely without feeling for what's happened."

"I don't think so. I doubt anyone thinks that."

"Because the only thing I know to do right now is move forward. I told the students we'd start back in tomorrow and that we'll try to make up for missing today."

"Good. I'll let the other volunteers know."

"Grace told them before they left."

*Grace.* Talk about a lack of feeling—I hadn't given her any thought, hadn't thought about how Phillip's death might affect her. "How's she taking this?"

"She came in this morning before I had a chance to call her. You just missed her. She and Wes stayed until the students were picked up, and then she went home."

I thought about the woman with Phillip the night before. "Were they still seeing each other?"

"Wes and Grace are seeing each other?" Nadine asked. "Where did you hear that? I really don't think they are."

"No, no, no, sorry. I meant Grace and Phillip."

"Yes, of course you did." She shook her head as if to clear it. "Still, I would say no to that, too, although I suppose stranger things have happened."

"Wasn't it awkward having them both working here?"

"They stayed out of each other's way when they could, and when they couldn't they were civil. At least within my hearing. And then, she's only here ten to fifteen hours a week. It helps, too, that their interests are quite different."

"What were Phillip's interests? Did he have any specific projects he was working on?"

"Kath." Nadine looked at me when she said my name—making it a demand, not remonstrating—and she didn't say anything else until she must have known I was uncomfortable. "I'm surprised," she said then. "Are you asking these questions for the deputy? Is that why he kept you so long? Or are you indulging your hobby that I've heard about, mounting an investigation of your own?"

"Nadine," I said, then waited, playing her game, which I won as easily as she had. But she didn't look any happier about losing than I'd felt, and that made me feel bad all over again. "You're partly right," I said. She pressed her lips together and I rushed to explain. "Not in the way you think, though. It's the skeleton, Nadine. I want to know who it is and I think I have a clue. Phillip was excited about the skeleton, too, and something I said made him think we might be on the same track. He said he was working on something I might be interested in, but then with everything going on yesterday, he didn't have time to tell me what it was. That's why I came out early this morning. He was going to fill me in and we were going to compare notes. Except that I don't know what those notes were."

"I apologize, Kath." She looked down at the binder on the desk and then tapped her fingernail on the keyboard of Phillip's computer. "I don't know what those notes were, either. After we hired him he threw himself into learning our basic history and preparing for this program. We talked about site interpretation in general, and he had some ideas about incorporating storytelling into one of the tours. He was full of ideas. That's one of the reasons we hired him. But I don't know what *that* idea was. And I cannot imagine what we're doing with an elbow or an arm or a whole person out there." She put her elbows on the desk, closed her eyes, and rested her forehead on her fingertips.

"There's no need to apologize, Nadine. I obviously did spend too much time in there with Deputy Dunbar if I sounded like I was interrogating you. His bad habits must have rubbed off on me." That minuscule joke at Clod's expense didn't raise a smile, but it did make me wonder about that session with Clod. *Had* he interrogated me? Not really. It was more like he'd interviewed me with intent. But with intent to do what besides irritate? He'd passed the time with a few questions and a smattering of accusations. He hadn't learned anything more earth-shattering than the fundamentals of retting linen, or that Phillip took an interest in local names, or that I didn't know someone named Fredda. He hadn't learned that there'd been a woman with Phillip last night, because I hadn't thought to mention it. Grace? Or could that have been Fredda? Was that why Shorty had asked me about her? Had they already talked to her? But she was a good liar . . .

A door closed down the hall or across the hall. Nadine stood up.

"Maybe that's Deputy Dunbar," she said, "and we'll hear something."

But it wasn't Clod; it was my idea of a better Dunbar.

"Hey, Kath, have you seen—oh." Joe stopped short of bending to kiss me. "Hey, Nadine." His hand settled in the small of my back. "Sorry to hear about Phillip, Nadine. He seemed like an interesting guy. I know he was going to make things easier for you around here. If I can help in the short term, just give the word."

"That's good of you, Joe. Thank you."

"In the meantime, has either of you seen Fredda?"

# Chapter 8

"Fredda had an appointment in Knoxville today," Nadine said. "She'll be back tomorrow."

"Her truck's behind the equipment shed." Joe's hand left my back. He'd caught sight of the banjo and went to pick it up. "Maybe under the circumstances she didn't go."

"Then if she's heard about Phillip, that's one less person I have to tell," Nadine said. "But I left her off the list I gave Cole of everyone who was here this morning."

"I think Cole already knows she was here," I said. "But, um, who is she?"

"You haven't met her?" Nadine asked. "I'm sure you've seen her around, though. She's our new caretaker. She took the job after Joe filled in that short while for us. It was Joe who recommended her."

"She used to have a lawn care business," Joe said. "Good with small engines. And animals." He plucked a banjo string. It jangled discordantly, and he put the banjo back next to the filing cabinet. "You've had your share of excitement out here in the past couple of days."

"It hasn't even been twenty-four hours," Nadine said, hugging herself. "Poor Phillip. He enjoyed stirring things up."

Clod darkened the doorway at that point. "Ms. Solberg? May I—"

*"Finally."* Nadine's terse greeting pinched off whatever else Clod had planned to say.

Joe and I took that as our cue to slip away.

"What would Fredda have to lie about?" I asked as we made our way to the excavation site. Joe wanted to see it—and the elbow if he could. Because Jerry and Zach had vacated the auditorium, we hoped they'd been given the go-ahead to start the careful work of uncovering the bones.

"What makes you think she has anything to lie about?"

"Something your brother bark—er, something he said."

"You shouldn't listen to everything he barks."

"You're right. You're a wise man, Joe Dunbar. With long legs."

Loping Joe adjusted his stride with a smile. Neither of us was a hand-holder, but we walked companionably across the site grounds. Joe hummed and I indulged myself by comparing and contrasting the Dunbar brothers. It was an interesting pastime, but not really fair, due to my personal bias. I also knew it might be dangerous to the relationship Joe and I were still working on.

Joe liked to say we were knitting our relationship— going forward, dropping a stitch now and then, unraveling a bit, then moving forward again. I thought of it more as weaving—one of us on either side of a huge loom, sailing shuttles of bright colors back and forth to each other—creating a tapestry we could both live with. But considering the pieces of each other's lives we were still discovering and exploring, with only our current Blue Plum pieces intersecting, maybe our relationship was more like a patchwork quilt coming together.

One of the differences between the Dunbar brothers

was in the way they responded to or asked questions. Joe withheld judgment until a situation or a misstatement was clarified. Clod and his world were always right. I thought that must make it harder for him to be happy.

When we rounded the end of the barn, we saw that Jerry and Zach had company in the form of another sheriff's deputy.

"Hey, Darla," I called.

"Hey, yourself. Come see what we're doing." Darla Dye, the sheriff's newest deputy on the beat, dressed in her regulation tan-and-brown uniform, sunglasses, and Smokey the Bear hat, was acting as an enthusiastic shovel and spade caddy for the archaeologist. "I might have to drop my needlework and grab a pickax. This is fascinating. But I'm on duty, so ya'll mind what you say and do."

"Darla?" Jerry Hicks looked up from showing Zach the correct way to peel sod from the underlying dirt.

"Yeah?"

"Do me a favor and don't ever come near one of my sites with a pickax. Deal?"

"Deal. Isn't he the cutest?" Darla's hands were full, so she pointed an elbow at Jerry. She might reach his underarm if he stood next to her, and he looked more piratical and sweaty than cute.

"Not much to see, folks," Jerry said. "What we're doing is peeling it all back, easy does it, sod, then the dirt, and we're documenting the process, the layers, every anomaly we bump up against—photographs, sketches, notes—until we see what we've got. Routine recovery work. Boring for now."

"No it's not!" Darla said.

"For now, for them," Jerry said. "So they might as well leave us alone."

\* \* \*

"For now, for the two of you, yes, the site is closed," Clod said. He'd crunched across the gravel parking lot toward us, interrupting Joe's rather delightful good-bye. Joe planned to go fishing, and I'd decided to stay at the farm for another hour and look through the archives. Clod scuttled my plans. "I am authorized to tell you to leave."

"But I'm already here," I pointed out logically, "and I've been here all morning. How am I going to hurt anything more than I already have?" I wanted to add that I'd been there first and that ought to count for something. Instead I tried appealing to his sense of justice or closure or mystery. Surely he had at least one of those senses. I couched my request in as much of his own kind of official-eze blather as I could stomach. "Deputy, I think you should take into consideration that I'm continuing a thread of research that will help your department solve a problem. But I'll need to be able to access the site's records to corroborate my findings up to this point."

"Do tell."

I took that as an invitation to continue. Not one of my brighter moments. He cut me off with a guffaw. Amazingly, he had the good grace to stop and apologize. My flaming cheeks might have prompted that.

"Sorry," he said. "I thought you'd realize the 'do tell' wasn't serious. And, seriously, the research, whatever it is, can wait."

"You don't even want to know what it is?"

Clod looked at Joe, then at me, making a decision. "All right, speaking now as someone who is not authorized to do so, I'll tell you what the sheriff will be releasing in his statement this afternoon. Unless or until we learn otherwise, Phillip Bell's death is being investigated as a murder."

"Wait, you mean it wasn't an attack by a—"

"No. Those wounds were not caused by the jaws of an animal. Person or persons unknown."

"With *what*?" I wasn't sure I wanted to know.

"Also unknown."

"That's horrible."

The brothers pursed their lips and nodded, Joe looking at the sky, Clod studying the gravel at his feet.

"You know Jerry and the kid, Zach, are over there digging, though, right? You're going to let them stay? Are they safe?"

"No need to worry yourself about any of that." Clod's gravel meditation over, he rolled his neck and hitched his belt. "The dig is official business, until we find out what he's got there, and a deputy will remain on duty at the site. And although you didn't hear it from me, we are not without a suspect or suspects."

"Who?"

"That is for *us* to know and *not* for you to run around trying to find out."

I stared at him. "Did you really say that? Did you say 'that's for me to know and you to find out'? Like this is a game?

"*Not* for you to find out. It's a small word that makes a big difference. *Not*. Remember that. Ten," he said, calling Joe a name almost no one else did, "you got a hot date with a cold fish?"

Joe put a warm hand on my shoulder. "Might go on up to Lower Higgins. I tied a Tardis Dalek this morning. Thought I'd give it a whirl." The hand on my shoulder gave a slight squeeze.

"Sounds good. Just don't let *this* one talk you into doing anything crazy." Clod smiled, jabbing a thumb at me, but he wasn't really joking and no one laughed. Then he raised his hand as though he meant to clap Joe on the shoulder, but before actual brotherly contact occurred, his hand changed direction and thumped Joe's truck instead.

"A Tardis Dalek?" I said, watching Clod's irritating back disappear into the visitors' center. "You might be a wise man, but you're also wicked."

"It's a safe joke. He won't turn into a *Doctor Who* fan anytime soon."

"Or a fisherman. What kind of fly are you really using?"

"Woolly bugger."

I started to laugh, then stopped and looked at him.

He shrugged. "A classic fly, appropriate for small creeks and veiled comments."

I finished my laugh. "Why does he still call you Ten?"

"Why do you call him Deputy instead of Cole?"

"I could say habit. Or I could be honest and admit to a trace of passive aggression."

"A bit of both probably covers it," Joe said. "Are we still on for Saturday night?"

"Wouldn't miss it."

Joe (born Tennyson Yeats Dunbar) was taking me up a creek to show me where he'd seen a family of otters. His brother (born Deputy Coleridge Blake Dunbar—he didn't really arrive in this world wearing tan, brown, and a badge; he just looked that way) could go jump in the retting pond.

# Chapter 9

Ardis sat on the tall stool behind the sales counter at the Weaver's Cat in what she called "cogitation mode." Eyes unfocused, tapping whatever came to hand against her lips—a double-ended crochet hook in this case—she listened to the details of my morning and the few facts I knew of Phillip's nasty death. She stayed in cogitation mode each time we were interrupted by customers and I stopped my narration to discuss patterns, materials, and notions, or to ring up a sale. When I came to the part about the bogus Tardis Dalek fly, Ardis tucked the crochet hook behind her ear.

"He should design that fly and we can sell the pattern and all retire in splendor. And if the BBC doesn't like it, he can shorten it to the Ardis fly and give me a larger cut of the profits. But all of that aside, the big question is, can we work on a hot case and a cold one at the same time?"

"There might be a few other middling to big questions besides that one, Ardis."

She waved other considerations aside.

"One of those being the fact that they do have a suspect."

She threw her hands up. "Now you tell me."

"Oops. But I wasn't supposed to. Deputy Dunbar specifically warned us not to say that."

"Then it's his fault," she said. "He shouldn't have told you in the first place. And when have we ever let Cole or the existence of an official suspect stop us before? Were you able to get it out of him *who* they suspect?"

"No."

"Because that might narrow the field; they're bound to be wrong. Boy howdy, do we ever know they can get it wrong. But do we have enough man—no, after your experience with Cole, I'm feeling offended by the term 'manpower.' But you know what I mean. Are there enough of us? The posse can only do so much."

"Instead of 'manpower,' should we call it 'staffing resources'?"

"Sounds bulky. How about 'posse power'?"

"Sounds like an exotic dance club."

"Let's not call it anything then and move on. How would you like us to proceed with the cold investigation? I think it's best we start there, don't you?"

Before I could answer, she brought out a notebook from under the counter.

"Having learned at your feet, I made an outline of what we know thus far." She opened the notebook and turned it so I could see. The heading on the first page read *What We Know Thus Far.*

"We don't know much, do we?"

"That might be the essence of a cold case. A brief story, only a few facts, and that's what makes it more of a challenge."

"I wonder how many cold cases start with something as brief as an elbow?"

"And a name. Geneva."

When Ardis said "Geneva," I glanced around. There was nothing. No shimmer or glint. No patch of fog or watery distortion. But I heard tapping . . . It was Ardis. She'd taken the crochet hook from behind her ear and was tapping it on the notebook, watching me.

"It will help if you can remember where you read the name. It has a sweet, old-timey sound to it, don't you think?"

"I like *Geneva* a lot."

"So do I, but there's no need to shout."

"Sorry." It hadn't done any good to raise my voice, anyway. There were still no ripples of mist. "You know what, though, Ardis, Phillip knew the name, too. That's why I went out there this morning. To find out what he knew and where he'd found it. He must have it in a file."

"Will Nadine let you look?"

"I don't see why not. We'll be adding to the interpretation of the site. What could be better than that?" I flipped to the next page of the notebook. "Wow. You made assignments?"

"Is it too much? It's only what you mentioned yesterday, hunting for names and whatnot, but did I overstep?"

"No, this is great. All I have to do now is call the others and hand the assignments out. Piece of cake."

Ardis shook her head.

"What?"

"It's already done. Ernestine, John, Debbie, and Thea are in. Mel was in the middle of a tricky chocolate galette and couldn't be disturbed. I left a message for her, but if we don't hear from her soon, I'll run over there and let her know in person."

"And sample the galette?"

"And bring back a slice for you."

"We're good, then." Melody Gresham—Mel—was the owner-operator of Mel's on Main, the best eatery in Blue Plum. Mel was opinionated, loyal, and a terrific cook. The mention of galette set my stomach growling. "Thanks for doing this, Ardis. How soon do you think we can call a meeting?"

"That's already done, too. We're meeting at seven tonight at my house so I don't have to find a sitter for Daddy. We might have to shout over the TV, but we'll manage. Debbie doesn't want to drive all the way back into town, but we'll catch her up."

Debbie worked part-time for us at the Weaver's Cat and more than full-time running her sheep farm, with the help of Bill her border collie, ten miles out in the county. Due to her time constraints, we considered her more of a consulting member of the posse.

"My first thought was to hold off on meeting for a few days," Ardis said, "to give our operatives more time for their assignments. But I knew you'd want to touch base, as a group, as soon as possible and start tossing ideas around the way you like to do." She started juggling what looked like a dangerous number of imaginary objects.

"We probably could have waited until the weekend."

She caught the imaginary objects and put them in the drawer behind the counter. "When I talked to Joe, he said he knew you were free tonight, but couldn't be certain about Friday or Saturday. Don't you love the word 'operatives'?"

"I do. Remind me to increase Joe's salary now that he's also acting as my social secretary. Is he coming tonight?"

"He wouldn't commit."

"That's my kind of social secretary." Despite his commitment constraints, Joe had proved his value as a posse member.

"Tell you what," Ardis said. Why don't I leave the notebook with you to make corrections or additions as you see fit, and I'll run over, right now, to see if Mel will be joining us this evening."

"With galette?"

"Hmm. Galette for now or for this evening?"

"Either."

"Or both. Good idea."

The fiber- and textile-buying public came and went the rest of the afternoon. Geneva did not. Argyle kept his distance. Ardis heard me calling him, softly and pleadingly, and sighing when he ignored me.

"It's in his contract to ignore people," she said. "He wouldn't *be* a cat otherwise. At least he's condescended to be in the same room with you, and he's behaving like a gentleman again. And if you watch his ears, you can see he's listening to us."

Or listening to someone. He was looking toward the shelf above the yarn bins along the wall—a space near the ceiling where Geneva liked to lie and watch the fiber- and textile-buying world go by. But I didn't see her, not even out of the corner of my eye or if I turned around fast.

As disappointing as being snubbed by cat and ghost was the bag Ardis brought back from Mel's. The virtuous, smug spinach salad staring out at me when I opened the bag looked nothing like the wicked galette of my imagination. But Ardis reported that Mel hadn't been satisfied with the first galette and wouldn't let any of it past her kitchen door. Mel did promise she'd come to the meeting, though, and bring version 2.0. I let Joe's phone know in a text. The chance to review a new recipe might be enough to entice him to our meeting.

The Three Stooges were blaring in the den off Ardis' kitchen when I arrived. I stuck my head in to wave hello to her daddy and found Joe there, too. The two of them sat side by side, in twin recliners, nyucking it up like old friends. Neither of them noticed me through the hilarity; I waved anyway.

"We might lose John in there, too," I said, "if the Stooges are still on when he gets here."

"I can't change the channel. Laughing's good for Daddy's chest. Take this in to Joe, will you?" She handed me a glass of iced tea. "But tell him not to let Daddy get hold of it or we'll both be up all night."

I'd planned to be at Ardis' well ahead of the others, the better to be their intrepid leader, even though I had neither called the meeting nor handed them their assignments. But the members of the posse were completely dedicated and serious, and I should have known they would all arrive early, too, ready to contribute.

Thea Green, our town librarian and the brains behind database searches, arrived shortly after I did. "I know I'm early," she said. "But I hope the sooner we get started, the sooner we'll be out of here. I've got books to read and places to go. Like my bed."

"It's not even seven," I said.

"My point exactly. Let's knock this thing out and go."

Ardis held a chair for her. "Sit, Thea."

Thea sat, and when I saw her kick off her three-inch heels, I knew we had her for the evening. She'd told me once that her shoes screamed high fashion while her feet just plain screamed.

Mel came in, her hair newly dyed midnight blue with turquoise highlights and spiked to attention. She hadn't bothered to change out of her chef pants—pink-and-black houndstooth. She handed me a box that smelled of fresh pastry, cinnamon, chocolate, and something . . .

"Raspberry," she said. "Knew you wouldn't get it. This galette is the important part of the meeting, Red, so if you haven't got anything momentous to tell us, we can cut straight to what makes the world get rounder."

The bottom of the box was warm. I passed it to Ardis before I drooled on it.

Ernestine O'Dell came in on John Berry's arm. They were the posse's senior members—Ernestine in her seventies, John in his eighties—and they watched out for each other. Ernestine was fond of wearing grays and browns and usually reminded me of a round old grandmother mole. Tonight she was decked out in green capris and a blouson top and looked more like a Granny Smith apple. John had left the mountains for the sea as a young man, first in the navy and then on his own sailboat. He'd moved home to stay, a month or so after I had, to care for his older, ornery brother, but when he occasionally talked about his boat, the blue of the ocean still lit his eyes. The boat hadn't been overly large, he'd told me, and it was trim and quick. That described John, too.

"Have you been shopping with that wild granddaughter of yours again, Ernestine?" Thea asked.

"She has an eye for color, doesn't she?" Ernestine peered down at herself. "Although I'm not sure the colors do so much for *me*. Kath, did you bring some of your wonderful notes and diagrams for us to look at this evening?"

"It wouldn't be an investigation without Kath's lists and flowcharts," Mel said.

"I only ask because I left my magnifier at home. I am so sorry." Ernestine's thick lenses shone at me as John steered her to a seat at the kitchen table.

I held up the messenger bag with my notes and Ardis' spiral notebook. "I brought copies, Ernestine. There isn't much to them, but you can take yours home and look at it when you get a chance."

"That's fine, then."

"If you don't have much for us, what are we doing here?" Thea asked.

"We are sitting down, hushing up, and letting Kath lay it all out," Ardis said, thumping a plastic jug of iced tea on the table. "John Berry, if you're going to stand there whistling Andy Griffith, you might as well go on in and join the other slackers. I'm closing the door, though, so you can't have it both ways."

"Ardis?" Joe said from the doorway. "Your ninety-six-year-old slacker daddy is asking for you. He wants to change the lightbulb in the lamp at the end of the sofa. He says it flickers. It looks fine to me. I can change it to humor him, though."

Ardis stood with her eyes closed for a few seconds.

"I don't mind sitting with him, if it'll help," Joe said.

"That would be a blessing, Ten." There was nothing but affection in her voice when Ardis called him Ten. She'd known him since he was too young to be picked on because of the literary millstones around his neck. "Here." She handed him a box of crackers. "Let him have a few of these. He thinks he's not allowed, and he loves getting away with it. And shut that door before I come in there and shoot Barney Fife with his only bullet. Kath, are you ready to get this meeting started?"

I moved to the head of the table. Mel gave me a thumbs-up. Joe waved and pulled the door closed.

"Although," Ardis said before I had a chance to open my mouth, "now that I think about it, I wonder if we're jumping the gun with this cold case." She pulled out the chair next to Mel but didn't sit. "All we have is an elbow, and for all we know that's all we'll have in the end."

"I love a short meeting," Thea said. "Pass the galette, and let's go home."

"But even an elbow deserves a name," John said. Ernestine and Mel murmured agreement.

"But maybe we should wait a few days" Ardis said. "At least until they finish digging it up and we see what we have to work with. It's already a cold case. It won't get any colder." She sat down and put her own elbows on the table. "But as long as we're here, tell them about the hot case, Kath."

"Is this some kind of bait and switch?" Thea asked.

"It's better," Ardis said. "It's bait and bait. We've hit the big time. We have two cases. Tell them, Kath."

"Do you all know Ardis is talking about the death, sometime last night or early this morning, of Phillip Bell, the new assistant director out at the Homeplace?"

"How could I?" Thea asked. "I've been in meetings *all day*."

"Pour soul," Ernestine said.

"Thank you, Ernestine."

"She meant Phillip Bell, Thea," Ardis said.

"Did you know him, Kath?" John asked.

"Only slightly. I met him yesterday when I was out there for the high school enrichment program."

"Limburger and raw onions on liverwurst," Mel said. "That's what he had the only time I remember him eating lunch at the café. We don't get an order for that too often."

I suppressed a shudder for Mel's benefit. "That fits. Nadine Solberg called him a showman, and from what I saw, she was right. He was . . . interesting. Very dramatic and intense."

"And you found him this morning, didn't you?" Ardis said. "And helped the authorities with their 'inquiries,' as they say."

"I believe they only say that when someone is a suspect," Ernestine said. "Oh my. *Are* you a suspect, Kath? I am so sorry."

"It's okay, Ernestine. I'm not a suspect."

"It sounds as though you aren't sure you liked him," John said.

"I *think* I did. I think I *wanted* to. He sure had most of the kids eating out of his hand. But it's funny, Nadine said the same thing about the Holstons when I asked her if *she* liked Phillip. She thought he was doing a fine job, and she hired him, of course. But she said the Holston jury was still out about him."

"And Holston money makes the Homeplace go round," Mel said.

"You only knew him by his coffee and the smelly cheese he ate," Thea said. "And Kath thinks he was 'interesting.' But we don't know him or the situation well enough to start throwing around motives."

"I was only making an observation," Mel said. "Legitimate and with no strings attached to any particular powerful, wealthy family. But money is a legitimate motive. We all know that. Money talks. Money giveth and money taketh away. The power of money corrupts."

"Yeah. Okay. We get it, Mel," Thea said with exaggerated punctuation. "I'd like to make an observation, too. The sheriff's department is not totally incompetent."

"The point of your observation being what?" Ardis asked.

The meeting was not turning out to be as tidy or friendly as our meetings usually were. It might have helped if Ardis had clued me in to her bait-and-bait tactic beforehand. Or if Thea had left her attitude in a book on a shelf back at the library. They eyed each other, Ardis' back straightening and Thea's shoulders squaring up. I wondered who would blink, then decided to step in before one of them spit instead.

The door to the den opened, and Joe stepped in first, accompanied by an air freshener jingle from the television.

"Sorry to interrupt, but you might want to come see this. The sheriff's coming on the news in a few seconds. Suspect in custody."

"We're not interested in Andy Taylor," Thea said. "Or Opie or Otis."

"Our sheriff," Joe said. "Haynes."

"You changed the channel?" Ardis squawked. "Daddy never lets me do that. He squawks!"

"I only flipped it for a second. Your daddy's in the bathroom. Come on, or you'll miss it."

Chairs scraped, and we crowded into the den after Joe

in time to see footage of two deputies, walking away from the camera with a suspect between them, heading for a side door of the courthouse.

"Who is it?" someone farther in the room asked.

A "hush" came from behind me.

Clod's posture and gait were recognizable on the right, and it looked like Darla on the left. They each had a hand around the upper arm of a woman who walked between them with her head bowed. Either we'd missed the suspect's name in the newscaster's narration of the footage or it hadn't been mentioned yet. The camera cut to Sheriff Haynes and we all leaned closer, despite the television's volume being turned up to the level of a bellow. Then Ardis' daddy tottered back into the room and the bellowing really began. It ended with Joe flipping the channel, Sheriff Andy Taylor tousling Opie's hair, Ardis settling her daddy back in his recliner, and her daddy telling the rest of us to clear out, sit down, or bring him a beer.

"I do not think beer is strong enough for what ails this posse," someone behind me said—the same someone who'd shushed us from behind moments earlier. "I will consider giving you some helpful management pointers. As soon as you apologize."

"Geneva!" I said. Out loud.

# Chapter 10

I wasn't facing anyone—anyone alive—when I had my "Eureka moment," as Ardis called it, so no one but Geneva saw me wince.

"They are all staring at your back," Geneva said, "except Ardis' older-than-dirt daddy. He is throwing daggers at your back with his eyes. And I have a confession to make. I have felt like throwing daggers at your back with both hands."

"Come on along, all of you," Ardis said, trying to be heard over Aunt Bee, but not so loud that she irritated her father. Avoiding that was a lost cause.

"Who *are* all these people, Ardie?" he shouted. "And why'd they let all the flamin' fireflies in the house?" He was looking toward Geneva. She preened.

"There are no fireflies, Daddy," Ardis said, kissing his bald head. "Ten, you stay with him, will you? And Kath, you come on back to the kitchen and we'll all try to behave better."

"Well, this is awkward," Geneva said, following me. "Now you will not be able to call me by name when you pretend to talk to me on your phone. You did not think of that when you started bandying my name about, did you? Our perfectly good ghost communication system scuttled like so much rubbish or some poor soul's left arm in a family garbage dump. And that was only your first mistake. I have been keeping track of your mistakes for you, and you can thank me later. But what are we going to do now? Of course, you could call me Ginger. That is what my daddy called me."

She followed me like a swarm of gnats—nattering gnats that I wanted to swat. I sat down at the table and tried to look normal, but probably didn't achieve it because my shoulders kept creeping up to my ears.

"Debbie just texted," Mel said. "The suspect we saw with Cole? It's Bell's ex-wife."

"Oh no, *no*," I said. Of course that was Grace we'd seen walking between Clod and Darla.

"Calling me by my daddy's pet name was merely a suggestion," Geneva said. "There is no need to be so theatrical about your aversion to it. People stare at you enough as it is. On the other hand, you could text me and I can read over your shoulder."

I sat up straight. Texting could work, and Geneva and I definitely needed to talk, if only so I could tell her to hush up and we'd talk later. "Um, guys? I need to get hold of someone. But I also met Grace Estes—Phillip's ex—yesterday, and I immediately liked her. I know that doesn't count for squat and, yes, I saw friction between them, but I can't believe she did this."

"Why not?" Thea asked.

"She was still in love with him." As soon as I said that, I knew it was true. That was the loss and the longing—the love and pain—that had jolted me when I touched her shirtsleeve after we collided. She might have been needling him, maybe maliciously, but she did still love him.

"That means *less* than squat," Mel said.

That was true, too.

"Hang on, though, okay? Um, discuss it among your-selves. This won't take long."

I pulled out my phone and tapped, *WHYB? WNTT. YH red hair?*

"My eyes are going to cross," Geneva said in my ear. "Please use all the letters God gave you."

*Sorry.*

"I have to tell you," she said, interrupting before I could type more, "that after the way you bludgeoned my heart, a mere 'sorry' is an unconvincing apology. It lacks effusion."

*Effusion later. Where have you been? We need to talk. You have red hair?* It was like conducting a weird, re-verse séance; instead of waiting for a spirit to rap, I was tapping messages to a ghost. It was also exceedingly un-comfortable, because she hovered right behind me and I was beginning to shiver. *Why don't I call you and not use your name in the conversation?*

"Do we have time to cover your many and varied queries?" she asked.

*Not really. Not now.*

"You are laborious and all thumbs with that thing."

*TTYL.*

She blew an unpleasant gust down the back of my neck.

*Sorry. Talk to you later. Walk back to the shop with me?*

"*A-Y-G-I-A-S-T-Y-A?*" she said, pronouncing each letter slowly, clearly, and annoyingly.

*?*

"Do you see why I think that is annoying?"

*Yes.*

"I will translate. Are you glad I am speaking to you again?" She pronounced each syllable as slowly, clearly, and annoyingly as she had the letters.

*Yes.*

"I will be gracious and assume that the hesitation of your thumbs before you answered was due to the up-welling of emotion you are feeling at having me once again at your side. I am overcome, myself, and feel I must go meditate. If you need me, I will be in the other room with Ardis' nearly dead daddy and your burglar beau."

*My burglar beau.* He wasn't one, really. Or much of one. Lately.

"Kath?" Ardis said. "Did you learn anything useful?" From the way she and the others looked at me, I got the feeling that they hadn't discussed anything among themselves while I'd been texting.

"Possibly." Would knowing that Geneva's father called her Ginger help find her in the records? She didn't strike me as a Ginger.

"That's unhelpfully nonspecific," Thea said. "Are we working on anything or not? One case? Two cases? I'm thinking no cases. Let's eat Mel's galette, tell her what we think of it, and hit the road."

"Not yet." I got up and went to the head of the table again. "Let me lay both cases out for you."

"Excellent, now the way I see it—"

"Ardis, let me take it from here, please."

She closed her mouth and sat back, hands folded in front of her. The model of comportment for all the third- and fourth-grade students she'd taught before she saw the light and became manager of the Weaver's Cat.

"Start with the name," John said. "Start with *Geneva*."

"Yes. Maybe there's something subconscious working

with that name, and that's why you suddenly felt compelled to shout it," Ernestine said. "Eccentricity aside."

"Hold on." I took a pen from my purse, and then rooted through the messenger bag, finding the notes and notebook, but no blank paper. Great preparation.

"What do you need?" Ardis asked.

"Nothing. I'll use these." I turned the pages over and tapped their edges to square them. I wrote *Geneva* on the back of the first and *Phillip Bell* on the second and moved them aside. "Geneva is a name I first heard out at the Homeplace. When I stayed in the cottage, in passing—that's as close as I can get to pinning it down. But"—I tapped the paper with Phillip's name on it— "Phillip seemed to know the name, too. He was working on something—researching something he was excited about—and from his reaction to the bones, they meant something or tied in to that research somehow. It's also possible that the last name we're looking for is Bowman. Geneva Bowman. But I'm not sure."

"I love the way you throw specifics around," Thea said. "*Somehow* they really *seem* to do *something* for me."

"That sounds like an old song, doesn't it?" I tried a smile on Thea. It didn't make the difference of a dent or a dimple on her brown face. "But that's how we always start, isn't it?" I said. "Someone did something. Somewhere along the line we get involved. Somehow we figure it out. We start with unknowns. This time we just have a few more than usual. We don't know the name of the body in the dump. We don't know the name of the person who put it there."

"We don't know that it *is* a body," Thea said.

"True. Hang on." I wrote *who buried the body* on another sheet and slid it out of the way.

"And we don't know if the person who buried the—arm or whatever—was in any way responsible for why he or she buried it." Thea clucked her tongue. "A 'few' unknowns. Yeah."

"What if it *is* only an elbow or an arm," Ernestine said, "and it was a farming accident? Or an amputation?"

"So you'd toss it in the household dump?" Mel asked. "Ernestine—ugh. I think you know I'm not the squeamish type, but that gives me the willies."

"They're theories, though," I said. "And coming up with theories is one of the things we can do tonight." I jotted *accident, amputation*, and *Bowman* on the Geneva sheet.

"We aren't entirely without specifics, either," John said. "We don't know who the bones are, but we know *where* they are. That gives us the name Holston, and the name Holston gives us a place to start looking."

"Back to the lords of the manor," Mel said. "Did they have an abundance of money and position back then, too, or was the house and land they had typical for the period?"

"Their fortunes might have ebbed and waned," John said, "and that's easy enough to check. I assume there are Holston family records of various types at the Homeplace. Phillip was working there. Isn't it likely that's where he started his research?"

"I asked Nadine what he might have been working on," I said. "Other than familiarizing himself with the site and jumping into the Hands on History program, he wasn't into anything that she was aware of."

"And we aren't going to find an entry in Great-Aunt

Sally Holston's diary saying, *So-and-so was buried too shallow in the family garbage dump this morning, and the Ladies Aid Society came for tea this afternoon.*" Mel ran her fingers through her spikes, then splayed her hand on the table. "There's something wrong about the whole body-in-the-dump thing and it's got me rattled."

"That's because you're kindhearted," Ernestine said, patting her hand. "You can't imagine disposing of someone that way, but your spikes aren't prickly enough to keep the pictures out of your head."

"But there might be clues in the records," John said. "We can sift for them while the archaeologist is sifting the dirt around the bones. Does Nadine know the materials well enough to help us narrow the scope of the search? Surely she'll appreciate our help in solving this puzzle."

"I would think so. She's understandably stressed about *everything* going on out there, but if we approach her the right way, I think she would welcome the help."

"We can take it to her in the form of a serious proposal. Directors are like captains and admirals, aren't they? Happiest when dealing with that kind of formality?" John rubbed his hands as though happiest when anticipating a good formal declaration of intent.

I jotted *Holstons* on the back of another page and shoved it aside.

"It seems to me we need to find Phillip's research notes," Ernestine said. "If we find them, won't we find out what he knew about Geneva?"

I pointed the pen at her. "Absolutely, Ernestine, and if he was any kind of historian, he made notes about where he found the information."

"But will Nadine let us look through his office? And the computer in his office?" she asked. "That might be trickier, due to privacy concerns."

"I'll add it to the proposal," said John.

"Nice device, John," Mel said when she saw him tapping notes into his phone.

"I'm an old sea dog and I love new tricks."

"When are you going to upgrade, Red? You're archaic there, with your papers strewn all over."

"I've got my own trick. Show you in a minute." I wrote *Phillip's research* on the Phillip Bell page. Then I almost started another page with a note about searching the cottage at the Homeplace. But I didn't, and I told myself it was because we were going to have enough paper and ideas on the table and it had nothing to do with the notion creeping around the edge of my higher motivations—the notion that if Nadine drew the line at some of us looking around the cottage and through Phillip's belongings for information he'd stowed there, then I knew a window, out of general view, that was easy to slide quietly open. And I had it on the reliable authority of my friend Not-Really-a-Burglar Joe that entering without breaking wasn't technically, too awfully, criminal. Especially if you did it only once.

Ardis noticed my hesitation. She'd been quiet—listening and giving me encouraging prompts. Now she had one eyebrow raised and looked at me with her *mm-hmm* face. I took evasive action.

"So, on to Grace Estes," I said, and all ears perked up. All eyebrows returned to normal levels. "They've arrested her, and I know we don't know what evidence they have against her, but I think they're wrong and that we still don't know who killed Phillip. This morning Cole

Dunbar said they didn't know *what* killed him. They couldn't identify a weapon. I thought it was an animal, a dog or something. When I found him . . . it looked like . . ." My hand went to the side of my neck. "It looked like multiple bites, to me. As though something had bitten and raked. Deputy Dunbar said it wasn't, but . . . the attack was vicious." The fingers against my neck curled into a fist and I bounced it off my lips a few times before continuing. "I hope Grace wasn't capable of doing that. Here's something else, though. I called Phillip late yesterday afternoon and a woman answered. They were, well, it sounded like they were having a good time. If you know what I mean."

"For heaven's sake," Thea said, "who answers the phone at a time like that?"

"The point is, I don't know who the woman was. I thought it might be Grace."

"Why?"

"Because I knew they'd been married. Nothing more than that. It could've been anybody."

"We need to know who she was," said Mel. "I'll start a few conversations at the café, see what I hear about Phillip. And Grace."

"Good." I turned to Ernestine. "I know you don't know Grace, but if she isn't released on bond right away, would you go talk to her? Not to pump her for information. Not obviously, anyway."

"Don't you want to do that yourself?"

"If she's out, I definitely want to talk to her, but I think Deputy Dunbar would find a visit from me highly suspicious."

"He would, dear, because he isn't nearly as obtuse as he lets on. But, oh my, I just thought of something. I can dress up like Aunt Bee and take cookies for Grace and her cellmates, if she has any. That would be a comfort, don't you think? And a hoot?"

"A hoot and a half, at least," Mel said. "Go for it. I'll supply the cookies."

"May I be Aunt Bee, Kath?"

"Mel's right—go for it." I looked over at Thea. She seemed to have nodded off. "Thea? Hey, Thea?" She jumped a bit, but then shook herself awake without being too surly. "Can you work your database magic and see what you can find out about four people?"

"Sure, I can tickle the keys and come up with the goods." She flexed her fingers and cracked her knuckles. "For two pieces of the galette."

"No one else asked for special favors."

She crossed her arms. "Four people, two pieces. One now, and one goes home with me."

I looked at Mel.

"If this investigation creates galette addicts, my work is done."

"Fine. Two pieces, but you're on call."

"Not indefinitely."

"For the duration of the investigation. We'll renegotiate for future investigations. Phillip Bell is the first name." I tapped the paper with his name on it. "Here are the others. Nadine Solberg, Grace Estes, Fredda Oliver, Wes Treadwell, and Jerry Hicks." As I said them, I wrote each name on the back of a separate sheet.

"I can't help but notice that you're a math moron," Thea said. "That's one-third again as many people as you stated."

"That's what 'on call' means. Added value for me. I

forgot Jerry Hicks, so in he goes, and Nadine is so obvious she should be a given."

"Who are they?" John asked. "Those last three?"

"Fredda's the caretaker at the Homeplace. I haven't
met her and don't know if I've ever seen her. According
to Cole Dunbar, she tells more believable lies than I do."
There was a poorly concealed snicker followed by a
grunt of pain.

"Go on," Ardis said, avoiding a glare from Mel.

"Joe knows Fredda. He recommended her for the job.
That's a point in her favor, I guess. Wes Treadwell is the
newest member of the Homeplace board."

"Somebody with money, then," John said.

"He dresses and acts like he has money. Jerry Hicks is
the archaeologist. I don't know any more about him than
that. Oh, except he's done recovery of unexpected human remains before, but that goes with the job. Maybe
none of these people fit into this picture, but I'm somebody who's pathologically nosy, and I want to find out."

"And Dr. Thea, though aggrieved at her workload,
will attend to your affliction," Thea said. "May I?" She
reached for the sheets of paper.

"Not yet." It was time for my trick. I pulled the papers
toward me and counted them—nine—good, that worked
neatly. I dealt them out on the table in rows of three.
"We're kind of crazy to be doing this, don't you think?
We've done it before, sure, but we've blundered and
we've gotten into some trouble. And Thea's right: The
authorities are competent. Up to a point. But it's at that
point that I can't help myself. Give me a puzzle and eccentric bits and pieces of information, and I want to
make a pattern—a pattern that solves the puzzle."

Ardis stood up and moved her hands above the grid of papers as though smoothing them. "You've conjured a quilt."

"She has," Mel said. "She's right about crazy, too. This might be the craziest case we've worked on yet."

That reminded me. "Speaking of crazy, have any of you ever heard Shirley or Mercy talk about a Plague Quilt?"

# Chapter 11

Mentioning the Spiveys and their Plague Quilt was a meeting stopper, though not a comment stopper. Reactions ranged from the spontaneous and heartfelt "Spiveys" spit out by Ardis, to the thoughtful but equally dismissive "If they were socially aware and civic-minded, I would assume they've made an AIDS quilt, but knowing them, I seriously doubt that, and in that case I can't imagine what in the world they are talking about" from Mel. Thea, continuing her irascible theme for the evening, reflected that Shirley and Mercy were a plague unto themselves and everyone around them. John asked if I *did* know what they were talking about. By then I regretted bringing it up and said as much. That put the *mm-hmm* look back on Ardis' face, where it sat until Mel served the galette.

Mel watched carefully as we sampled, then dug into the dark chocolate and raspberry nestled into the buttery, flaky . . . "What do you think?" she asked.

"You could negotiate world peace and tame wild beasts with a slice of this heaven," Ernestine said. "Bless your heart, Mel Gresham."

Judging by the soft moans of satisfaction rising around the table, we all agreed. But when the last crumbs disappeared from her plate, Ardis crooked a finger, inviting me to lean closer.

"There's more to that Plague Quilt than meets the eye, mark my words. And you know more about it than you're letting on."

That seemed like a good time to leave. When I looked in the den to see who might like to leave with me, Joe, Geneva, and Ardis' daddy were glued to an old episode of *Law & Order*. It was one with Lennie Briscoe offering his glib take on the world—shouting his glibness because the TV volume was so high. Geneva lay like a mist on the floor between the two recliners, her chin propped in her hands.

I waved to catch Joe's attention. "I'm taking off. See you tomorrow?"

He started to get up. "Why don't I walk with you?"

"Sit yourself back down, son," Ardis' daddy yelled. "You'll miss the best part. Lennie always gets his man."

"Oh, *great*," Geneva said.

"I'd better—" Joe tipped his head toward Ardis' daddy.

"*Quiet!*" Ardis' daddy yelled.

"It's too *late* for quiet," Geneva roared back. "You spoiled the ending. Now we *all* know Lennie gets his man!"

Joe, looking sheepish, mouthed "sorry" and dropped back into his chair. Geneva swirled out of the room in a huff. I waved again and closed the door.

"If Daddy didn't like having Ten there so much, he wouldn't yell," Ardis said. "They're getting along fine."

"I do not know when I have run into a more peculiar family," Geneva said. "I suggest we get out while the getting is good."

"Do you think we can have progress reports for Fast

and Furious on Friday?" I asked the others before they got away. "That gives us two and a half days, and maybe by then we'll hear something from the archaeologist."

John said, "Aye, aye, Captain," and took Ernestine's arm. As they went out the back door, I heard Ernestine asking him if "captain" was really the right word for the person in charge of a posse. Ardis started singing about the foot bone being connected to the ankle bone, and I hurried to collect my notes before Geneva caught on and took further offense. I saw Thea put not one, but two more pieces of galette onto a paper plate. When she looked up and saw me watching, she put her nose in the air and said, "Special compensation for rush orders."

"It's her waistline, Red," Mel said. "Let her watch it and you can watch your own." She handed me a plate covered with a paper napkin. Under the napkin were two pieces of heaven all my own.

"No," Geneva said.

We were headed for the Weaver's Cat—one of us walking, the other doing a meandering float, as though a capricious breeze were blowing an eddy of fog back and forth across the sidewalk. Breezes didn't affect Geneva that way, though; her own whims did. For instance, answering a question I hadn't asked. I looked around before speaking, but didn't see anyone else nearby. Blue Plum generally rolled up its streets by nine or so, even on a pleasant late-summer evening. It was probably safe for me to talk without resorting to the cell phone subterfuge.

"What question are you answering?"

"Your nosy question about my hair. It is not red."

"Really? Not even strawberry blond? Then why did your father call you Ginger?"

"I am not sure I should answer any more questions until you apologize effusively for your heartless treatment of me."

"I have never wanted to hurt you, Geneva, and I'm sorry I did."

She stopped wafting to and fro and floated beside me. "You are not very good at effusion, but you are honest. I forgive you."

"Thank you."

"Thank goodness that is blown over, then." She billowed in and out, as though that cleared the air, and then she settled in beside me again. "I am glad we are friends again. Argyle will be, too. He missed sitting in your lap."

"Did you have something to do with him not sitting in my lap?"

"I was angry." She made a sound that could only be described as a nervous titter. It wasn't pleasant. "And that reminds me. There is another point that needs to be corrected. For the record."

"What point is that?"

"I would have brought it to your attention earlier, but I was caught up in your dramatics."

"Okay—"

"But it is not okay, and that is why it needs to be corrected. Mattie and Sam are the posse's first cold case, not this skeleton in the dump."

Mattie and Sam. As misty as Geneva's memories were, she was convinced—and she'd convinced me—that sometime in the past she'd seen a young couple lying dead in a green field. A hundred years ago? A hundred and fifty? She didn't know, and I'd never found any record or reports of a sensational double murder. But she'd recounted the incident in such vivid, painful detail that I'd promised to help her find her Mattie and Sam.

"You're right, Geneva. I'm sorry I forgot that."

"You are forgiven," she said. "Now the record is straight. Everything is fine, and I am overjoyed that you have given up that wretched, horrible, insulting idea that I am buried in a garbage dump."

After gulping, I walked the rest of the way to the shop with Geneva, saw her in, and nearly melted when Argyle twined around my ankles, but then I skedaddled home with a "sick headache."

And nearly had a genuine sick headache when I saw Clod Dunbar's patrol car parked under the streetlight in front of my sweet little yellow house. Worse, he wasn't in the car; he was sitting on my front porch swing, the mellow porch light softening his starched corners. *Drat.* He was the kind of surprise porch guest that made me seriously consider taking the swing down. But I loved that swing, and the house and the swing had been Granny's, and Granny would have been gracious to her uninvited guest and offered a glass of sweet tea.

Although, if Clod hadn't seen me yet . . .

"Evening," he called before I could turn and creep away into the shadows. "Why don't you come on up and sit a spell?" He followed the invitation with a warm chuckle. Points in Clod's favor—he didn't hold a grudge, and he amused himself.

"Hi." A point in my favor—I knew when to be wary. I climbed the steps but stayed on the top one, and I put the back of a hand to my forehead where I hoped to feel that headache popping up any second.

"It's a warm one." He was still in uniform.

"Sorry," I said, wondering if the uniform was good news or bad, "I know I should offer you tea, but I don't have any made . . ."

Clod stood up. I tittered nervously. *Drat.*

"A glass of something cold would be nice, but don't worry about it. I'm not here for refreshments." He hooked his thumbs on his belt and didn't say anything else.

"Okay, um, why are you here, then?" Maybe not sounding as gracious as I imagined.

"I thought you'd like to know, so that you can spread the word to your gang, and you don't have to waste any more of your time, especially your evenings, nosing around—"

"You thought I'd like to know what, Deputy?" Graciousness went right out the window.

"Grace Estes was arrested tonight."

I crossed my arms. "It was on the news."

"I thought you'd like to know on what grounds."

Now the porch light wasn't being any more kind to him than I was. Even though it wasn't terribly bright, it highlighted his wrinkled uniform and tired eyes. The light didn't have anything to do with his voice, but his syllables were less starched, too. Less . . . abrasive. He stepped closer. A hint of cigar surrounded him.

"She told us where to find the weapon."

"You smoke?"

"Didn't you hear me? Or are you ignoring me?"

"I heard. But remember what you said this morning? You said I'm nosy. Do you know what else I am? I'm also a skeptic. So, what is it and where was it?"

He tilted his head, as though that made it easier to

read my face or my mind. But he didn't answer my questions. "You and your bunch up there at Ms. Buchanan's tonight, you can call them off, tell them to stand down. There's no need for you to mount your own investigation." He sucked in a huge and noisy breath before continuing. "I will admit," he said, "that you have, upon occasion, found out the truth before the department did." The pain behind that admission worked for a few seconds on his face. "But not now. Not on this one. We have it covered. We are satisfied and the D.A. will be satisfied, too."

"But not yet?"

"Pardon?"

"You said the D.A. *will* be satisfied. Does that mean she still has questions?"

"No."

"It kind of does."

"No. That's not what I meant."

"Are you saying I twisted your words?"

"Yes, because you did."

My anti-sarcasm program flew out the window after my graciousness. "You mean that can happen? Words can be twisted to mean something else? To prove something? To satisfy someone's need for an easy answer?"

He started to growl.

"And what we were doing at Ms. Buchanan's tonight, Deputy Dunbar—and I'd *love* to know how you know where my friends and I were—what we were *doing* was taste-testing a new dessert for Mel. And if you don't believe me, *here*." I shoved the paper plate at him. "Try it *yourself*." The paper napkin fluttered off, and he gazed down at those two luscious slices of galette sitting side by side. Under the porch light they appeared to be one huge, heartbreaking helping.

Clod accepted my belligerent generosity with a surprised blink.

"And now, Deputy, if you don't mind, it's been a long day. A long day that started out badly for me, but even worse for someone I liked. And nothing about the day has, in any way, improved, because now someone else I like has been accused of murder. Good night. Enjoy your galette."

"My what?"

I pointed at the plate, then turned my back and fumbled for my keys in my purse so I wouldn't be tempted to grab it away from him.

"Well, thanks. Good night."

*Dratted man.*

I desperately wanted to know what the weapon was and how Grace knew where to find it. And to know if she'd confessed, a detail Clod hadn't included in his goodwill visit. I was almost desperate enough to scan the darkened street for sneaky, loitering patrol cars, and if the coast was clear, to hop in my own car and drive over to the jail to ask her. But if the jail had visiting hours, they were probably over. What time was it, anyway? Going on nine. Was I desperate enough to hop in the car and drive over to Mel's to see if the galette's visiting hours were over? No. I might have lost the sarcasm battle at the end of the day, but surely I had *some* self-control. Also, I had a recipe for one-minute chocolate cake in a mug—invented by some desperate genius for just such moments of sudden deprivation.

A call from Nadine Solberg saved me from myself and a one-minute mugging.

"I hope I'm not catching you at an inconvenient time," she said.

"Not at all, Nadine. I heard about Grace."

"In regards to that, I'm calling to let you know nothing has changed from this morning. Hands on History will take place tomorrow as planned."

"Oh, gosh, I hadn't even thought—" Or had I?

Nadine interrupted my words and distracted thoughts. "Students will arrive at nine. I'd like volunteers to arrive at least half an hour before their units are scheduled to start." She sounded as though she was reading from a script. Under the circumstances, who could blame her?

"Thanks for calling. I know you've had to make some quick changes to the program."

"The program will take place and continue as planned," she repeated. "We've made some personnel adjustments—"

*"Adjustments?"*

My outburst finally jogged her loose from her rehearsed content, but not in a useful or friendly way.

"I have more calls to make, Kath. I don't have time to discuss decisions or vocabulary. If my choices have offended you, then you should be aware that volunteers who wish to withdraw may also do so at this time."

"Has anyone withdrawn? Students *or* volunteers?"

She didn't answer.

"Nadine, I'm asking so I know how to plan for tomorrow, not because I'm backing out. If I need to, I can rustle up more quilters. I wasn't offended, and I didn't mean to offend *you*. I'd like to help in any way that I can."

"Five students have withdrawn. Well, no. Let me rephrase that. Their parents withdrew them."

"That's a shame."

"But understandable."

"It is."

"I do have more calls to make, Kath."

"I'll let you go, then. But Nadine? Try not to worry. Do you know what my grandmother would have said? She was a great one for working through problems. She would have said 'Go for the smooth.'"

Nadine responded with a short, exasperated snort. "I'm sure your grandmother was a wonderful person, full of wise country ways, but I have no idea what that means. I need to go."

She disconnected before I could say anything pleasant like *See you in the morning*. Just as well. Something unpleasant about her dismissive opinion of Granny might have come out instead, and she didn't need my snippiness added to her problems.

The next morning started out feeling like a replay of the day before—gathering my notes and courage for the first textile and quilt session with the teenagers, driving to the edge of town through a soft summer morning toward the mountains and the Homeplace. As before, the gate stood open and I drove slowly through, crunching along the gravel. I didn't realize how tense I was over this rerun until I felt the relief of seeing four other vehicles already parked in the lot beside the visitors' center. My hands relaxed on the wheel, and I rolled to a stop beside a car twice as big and ten times shinier than my trusty, dusty Honda.

The relief was short-lived. Two of the vehicles were sheriff's cars. Their presence probably wasn't unusual— deputies were surely still investigating Phillip's death and tying up loose ends. But as I got out of my car, a third sheriff's car rocketed down the drive and braked into a short skid. There'd been no siren, but from the way Shorty jumped out, slammed the door, and took off running toward the barn, it was clear something else had happened. I left my notes and materials behind and took off after him.

# Chapter 12

Shorty ran like a jackrabbit. I followed, but not with any hope of catching up or keeping him in sight if he didn't slow down. It didn't matter. When I rounded the barn, he'd joined a tableau posed along one side of the newest excavation square—a tableau of tan, brown, and starch. Shorty, Darla, and Clod, Smokey Bear hats in place, stood in a row at the edge of the pit, fists on hips, bent forward at the waist, staring at a feature Jerry and Zach were pointing at like proud parents. Jerry was on one knee, one long arm and index finger extended. Zach looked electrified. He stood, legs spread wide and with all ten fingers of his palms-up hands splayed toward the feature. The tableau became vivant when Zach said something I didn't hear, since by then I was winded and puffing. It sounded as though he said, "Bite me."

I did hear Shorty's disgust when I panted to a stop on the adjacent edge of the pit.

"I friggin' don't believe it." He took his hat off and slapped the brim against his thigh.

Zach fairly danced as he turned to make sure I appreciated their work. They'd dug down to the level of the elbow, only deep enough to see, not enough to rescue—

the elbow connected to the arm bones, the shoulder bones, pretty much the whole shooting match . . .

"Was she shot?" I asked. None of the "grown-ups" answered my question. Zach shrugged and bent to brush dirt from a scapula. I stared and couldn't stop staring at the back of the skull, the framework of bones emerging from their pit. Thin. Fragile. Exposed after years under clay and unknowing boots and hooves and bare feet crisscrossing through lush grass above. They lay in the warm morning sun. Why didn't they shiver?

"You had insider information," Shorty was saying. He straightened and looked over Clod's still bent back at Darla. "Had to be."

"No, she did not," Jerry Hicks said. "There is no insider information possible in an excavation like this. Darla won the bet fair and square."

"Darla was *here*." Shorty shot a finger at the pit. "And I was stuck looking for—"

Clod laid a hand on Shorty's shoulder, and then he used that shoulder as though it alone helped him rise to his full height so that he looked down at the top of Shorty's head. He took his hand off Shorty's shoulder and took a moment to readjust Shorty's sleeve. Shorty tightened his lips and made no further comment.

"What Shorty means to say, Deputy Dye, is that he'll be happy to pay up. He's a man of his word. And that's the end of it."

"What were you betting on?" I asked.

Darla gazed off into the trees to her left. Shorty clapped his hat back on his head. Zach, eyes bright and wide, looked from one to the other of the four and started to open his mouth.

Clod's voice bulldozed right past Zach. "That's the end of it. Nothing more to discuss. How much more time do you need, Hicks?"

"Until there's nothing more to dig."

"*Two* so far," Zach exploded. "Darla guessed more than one and wins twenty bucks."

"What?" I asked. "Two what?" But I already knew. *"Where?"*

"Second skull." Jerry showed me the rounded bone breaking the surface of the clay not more than a foot from the first skull. Occipital lobe? Parietal? Zach probably knew. "Deeper than our first guy," Jerry said. "Maybe partially beneath. Too early to say."

"Him?" I asked. "Male?"

"A guess."

Our words clattered, as spare as the bones, but in my case that was because the images and possibilities the bones conjured ran wild and I had trouble holding them back.

"How many . . ." I waved my hands to finish that sentence.

"As I said." Clod didn't move, but his words crossed their arms and lowered their brow. He waited. When we were all looking at him, he said to Jerry, "Keep me informed." Then he looked at me. "I meant what I said. There is nothing more to discuss. When we do know more, the sheriff will issue a statement. I'd appreciate your discretion in this matter. That goes for you, too, Aikens."

Zach brushed dirt from between two ribs, bending close.

"You're Ty Aikens' boy, aren't you?" Clod asked. "And Isaac's little brother? Your daddy's still in for misdemeanor theft, isn't he? Third offense? But I hear Isaac got out last month. My advice? Stay away from both of them."

Jerry got down on one knee and faced Zach on the other side of the skeleton, his broad back making an effective barrier between Clod and the teen. "Let me show you how a professional does it, dude." He took his own stiff brush from a back pocket. "Concentrate on the surface and the shape." He brushed around a kneecap, speaking loudly enough for the three deputies behind him to hear. "Be aware of what's going on around your artifact, but focus your attention here. After a while, it's like the rest of the world goes away. Been my experience, anyway."

If a smile touched Zach's lips, it disappeared before Clod or Shorty saw, when they passed him on their way back to their cars. I waved to Darla, who remained on excavation sentry duty, and followed Clod and Shorty.

Clod had said he'd appreciate my discretion about the second set of bones. I understood his request. Of course I did. That's why I waited until he and Shorty were far enough ahead that they couldn't hear me. And then I made a discreet call to Ardis.

"Two," Ardis said with a disbelieving cluck. "Will this make it easier?"

"Or twice as hard? I don't know."

When I got back to the parking lot, two of the sheriff's cars were gone. The day looked brighter already. I carried my materials inside and dropped them off in the education room, then went to find Nadine. Her office door was closed and she didn't answer a knock. Yet she must be in the building. The front door wasn't locked. The lights were on.

I stood in the long hall listening and heard muffled voices. In the auditorium to my left? Or down the hall to the right? Down the hall, to the right, in Phillip's office? Without much effort, I convinced myself the voices might be coming from Phillip's office. And I should go check. Make a security check. As a good volunteer.

Hesitating only slightly, I turned my back on the more obvious voices in the auditorium and walked quickly to Phillip's office door. Nothing stirred. I put my ear to the door to be sure—quiet inside—then tried the knob. It turned. I cast a clichéd look left and right, slipped inside with another scan of the hall over my shoulder, and pulled the door shut behind me.

Clod sat at the desk.

"Oh." I could be remarkably eloquent. Eloquent enough to stun Clod, anyway, because he didn't say anything. Or maybe his silence was due to my sudden, not to say sneaky, appearance in the office of a dead man. Clod looked at home behind the desk and oddly academic, pulling a pair of half-lens reading glasses to the end of his nose. He almost looked safe. "You should wear those more often," I said. "Suspects will probably relax and tell you more."

"Is there more *you* want to tell me?"

"Oh. No." I tried to look and sound offhand. "I came to check on the copier. Because I'll need to make copies later. For my quilting program." I pointed to the machine I'd seen sitting on the filing cabinet the day before. I followed my pointing finger over to it. "Ah. A copier and printer combination. That's a nice feature. Looks standard. We shouldn't have any problems." While I driveled, I glanced down the front of the filing cabinet. Nothing about the labels on the three drawers jumped out at me.

Loan documents in the top drawer . . . But what did I think I'd find? A label pointing me in the direction of a letter marked "In the Event of My Murder"?

"Now that you've hunted down the elusive copier, can I help you find anything else?"

"No, thanks. I'm good. This should work." I lifted the lid of the copier in a last effort to lend verisimilitude to my terrible acting. A document lay on the glass. It took all my willpower not to react, not to pick it up, to lower the lid, and turn around.

The long arm of the law intervened. "Interesting," Clod said. He'd moved fast, coming up behind me. His arm reached over my shoulder. His hand kept the lid from closing. "Were you looking for this?"

"No. But people leave things in copiers all the time." He was standing too close. I moved sideways. "What is it?"

"Did you know your voice gets tighter and higher when you're telling stories?" He turned toward me and held his hand up. "Before you go off on me, I did not say 'lying.' Your song and dance about looking at the copier might be true enough. But what you said about people leaving documents in copiers? That's when your voice sounded normal for the first time since you broke in here."

"I *didn't* break in."

"And now you're showing honest, spontaneous emotion. Makes your voice huskier."

He still hadn't taken the paper off the glass. He looked from me to the copier, then smiled and closed the lid. "It's probably not the clue you're looking for. A document left in a copier? Not usually a case-breaker."

"You're not going to look at it? Phillip thought he

knew who's buried out there. He was going to share his notes with me. What if that's one of his notes? What if it tells us something?"

"*Me*. It might tell me something. Highly doubtful, though. And *I* will look at it after I finish with the desk. Call me a methodical plodder, but I like doing things in order. These are all bona fide detective tips, by the way, in case you want to write them down."

Calling him a methodical plodder wasn't the first thing that came to mind. "I thought you had Grace all stitched up for Phillip's murder. What are you looking for?"

"Stitched, huh?" He put his fist on his hip and leaned artfully to one side, as though he'd practiced his John Wayne look in a mirror. "Clever. And quilting? That's why you're hanging around here again? I'll put this in terms you'll understand, then. I'm looking for the odd pieces. Tying off loose ends. See? I know your jargon. I used to watch my grandmother quilt. I'm not without needle skills."

"*Needle* skills? Good for you." That sounded only half sarcastic. "Why were you needling Zach Aikens out there? Why did you embarrass him like that?"

"You don't know his family."

"He can't help who he's related to, and he's a smart kid."

"Then he'll take my message as cautionary. But you met him, what, yesterday? Day before? You don't know *him*, either. Now, if you don't mind, I have official business to attend to. Please shut the door on your way out."

It took most of my self-control not to slam the door. It took a soupçon of what was left to leave the door very . . . slightly . . . open, and walk away.

*       *       *

With my nerves hovering on the brink of a Clod-induced simmer, I went back down the hall to the education room to see if my volunteers had arrived. Shirley Spivey, or it might have been Mercy, hovered inside the door as though waiting to pounce on me. When the twin saw me, she struck a pose with one hand artfully indicating the mobcap on her head and the other spreading the fabric of her ankle-length patchwork skirt for maximum effect. Mercy's unpleasant cologne didn't spread in cloying waves with the spreading of the skirt, so in my role as keen detective, I deduced that this was Shirley.

"Oh." Really, my eloquence knew no bounds.

"Good!" Shirley exclaimed. "You like it. We weren't sure you would. But we thought we should rally to the spirit of the program and dress the part. It's good for the kiddos to see how we did things in the olden days."

"You used to dress like that? When?"

"Not us, per se, but you know what I mean."

No, I didn't know what she meant, and even my eloquent "oh" failed to cover for me. I tried blinking as though in accord, instead. Then I looked more closely at Shirley's skirt—eccentric pieces of embroidered velvets in colors so deep they approached black until they caught the light as Shirley moved. "Shirley, your skirt's beautiful. Where did it come from?"

Mercy marched over before Shirley answered. Her mobcap had slipped down the back of her head, revealing her badly permed gray hair, and she wore the twin of Shirley's skirt. Both skirts looked as though they'd been fashioned from an antique crazy quilt.

"The kiddos have started arriving and that woman with the bee up her nose—"

"Mabeline," Shirley said.

"Nadine," I said.

"She asked where you were," Mercy said. "Is she always that uptight? Or do you think that's because of the murder? Come to think of it, that's probably it. Some people can't handle that kind of stress. Anyway, don't worry. We covered for you."

"We found the notes and materials you left in here," said Shirley. "I organized the notes, and Mercy distributed the needles and fabric around the tables."

That worried me, but I had another question for them. "Should you be wearing those skirts?" I asked. "Aren't you afraid something will happen to them? Where *did* you get them?"

"Tell her," Mercy said, nudging Shirley with her elbow. "We made them. As for wearing them, we don't like to keep our light under a bushel."

"Crazy quilting is our forte," said Shirley.

"I'll say. I'm . . . I am so impressed. Why haven't I seen these skirts before?"

"You might be surprised how few occasions there are for taking our light out from under the bushel," said Mercy. "New Year's Eve is about it. This seemed appropriate."

Hardly. There was nothing historically accurate about the skirts as clothing and they weren't practical for working—or volunteering—at a historic site. But I wasn't about to argue. I wanted to fall into the blue blacks, inky emeralds, and deep purples of those skirts. I wanted to trace their feather stitches and running daisies.

"What else have you made?" I asked. "May I?" I backed into a chair at one of the tables, and sat, leaning forward, my elbows on my knees. Shirley swished closer and stood in front of me. Mercy moved in beside her. Their crazy quilt velvet skirts took up my entire field of vision. Even Mercy's cologne didn't matter. I clasped my hands between my knees and drank in those skirts. "This velvet is silk, isn't it? I mean, with no synthetics. Is it old? And what about the embroidery threads?"

"Our mother had a box of silk threads. Go on and feel it, if you want," Shirley said.

"She won't, I told you," said Mercy. "It's her training."

My textile training, yes, but also my new fear of "feeling" when touching certain fabrics.

"The velvet and threads were handed down from Rebecca," Shirley said.

I glanced up. "Rebecca who made the Plague Quilt?" I tried to look around the skirts. "Where is it? Did you bring it?"

"Backseat of the car—*oof*." Shirley's skirt shifted to the left.

"It's safe at home," Mercy said.

"As I was saying," Shirley said, "our velvet came from Rebecca. She had two daughters and a son. Her wedding present to each of them, her daughters and the daughter-in-law, was six bolts of velvet and silk threads in enough colors to embroider a garden."

"Granny's mother was the daughter-in-law, right? Rebecca was Granny's granny? I've never heard that story about the velvet and threads. How cool. But that would have been ninety or more years ago. And you made these skirts from some of that velvet? You still had some of it?"

"Ours is the thrifty side of the family," Shirley said.

"No telling how the rest of it was used," said Mercy. "Or wasted. Here, forget your dang training."

I only half listened, so I wasn't prepared for Mercy's sudden move. She twitched a handful of her skirt, flipping the bottom up and into my lap.

I caught it in my hands.

# Chapter 13

I was lying on the floor, looking up into the faces of a dozen curious teens and an anxious Nadine. I felt as though I'd been lost in a complicated embroidery pattern, as though I'd watched a stop-action video of . . . of what? The history of the Spivey family? Because I'd held the hem of Mercy's skirt in my hands . . .

I realized Clod was holding my hand. I yanked my hand from his and worked very hard not to wipe it manically on my pants leg. Shivers went through me and I jammed both hands in my armpits. I heard an odd, gurgling noise and realized it came from me. I stopped when I also realized one of the teenage girls standing near my feet was crying.

"Hey, I'm okay." I sat up. "See? I'm fine."

Clod was still too close and everyone else was staring. Except the twins. I didn't see them. And I couldn't smell Mercy. Where had they gone with those skirts as dark as night, velvet night . . . nightmares . . .

"Did you hit your head?" Clod asked. "Come on, we should get you checked out." He put his hand out to help me stand.

"What? No. No, really, I'm okay." I was, too. Head

clear again, breathing easily, steady hands. I stood up. "I'm okay now. Thank you, though."

"All right, everyone, the drama is over," Nadine said. "It *is* over, isn't it?" She glared at me, looking and sounding more angry than anxious. "The quilting *will* take place?"

"Sure, Nadine. Of course. Give me five minutes?"

She leaned close, still glaring. "You were supposed to be ready to start," she hissed, "and this is turning into my personal nightmare. You need to start and finish, on time, so that Wes can start and finish on time. He's stepping in for Phillip, but he is a busy man, with other commitments, and we cannot *waste* his time."

*And I frittered my own copious hours away, lolling on cold linoleum floors.* I leaned closer to Nadine, reducing the comfort gap further, and stared without blinking until she pulled back. I'd used that technique before, and found it effective for unnerving confrontational colleagues. I thought of it as my "dead-eyed shark look." Considering how often Geneva used it effectively on me, I decided I could probably rename it my "dead-eyed ghost look."

"Fine, Nadine. No problem. We'll start immediately. But may I make a suggestion? *You* should take five minutes and get a grip." Ah, no, I should not have made the suggestion. Too late—mouth opened, tongue disconnected from brain. Granny would not have been proud, and neither was I.

Nadine gave me the look of an antagonized site director. It was a look that didn't bode well for gaining her confidence and permission to snoop in her domain. I should have slapped my forehead and apologized instantly, but Clod stepped between us in one of the smoothest moves I'd seen him make. Or maybe he'd missed the tension he'd interrupted, and he was taking the shortest route to the door. In fact, from the tilt of his head and the direction of his nose, it looked as though he'd seen someone or thought of something . . . Without another glance at Nadine or me, without another word, he quickened his pace and disappeared out the door.

And then I was torn. I wanted to follow him. He'd just reacted in an interesting way. To what? Why? I wanted to know where he was going. But Nadine was right—I needed to get the students engaged in the quilting. I needed to put my nosiness in check. Besides, Nadine saw Clod leave, too, and she was already going after him.

Nadine had either fudged on the number of teens who'd withdrawn from the program, or more had dropped out since she'd called me the night before. It didn't matter which was true. The first day, two dozen students sat in the auditorium listening to Phillip's introduction and followed him on the tour of the site. Now—one death, two skeletons, and two days later—half that many sat at tables in the education room, waiting for me to begin the quilt unit. I wondered if, in the name of public relations, Nadine had offered to refund the hefty chunk of money the dropouts had paid for the program.

I also wondered where Shirley and Mercy were. I didn't like to admit it, but I needed them; none of my other volunteers had shown up. I wasn't quite ready to agree with Nadine that the program was a disaster, but it couldn't take too many more body blows. And then I wished that turn of phrase hadn't popped into my head.

"Hi, welcome to the crazy quilt portion of Hands on History. It's nice to see all of you again. I'm Kath Rutledge. You can call me Kath or Ms. Rutledge; either works for me. I'm going to give you a short introduction to crazy quilts, we'll look at examples of quilt blocks and a few other artifacts, and then if we can, we'll jump right into the project." We would if the irritating Spiveys came back or the other volunteers arrived. I glanced at the door. That didn't make any of them magically appear. "Along the way, I'll work in information about nine-teenth- and early-twentieth-century textiles, and I'll do it in such a brilliantly seamless way that each of you will develop a burning desire to pursue advanced degrees in textile conservation." I looked around at them. "Didn't you have lanyards with name tags on Monday?"

"Mr. Bell collected them."

"Ah. Well, we're going to talk about autograph quilts anyway, so let's start by making one." I sketched a chart on a blank piece of paper—rectangles for the tables, squares for the students, and then added a frivolous saw-tooth border all around. "Quilts with embroidered signa-tures were popular keepsakes and going-away presents in the nineteenth century. They were a functional, deco-rative way of remembering friends. This will be my keep-sake, and at least for this morning I'll know your names." I held the paper up. "Your piece of the quilt is where you're sitting. Find your square on our seating quilt and put your name in it."

"Should we put our last names, too?"

"First and last names will be great. And neatly, please, so I can read them."

While they passed the seating chart, I stewed over the missing volunteers. The TGIF quilters were experts—artists who enjoyed hooking other people on their art. Our plan called for me doing my academic bit, but the

Hands on History quilt sessions really belonged to them. They'd be guiding the students through the steps of making a quilt—albeit a small one—from start to finish. Most of the volunteers had committed to quilting with the students each morning through the whole two-week program. Surely they hadn't all backed out in reaction to Phillip's death—not without telling either Nadine or me. So where were they?

Oh. I looked at the communicating door at the back of the room and felt like a fool. In the confusion of . . . everything . . . we'd no doubt crossed wires, and I would find them sitting in the auditorium, chatting happily and wondering where the heck *we* were.

But the auditorium was dark. Empty, too, unless the Spiveys hung like a couple of old bats from the ceiling. On my way back to the front of the room, I pulled out my phone and called Ardis.

"I haven't heard anything on this end," she said when I told her what was going on. "Don't send anyone looking around for them."

"It isn't dangerous, Ardis."

"We don't know that, but I can find them faster with a few phone calls than a teenager will traipsing around the Homeplace. I'll hunt, you punt, and I'll call you back."

I disconnected and one of the girls handed me the completed chart. "Thanks . . ." I waited to see where she sat down. "Thanks, Barb. This is great. All right, let's get started with a question. What do zombies and yoga pants have in common with bacon-flavored ice cream?"

And there wasn't a single peep. *Zach would have gotten that riddle,* I told myself. But he'd attached himself to Jerry and the skeleton. Skeletons. Two skeletons. Did these kids know there were two? Two and counting? Did that mean it wasn't Geneva out there? Or was it Geneva and someone else? Two bodies where they shouldn't be . . . the memory of two bodies haunting Geneva . . .

"Ma'am? Are you sure you're all right?" Ethan, according to the chart.

They really were a nice bunch of teenagers. They continued staring at me, but now they looked concerned instead of clueless.

"Sorry." I gave myself a shake and smiled at them. "Zombie walking over my grave. What do zombies, yoga pants, and bacon-*anything* have in common? They're fads. Everyone agree with that?" They did. "Good. People followed fads in the 1890s, too, and making crazy quilts was one of them. Quilters—men as well as women and girls—made crazy quilts for a variety of reasons, and not just to sleep under. This was the height of the Victorian era, and people loved clutter. They filled their parlors with curios—" I stopped. "Do you know what a curio is?"

"I don't, but I'm curious." That wag, sitting next to Ethan, was Nash. They fist-bumped and sat back, looking pleased.

"Kudos for being curious. The term 'conversation piece' was coined at that time. They filled their parlors with objects—natural and man-made—from around the country and around the world, and crazy quilts fit into that trend. You saw the crazy quilts on display in the museum here on Monday. Did their crazy—their crazed—pattern remind you of looking through a kaleidoscope? Because the Victorians loved kaleidoscopes, too, and some historians see a connection between that love and the love for crazy quilts."

"I can see that," Barb said.

"Good." And then I realized that I *had* seen that—the weird patterns that spun through my head when my hands touched Mercy's skirt were completely kaleidoscopic. Thinking about it, trying to anchor those fractured, spinning images, trying to bring them into focus, threatened to make my head spin again. I needed to concentrate on what I was doing.

"Crazy quilts," I said on a deep breath, "were *it*. And the Gilded Age Victorians put them everywhere. They covered pianos with them and draped them on tables and on the backs of sofas. And the quilts weren't just part of the clutter. With their lush fabrics, lack of symmetrical or repetitive patterns, and elaborate embroidery, the quilts themselves were cluttered. Quilters created them out of scraps of velvet, pieces of favorite dresses, handkerchiefs, men's ties, silk cigar bands, ribbons commemorating special celebrations and events, and out of the clothes of loved ones who'd passed on."

"They recycled," said a boy sitting behind Barb—that would be Tyler.

"They did, Tyler. But not always. Companies were as sharp in 1880 as they are today, and some of them capitalized on the crazy quilt fad. You could go down to the mercantile in Blue Plum and buy bags of velvet and silk scraps packaged specifically for crazy quilts. Or you could buy them through mail order. And you could buy magazines with quilt patterns and embroidery designs."

I held up a scrapbook I'd borrowed from Ernestine. Her granddaughter had started it when her first baby was born. I flipped through the pages so the students could see the decorative papers and colorful borders highlighting the story of the baby's first year.

"Do any of you know someone who scrapbooks?" I asked.

This time a few hands rose.

"Fad," one of the girls called. Megan.

"Yes, it is. And scrapbooking was a fad with Victorian women, too." I put Ernestine's scrapbook down and held up a pair of thin white cotton gloves. "Watch this." I put on the gloves and picked up another scrapbook, older and more fragile. "Why the gloves, do you think? To protect my hands from old paper and glue?"

"To protect old paper and glue from *you*," Zach said from the doorway.

"Absolutely right, and a hank of embroidery floss goes to the unexpected young gent in the doorway. Are you taking a break from digging, or are you joining us?"

"Jerry said he only needs a skeleton crew right now," Zach said with the ultimate deadpan. He slunk into the room to a chorus of groans from the other students, and sank onto his spine in a chair at a table by himself.

An interesting kid, Zach Aikens. As far as I knew him, I liked him. And I heartily resented Clod for planting the doubt in my mind that made me add that qualifier. I couldn't think of anything about Zach's behavior that wasn't part of the typical growing pains of teenagers anywhere or from any family. He was a bright kid who shouldn't be considered dubious just because he had law-breaking relatives. Nor should he be dismissed merely on the say-so of a deputy who had his own iffy brother. Not that I thought Joe was really all that iffy.

"Burglars," I said, regaining the teens' attention. "Burglars and museum professionals also have something in common. We wear gloves because we don't want to leave fingerprints behind. Hands, no matter how clean, leave oils that attract dirt. *This* scrapbook"—I held the clothbound book higher—"comes from the collection here at the Homeplace. Lillian Holston started it in 1876, pasting swatches of silk, velvet, cotton, and linen fabrics in it, and also samples of embroidery stitches. It started out as her quilting scrapbook. Her friends might have made quilting scrapbooks, too, because scrapbooks *about* quilting were as much a fad as quilting itself. Lillian dated some of the pages, and she wrote notes on others with ideas for color schemes and patterns. Toward the end of the book she began pasting in newspaper articles that must have caught her eye, mostly about parties and social functions. Again, some of them are dated and some aren't, but she seems to have worked on the scrapbook for about three years."

I walked around the tables, turning pages so the students could see the fabrics, stitches, and newspaper articles.

"Did she ever make the quilt, and do we have to make those fancy stitches?" Megan asked.

"I don't know if Lillian made the quilt," I said.

"Why not?" Zach asked.

"That's a good question. I might know if she made the quilt if I knew the collections better. As a volunteer for this program, and because of my professional background, I was allowed to look through the collections. But the collections are fairly extensive, and I only had time for a brief survey of the records to find appropriate artifacts to illustrate what I'm talking about."

"She means it was a rush job, but she looked around and found stuff for show-and-tell," said Ben.

"You're right. That is what I meant. Thank you for abbreviating and clarifying. The bottom line is, any number of things could have happened." I ticked them off on my fingers. "If Lillian made the quilt, it might be here, resting safely and comfortably in storage. Or she might have made it and given it away. Maybe it's lying somewhere in sunny California, even as we speak. Or she might have been big on making plans but not so much on following through. Or maybe she made the quilt and it was well loved, well used, and completely worn out. It might have ended up, along with so many other things, in the household dump behind the barn."

"Wrapped around one of those other things called a human body," said Ben.

I could have thought that last supposition through better. While I kicked myself, Zach offered his observations.

"The bones in the dump are clean. If the dudes we found out there were wrapped in a quilt, then the quilt rotted with them. They're dead. The quilt's gone. And so far the bones aren't talking." If he'd been wearing a fedora, he would have pushed it low over his eyes at that point and put his feet up on the table, crossed at the ankles. He settled for crossing his arms and sinking his chin onto his chest.

*"Them?"* Megan asked.

The girl I'd seen crying earlier, when I'd caught Mercy's skirt and done my momentary flake-out, was sniffling quietly again and staring at the table. Her name was Carmen, and it seemed a good bet she wouldn't come back after today, or even after lunch. Barb moved over and put an arm around her.

"Why don't we take a break from quilts for a few minutes." I put the scrapbook down and peeled off the gloves. I wasn't sure what to do, but it seemed pretty harsh to ask these kids to continue with the program as if nothing had happened. "Carmen, would you rather go home? Do you want to call someone?"

She shook her head no.

I looked around at the rest of the students. Some of them watched Carmen, and others seemed to be avoiding looking at her. Zach doodled long bones on the back of one of the handouts I'd given them. What I was about to do might not be the wisest idea, but it couldn't be worse than plowing straight ahead with the program and ignoring obvious distress.

"Has anyone talked to you guys about the bones or what happened to Mr. Bell? Did Ms. Solberg or Deputy Dunbar say anything?"

"Is there more than one skeleton?" Ben asked.

Clod had told me not to say anything about the second skeleton. He probably thought he had a good reason. I didn't know what it was, though, and I couldn't see what difference it would make. Lying sure didn't seem the right thing to do.

"Yes. It looks as though there are two."

Without looking up from his doodles, Zach held up two fingers.

"Would it help if we stopped and talked about what's happened? About what's going on with the dig? Carmen, is that okay with you?"

She nodded and wiped at her nose with the back of her hand.

Barb pulled a tissue from a pocket and handed it to Carmen. "Ms. Solberg said we aren't supposed to talk about any of it, if tourists ask us while we're here at the site," she said.

"This has been a rough, unusual, and emotional start

to a program," I said. "And Barb, I want to thank you for being a good friend to Carmen. You're all showing how resilient you are by being here. I'd like to thank all of you for that, too. So, what did you think of Ms. Solberg telling you not to talk with visitors?"

"She said she was treating us like professionals and professionals wouldn't engage in idle speculation with visitors," Barb answered.

Several of the students sat up straighter, as though trying to look more like professionals. Zach sank lower on his spine.

"That's a good point," I said. "Rumors are quick to start and hard to stop, and it's better not to be the source of them, or the place they splatter when they land. You can call that professional ethics. Or plain old everyday ethics. Ethics aside, though, has anyone said anything specific to you about the skeletons or Mr. Bell's death?" My possibly unwise plan to offer comfort was skating closer to the thin ice of snooping and prying. "Were any names mentioned? Any theories? Suggestions of a motive? Or a weapon?" Definitely unwise now.

Carmen and Barb looked at each other and shook their heads.

"They wouldn't tell us anything like that," Megan said. "They want us to act like professionals, but they still treat us like kids. Which is, technically, what we are."

"Point taken. They didn't tell you. But did you happen to *hear* anything?"

Ethan raised his hand. "Mr. Bell said something about the skeletons. He said, 'Up until cemetery dude found the skeleton, this was going to be a good program. Now it's going be a great program.'"

"He didn't say 'great,'" Nash said.

"Yeah, he did."

"Nope. He didn't. He said 'incendiary.'"

*"Dude."* Remembrance and enlightenment lit Ethan's face. "And that was *before* he knew there were two skeletons. So what's better than incendiary? Maybe he thought it would go, like, thermonuclear."

"Why, how, and what?" Nash asked with dampening rationality. "Dude, we're at a two-week history-geek fest at the Homeplace. In Blue Lump, Tennessee. Big whoop. There's nothing close to thermonuclear here. Besides, he never knew there were two. He was dead before they found the second one." He turned to Zach. "When did you find the second one?"

Ethan didn't give Zach a chance to answer. "But maybe that's *why* he was killed. Because he *did* know there was more than one."

"Whoa, whoa, whoa, guys." I interrupted before Ethan got too carried away. "Remember the ethics thing? Going off on 'what ifs' is what Ms. Solberg meant, and why she doesn't want you discussing this with visitors."

The faces of both teens closed a bit.

"On the other hand, I'm not a visitor and I love 'what ifs.' But are you sure Mr. Bell used the word 'incendiary'? It's not as over-the-top as 'thermonuclear,' but it still is over-the-top."

"So was he," Zach said without looking up from his doodles. He'd started a row of toothless jawbones.

"No, he wasn't. He was *cute*," Carmen blurted, and immediately clapped a hand over her mouth, her cheeks glowing.

"Does anyone have any idea what he meant by 'incendiary'?" I asked, moving away from Carmen, so that eyes might follow me and give her a moment to get her flames under control. "Did he say how the program would change or be different? Did you get the feeling he meant it would be better? He seemed pretty wired after Zach found the bones. But did he say anything that gives us a clue to what he meant?"

Those questions got nothing but shrugs. Then my phone rang. It was poor form, but I checked the display. Ardis.

"News about our quilting volunteers," I said to the teens. "Excuse me for a second."

Ardis didn't wait for a hello. "You'll never guess who it was who told your volunteers you didn't need them," she said. "Flat-out said you wouldn't need them. You'll never guess."

"Then I won't try. Who was it?"

"Nadine."

# Chapter 14

"*What?*" I quickly put my reaction in check and smiled for the students' benefit.

"The message came from Nadine."

"What kind of sense does that make?" Incredulity fought for the upper hand, but I managed to keep my voice low and even.

"Heaven only knows. There's a lot going on, and she might not be thinking. Maybe she was confused."

"Right. Thanks for checking, Ardis. I'll see you later."

I disconnected, still smiling for the students' benefit, seething for my own. Did Nadine *want* a disaster? If she'd called the volunteers, then that was why Shirley and Mercy disappeared, too. She must have cornered them and sent them packing. With the Plague Quilt. Did that mean I'd have to strike some other bargain with the twins? Talk about disaster! I felt like hunting Nadine down and asking her what her game was. But maybe it really was a game. Maybe Ardis was right and someone misinterpreted Nadine's message like an old-fashioned game of telephone. That seemed idiotic, but about as plausible as Nadine canceling the volunteers without warning or telling me.

I talked myself down from my high horse, deciding to give Nadine the benefit of the doubt, or at least a chance to deny or explain. And I knew I'd better find my cool before asking her. We didn't need more tension, or outright antagonism.

"Interesting news about our quilting volunteers," I said to the students. "And that news is we're going to start our hands-on quilt project with the basics—so basic we don't need volunteers. Our goal is to end up with a small signature crazy quilt."

Ethan raised his hand. "Who gets to keep it?"

"It'll be one of the featured items in a gala auction, raising funds for the Homeplace, later this fall."

Ethan's hand stayed up. "Whose signatures?"

"Yours for starters. And maybe some local celebrities will contribute theirs."

"Like who?" Barb asked.

"Ms. Solberg is working on that. What we're going to work on, today, is a basic embroidery stitch." Because I'd never pieced a crazy quilt in my life. But there was time for piecing later, after I reassembled the volunteers. This program, and especially the quilting portion of it, was *not* going to be a disaster. "How many of you have ever threaded a needle?"

Without too many fumbles or pricked fingers, I left them practicing their chain stitch. I had to exact a promise from Ethan and Nash that they'd stop using their needles as miniature épées, and then I went hunting, wondering if I needed a sword in case Nadine turned into a dragon. If not a sword, then maybe an apology would do the trick.

Nadine and Wes stood in the visitors' center lobby talking to a woman whose back was turned to me. The woman had her hands stuck in the back pockets of her jeans, reminding me immediately of Grace, and for that instant, I thought the sheriff had released her. But this woman had more curves than Grace, and hair falling to her shoulders instead of Grace's shorter hair tucked behind her ears.

I waited at the corner where the hall I was in met the lobby, not sure if I should interrupt. When I heard Nadine mention the police and Phillip's cottage, I stayed put.

"All I can tell you is what they've told me," Nadine said. "They haven't finished and they aren't ready to let anyone else go in to pack or clean."

While she listened to Nadine, the woman gathered her heavy hair and lifted it off her neck, exposing a small tattoo below and behind her ear. From where I stood, it looked like a cardinal's feather. She put an elastic band around her hair and let it fall in a low ponytail.

"When I hear anything, I'll let you know," Nadine said.

The woman said something in return that I didn't catch. But I did catch her laugh—not a happy laugh, but low, throaty, and familiar. I was sure I'd heard it before, when I called Phillip. This had to be the woman who'd answered his phone.

Nadine caught sight of me then. I really wasn't trying to be invisible. Or surreptitious. Much. I smiled to cover a lingering sense of sneakiness, though, and went over to join them. Wes Treadwell, looking serious and concerned, nodded. Nadine didn't return my smile or nod, but she didn't snarl or bite my head off, either. She did introduce me to the woman.

"Kath, you wanted to meet Fredda Oliver, and here she is. Fredda is our wonderful and valuable site caretaker. Fredda, I'd like you to meet Kath Rutledge. Kath is one of the volunteers for the Hands on History program.

Fredda was . . . steamy. Not just her curves, throaty

voice, thick dark hair, and the long-lashed, sleepy eyes with which she regarded me. She was sweaty, too. Apparently she'd just finished mowing the back forty. Or something. I was at least ninety-five percent sure she was the woman laughing and answering Phillip's phone that night, but she gave no flicker of recognition when Nadine introduced us. What had Clod and Shorty said, though? That Fredda told more believable lies than I did. Or than my face did. So, again, there was the question I'd asked Joe that he hadn't answered—what did Fredda have to lie about? And what, if anything, did that have to do with Phillip's death? Being able to lie wasn't necessarily the first step on the road to ruination and murder. Still, if she lied to Clod and Shorty . . . I decided to put her face to a test.

"It's nice to meet you," I said. "I think we might've spoken on the phone, once."

She appeared to think back, but all she came up with was a shake of her head. "I can't think why we would have."

And I couldn't see how I'd learned a thing from that dumb experiment. She didn't look as if she was lying, but how was I supposed to know? I hadn't chosen my question wisely.

"Any particular reason you wanted to meet me?" Fredda asked.

"Someone mentioned your name. I guess I was surprised I hadn't bumped into you before."

"And now you have. Nice to meet you, too."

I couldn't tell if that was true, either, but somehow I doubted it. Her greeting didn't leave me all warm and fuzzy, anyway.

"I'll talk to you later, Nadine," she said. "You're right; I am curious to see the inside of the place. So, yeah, give me a call when you know his folks will be here, and if it's after hours, there's no need for you to come all the way out. I'll let them in."

"I'll come out no matter what time they arrive, Fredda," Nadine said. "I'll want to offer my condolences in person. I can't imagine what they're going through right now."

Wes put a hand on Nadine's elbow. She didn't quite jump at his touch, but for a second her back straightened, then relaxed.

I didn't know if Fredda saw that tiny interaction, too, but as she passed me on her way out, she gave me the hint of a wink. "I understand we have a friend in common," she said, her husky voice low in her throat. Before I could ask her who, her voice chuckled even lower. "That would be the more delicious of the two Dunbars."

I sort of lost my train of thought at that point, and it was all I could do not to stare after her with my mouth hanging open. Did she call Joe delicious and imply . . . what? Nadine's voice snapped me back.

"Did you need something, Kath?"

"To apologize for being short with you earlier, Nadine."

"We're all on edge," she said, sounding on edge and not entirely forgiving. "Is that all?"

"Also to run something by you." I'd thought of something I could do to punt the rest of the quilting session for the day. I slowed my breathing, trying to follow Clod's advice on relaxing one's vocal cords when lying. "Phillip suggested that I take the students on a tour of the storage area and archives, taking half the group at a time. Now that we're down to half as many, I thought I might as well take all of them at once. That won't be a problem, will it?"

"As long as they're ready to break for lunch and Wes' presentation, I don't see why that should be a problem."

"Thanks. Phillip didn't tell me where the key for the storage room is, though." I felt entirely honest saying that, and must have sounded it, too. I should remember to thank Clod.

"There's a key box on the wall behind the door in his office."

"And I won't need a key for the box?"

"No."

Wes looked bored with our housekeeping details. That shouldn't have bothered me; I didn't know the man and didn't need to care about what he thought. But I'd known men like him. Administrative types who couldn't be bothered to take, or at least fake, an interest in what the women standing with them were talking about. If Wes had looked contemplative or preoccupied, I might have given him a pass. He'd ignored me the other day, when he and Nadine came to see the bones, though, and now he looked on the verge of rolling his eyes, and that was too much. I wanted to wake him up, and it was tempting to tip him over the eye-rolling edge by asking him something to do with fibers or textiles or some other "woman's" subject. Instead I asked him what he planned to talk about over lunch during his presentation for the students. My ploy might have worked, too, but Nadine answered first.

"Wes has graciously come to the rescue by stepping up to the plate and stepping in for Phillip."

That didn't tell me what he was going to talk about, but it did tell me he was a verifiable home-run king and superhero all rolled into one. Or maybe that was too sarcastic. Maybe it just told me that there were interesting dynamics between Nadine and Wes. Suspicious dynamics? Who knew?

I'd left the students for longer than I meant to, and turned to go, and then I remembered what else I wanted to ask.

"One more question, Nadine. When you talked to the volunteers last night, you didn't tell any of them we didn't need them, did you?"

"Why would I do that? Is there a problem?" she demanded.

I waved her concerns away. "No, one of them said she'd heard something, and I said I'd ask. You know how these things go." Interesting. But if Nadine hadn't told the volunteers we didn't need them, who had and used her name? Or was Nadine as good a liar as Fredda? I'd watched her face and listened for tightening in *her* voice, and hadn't detected either. But maybe I wasn't so attuned to those clues as Clod was.

I dashed back to the education room, hoping to find a dozen teenagers bent industriously over their stitching. They weren't. They'd abandoned their needles and floss and were gathered around a table, transfixed by whatever they were looking at. All of them except Zach. He sat in his own world of tiny white bones that he'd chain-stitched on a scrap of black velvet. At first, I didn't see what held the other students so engrossed, but it didn't take more than a few breaths before the clues smacked me upside my nose. Then the students shifted, and there were Shirley and Mercy, hovering on the other side of the table. And there was the Plague Quilt, its deep colors and rich embroidery shimmering the way the surface of water does when it's far, far down in a well.

Barging in and wresting the class away from the Spiveys

was an option. In another situation, saving teenagers—or any innocent bystanders—from the twins' clutches might be the only option worth considering. Not this time, though. I crept in, on stealthy Kath feet, giving Zach a thumbs-up for creativity in embroidery on my way past. He was still cool, though, and didn't acknowledge my thumb.

The Plague Quilt drew me, and at the same time it worried me. What would happen if I touched it?

One of the students—Barb?—saw me and waved me forward.

"Look," she said, "it's got autographs."

In the one quick look the twins had allowed me the other day, I hadn't noticed signatures on the Plague Quilt. I'd been too caught up in the colors.

"They aren't signatures," Zach corrected.

"They're names," said Barb. "Same difference."

"Big difference," Zach said. "They're all in the same handwriting, so they aren't real autographs."

Barb made a face at Zach. He was more invested in his embroidered bones and didn't notice. *I* noticed the twins starting to refold the quilt.

"Wait," I said, practically leaping forward.

They folded faster, sliding the quilt back into its muslin bag and setting the bag on the table behind them, all in an annoying Spivey twinkling. And then they bossed the students back into their seats, clapping their hands and chivying them along by telling them time was wasting and quilts weren't made in a day. Oddly enough, their efforts were effective—the students complied without complaint.

But while they were being officious and efficient, the twins kept darting glances at me. If I moved to the left, one of them mirrored that movement. Through some secret Spivey sense, they tracked me and one of them faced me at all times. It was as though they didn't know what to expect from me. As though I might suddenly . . . what? Pounce on them? Grab the quilt and run?

They were in good company; I didn't know what to expect from me, either. I had questions for them, but I was wary, too—wary of upsetting them so that they'd take the quilt away and I'd never see it again, and wary of the quilt. Was there a connection between it and the twins' skirts, beyond the velvet coming from Rebecca? Did that matter? But I had two bigger questions. First, if Nadine hadn't told the twins we didn't need volunteers, then where had they disappeared to? And second, why was it called the Plague Quilt? The answer to the first question might be simple. They'd gone out to the car to get the quilt. But why had it taken so long? What had they been up to? "Up to" as opposed to "doing"—of that I was sure. I decided to treat the twins the way I did Geneva when she was skittish—act as though everything was going as planned. Go for the smooth. Nadine might not have known what that meant, but I was sure Zach would. Going for the smooth with the twins might be the only way to learn more about the quilt.

They were showing the students how to arrange various sizes and shapes of cotton scraps on squares of muslin for backing, looking at colors and patterns. The students were attentive and enjoying themselves, all of which put me in a quandary. Did I let the twins continue, or did I interrupt and take the students on the spurious tour of the storage area? Or . . . did I let the twins do their thing while I went on a solo reconnaissance tour of the storage and archives? I approached Shirley slowly, calmly, smoothly. I knew it was Shirley because I could breathe easily.

"I'm really glad to see the two of you, Shirley." I meant that, which surprised me. I felt bad about being surprised, but at least I was honest about it. Honest enough to know this happy-to-see-the-twins interlude probably wouldn't last and I should take advantage of it. I checked the clock. "You and Mercy are doing a great job."

"It's our passion," Shirley said.

"It shows." *She* didn't seem surprised either by my compliment or by my saying I was glad to see them. But maybe that was the way they got through life—and why not? If living in an oblivious, happy bubble really worked for them, more power to them. "The kids are supposed to break for lunch and a presentation from Wes Treadwell in half an hour."

Shirley made a choking noise.

"Are you okay?" I asked.

"She's fine," Mercy said. "Knee-jerk reaction. Skip back to the part about us doing a great job and leave Less-and-less Treadwell out of it."

"You know him?"

"We'd rather not."

"Oh. Well—"

"And we'd rather not talk about him."

"Okay. So, not talking about Wes Treadwell, are you two happy in here until lunch? Because if you don't need me, I thought I'd go into the storage area and scope out what to show the students."

"You mean snoop," said Mercy.

"Don't worry," Shirley said. "We'll cover for you."

# Chapter 15

The only wrinkle in my scheme, other than the Spiveys' seeing right through it, was noticing that Zach was gone. So were his embroidered bones. Phillip hadn't covered wandering students in our volunteer orientation. Nadine was aware he'd been helping Jerry, though, and she hadn't insisted that he stay with the rest of the group, so maybe I didn't need to worry. Unless I needed to worry about law-breaking. Doggone Clod for putting that in my head. And doggone Zach for disappearing.

As I went down the hall, Zach came out of the restroom. I felt like a jerk.

"Are you through embroidering for the day?" I asked.

"Are you abandoning the class to the old lady twins for the day?"

I looked left and right, but didn't see anyone else. "The Spiveys are experts in the actual art of quilting. I'm not. I'm taking this opportunity to look around the storage area and the archives."

Zach seemed to think that was an invitation to join me. Maybe it was. He was a student, after all, and my cover story was showing the storage and archives to students. *Way to take advantage of minors, Kath.*

"How old are you?"

"Seventeen."

"Sounds right. I need to stop in here."

Phillip's office door was open, with no deputies in sight. The copier lid was open, too, with no documents in sight. Dratted deputies. The key box—gray, metal, about the size of a phone book and several inches deep—was mounted on the wall behind the door. The storage room key hung inside on a duly labeled hook. I grabbed it and realized that Zach had hung back at the door, hands jammed in his pockets. Interesting that he was fine with sweeping dirt from old bones but reluctant to invade a dead man's office space.

"That his?"

I looked to see what he meant. "The banjo?"

"Banjos are cool."

"Do you play?"

His shoulder movement didn't tell me much. Banjos were cool, but discussing them obviously wasn't. Casual conversation probably wasn't cool, either, but as I led the way to the storage room, I tried anyway.

"What did Ms. Spivey and Ms. Spivey tell you about the quilt they showed you?" Okay, so the question wasn't all that casual. But I didn't ask leading questions. "Did they have a name for the quilt?" Okay, so I did ask a leading question, but at least I didn't suggest an answer.

"What do you mean, a name for it?"

"Some well-known quilts have names, the same way paintings or statues do. There's a famous one called the Kaleidoscope Quilt. Did the twins call theirs anything?"

"Like what?"

"That's what I was asking you." I unlocked and opened the storage room door, reaching around the frame to flip the light on. Ahead of us and stretching to the left for the length of the building were four ranks of six-foot-tall gray metal shelves—one row down each wall and two sets back to back down the middle of the long, narrow space—all laden with bundles and boxes large, medium, small, and enticing.

*"What do you see?"* I asked. But it wasn't a question for Zach, and I answered it myself. *"Wonderful things."*

"Huh?"

"It's a quotation. It's what Lord Carnarvon asked and what Howard Carter answered when he first looked into King Tut's tomb."

"Cool." He tried to see around me. "They got mummies here?"

"No. It's just something that always goes through my head when I open a door like this. Wait, though." I stayed in the doorway so he couldn't go past. "What *did* the twins say about the quilt? Humor me on this, okay? Old quilts are to me like Tut's tomb was to Carter and Carnarvon."

"I think I'm on Tut's team. The old ladies wouldn't let anyone else touch the quilt."

"It might be fragile."

"They talked about their great-grandmother. Could've been their great-great-grandmother. Whatever. *They* thought she was great, anyway, and they talked like they actually knew her, which I guess could be possible. How old are they, anyway?"

"That's an impolite question."

"You asked how old I am."

"They're somewhere in their early seventies." He didn't look impressed. "Anything else about the quilt?"

"The Tut connection."

"You've lost me. Is that something they said?"

"No. I did. It's a game. Connections. The connection between King Tut and the quilt is coffins. And you know, if you need to have a name for it, you could call it the Old Lady Quilt."

"Coffins?"

"Tiny coffins in a row on one edge. Thirteen of them."

I'd missed the signatures, and I'd missed the coffins. I hadn't been given enough time with the quilt. "Did the Spiveys say anything about the coffins? Or the signatures?"

"No. Are we actually going in there? Because, I'm like—"

"Yeah, come on. I'll show you around."

Phillip had given me a brief tour of the storage area when I'd agreed to be part of Hands on History, although he'd apologized for the "small-town, small-time" facilities.

"It's not what you're used to, coming from a state museum, is it?" he'd asked.

"It's exactly what I'm used to. Old things, lovingly cared for," I'd said. "And professionals doing the best they can with the resources they have."

"Then I'll put it another way," he'd said. "It's not what *I* plan to become used to."

I enjoyed showing Zach the eclectic variety of artifacts—from clay marbles to several dozen pairs of mule shoes to lace-edged antimacassars to an apple butter kettle and paddle—but I couldn't help feeling the loss of Phillip's joy and dramatics. I'd always thought of museum artifacts, resting quietly in their boxes and drawers, as waiting in suspended animation for the right interpreter to come along and tell their stories. And these artifacts—the Homeplace—lost a voice when Phillip died. Others would come along, but how sad that we'd missed out on his interpretations of those stories.

"Are you allergic to dust?" Zach asked.

I blew my nose.

"Because I don't see any, but if there is some, it might be so old that it's toxic."

"I'm sure that's it. There's probably toxic dust in these, anyway." I pointed to the filing cabinets and shelves of boxes that made up the archives. "It's hard to avoid a certain amount of dust in old papers."

"What's in them?"

"Artifact records, here," I said, pointing to the accession files cabinet. "Whole lives and fragments of lives, in the rest of it. The history of the Holston family in letters, deeds, newspaper clippings, ledgers, receipts, recipes, photographs, and who knows what else. So, what do you think?" I took the cotton gloves I'd worn earlier out of my pocket and put them back on, then pulled the top drawer out of the first archive cabinet and started flipping through the files. "Storage and archives are reasonably cool, right?"

He didn't answer, which was cool, and I continued flipping. Then I realized I was being rude by suddenly ignoring him, or at least being un-instructor-like. "That's the end of the tour, I guess. Any questions?"

"Yeah. What are you looking for?" He pointed at the open drawer, at the file in my hands, at my eyes, which kept returning to the clipping in the file.

"Elbows."

He looked down his seventeen-year-old nose at me.

"Access points." I ticked the points off on my fingers. "Names. A Holston family tree would be nice. Names of Holstons who lived here. Names of *anyone* who lived at the Homeplace. That kind of information shouldn't be too tough to find."

"Isn't all that in one of those guidebooks they sell in the gift shop?"

"Some of it. Histories are usually abridged, though. Looking for that information, and finding it easily, will tell us something about the site, too. About how much research has been done and about the state and extent of the archives. About what might be missing. I want to know what kinds of primary source materials are here. Someone else, with more time, is coming in later to do more thorough research. I'm just—" I checked the time on my phone. "We still have time before lunch, so if you want to stay and help, then you and I'll be the scouting party, finding likely access points, to save time later. What do you think?"

"I think I'm confused. Who are you trying to be, Harriet the Spy or Marshal Dillon?"

"You're too young to know Marshal Dillon."

"I'm not too young to know anything."

A box of white cotton gloves sat on top of the filing cabinets. I handed a pair to him. He curled his lip, but put them on.

As he opened a drawer in the second cabinet and started flipping, I wondered what Geneva would think of Zach. From the way she talked about Matt Dillon, she had a crush on him, thanks to her years of nonstop television watching during the time she'd haunted the cottage. Would she like Zach, because of that, and think of him as a *pardner*, or see him as an indecipherable modern kid? But being indecipherable was a teenager's general lot in life, and probably not so different from a ghost's lot in death.

I stopped my own flipping when I came to a file holding a clothbound book. Clothbound. What would happen if I touched it? Probably nothing. It was cloth but not clothing. Was that what made the difference with this weird extra and extraordinary "sense" I'd developed since Granny's death? Textiles were safe, but some textiles, made into clothing, somehow "radiated" the emotions of the person who wore them? Would the cloth-but-not-clothing rule make the difference so that I could touch the Plague Quilt? Maybe not if the quilt incorporated scraps from dresses. Did I dare touch it? Did I dare touch the book in the filing cabinet? Why not? I touched textiles all the time without flaking out and nothing would happen this time, either.

I pulled a glove off and dabbed a fingertip against the book. Nothing. I put all my fingertips on it. Nothing again. I put the glove back on and picked up the book. It turned out to be a household account book, kept between January 1874 and September 1875. I heard the absence of flipping from Zach and glanced over.

"Why'd you poke it?" he asked. "Did you think it would bite?"

"You can never be too careful. Have you found anything interesting?"

"To me? No."

Zach slid his drawer closed. I put the account book back in my drawer and thought about making a note for John about it. I patted my pockets. No paper. I turned to Zach. No Zach. But I heard quiet steps behind me, down one of the rows of metal shelves.

"Zach?"

"Yo."

"Be careful what you touch."

"Not an idiot."

"Neither am I." I checked the time again, opened the second drawer.

Then I heard an exultant cry from Zach. "Wicked."

"What'd you find?"

"No idea," he said, carrying his treasure toward me cradled in his gloved hands. "It's like a miniature bed of nails. What do you think it is?"

I knew what it was. And what it could be. A perfectly wicked murder weapon.

# Chapter 16

"That's a flax hackle, Zach."

Zach looked skeptical, as though I'd pawned a Dr. Seuss rhyme off on him. What he held was a heavy board, six inches wide and a foot long, about an inch thick, with four or five dozen six-inch-long sharp spikes sticking up out of it in even rows—exactly like a miniature bed of nails.

"A hackle is what you use to comb the last pieces of straw from flax when you're processing it. Sometimes they're called heckles." I tried to get a closer look at the spikes without being too obvious. I couldn't see any signs of . . . of recent use or hasty cleaning. "Where did you find it?"

"Back there."

"Show me."

I followed him along the row of metal shelves, looking at his back, wondering if he had any idea what he carried. Except that it wasn't this one, couldn't have been. Zach stopped and shrugged his shoulder at an empty space on the middle shelf of the unit along the wall. The space was large enough for several hackles, and the last time I'd looked, when Phillip and I had talked about involving the students in the flax processing, there had been two.

"I didn't hurt it," Zach said.

"Did I say you *did*?" I retorted, and immediately felt bad. "Sorry, Zach. I didn't mean to snap at you."

"Why's it such a big deal?" He put the hackle on the shelf and peeled off the cotton gloves.

"It isn't such a big deal." That statement could not have sounded like anything but a patronizing lie. Of course *his* touching one of the hackles wasn't a big deal. But that someone *else* had helped him- or herself to the *other* hackle was a humongously huge deal. Because I was sure that's what had happened, and I was also sure that the other hackle had been used to kill Phillip. It had to be. But if Clod and his buddies knew that, and if they had the murder weapon, then why weren't they crawling all over the storage room looking for more evidence? Or had they already crawled?

I glanced around. I didn't see any evidence of cops crawling around, but I wasn't really sure what such evidence would look like. Nadine wouldn't have let them leave fingerprint dust everywhere.

But that brought up another question. If Phillip's murder was some kind of inside job, why was the site still open?

Oh, right. The answer to that and most of my questions was that they already had their murderer. Grace. "Hmm."

"Hmm, what?" Zach asked.

"Did I say that out loud? I was thinking about how sorry I am that the flax production part of Hands on History has been axed."

Cool Zach actually winced at the word "axed," and didn't ask any more questions. Just as well. We needed to get out of the storage room. There wasn't a chance in a million that a villain with another hackle lurked in a corner, but the less we disturbed anything else in there, the better. Even if the professionals from the sheriff's department didn't have plans to crawl all over it. One more thing, though. I went to the accession file and looked for the records for flax hackles. As I thought—the site owned two, both listed in storage.

"Come on, Zach. Time we were out of here. I need to check in on the quilting, and it's almost time for lunch. What are your plans for the afternoon?" He might not have any more questions, but I swept him ahead of me with my own. "Are you bored with the dig, or is Mr. Hicks going to let you continue helping out there?"

"I'm not bored with the excavation," he said, sounding offended. "Jerry had to take off for a while, that's all. He'll be back after lunch and I'm going back, too."

"And are you coming back to the education room now?"

"That's where lunch is."

Which answered my question as clearly as a "yes." He walked back with me, and when we got there, the other students were putting away the quilt project for the day. Under Spivey direction, they tidied away the scraps and needles and threads, talking and laughing as they did so, no one casting sulky or heavy glances toward the twins. The twins, though, gave an in-tandem jump when they looked up and saw me in the doorway. Why did that make me suspicious?

"Shipshape," Mercy said when I went over to thank them. "That's the way we're leaving things."

"Back in the morning, though," said Shirley. "Making excellent progress."

"Um, good. That's great," I said. "Say, did anyone call

you late last night or early this morning and tell you that we didn't need volunteers for the program after all? I'm only asking because I'm trying to track down an odd message some of the volunteers got." And because it would be just like the Spiveys to ignore the message if someone *had* called them.

"No," Shirley said.

"Huh. Well, I guess that's good, then. The morning wouldn't have gone as well without you. Thanks, and we'll see you again tomorrow."

They turned to get the Plague Quilt, safe and secret in its muslin, from the table behind them. One of the teens—Carmen—offered to take it to the car for them. They thanked her, but said no. They saw me watching, and I must have been too close to the quilt for their liking. Shirley carefully took the quilt, Mercy grabbed their pocketbooks, and they scuttled.

Interesting that they hadn't received the cancellation phone call. But their names weren't on the original roster of volunteers. So who had access to the roster besides Nadine? Grace. And Grace also had access to the hackle. But Grace was already in jail when the calls were made. I didn't like that. I didn't like the way this was going at all. I needed to find out a number of things, but first on the list was whether Ernestine had been allowed to see Grace at the jail.

Geneva heard the back door at the Weaver's Cat "baa" when I arrived, and she swirled into the kitchen to meet me—in high-excitement mode.

"Quick!" she said, whirling around me. "Run out there yelling 'Stop action.' You do not want to miss a single minute!"

"Out where? Why?" Her excitement caught me by the throat. I jerked back around to look out the door, saw nothing. "Where? Miss what?" I turned back, my heart racing.

Joe stood in the kitchen door. "I don't know. Miss Connection?"

"Mistimed," Geneva moaned. "Now I will lose you to canoodling and common misbehaving."

"Miss Understood," I said, trying for a laugh. But there were those darn tight throat muscles again. And since when had Joe and I ever scandalized Geneva, or anyone else, in the shop with any amount of "canoodling"?

"How'd the program go this morning?" Joe nuzzled my ear.

Geneva said, "Eep," and turned her back on us. Then peeked over her shoulder. Romance in the presence of a ghost—*anything* in the presence of a ghost—posed problems I'd never dreamed I would encounter.

"The program went well, mostly thanks to Shirley and Mercy."

"Mystifying."

"That about sums it up. Who knew, but they're good with the teenagers and have a knack for quilting. More than a knack—they're artists. Is that something that's generally known? Have you seen their quilted skirts?"

"I've seen their yoga pants."

"Gah."

"Ernestine's out front."

"As I was trying to tell you," Geneva said with a sniff, "before you fell for his rakish ways."

Ardis and Debbie sat on the high stools behind the sales counter admiring Ernestine as she modeled her Aunt

Bee outfit. She looked perfect, turned out in a paisley shirtwaist dress in shades of lavender, a string of pearls, stockings, and sturdy, low-heeled shoes. With her usual attention to detail, she'd worn hose with seams up the back. She completed the Mayberry impression by carrying a large pocketbook on one arm, which she held at her waist. She twiddled a wave with her fingers when she saw Rakish Joe and me.

"How'd the quilting go?" Debbie asked. She organized most of the classes we held at the Cat. If she could spend more time away from her sheep, she would have loved to teach all of them, too.

"Surprisingly well."

"How so?"

"Tell you later." I shouldn't have added the interest-piquing adjective and hoped I wouldn't regret it. I hadn't told Debbie or Ardis about the twins' helping with Hands on History and didn't feel like introducing that freighted subject yet. Debbie was her usual sunny self, though, and didn't look for any subtext in my comment.

The bell over the front door jingled. A couple of regular customers came in and Debbie hopped off her stool.

"It's about time for you to take off, isn't it?" I asked her. "Why don't you go on? I can get this."

"You'll want to hear Ernestine's report, and I can stay a little longer." The customers waved and went into the next room. Debbie followed.

"Are your fly-tying boys finished?" Ardis asked Joe.

To Ardis, anyone who'd been in her third- or fourth-grade classroom was still a boy, a girl, or a hon. She was referring to the weekly session Joe led, mostly attended by men who came in during an early lunch hour. They used the TGIF workroom on the second floor, and gath-

ered around one of the oak worktables with their dub-
bing needles, hooks, bobbins, loop spinners, scissors, fur,
feathers, and fly-tying vises. Ardis thought they looked
cute, arriving with their toolboxes full of gadgets and giz-
mos. She got a kick out of watching them test the weight
and feel of fluffy and sparkly yarns, and she loved listening to them discus the merits of one eye-killing color of
frothy marabou over another for attracting the wily fish
they went after.

"Phooey on the fly-tying fellowship," Geneva groused.
"Aunt Bee is going to tell us how she infiltrated the
hoosegow."

"Did you get in to see Grace?" I asked Ernestine.

"I did, although I had to wait for Cole to leave. I sat
outside on that shady bench at the courthouse knitting
baby hats. I finished a pale peach hat and started another
one in lilac that looks pretty next to my dress." She put
her pocketbook on the counter and brought out the hats.

"You finished *both*?" I was definitely the slowest knitter in Friday's Fast and Furious. Before I'd taken over
running the Weaver's Cat—before I'd joined TGIF—the
group had set a goal to knit one thousand hats for pree-
mies and hospitalized infants by the end of the year.
Thank goodness there were enough knitting whizzes in
the group to make up for my dawdling needles.

"It was a lovely morning," Ernestine said modestly,
"and I thought Cole must have a lot of paperwork."

"He was out at the Homeplace before nine," I said.
"They found the sec—" I stopped and looked for Geneva. She sat on the sales counter in front of the cash
register, kicking her heels and watching Ernestine, her
eyes wide. This might not be the best time to mention the
second skeleton, either. "He was already there when I

got there. I think he went out kind of early," I ended clumsily.

"Which is what I found out when I got tired of waiting and went inside," Ernestine said. "I was glad I didn't run into him, in any case. And the sweet young deputy behind the desk let me go back to see Grace immediately. After I said I was her grandmother. I apologized to Grace for impersonating a loved one."

Geneva moved closer to Ernestine, looking askance at Joe, who'd snorted. "What happened next?" she asked. "Did you inveigle your way into her good graces? Ha! Did you hear my wonderful joke? Good gracious—Grace's good graces!" She rocked on the counter, slapping her thigh. But when no one else laughed—because no one heard her joke but me—she drew her knees up, sinking her chin onto her crossed arms. "What is the sound of one ghost laughing?" she asked forlornly. "Dead silence."

Sometimes her solitude was heartbreaking. I tried to signal her, using one of the signs we'd come up with for when I couldn't speak to her. Putting a hand on my heart meant that I promised I'd talk to her, or fill her in, later. But now she'd sunk so far into her doldrums that she didn't see me. Even though I tried catching her eye and put my hand to my heart, and even thumped it several times, she didn't notice. Neither did Ernestine, whose thick lenses helped only so much. And Joe had wandered over to a display of the new purple and black marabou we'd ordered on his recommendation—apparently bass went gaga over anything purple and black. Ardis, however, did notice.

"Hon?"

"Thinking," I said. "Just thinking." I drummed my fingers on my chest a few more times to prove it.

"About Ernestine's question?"

I stopped drumming. "No. Sorry. About something else. What was your question, Ernestine?"

"When Cole told you they'd arrested Grace, and told you about the weapon, did he say they'd *found* the weapon, or that Grace had told them *where* they could find it?"

"Wow. Ernestine, that's a great question, and it parallels something I think I discovered this morning."

"What did you discover?" Ardis asked, almost as wide-eyed as Geneva had been.

"Can we *please* let Aunt Bee *finish*?" Geneva said. Being sunk in the doldrums didn't keep her from being impatient. Or bossy.

"Let me answer Ernestine's question first, Ardis, and then let's hear the rest of what she has to report. We don't want to lose track of details."

"Rapid developments and ramifications?" Ardis did an abrupt switch from wide-eyed to serious. "Excellent. I'll take notes."

"Good idea." I turned to Ernestine. She smiled and touched her hair, and I saw that she'd swept it back in the signature Aunt Bee hairstyle. "You look perfect, Ernestine." She gave a half curtsy. "Okay, so you asked if Cole said they'd found the weapon? I don't think so." I drummed my fingertips on the counter—actually thinking, this time. "No, I don't think he said that. Why?"

"Grace is clear on that point. She says she doesn't know what the weapon is and that she didn't tell the deputies what it is. What she did tell them is advice supposedly dating from centuries past, the sort of half-serious advice you might read in an almanac, and it's this—*If you need to hide or get rid of something, throw it in the retting pond.* Apparently they smell atrocious. But she says she didn't tell the deputies the weapon *is* in the retting pond, and she didn't tell them where they *would* find it. She says she only told them where to *look.* She didn't give them a fact, she gave them a possibility, and facts and possibilities aren't the same thing. Nuances are sometimes lost on thick skulls, though, don't you think? Begging your pardon for the slur on Cole's skull, Joe."

"Not a problem."

"How's Grace holding up?" Ardis asked. "And what's your impression of her?"

"I think she's very brave. She's frightened, but she's a strong young woman. She's holding up better than I would in those circumstances, I'm sure of that. I took her a care package with packets of nuts for stamina, some of Mel's chocolate cookies for something to look forward to, and a book of crossword puzzles to keep her mind occupied."

"You're a peach, Ernestine. You didn't happen to . . ." I looked around hopefully.

"We all need something to look forward to," Ernestine said. "There's a plate of cookies behind the counter with Ardis."

"Which I have virtuously left untouched," Ardis said. "Anything else to report, Ernestine?"

"Only that I agree with you. Grace is likable, and I believe she did still love Phillip."

"But that's not enough to get her off," Ardis said.

We heard a sob. Scratch that. *I* heard a sob. Geneva was crying and using her sleeve to blot the ghostly tears that must be running down her cheeks.

"Love stories are the saddest stories in the world," she said through her snuffles. "I can hardly bear to hear any more about the poor hopeless thing's plight. Except—" She sat up and leaned toward me. "It would be far more exciting if Aunt Bee could spring the lovelorn lass from the calaboose. Won't you please send her back to try? Or put your burglar beau to good use? Send him in to sneak her out under dark of night."

"No," I said. I waited a couple of beats, then added, "No, you're right, Ardis. That isn't enough to get her off."

"She *shouldn't* have," Ernestine said with sudden vehemence.

"What do you mean?" I asked. The only other time I'd seen her that worked up was the first time I met her and the Spivey twins had tried to bully their way past her. "She shouldn't have what?"

"Loved him," Ernestine said. "She should have stopped that when she left him the first time. She didn't come right out and say it. She wouldn't. But I know what she was saying. I heard it in her voice and the way she chose her words." Ernestine slashed a hand through the air. "I've heard that kind of wretched, sad nonsense from one of my granddaughters. Grace said she left Phillip and divorced him because he wasn't always 'nice.'"

"He hit her?"

"I'm sure of it."

"Then why did she follow him here?" I asked. "And you said it, too—she still loved him. How could she?"

"The police are bound to know all this," Ardis said. "If they didn't when they arrested her, they do now."

"But the weapon," I said. "Unless the deputies have it, then they still might not know what they're looking for."

"And in that pond, good luck finding anything," Joe said. He came back to the counter with a skein of electric pink marabou. "Put this on my tab, will you, Ardis? And may I have one of Mel's cookies to go?"

"You have someplace better to be?" Ardis asked.

"Thought I'd go scare some fish. Maybe head up Sinking Creek a ways."

"At a time like this?" Ardis demanded.

"Can't think of much else I'd rather do." He tucked the marabou in a pocket and smiled at her. She didn't return the smile. "Ernestine," he said, "your Aunt Bee is good. Better even than your Miss Marple."

"Thank you, dear."

"I'll call you later," he said to me on his way to the door. "Let you know what I catch."

Ardis waited until the door shut behind him, then boiled. "For years I've heard people call Tennyson Yeats Dunbar a lazy, ne'er-do-well so-and-so. Some of those people being related directly to him. But I have always stuck up for him, and I will continue to do so, if for no other reason than that I enjoy being contrary. But there are times . . ." She stopped, breathing hard.

Hearing Ardis' anger, Geneva came out of her funk. She floated over beside Ardis and shook her finger at the departed Joe. Invective stirred her.

"There are times," Ardis repeated after taking a few angry breaths, "when that man tries even my forgiving soul."

"Sinking Creek loops around past the Homeplace," I said. "It kind of trickles in one side of the retting pond and out the other." With my recent interest in small-creek fishermen, I'd also taken an interest in the geography of small creeks.

Ardis blew out one last breath, deflating a notch or two, and brought the plate of cookies out from under the counter. "Be sure you take two or three of these to Ten, because I seem to have forgotten to give him one. And henceforth I will remember to trust my friends. I have no doubt that Ten is the best kind of fisherman, who knows enough not to alert the fish, or anyone else in the vicinity, by crashing through the underbrush."

"I've heard that the brook trout call him Stealthy Joe." I reached for one of the cookies. Mel called them Double Dark Chocolate Devastators. Stealthy Joe would be lucky if he got the two or three Ardis told me to take him.

"I'm afraid I didn't get us very far forward," Ernestine said. "I may have set us back."

"You brought us information," I said. "Even if it's bleak, information is gold."

"We might not know what the weapon is, and we might not know if it's in the pond," Ardis said, "but the pond is as good a place as any and better than most. And thanks to semantics, I think we have proof, slender proof but proof all the same, that Grace is innocent."

"Unfortunately, what I found this morning also falls in the bleak column. It doesn't help her at all. Actually, it's what I *didn't* find that doesn't help." I'd been about to take a bite of my cookie, but had to put it down. Decadent chocolate didn't go with what I needed to tell them. "A couple of weeks ago I saw two flax hackles in storage at the Homeplace. This morning there's only one."

"Misplaced," Ardis said. "Moved somewhere else for the program."

"No," I said. "There's no note in the accession records indicating a change of location. Making that kind of note is standard museum practice. The hackle isn't in the education room and I didn't see it in Phillip's office."

"In Nadine's office?" Ernestine asked.

"Possibly. Again, she would have made a note in the accession file."

"But a hackle," Ardis said.

"Grace had access to storage, Ardis. And remember, I saw the wound. A hackle's got a whole lot of teeth, and if you swing it just right . . . ?"

"Lord have mercy," she said softly.

"And then toss the nasty thing in the pond." Ernestine looked at her Aunt Bee pocketbook, put it on the counter, and folded her hands. "I don't want to believe Grace did that, but perhaps I was too caught up in my playacting and didn't see through her own act." She reached up, unclasped her pearls, and put them away in the pocketbook.

"Wait, what's happening?" Geneva fluttered around Ernestine. "Don't let her turn back into that dumpy, nearsighted old lady."

Ernestine looked at the floor. Ardis sat on the stool behind the counter, hands clasped to her lips, head bowed.

"Do something!" Geneva said. Her agitated fluttering turned into swooping. She flew from one end of the sales counter to the other, then swooped up to the ceiling and down past my left shoulder, around to the front door and back, stopping in front of me. And billowing—never a good sign.

"Do you realize how serious this situation is?" She billowed to within inches of my nose. "*Look* at that plate of cookies. *Look* at that cookie you left sitting on the counter. *Abandoned*. Don't you see what that means?"

"Shh." I stepped back. She followed.

"*I* can only enjoy those cookies through the vicarious moans that approach indecency when the rest of you eat them. *You* are so in love with them you would have a hard time putting one down even to save a damsel tied and flailing on the railroad tracks. *Ardis* never met a cookie she did not take one look at and devour whole."

"Hush."

"I will not. Those abandoned cookies are the case."

"What?"

"You have given up."

"No, I haven't."

"You have. First you insulted me by saying my body lies a-moldering in a garbage dump. Now you have abandoned the case and abandoned Grace. And that means there is only one course of action left. I shall take over and I shall solve the crime. No, do not try to stop me. The time for arguing is past. I have spent hours, if not months and years, being trained by the best detectives in the world, including Kate Beckett, Matt Dillon, Joe Friday, Lennie Briscoe, Cagney *and* Lacey, Aunt Bee, and a cast of thousands. You had your chance, so go ahead and hide your eyes in shame."

My hands were over my eyes so I wouldn't get seasick from her pulsating billows in such close proximity.

"You may congratulate me when I return. For now, farewell. I said farewell. You could at least wave good-bye."

I waved one hand, keeping the other over my eyes. And then there was silence. I dropped both hands and looked around. She was gone. *Poof!* For the second time in not so many days, Geneva had disappeared. The first time, I'd felt as though I'd failed her in some essential way and then lost her. This time, I felt as though I'd failed again, but instead of losing her, I'd lost control of her. If I'd ever had control, which I really hadn't—no more control, anyway, than a parent had over a headstrong, self-righteous teenager.

There was another difference, too. This time she was a hyped-up, headstrong ghost on a self-righteous mission.

# Chapter 17

The bell over the front door jingled again. Three more customers came in, waving away assistance. Then Debbie's customers made their way back to the counter, cradling armfuls of pastel baby wool. That was enough to rouse Ardis from her meditative slump. She whisked the cookies from the counter and assumed her warmest customer service smile.

"First grandchild," one of the baby-wool customers said, stroking the cheek of a rosy pink skein. "Getting an early start."

"No grandchild in sight," the other said, "but can't help jumping the gun."

Ardis rang them up while Ernestine congratulated them on their good fortune and foresight. Debbie got her purse from the office and paused next to me before taking off for the day.

"What's happened?" she asked quietly. "You look worried."

"Complications. But that's the usual pattern of our cases, right? So, nothing more than the usual, I guess. That and wondering about obligations."

"Well, you're not obligated to say yes to this, but if it'll help free you up, I can work two or three afternoons this week or next. I sure wouldn't mind it. I've had the vet out to see the girls a few times more than my budget likes."

"Good to know. Thanks." I'd have to check with Ardis before agreeing, though. We were already paying Debbie for extra hours while I helped with Hands on History. We had wiggle room, but if we wiggled too much, our budget wouldn't be any happier than Debbie's.

While Ardis finished with the new and potential grandmothers, I went to see if the other customers were still happy browsing on their own. I found them sitting in the three comfy chairs in one of the front rooms upstairs, three young women about Grace's age, knitting and talking companionably. All was right in their world. I didn't bother them. When I got back downstairs, Ernestine and Ardis were waiting for me, again looking doleful. I squared my shoulders and marched over to the sales counter.

"Ardis," I said, "break out the cookies." I patted the counter. "Put them right here." She did, giving me a sidelong look that would have done Geneva proud. "Now everybody take one, raise it high, and let's have a toast to solving this crime." I started to raise my cookie, then thought better of it and took a bite. I couldn't help a barely decent moan. Again, Geneva would have been proud.

"Ernestine, what was it you said about facts and possibilities?"

"They aren't the same, despite what some . . . well, perhaps I shouldn't repeat the rest." She ate her cookie to cover her discomfort.

"What are you getting at?" Ardis asked.

"We have to remember the difference between facts

and possibilities. That Grace is guilty is only a possibility. That we are capable of solving crimes is a fact."

Ardis took another cookie. "Hear, hear."

"Possibilities mean hope," Ernestine said. She took her string of pearls out of her pocketbook and put them back on.

"And facts are facts," Ardis said. She finished the cookie, picked up her pen. "And before we're interrupted by more of the fiber-inclined public, let's discuss one of those facts. Other people had access to the storage room. A fact—am I right?"

"Fact."

"In *fact*, it seems to me that if you've been traipsing in and out of their locked storage, then they aren't exactly operating under high security. So who else, besides Grace, has access? No need to answer until you've finished chewing."

Geneva had been right. We never should have abandoned the cookies. They were putting us in the proper frame of mind and giving us strength to continue the investigation. I glanced around, wondering if she'd really left, and if she had where she'd gone. To the jail to haunt Grace? The Homeplace? Would she know the way? Would she be okay going either place on her own? She hadn't ever done this before. Would she come back? I took a third cookie without answering Ardis' question. She moved the plate out of my reach.

"Thanks, Ardis." I stepped away from the counter as a further precaution against overdosing on proper frame of mind and strength, although I couldn't help noticing that she continued strengthening herself from the rapidly diminishing contents of the plate. "You're right. Security is lax." I told them about the unlocked key box in Phillip's unlocked office. "That kind of security isn't un-usual in a small place, though. They aren't locking the artifacts away from each other; it's to keep other people—from outside—out. That laxity helps Grace, but it doesn't help us eliminate anyone from the field of sus-pects. If you're still taking notes, put down Nadine, Wes Treadwell, and Fredda Oliver. She's a piece of work, by the way."

"Is that a fact or possibility?"

"Pretty sure it's a fact." I was also pretty sure I needed to ask Joe if he knew Fredda called him delicious.

"Interesting," Ardis said, cutting into that uncomfort-able thought. "Here's another question, then, and it's fraught with possibilities. Are we obligated to tell the police about the missing hackle?"

"Do you think that's a moral dilemma," Ernestine asked, "or more of our semantics? Because we don't know, for a fact, that the hackle is guilty or innocent."

"And that *is* a fact," Ardis said. "All right, tell me what you think of this line of reasoning. Let's see if I can keep it straight. What you've told us about keys, and about artifacts that might or might not be missing, amounts to some of the best hearsay I've heard said in ages. But hearsay, like possibilities, is next to rumor and gossip in my book. Not that I don't love my book, but I venture to say that Cole Dunbar does not like my metaphorical book. In fact, I'd go so far as to say that my book irritates the snot out of Cole Dunbar. Because of that, and be-cause I like to be an upright citizen, helpful to the au-thorities in whatever way I can be, I would say that I also have an obligation to not purposefully set out to irritate them. So my conscience is clear. I will not be telling Cole, or anyone else in authority, about a hackle, missing or not. Now, I believe I've had enough sugar and caffeine for several days, and I would appreciate it if you take the rest of these away from me."

There were only three cookies left. Ernestine handed me the plastic wrap that had been over the plate and I wrapped the survivors for Joe. Ardis watched sadly, then sat down on the stool behind the counter, looking exhausted.

"Did I make any sense?" she asked.

"You stitched around the question of obligation beautifully," I said, "piecing together several somewhat eccentric points."

"Very nicely embroidered," Ernestine agreed.

"Thank you," Ardis said. "I do my best. Now, where do we go from here?"

"Let me try my hand," I said. "Because we don't really know anything, because we don't have enough facts, why don't we give ourselves until we meet Friday for Fast and Furious—"

"A *grace* period?" Ernestine asked. "Oh, please excuse me for interrupting."

"A grace period. Yes, and during that grace period, we'll either discover someone who looks guiltier than Grace, or Deputy Dunbar and his buddies will come up with the weapon all on their own. And if they haven't done that by the end of the grace period, then we'll tell them the hackle theory. We'll do it this way because, after all, we're amateurs. We didn't set out to investigate Phillip Bell's murder. We're looking into the curious incident of two skeletons in a dump. It seems obvious to me that what we're looking into is the fairly old murder of two people . . ."

*Old murder of two people.* Mattie and Sam. The double murder Geneva had nightmares about. What if the skeletons in the garbage dump were Geneva's Mattie and Sam?

And my headstrong, hyped-up, self-righteous, emotionally vulnerable ghost might be on her way out there right now.

# Chapter 18

"I should've seen it sooner," I said. "Why else would there be two skeletons in the dump? They were murdered. They were dumped. And we know there was a double murder back . . . sometime back then, and the bodies were never found. It has to be them. Mattie and Sam."

Ardis and Ernestine exchanged looks.

"I didn't know they'd found a second skeleton," Ernestine said quietly.

"I'm sorry I didn't say anything, Ernestine. They found it this morning. And the fact is, Cole Dunbar told me not to say anything."

"Speaking of facts," Ardis said, none too casually, "you never have told us how you know about this murder or know the victims' names."

"That's not important right now."

"It might be."

"It isn't."

"It is."

"Would you look at the time?" Ernestine said. "I am so sorry, but I really should be going."

She did, and I started to leave the room, too.

"Don't do this to me, Kath," Ardis said before I got away.

"Do what?"

"Shut me out. It's what Ivy used to do sometimes. As though she didn't trust me."

"What are you talking about? Of course she trusted you."

"Not always. And it hurt. But even after all the years we worked beside each other here at the Cat, after all we went through to make the place a success, there were times she hid things from me. Not often, and when she did I didn't say anything. But do you know why I didn't?"

I shook my head.

"Because what she hid were things that couldn't quite be explained. They were the kind of things that prompted small-minded people to call her Crazy Ivy. And I saw how that hurt her, even though she put up a good front."

"I'm sorry you felt shut out, Ardis."

"Don't you do it to me, too."

"Ardis—"

"But you can't help it, can you? I can see that in your eyes. They're Ivy's old blue eyes, and I can see Ivy looking out at me, not letting me in. No one your age should have such old eyes, Kath."

"I'll be right back, Ardis."

Great. How had I managed to alienate my two best friends—Ardis, my rock, and Geneva, my flighty ghost—in one short afternoon? Upsetting Geneva didn't take much skill, but this was the second time in not so many days I'd managed to do it, so my skills must be improving. Granny used to say the old adage about a thing worth doing being a thing worth doing well was nothing but a crock of codswallop. *Everything is worth doing well,* she'd said, *even if what you're doing is making a crock of codswallop.* I'd certainly made a crock of well-done codswallop that afternoon.

I would have stomped up to the study in the attic, but Ardis didn't deserve my selfish tantrum. Neither did the customers. Once again, when I got to the study, I hoped to find Geneva. I didn't, but I did find Argyle. He sat curled in the window seat and chirruped when he saw me, wrapping me around his little paw instantly.

"Hey, sweetie puss. Is our old girl here?"

Argyle stood and stretched, shivering his tail upright, then jumped to the floor. He didn't gaze into a corner and chirrup again, and he didn't walk over to sit in front of the hidden cupboard that was Geneva's "room."

"Ghost on the loose, Argyle. She's a vigilante ghost and I don't know what's going to happen."

He leapt up on the desk and yawned.

"Really? You think not much?"

He looked around the desktop, found a pencil, and dribbled it with his paws to the edge. He gave the pencil one last swat and watched it hit the floor, then he flopped on his side and yawned again.

"A little excitement and then a nap? I hope you're right. Would you mind napping on another pile of papers, though? I need these."

He graciously let me tug the papers carefully out from under him. After I had them, he jumped down and headed for the door with a more demanding meow.

"Yeah, okay."

I followed him down to the kitchen and tipped crunchy, fishy kibbles into his dish. Then I went back out front to face Ardis. She was with a customer, listening to an animated story about the woman's first attempt to use circular needles. Ardis wiped tears from her eyes and told the woman she was lucky not to have garroted herself. The woman agreed and left with a bag full of alpaca. When Ardis saw me watching from the hall doorway, the smile she'd had for the customer disappeared.

"I want you to see something, Ardis."

"You don't need to show me anything. I'll keep my nose out of your business." She turned her back to me.

I moved down the counter so I could see her face. "Did I say I wouldn't tell you how I know about the double murders?"

"As good as."

"What happened to the vow you made about henceforth trusting your friends?"

"A hasty decision if there's no two-way street."

"I said it wasn't important how I know about them. And in the great scheme of things—"

"There *is* no great scheme. There's only what we have right here, right now." She shifted around the other way, so her back was to me again.

"Then let's deal with what we have. What I *have* is not much information about the woman who told me about the double murder. I'll tell you what I can."

"What you *can*. Is the rest top secret?"

"*Ardis*. I honestly don't know her very well. I don't know her full name. I don't even know how to get hold of her right now."

"What part of her name *do* you know? I might know her."

"She doesn't live around here . . . anymore. She told me she doesn't know anyone. I met her when I was staying in the cottage at the Homeplace in the spring, after Emmett Cobb died. She knew him."

"Emmett was a first-class wretch. Was she a friend of his? I don't know that we should trust her."

"No, she just knew him. They weren't friends." How could they be? Emmett had lived in the cottage Geneva haunted, but he never saw her, heard her, or knew she existed.

"Hmph. Well, then."

"And then, after Will Embree and Shannon Goforth were killed, I saw her again, and she was terribly upset. Reading about Will's and Shannon's murders triggered something, and she suddenly remembered seeing a photograph of two murder victims. This would've been years ago that she saw it. She remembers the picture showing two bodies, a young couple, lying faceup, head to head in a green field. She was so specific. She even described the woman's dress. She said it was white lawn. And she remembered the color of blood."

"I don't want to hear about blood."

"No. I know. But the picture must have shocked the poor thing horribly so that she repressed the memory. You believe that can happen, don't you?"

Ardis shrugged one shoulder.

"And the article about Will and Shannon in the *Bugle* brought it all back. She described the scene in the photograph so vividly—it was horrible for her all over again."

"Like post-traumatic stress disorder?"

"I guess so."

Ardis twisted partway around, still not quite facing me. "No one around here talks of such a dreadful thing happening. I've never heard about it, anyway, and you know how much I manage to hear. When was this supposed to have happened? Did she tell you that much?"

"No. But from her description of the clothes, late eighteen hundreds."

"Then a color photograph makes no sense whatsoever. How did she know about green grass and the color of blood? Are you sure this woman isn't delusional?"

A color photograph *didn't* make sense. That had been the problem with Geneva's story about the double murder from the beginning. But when the memory had started coming back to her, she'd been looking at photographs of Will and Shannon in the *Bugle*. Maybe the memory came back to her as a photograph—because a photograph was safer than the real memory. Her trauma definitely *was* real. Somewhere, somehow, sometime she'd internalized a traumatic incident, and she absolutely believed she'd seen a couple she knew—Mattie and Sam—lying dead in a field in Blue Plum.

"She absolutely convinced me, Ardis."

Ardis twisted the rest of the way around and faced me.

"I asked both Cole Dunbar and Thea to look for a record or mention of the murders," I said. "Or a photograph."

"I remember. Cole was more rude than usual about it."

"But Thea found something."

"Bless the Goddess of Information. What did she find?"

I handed Ardis the two pages I'd brought down from the study—photocopies of the *Blue Plum Bugle*, one page from the October 7, 1872 issue, and the second from the week following.

"This isn't much." Ardis turned the papers over. The backs were blank.

"I know."

Both photocopies were of pages from the Personals

section of the *Bugle*'s classified ads. As Thea had explained it, the Personals were the social media of that time. If a person had no better way of communicating with someone, then paying for a message in the Personals was the way to go. The first ad read, *Mattie Severs, please forgive and contact the ones who will always love you.* The second was simpler and sadder, asking anyone who'd seen Mattie Severs or knew of her whereabouts to contact a post office box.

"There's only the one name," Ardis said. "This could be your Mattie, but where did the name Sam come from? How did your mystery woman know that name?"

"It's from somewhere in her memories. Ardis, I wish I knew the whole story. I *want* to know it. That's why I've been trying to find out. If I ever see her again, I'd like to be able to tell that woman whatever I do find out. Knowing the rest, or knowing more, might help her."

"But if she doesn't live here, how do you know you'll ever see her again?"

"I hope I do. I have to believe it's a possibility."

"Ivy believed in all kinds of possibilities," Ardis said. She laid the photocopies of the *Bugle* on the counter and looked at me with an interesting, assessing sort of glint in her eye. The kind of look that made me nervous. "And you certainly are your granny's granddaughter. In so many ways."

"Well, so"—I picked up the photocopies and tapped their edges on the counter—"that's what I know about the double murder. And this is what I think. Unless Jerry Hicks uncovers a bunch more skeletons, or unless there have been an unusual number of double homicides in and around Blue Plum that nobody knows anything about, then I think we've found Mattie and Sam."

"What's the *possibility* of positively identifying them?"

"I'm not sure." I was beginning to think I liked it better when she'd kept her back to me. There'd been a few times, over the past months, when Ardis seemed to be skirting a suspicion or on the verge of voicing one. She might not be able to see or hear Geneva, but, as careful as I tried to be, she couldn't help seeing and hearing me reacting to Geneva.

And then there was the Crazy Ivy thing that Ardis mentioned. I'd been aware of the nickname, mostly whispered. Granny had always brushed it aside, but then she'd left a letter for me to read when she died that gave me reason to wonder. *I'm a bit of what some people might call a witch,* she'd said, although apparently she hadn't liked the word "witch." *I prefer to think of the situation more in terms of having a talent. I have a talent which allows me to help my neighbors out of certain pickles from time to time.* That sounded so friendly, so gentle. Innocuous and something to smile at. I could almost have brushed it aside, as she had the name Crazy Ivy, but she'd also left me her secret dye journal—a notebook with her recipes for natural dyes that would let me continue her good work—and then she told me I was a bit of a witch, too.

Was it all just so much codswallop? My science-trained brain had been sure it was. Then I'd met Geneva . . . and started feeling the occasional jolt of emotion from a piece of clothing . . . and couldn't keep myself from trying a few of Granny's dye recipes. And started catching Ardis eyeing me with "interest."

Talk about being in a pickle. Maybe I could find a recipe in Granny's dye journal for laying aside suspicions. And if I didn't watch out, Ardis and everyone else would start calling me Crazy Kath.

"Here's another *possibility*," Ardis said.

"What?" That came out squeakier than I'd wanted. Darn tight throat muscles.

"When you're out at the Homeplace in the morning, why don't you look through the guest register for those few weeks you stayed in the cottage. You might find your mystery woman's name. Her address, too."

"Oh. Yes. Good idea. I hadn't thought of that."

"That way you can contact her. For further information. Or to pass it along."

The three young women who'd been knitting upstairs came down at that point and I practically leapt across the room to see if they needed any help. No, they didn't; the front door hadn't moved since they'd arrived, and it looked as though they hadn't forgotten where to find it. I thought about following them out onto the porch, in a further show of friendly customer service. But I was saved from going overboard by the arrival of a tour bus of senior citizens, many of them bent on spending time and, better yet, money in the Weaver's Cat. They kept us busy and let me avoid Ardis' scrutiny for the rest of the afternoon.

There were still a few straggling shoppers at closing. I magnanimously told Ardis I would stay to balance the register, lock up, and say good night to Argyle so that she could go home and her daddy's supper wouldn't be late.

When I got home myself, I dropped my purse and sprawled in one of Granny's faded blue comfy chairs in the living room. My head nestled where her head and gray braid had. *It's a good thinking position,* she'd said,

*because your head and back are supported and all the
thoughts or pictures running through your brain won't
unbalance you.* I wanted to feel myself relax. I wanted to
feel answers to my questions bubbling to the surface.
Neither my muscles nor the answers cooperated, though.
I sprawled harder, but there was no noticeable improve-
ment.

Granny had bought this old frame house shortly after
Granddaddy died, saying it was her way of letting go and
holding on at the same time. *It gives us both room to
breathe,* she'd told me over the phone, the other half of
that "us" being the other love of her life, the Weaver's
Cat. She'd taken some furniture and her looms and
books with her to the new old house, giving the growing
Cat permission to stretch and fill all the corners of the
space she'd shared with Granddaddy since they were
married. I was lucky enough, now, to own both places
and to have stewardship of the loving memories woven
between them. I'd hated losing my job and my life in Illinois, but I loved the safety net of Blue Plum that I'd
fallen into. My move to this house had been, like Granny's, one of letting go and holding on, at the same time.

Phillip had moved to town not much more than a
month and a half earlier. New like me. By all accounts,
he'd loved his job and profession. But someone in town
had come to hate him enough to kill him. At least to hate
him enough at that one crucial moment—at the swing of
that wicked hackle. Did that make it a crime of passion?
A momentary loss of humanity? Or had someone
planned to kill him with the hackle there and then? Was
it reasonable for anyone to think they could be accurate
and forceful enough to kill with the swing of a hackle?
But if the murder wasn't premeditated, who'd taken the

hackle to the retting pond? Phillip? And if he had, then it didn't matter who had access to the storage area. It only mattered who knew where to find him, or happened to find him, that morning, at that hour. And what had that person gained by his death? Or what hadn't that person lost?

Sprawling in the faded blue chair wasn't producing the coherent answers I wanted, just more confusion and questions. On the theory that comfort and better accessories might make a difference, I went to change out of my presentable shopkeeper khakis and knit top into dark jeans and a black T-shirt. Then I took the ultimate accessory out of the drawer in the bedside table—a notebook from Ernestine. She, who always carried the perfect props, had given me a "casebook" suitable for a sleuth from the Golden Age of Detective Fiction—chocolate brown leather, the size of a deck of cards, dark red ribbon bookmark, and an elastic band bound into its cover to keep it closed. I felt almost indecent every time I stroked it.

My little beauty and the sheaf of notes from the meeting at Ardis' went with me to sit on the front porch swing. There we swung gently to and fro, and I read and thought and made more notes. None of that helped, either, except to pass the time until it was too dark on the unlit porch to read. A good supper might have helped, considering I'd eaten only Mel's cookies since breakfast, but I'd decided to skip eating until later. Not that I wasn't hungry, but nothing I ate was going to sit well. The thought of driving out to the Homeplace and breaking in was giving me the heebie-jeebies.

# Chapter 19

I was "visiting the Holston Homeplace Living History Farm after hours." That sounded better to my rationalizing ears than "I was breaking in." And I left my car at the Quickie Mart, a quarter of a mile away from the site, not because I planned to sneak in on foot, but because the warm evening reminded me of the first night I'd spent in the cottage. On that night I'd walked to the store for milk, so on this night, walking in the shadows along the edge of the dark, winding country road was a pleasant nostalgia tour. Although, after thinking of the phrase "nostalgia tour," I wished I hadn't, because I'd first heard it from Clod. Still, "nostalgia tour" sounded better than "breaking in," too. So did "looking for a lost and fragile friend."

And entering the grounds of the Homeplace hardly involved breaking in. *Anyone* could walk around the locked gate that barred the drive. "Stroll" was more like it. And most people would only need to duck behind a rhododendron if a car came along the road. And a smaller person hardly even had to duck, because some of the rhododendrons in east Tennessee were huge.

Once around the gate (and after brushing off a few rhododendron leaves), I headed for the caretaker's cottage. Geneva, if she'd made it out to the site, might have gone to one of the other buildings. But as far as I knew, she'd never left the cottage once she'd started haunting it, so that was the first place to look for her. That it was also a place I wanted to look around because Phillip had lived there was only a coincidence.

Since meeting my less-than-corporeal friend, I'd done some research on ghosts. I'd read both that lavender kept ghosts at bay and that it attracted them—contradictory and confusing, like so many pieces of my life lately. The bees I'd seen buzzing in the lavender the other morning were all home and in bed when I walked past Phillip's door and around to the side that was hidden from view. I put on the white cotton museum gloves I'd so handily stuck in my pocket. Then I checked to see if the window in the pantry was still in the habit of being unlocked, and I smiled. Yes, it was.

It occurred to me, after I'd climbed less than gracefully through the window, that it was now possible I'd broken into—that is, that I'd entered unlocked premises—more often than Joe had. It also occurred to me that long, lithe legs built for ambling were an advantage during such activities. So was the small LED flashlight on my key ring.

The pantry opened into the kitchen, which wasn't as neat and clean as when I'd stayed there. Phillip hadn't done his dishes before he died. I admired the variety of spices he'd left out on the counter—cumin, coriander, turmeric, garam masala, rosemary, smoked salt, basil, dill—the inventory was wasting time and making me hungry. There wasn't a hackle sitting on the counter or table or on top of the refrigerator. No ghost wept in a chair at the table as she had the first time I met her.

I moved into the living room, still furnished with the shabby sofa and upholstered rocker. Phillip had squeezed a desk into the corner near the window seat. Stacks of books surrounded a laptop-sized space in the middle of the desk.

No ghost or hackle sat on the mantelpiece. The fireplace tools stood handy, where I remembered. I thought about using the shovel to pry the cap off the newel post at the bottom of the stairs, the way TGIF and I had before. But the note Elihu Bowman left in the hollow post when he finished building the house didn't answer any of my questions, and having it in my hand wouldn't either, as far as I could see. I put my hand on the newel and looked up the stairs. There was a low-ceilinged bedroom up there and a small bathroom. I put a foot on the first step up, but stepped down again. Was that my inner prude hesitating to intrude in a dead man's more personal space? Maybe. Instead I went back to the desk.

The books on Phillip's desk were less interesting than his herbs and spices. Less varied and less exotic, anyway. *The American Resting Place: 400 Years of History Through Our Cemeteries and Burial Grounds* piqued my interest, but the rest of the books looked like textbooks he must have used in his graduate museum administration classes. A manila folder under one of the stacks intrigued me more than the books, and the stack of books sitting on the folder cooperated more quickly than Argyle had when I'd asked him to move.

I considered the ethics of opening the folder. It was thin, light. There couldn't be more than two dozen sheets of paper in it. Or three dozen. If I leafed through them quickly, my ethical lapse would be over in a twinkling—ignoring the fact that I was still inside the cottage without invitation. But, after all, it was that kind of cottage, and I knew from personal experience that people frequently turned up in the pantry or the kitchen uninvited. Ghosts, too.

Inside the file, right on top—I caught my breath. A photocopy of Elihu Bowman's note looked up at me.

> *Finished this house this day for this family*
> *My dear wife and our dear children*
> *Elihu Bowman*
> *29th April 1853*

Good for Phillip for not falling into the camp of architectural historians and preservation experts who pooh-poohed stories of people finding documents stashed in newel posts. I'd known a few homeowners who'd found the blueprints of their houses in newels. Elihu's charming note, even in facsimile, was a pleasure to see again.

The next page in the file was a photograph—but again, it was a copy, not an original. It looked as though Phillip had done a cut-and-paste into a document and printed the document page. He'd printed it in gray tones, instead of color, and the lack of contrast made it hard to decipher. But there appeared to be names scrawled on a lined surface. Not paper—it was too dark to be paper, and the lines looked more like dimensional spaces than something ruled onto a surface. The scrawls were a childish mix of upper- and lowercase letters, one short name per line. *Ezra, Thos, Uley, Whit*—four little boys leaving behind their marks? Without any reference points—who, what, when, and especially where it had been taken—the photograph didn't mean anything to me. It wasn't worthless, though; it gave us names, possible access points.

The rest of the papers in the file were photocopies from county record books—ledgers dating back to when they were kept by hand in spidery script, their ink now fading. They looked to be a combination of census, deed, and land records. Maybe tax records, too, but it would take time to decipher the handwriting and interpret some of the abbreviations and jargon. There were more like four dozen pages in the file. The first date on the first page was July 30, 1814. I turned to the last page and saw March 11, 1918, but scanning through the pages in between showed dates drifting back and forth and possibly beyond in both directions.

Phillip had highlighted certain names throughout. He'd been thorough and systematic, using a different color for each surname. The name Holston rated blue. I saw a couple of Bowmans, but they were a Francis and a Benjamin, not Elihu. With more time and more care, I might find Elihu, but I didn't want to get caught up in details. I didn't want to get caught, period. Murphy was a name new to me, and it showed up several times in green. And Severs in yellow. Related to Mattie Severs? Levi Severs had sold a fifteen-acre tract of land in 1872. Why had Phillip thought that was significant? Why were any of these documents significant?

"Your life of crime is much less exciting than mine," a voice said in my ear. It was a familiar voice, but that didn't matter. I jumped and scattered photocopies from the file as I spun around.

"And although I am not as easily spooked as you are, I do not sound like a startled kitten when I do scream. Let me show you." Geneva kindly demonstrated a blood-curdling scream.

The photocopies I hadn't initially strewn, hit the floor

when I dropped the file to cover my ears. When I opened my eyes, she was floating in front of me.

"Have you found any clues yet?" she asked.

"I'm not sure I have any memory of my life before your scream."

She tipped her head and looked thoughtful. "Perhaps that is what happened to my memory, too." She said that without any of the usual signs of distress she showed when she talked about trying to remember.

"Did you have any trouble getting here?" I asked.

"I did wonder if I would get lost and be left to wander as though in a wasteland. But no, I knew the way here without thinking. And then I wondered why I ended up haunting this house—uselessly, I might add, if one measures one's success by traditional haunted-house stories. I thought perhaps the reason I came to *live*, as it were, here, and the reason I was drawn back so easily is because I am buried in the foundation."

"You *are*?"

"Of course not; this house is much older than I am. But I looked around the foundations anyway, and under the house, too. As a theory, that did not pan out."

"You're handling this all very well," I said. "How do you feel being back here? Do you miss the place?"

"It is not a happy house."

"You weren't happy when I met you here, but the house is cute and comfy enough."

"It is not easy to be comfy or cute when one is dead and gone. You should try it sometime. In fact, you probably will. But I remember that you were not happy living here, either."

"For other reasons, though. For good reasons. Not because of the house. You had good reason, too."

"That is true. It is not any easier being happy than it is being comfy when one lies moldering graveless, so perhaps you are right, and everyone's unhappiness here has nothing to do with the house. What are all these papers you threw around with such wild abandon?"

"Something Phillip Bell was researching." I started gathering the photocopies. Getting them back in their original order would be impossible. I was more or less shoveling them back into the file when the name Levi Severs caught my eye again. I sat back on my heels. "Geneva, did you really look around the foundations of the house for your body?"

"Yes."

"And it didn't upset you? Talking about your death and trying to remember your life usually do."

"Trying to remember and failing is depleting. Searching for clues and answers feels like strength."

"That's a good way to put it. Have you found any clues or answers?"

"Only if you count the woman who arrived here before you did. Oh, now look. You have gone and thrown those papers all over the room again. Are you having a heart attack?"

We cleared up her mistaken notion that I was having a heart attack fairly quickly. Finding out what she meant about another woman took some frenzied whispering on my part and affronted huffing on Geneva's. She thought I was overreacting by accusing her of underreporting. From her description—unless more than one sultry woman in Blue Plum had a red feather tattoo behind her ear—the other woman was Fredda Oliver.

"I would have told you immediately that you were

not alone, when you climbed so clumsily through the window, had that been true," Geneva said.

"You didn't tell me *you* were here immediately."

"But we are here together, now, and Fred is not here, and that is all that matters, except that she has an unusual name, which must be hard on her, so perhaps *we* should not be so hard on her."

"Her name is Fredda, and she might have killed Phillip. That was kind of hard on *him*."

"And you should not be so hard on me, either, because I am the one who was Geneva-on-the-spot to see everything she touched and took. Unlike some, who had given up and turned their backs on crime solving."

"What did Fredda touch and take? Anything on the desk? Was there a computer on the desk? Did she take it?"

"She went upstairs first."

"Darn. I've been here longer than I should have already. How long was *she* here?"

"I have no idea."

"Do you know how she got in?"

"No."

"But you said she arrived—"

"Well, she must have, because she was here."

"You mean she was here when you got here?"

"Yes."

"This isn't getting us anywhere. Can you show me what she did upstairs? Then we'd better scoot."

This time I didn't hesitate at the stairs. I dashed up them to the room under the eaves and flashed my light around. It was not the room as I remembered it. The narrow iron bed frame that had made the room look like a Victorian housemaid's garret was gone. Now it had the air, figuratively and literally, of a college flophouse. A pizza box and beer bottles, empty except for their stale smell, shared the floor with strewn clothes and a queen-sized mattress.

"Geneva, what did Fredda do up here? This is important. If she took much, I should make a list."

No one had made the bed the morning Phillip died. The top sheet and blanket were twisted together near the foot. The wrinkled bottom sheet looked cold. He hadn't closed the closet door, unless Fredda left it hanging open.

"Geneva?"

She didn't answer, and when I looked around, she was sitting between the pillows at the head of the bed.

"Do you remember what she took?"

"I'll have to think," she said.

"Okay." I went into the bathroom and looked in the medicine cabinet. Didn't see anything interesting. The usual assortment of personal hygiene products and over-the-counter stuff. But what had I expected? Empty spaces labeled with Fredda's initials? I stuck my head back into the bedroom. "Did it look as though she knew her way around? Was she hunting for something, or did she go straight to the things she touched and took? This morning, she told Nadine she'd never been inside. But Deputy Dunbar says she's an excellent liar, and the night before Phillip died, I called and a woman answered his phone. I'm almost certain it was Fredda. She could've answered his phone while he was at her place, but he said "I live here," and he joked about how awkward it would be for me to meet him here for breakfast. Have you remembered anything yet?"

"Hmm."

What was up with her? She sat there, just staring at

the wall. No. At a television. Phillip had mounted a flat screen on the wall above the bureau. I'd missed it by staring at the bed and dashing into the bathroom.

"Geneva, when Fredda was up here, did she turn the TV on?"

"It is high quality and high def."

"Did you see *anything* Fredda touched or took?"

"I saw her turn the television off in the middle of *Magnum, P.I.*"

Why had she even turned it on? If she was sneaking around like me, why would she want the distraction of background noise? Wouldn't she want to be alert to any other sounds? So—maybe she wasn't sneaking around. Maybe she was comfortable here.

"Are you coming back to the Weaver's Cat with me?" I asked.

"Yes. Unless you think she might come back and turn the television on again."

It was torture leaving the file of photocopies behind. I didn't know what they meant, and now they were scrambled, but they represented a lot of time spent poring over old ledgers and a small investment in copies. It looked as though Phillip had been making connections between the names, and I would have loved trying to make the same connections, or asking one of the posse members to work on it. Before tapping the photocopies back into a stack—which might have been easier to do and neater without the gloves—I took pictures of the first ten pages with my phone. They weren't the first ten pages as Phillip had arranged them, but there wasn't anything I could do about that. I did find the photo with the names and Elihu Bowman's note and put them back on top. I patted the note for old times' sake, then tucked the folder under its pile of books.

Other than snickering when I heaved myself inelegantly back out the pantry window, Geneva was quiet and stayed close on the way down the dark road to the Quickie Mart. When we reached the car, she apologized for not finding any important clues.

"I wanted to bust the case wide open," she said.

"Busting would've been nice, but I wasn't really expecting that to happen tonight."

"Busting what?"

That wasn't Geneva. It was another familiar voice. Not quite in my ear, thank goodness, or I couldn't have been responsible for what I busted.

# Chapter 20

"What *is* it with you?" I swung around on Clod—both hands open and firmly on my hips so there could be no chance of his misinterpreting one of them as a fist. Also to hide the white museum gloves that might be sticking out of the pocket of my dark jeans. "Why do you always show up when I—" With effort, I swallowed the rest of my words. *When I'm in the middle of an investigation* would have been a bad way to end that sentence. *When I've just snooped around a murder victim's property after illegally gaining access* would have been a worse way.

"When you've been out for a moonlight stroll with the invisible friend you were talking to?" Clod asked.

Geneva floated over so that she hovered next to him. "Do you think he can see me?"

I answered both of them. "No."

"Then what *were* you going to say?" Clod asked. "Really. I'd be interested in knowing."

"You should count to ten before you answer," said Geneva, "so that you do not say anything I will regret. For instance, if you are arrested and cannot drive me back to the Weaver's Cat, then I will regret having to find my own way back there alone. Alone in the dark."

"You surprised me," I said to Clod. "You scared me. That's all."

"A woman out walking alone at night should be aware of her surroundings so that she *isn't* surprised," he said.

"My darling mama warned me about the foolishness of young women walking out alone," Geneva said. "My dear daddy, too. They were right, I fear, and I am dying proof of that. Although broad daylight is just as dangerous, depending on who sees you, and what terrible thing you have seen him do." Her voice quavered toward a higher pitch.

Clod stepped between Geneva and me. "Hey, are you all right?"

"I'm fine." I tried to move around him. Geneva was beginning to keen, and I thought if she could see me, it might calm her. It might give her something to hold on to in this time—here and now. It might give her back some of the strength she'd felt when she came looking for clues. "Everything's fine," I said.

"No," Geneva wailed. "After he follows you into the dark wood, you will never be fine again."

These were her nightmarish memories resurfacing— her memory of Mattie and Sam lying dead in a grassy field, and what must surely be the fractured memory of her own death. She hadn't just seen a picture. She must have been there that day and must have seen Mattie and Sam. She either witnessed the shooting or she came upon the scene immediately afterward. The murderer must have seen her there, and then killed her, too.

Reliving the deaths and the grief was almost too much for Geneva. Watching her relive them was almost too much for me. And if she dissolved into a gray fog of weeping, what could I do? I couldn't scoop her up and pour her into the passenger seat of my car. I couldn't leave her there in the parking lot of the Quickie Mart. But maybe I could get through to her by using Clod's stubborn faith in his own conclusions.

"Deputy, how is your case coming?" I asked. "You caught the *killer*, right?"

A wrinkle of suspicion at my emphasis creased the starch in Clod's face.

"You've got the *killer* behind bars, right?" I looked at Geneva each time I said "killer," hoping to catch her attention. "The *killer* isn't still at large, following innocent women into the dark woods?"

"But he got away with it," Geneva wailed.

"What are you playing at?" Clod asked. "You're up to something, and whatever it is, don't think you're going to get away with it."

"That's right. You're right, Deputy. *No one* gets away with *anything*. So we can all get in our cars and go home now."

Clod looked left and right. That made me look left and right, too. But the three of us—the two of us, as far as Clod was concerned—were alone in the shadows at the edge of the parking lot. Not even the clerk in the Quickie Mart paid us any mind. Then Clod leaned close and asked, "Have you been drinking?"

"Absolutely not."

"Because I can give you a ride home if you need one." He stayed close and took a large sniff. I could hardly blame him.

"Are you *happy*?" I asked, giving him an extra gust of breath on the word "happy" to help him out. "I am stone-cold sober."

Clod pulled back, one eye narrowed.

"I am not happy," Geneva moaned. "I am stone-cold dead and nothing can change that."

"I've changed my mind," Clod said. "Maybe you haven't been drinking, but you are definitely craz—"

I held a hand up. It might have looked ready to slap. "Don't say it, Deputy. Don't. Thank you for stopping by. Thank you for your concern for me and my 'invisible friend.' Shall I tell you a story about her? Once upon a time, a long time ago, my friend's dear mama warned her against strange men in dark places. And her dear mama was right."

"Mamas usually are," Geneva said. "The end."

"The end," I echoed. "Again, Deputy, thank you for stopping to see that *everything is safe*. Now it's time to get in the car and go home. There isn't anything else to say, except for this—although nothing can change the fundamental truth of our individual situations, home and the love of a warm cat can do wonders."

I'd been speaking for Geneva's benefit, of course, but glanced at Clod. Expressions flitted across his face almost too fast to read. Suspicion went past again. And confusion sped by, followed by alarm, so I took pity on him and didn't rub it in by walking around the car to open the passenger door for my "invisible friend." Tempting though that was.

Geneva shimmered through the windshield and huddled in the front passenger seat. She looked like a heap of damp gray laundry. After I got in and started the car, Clod rapped his knuckles on the window. I lowered it.

"You are the most—" He stopped when I started raising the window again. "Hold on. Hold on. I'm sorry."

I stopped the window and waited, leaving my finger on the switch, ready for action.

"Believe it or not," Clod said, "when I saw your car here, I didn't stop to harass you or to get into an argument. Doggone it, I wish you'd—"

I powered the window up another inch but stopped when he put his fingers on the top edge.

"If you close the window on my fingers, you'll be assaulting a peace officer."

"Been there, done that" danced on my tongue, but I held it in.

"Just listen, will you? I stopped to let you know I saw Jerry Hicks at Mel's over dinner. He uncovered more at the dig today."

I cut in. "More what?" *More bones? Geneva's bones?* I looked over at her. She sat silent, listening.

"Associated artifacts. They might be helpful in dating."

"Or identification?" I shivered and out of the corner of my right eye saw Geneva wavering next to me. She'd draped herself over the steering wheel and looked up at Clod. She put her hand to her throat.

"What shape is her cameo locket?" she asked him. "What shape is it, and what initials are engraved on the back?"

"Hicks'll know better what he's got and what it means when he's had a chance to clean everything," Clod said.

"Did you find the curl of hair inside?" Geneva asked. "A sweet, dark brown curl." When Clod didn't answer, she said in my ear, "The law is deaf to those long dead. It is a sore affliction."

I gave her a small nod, then said to Clod, "Could one of the artifacts be a cameo locket?" I put my hand to my face and pretended to rub my nose. From behind my hand I whispered a question to Geneva. "What shape is it?"

"Oval," she said. "A rosy cameo that brought out her

rosy complexion, mounted on an oval locket made of gold."

"A cameo locket?" Clod tipped his head. "You want to tell me why you think we'll be finding a cameo locket?"

"Given the time period, a piece of jewelry like that wouldn't be so unusual," I said.

"And what time period would that be?"

"Go ahead and pinch his fingers with your electric window," Geneva said. "I do not like his attitude this evening."

I almost never liked his attitude, but I didn't run the window up. "It's probably wishful thinking on my part, Deputy. A locket, on its own, could be from almost any period. They don't go out of fashion. But if a locket had initials, that might be another story, and that might tell us something. I've been trying to think what personal effects might have survived that burial climate—with that layer of clay—and a locket occurred to me."

"Uh-huh. Burial climate. That's good. I like that." He took his hand from the window and tapped the roof of the car—not the clichéd, cop-show thump, though. It was more of a pat, and a condescending "good dog" pat at that. "Uh-huh. Okay, you're free to go."

He might have said something else, but his radio spit static and I didn't hear. I wouldn't have heard, anyway, over my grinding teeth. *Free to go?* I'd show him free to go. Grinding my gears as well as my teeth, I threw the car into reverse, not really caring if he knew when to jump clear of a moving vehicle.

The speed at which I drove the dark, winding roads back into town terrified me, but careening around curves perked Geneva right up. First she peppered me with questions. Then, when I didn't answer with anything but yips on the hairier bends, she sat forward and imitated a siren. We pulled up in front of Mel's in record time. Sadly, the café was already closed.

"I wish I had lived long enough to drive a car like a bat out of you-know-where," Geneva said. "Hanging on to a runaway mule for dear life is exciting, but it jars one's teeth. Why were we in such a blazing hurry to get here if you are only going to sit in the car muttering and pounding the steering wheel?"

"It was stupid to drive like that, but I wanted to see if Jerry Hicks was still here. Maybe he knows more about the artifacts he's found than he told Deputy Dunbar. But a cameo locket, Geneva?"

"Maybe." She rippled and wouldn't look at me.

"Whose locket? What made you think of it?"

"You sound as unbelieving as the deputy."

"No! No. I believe you. The problem is, we don't know if they've found one."

"Yet."

"Yet. Right. Tell you what—let's not sit here on Main Street discussing it."

"Where all the world's a stage?"

"All Blue Plum, anyway."

I drove—sanely—to the end of the block, around the corner into the alley, and parked under a security light behind the Weaver's Cat. Between the stark shadows created by the light and the hollow sound of my feet on the wooden steps up to the Cat's back door, that town alley struck me as more ominous than the Quickie Mart's parking lot bordered by woods.

"Did you know that I once read Shakespeare?" Geneva asked.

"No."

"Frankly, I am surprised that *I* know it; I seem to know so little about myself. I can picture a volume of tales, green with gilt decorations." She followed me into the shop, and when the door chime said "Baa," she baaed back. "That is a nice coincidence. The authors of my *Tales from Shakespeare* were Charles and Mary Lamb."

Argyle roused himself from somewhere and came to meet us, his tail upright and shaking. He said something suspiciously like "baa," too. They both followed me up to the attic. The light from the landing spilled into the study, making it cozy and almost secret. Geneva and Argyle settled in the window seat, the two of them looking at me expectantly. I switched on the banker's light that sat on a corner of the desk and pulled out the oak teacher's chair.

"The love of a warm cat *is* a fine thing to come home to," Geneva said. "Are you any good at drawing?"

"Why?"

"I can describe it for you. You can pretend that you are a police sketch artist."

"The cameo locket?"

"Yes. I will describe it while you attempt to draw it, and then I can critique your work and tell you where you get it right and where you make a hash of it."

"May we talk about something else first, Geneva? If you don't mind, I'd like to talk about you. I mean, look at how you are right now."

"Do you realize that you and I are the only two people in the whole world who can do that?" she asked. "Who can look at me, I mean. The only two people and a cat."

Argyle blinked and settled into a contented meat loaf shape.

"I meant do you see how you're behaving? Back there, in the parking lot, you were . . . upset. You were emotional. Now you're rational."

"Which proves my theory beyond the shadow of a reasonable doubt; searching for clues and answers gives me strength. I think it clears my mind, too, because if I am not mistaken, that shadow, whether it is reasonable or not, is the gold standard for evidence if you want something with a leg to stand on in a court of law. So pick up your pencil and we will get started. The cameo locket is a very important clue. I hope you have a large eraser, in case you are not a good artist."

I pulled a few pieces of scrap paper toward me and found the pencil Argyle had knocked onto the floor earlier. "Can I ask you a few questions before we draw the cameo?"

"Are they tedious?"

"No, but you might have to think hard before you answer them."

"Then you probably should not waste our time by asking them."

"Your answers might give me clues."

She didn't say anything.

"I think they'll be very important clues, Geneva. Clues that might help us find out what happened to Mattie and Sam. About what happened to you. But I don't want to risk upsetting you the way you were upset back there in the parking lot. You and I were there together, and you were fine, and then you started remembering your mama's advice about walking alone and you were slipping away—"

"But I came back."

"You did. You did, and I was relieved, Geneva. And then you brought up the locket, and talking about that didn't upset you. Why not? Whose locket do you think they'll find and why do you think they'll find it?"

She wavered in the window seat, but she didn't answer.

"It's okay. We can come back to that." I watched her, trying to gauge her state of mind—wondering if I should be gauging my own state of mind—wondering how far I could press her for "clues." "Do you remember when you and I first met?"

"You did not believe your eyes."

"I don't think you believed yours, either."

"It had been so long, I was not used to being seen. But I think it was the beginning of a beautiful friendship, don't you? Although you will have to be the fishy Frenchman, because I believe you are shorter and rounder than I am, and I am more mysterious, like Humphrey Bogart, and I would look the best in a trench coat. And then you can call me Geneva Boggart, with an extra *g*. *Casablanca* will be on later tonight, in case you are interested. I know I am. I saw an announcement for it on Phillip's flat-screen television. Did I tell you his television is high def? That means it is very good." She heaved a sigh that turned into a moan and then trailed off with a few notes of "La Marseillaise." "Oh dear," she said after another sigh. "Do you remember what we were talking about?"

I rested my chin on my clasped hands and held my breath to keep from sighing, too.

"Well, memory is a funny thing," she said. "Before you go, will you please turn on one of my recorded books? Argyle and I would like to hear more about Jessica Fletcher. She is almost as wise as Shakespeare. She is a good role model for me, and Argyle is waiting to see if George will kiss her."

"Would you like me to find Shakespeare on audio

sometime?" I'd flatly refused to put a TV in the study for her. She might deserve special consideration because she was dead, but I wasn't willing to share her idea of heaven—television twenty-four/seven. Audiobooks were our compromise

"I would not mind," she said, "but Argyle prefers cozy mysteries."

I'd have to take her word for that. Argyle was sound asleep and didn't wake when I put on the first CD. Geneva was rapt and didn't wave when I turned out the light and went home.

By the time I pulled into my driveway, I was starving. I also had company. The kind some people referred to as delicious.

# Chapter 21

"Hey," Joe said. He was sitting in the dark on the front steps. I joined him. "I saw the light on at the Cat."

"And you didn't see a light on here, but here's where you decided to wait?"

"I thought you might be busy. If it's a problem—"

"It's not."

We explored that lack of a problem until we were interrupted by a growl from my stomach.

"Sorry. Except for a few of Mel's cookies, it's led a deprived life since breakfast. Are you hungry? I've got a couple of curried sweet potato pasties in the freezer. It won't take long and they're delicious." That word again. It made me nervous and I stood up. "While they're heating, you can tell me how the fishing went this afternoon. And what you know about Fredda Oliver." I tried to lay the Fredda line as artfully and gently as a trout fisherman working a clear mountain stream. Joe held the screen door for me while I unlocked the front door, so maybe I had.

It hadn't been a good day for fishing along Sinking Creek. Rainbow and native brook trout—brookies to those of us in the know (or to those of us who knew people in the know)—didn't like hot, bright afternoons. Neither did the fisherman. He'd emulated the trout and retreated to deep, cool shade. In Joe's case, that was a quiet and private place in the woods near the retting pond.

"Upwind, too," he was happy to report. "The deputies have got a mess on their hands looking for anything there. I told them how they could temporarily re-channel the creek and see if the pond will drain. That should help. Mind if I take a rain check on the pastie? Mel had a special on her fresh tomato tart."

"You *talked* to them at the pond? I thought you were being clandestine."

"We do want them to find the weapon, though."

"Oh, right. Huh. I didn't think I was so competitive. Your brother brings that out in me." I tossed the frozen pasties back in the freezer and took a bag of salad from the fridge instead.

"He called this evening."

"With news?"

"With concerns."

"Ah." Deputy Clod must have called Joe *after* my invisible friend and I left him in our dust. Interesting. I tossed the bag of salad back in the fridge and looked at Joe with a smile that was supposed to show how unconcerned I was about concerns.

"Are you all right?" His angled brows and soft voice proved *his* concern, but I had to clear something else up before I could concentrate on that.

"Waiting on my front steps—was that your idea or Cole's?" I was proud of myself for holding back the sarcastic questions I'd rather ask. *Was this a social welfare visit? A psych evaluation by an untrained professional? Or was this more of a guard-dog-on-duty kind of thing?*

"It's okay for people to worry about friends."

"Ah."

"You keep saying that."

"It covers a lot."

He let it cover a few moments of looking at each other, and then he said, "Why don't you sit down and let me make an omelet for you?"

I didn't immediately sit, and I wasn't sure why. And then I could hear Granny, in one side of my head, telling me that being mule-headed was fine as long as I didn't make a complete mule of myself. And Geneva was there in the other side of my head telling me about the tooth-jarring excitement of hanging on to a runaway mule for dear life. Contradictions. My life was full of them, and while I tried to sort a few of them out, I sat down at Granny's square maple kitchen table.

Joe went to more trouble for an omelet than I would have, browning cumin seeds in the cast-iron skillet before adding diced onion, jalapeño, fresh ginger, and a couple of beaten eggs. Stubborn as I was, I had to admit it was nice having him there. I'd lived on my own, alone, for years in Illinois. But I hadn't quite gotten used to the stillness of living in Granny's house without her footsteps, her laugh and snatches of song, or the sounds of her loom and spinning wheel. I loved having her things around me, but I missed hearing the rhythms of her life.

When the omelet was set and golden, Joe folded it onto one of Granny's pretty painted china plates, sprinkled fresh cilantro and diced tomato over it, and put it in front of me. My stomach growled a brief grace.

"There's a cheap Cabernet in the cupboard."

He poured us each a glass and came to sit across from me. He rolled his glass in his hands, then took a sip. "It might be cheap, but it's not tawdry. Do you want to talk?"

"No, I want to eat. You talk. Talk about Fredda. How you know her. How long you've known her. How well you know her."

He listened to my questions and took a larger sip of wine. "Do you have any particular reason to be suspicious of her?"

"We don't have any particular reason to be suspicious of *anybody*, so I'm being ecumenical and cultivating my suspicions of everybody. But I'm starting with Fredda because I think she was with Phillip the night before he died and because Cole says she's a good liar. I'm not saying she killed Phillip. I have no idea why she *would* kill him. But now my lovely omelet is getting cold, so you talk. Tell me about Fredda."

"She's been around for a few years. Three or four. She moved over here from Asheville."

"Did you know her there?" He'd lived in Asheville for a while.

"Not well."

"What brought her here?"

He hesitated. "Getting away from a bad relationship."

"Like Grace."

"Like you?"

*"What?"*

"When Cole called, he said something—"

*"Oh my gosh.* He thought I was talking about *myself*? No, no. Oh, for—I should've known better." I shook my head, took a deep breath and let it out again. It didn't help. "I should have known he'd get it wrong. Doggone it—he scared the bejeebers out of me in the parking lot at the Quickie Mart. I got mad. He made fun. And then

I thought I was being so smart. I told him part of a story about something that happened to a friend of mine, and he must have thought I was using the old 'it's not me, but I have this friend' routine. What an idiot."

"You or Cole?"

"Both of us. Okay, so no. No, not like me. But Fredda and Grace both left bad relationships."

"Grace followed her bad relationship."

"And Fredda might have fallen into another one. If the police are using abuse as a motive for Grace, it works for Fredda, too. How is it you came to recommend her for the caretaker's job?"

"I ran into her a time or two. She'd started her lawn care business. She worked hard and the business let her get by, probably just barely. I knew she'd be good out there at the Homeplace and she could use a more reliable income."

"I'm glad you were able to help her."

"It helped me, too. I didn't mind filling in out there short term, after Em died, but I didn't want to be tied down."

"You have a reputation to uphold?"

"Renaissance Appalachian Idler. It's a low-maintenance facade."

"And you do it well. You even had Ardis fooled for a while this afternoon with your fishing trip. But you can't fool all the people all the time."

"What about fooling around with some of the people some of the time?"

It flashed through my mind to wonder if his "some" was just wordplay or if "some" included Fredda. But Joe had been completely matter-of-fact talking about her, not evasive or uncomfortable, and he wasn't *with* Fredda.

He was with me. Reaching his hand across the table for mine.

That weird sensory business that made me leery of brushing against a sleeve, or of resting my hand in the small of a back, wasn't a problem at all when clothing didn't get in the way.

Due to one thing or another, telling Joe about the missing hackle slipped my mind that evening and the next morning, too. Or maybe that happened subconsciously on purpose, because what he didn't know wouldn't be something he might or might not feel obliged to pass along to his brother. Not that TGIF was in competition with the sheriff's department, and not that we didn't want Clod to find the murder weapon. But by letting Joe go off and do his Appalachian Renaissance thing without the worry of weighing moral decisions, I felt I'd done my first good deed for the day. Two, really. Because by keeping the rumor about a missing flax hackle from percolating through to the sheriff, I was continuing to be a good, non-interfering citizen. No deputy was going to catch me making reports that couldn't be backed up by facts.

After a cup of coffee, that logic still made sense to me. I left for the Homeplace and another morning of Spiveys, eager teenagers, quilting, and Hands on History with a clear conscience. But first, I stopped by the Weaver's Cat to check on Geneva.

Argyle met me at the back door. He twined around my ankles to make sure I knew the way to the cupboard and from the cupboard to his bowl. Geneva floated down the stairs while he supervised portion control. She circled me. Twice.

"You look . . . happy," she said, going around one more time.

"You make that sound like a questionable activity. The morning is beautiful, Geneva. I'm happy and enjoying it."

"A good weather report does not usually give you such a self-satisfied look."

"I, uh, I slept well. How about you?"

"To sleep, perchance to dream," she said. "There, Argyle wants a rub."

He butted his head against my ankle and said, "Mrrph." I knelt and scrubbed him between his ears.

"Rather than sleep or dream," Geneva said, "I thought of a clue. The other woman in the cottage—"

"Let's call her Fredda instead of 'the other woman.' What about her?"

"I am trying to tell you. She turned off the high-quality, high-def television halfway through *Magnum, P.I.*"

The TV again. I didn't groan; the morning was that beautiful and Argyle's attention that sweet. "You told me about that last night."

"She turned it off at the halfway point."

"Yes. And *your* point?"

"She turned Thomas on at the beginning. She turned Thomas off halfway through."

"Thomas?" All I could think of was tank engines and the fact that Geneva was stuck on a one-way track.

"The beautiful morning and the love of a shedding cat have addled your brain. I will try to simplify the clue so that you can follow along. Please pay attention." She hovered in front of me, back straight, hands clasped—a foggy gray schoolmarm. "Thomas Magnum is a brave man with a moustache, a current P.I. license, and an exciting caseload. Fredda was in the cottage for half of one case, including commercial breaks for products that made me blush and watch between my fingers. A whole case is solved in one hour—Thomas is that clever. Do you see how this is like a math problem? If a whole case is a whole hour, a half case is a half hour. Fredda was in the cottage for one half hour, and during that time she could have touched or taken any number of things. Unfortunately, we will never know what things, because I did not know she was a suspect. You did not tell me, and I cannot take responsibility for your lapse in judgment."

I sat back on my heels. "That's a good clue, Geneva."

"Thank you. After listening to my audio episode with Jessica last night, I rehearsed my clue so I would not have a lapse in memory the way some people have lapses in judgment. What do you think the clue tells us?"

"I wish I knew."

"I wish you knew, too. I put a lot of work into it."

"Thank you for all your work, Geneva."

"And my attention to detail. Did I remember to mention his moustache?"

"You did."

"I should have also remarked on his muscles."

"Speaking of muscles, I liked what you said last night—that searching for clues and answers feels like strength. I think searching for concrete clues really is doing something for you. And that gives me hope that we'll find answers. Maybe to a lot of our questions."

She held one arm up in a muscleman pose and prodded her biceps. "Do I appear stronger?"

Oddly enough, she did appear stronger, though not in the sense she meant. I could see her better. She wasn't as watery or filmy. She was still gray, but she appeared more . . . dimensional, more solid, and there was something about her face that I could almost see clearly.

"Geneva, pull your hair back from your forehead, will you?"

She lifted her hair and held it just long enough for me to see a frightening crimson streak. But in the next second she cried out, jerking back as though she'd been struck, and she sank toward the floor, falling in terrible slow motion, her hands reaching up to catch hold of something, anything, nothing.

"Geneva?"

She started to fade and, still in slow motion, she collapsed on the floor.

"Geneva! What's happening? What happened?"

She'd been strong, searching for clues. She'd even been happy. But then what? Had she remembered something?

She lay like a shadow on the wide boards. Like a ghost. Argyle and I sat beside her until I had to leave for the Homeplace.

"Keep watch until I get back," I told the cat. "And you," I said to the ghost. "You stay with us."

As I turned the corner to head out of town, I saw Thea leaving Mel's with Wes Treadwell—Thea laughing, her hand on Wes' arm. That echoed Nadine's habit, and I was oddly comforted knowing I wasn't the least bit tempted to put my hand on his arm. I waved as I went past, but neither of them saw me. No matter. That Thea was engaging one of our unknown quantities—up and detecting well before the library opened—could only be a good sign.

Nadine opened the door for me at the visitors' center, a coffee mug in one hand. "Good morning, Kath."

"How are you, Nadine? Oh, sorry."

I'd caught her with the mug to her lips. She finished with a gulp and a smile. It was nice to see that some of the strain of the last few days had left her face.

"I'm doing better. Thank you for asking." Some of the sharp tones were gone from her voice, too. Wearing jeans, a T-shirt, and old sneakers might have helped that impression along. Looking forward to working in the herb garden—with a heady mix of green growing things and budding historians—might have helped, too.

"Any changes in the schedule today?" I asked.

"Not unless you want to help us weed and water the garden after you finish quilting."

I looked down at the knees of my pressed khakis and back at Nadine.

"I'm kidding, Kath. You're doing enough for us already. I would like to talk to you sometime, though, about the natural-dye classes you have at your shop. I'm putting together a grant proposal for an herb festival next spring and I thought your shop and the members of your group would be a natural fit."

"Interesting. What are you thinking, a demonstration? A workshop?"

"A workshop—hands-on like we're doing now— would be an attraction, don't you think? I want to line up presenters for a variety of topics. I'd definitely like to cover cultivation and traditional herbal medicine, and get someone in for a cooking demonstration. All of that's a conversation for another time, though. Your quilting volunteers beat you here this morning. They're already in the room setting up. I'll call you about the grant. Better yet, I'll stop by the shop sometime."

"Sure."

I put the brakes on at the door to the education room, too chicken to set foot inside. The place looked dangerous. John Berry and Ernestine stood on one side of one of the long tables, staring at Shirley and Mercy. Shirley and Mercy, immobile and belligerent, stood on the other side of the table, staring back. None of the four spoke. None of them needed to. Their nonverbal volleys screamed across the chasm of that thirty-six-inch-wide table with expert precision.

Their silent skirmish was my fault. I hadn't told Ardis or Ernestine—I hadn't told anyone in the posse—that the twins had volunteered for Hands on History and were entrenched. Clearly, I'd made a huge tactical error.

"Why didn't you *tell* me the darling twins would be here!" Geneva's joyful exclamation exploded in my ear.

"Gah!"

The four combatants in the room hadn't noticed me standing in the doorway. My sudden leap in the air and wide-eyed shriek was all it took to break the tension around the table.

"Hi," I said, somewhat breathlessly, one hand holding my hair to my head and the other holding my heart behind my ribs. "How nice to see all of you." I smiled at each of the five in turn, so they would all feel included and welcome. Geneva had floated over to hover between the twins. That was good; if she'd been floating five or ten feet to either side of the group when I'd smiled at her, I would have looked more like a loon than I already did.

"If we aren't wanted," Mercy said with icy petulance, "we won't stay."

"We don't want to stay if we aren't needed," said Shirley.

"Shirley, you are needed," I said. "Mercy, we do want you here."

What extraordinary statements I'd just made, although they were extraordinary only because I'd made them to the Spiveys. Even *they* hadn't expected me to say anything of the kind. They were slower to recover from their shock than Ernestine and John. Geneva *wasn't* shocked or surprised, but she was also the only person I'd ever known who was always happy to see the twins. That was because she was superstitious and thought they must be good luck. It was also because, being unseen and unheard, she couldn't really interact with them and never felt the full Spivey effect.

"Shirley and Mercy, why don't you show Ernestine and John the Plague Quilt?" Knowing how uneasy the twins were when I got too close to the quilt, I stayed where I was, just inside the door.

Shirley and Mercy exchanged looks with each other, but avoided Ernestine's and John's eyes. As well they might, considering their bullying history. But I needed this to work, for the program's sake.

"Ernestine, John, you really have to see this quilt. Their great-grandmother—my great-great-grandmother—made it. It's an embellished crazy quilt, velvet and—well, let them show you and tell you about it. They're the ones who know it. But it's gorgeous. And you have to believe me, as truly gorgeous as that quilt is, Shirley's and Mercy's own work is even more beautiful." My compliments *did* impress Geneva.

"You do not usually gush over the twins," she said. "More often you say something rude under your breath and run the other way. Unless Ardis sees them and runs first. Or unless they sneak up on you, which they are very good at doing."

"I don't often gush," I said to all of them. "I've seen a lot of amazing textiles over the years. Amazing for a variety of reasons that don't necessarily have anything to do with appearance or artistry or value. But there's something special and touching about this quilt." I hesitated for a gnat's breath at the word "touching," then went on. "This quilt has more heart and story sewn into it than most I've seen. You two show," I said to the twins, "and you two look," I said to Ernestine and John. "I'll go meet the students and then we'll get started."

Geneva came with me into the hall and I took out my phone so we could "talk."

"Remember not to use my name," she said before I got the phone to my ear. "You blew my cover when you shrieked my name at Ardis' the other night. And speaking of shrieking, you should warn people before you shriek and jump the way you did just a minute ago. Why were you so surprised to see me?"

"Why wouldn't I be?" I said into the phone. "When I left, you weren't exactly lively. Even the cat was worried. What *was* that? What was happening?"

"A bad moment."

"A memory?"

"I do not know. I am not sure. I felt different. My head felt . . . full."

"You *looked* different." She was back to her normal appearance now—watery, cobwebby, and slightly out of focus. "How do you feel now? Are you still feeling strong?"

"I was. And then I lost my hold."

"I could tell. I saw you falling."

"Falling, falling, falling . . . but I heard you say, 'Stay with us,' so here I am. Did you forget you told me that?" As simple as that—my literal ghost. "Now that we are both here," she went on, "would you like me to dodge here and there like a shadow or a spy, moving as silently as a ghost on sneaking cat feet, to see who is up to nefarious no good?"

"That hasn't worked out very well for us in the past."

"Practice," she said, emphatically smacking one fist soundlessly into the other. "What I need is practice."

"Are you sure you're okay being out here today? That it won't prompt another traumatic memory?"

"I have no idea, but I am game if you are."

"Huh. Well, I guess we'll find out. Come on this way." I started toward the lobby. She followed. "Practice isn't a bad idea," I said, "and I know where you can start. You'll enjoy it, too, which will help, because then you'll be less likely to lose interest and wander off."

"Please do not be insulting."

"I don't mean to be insulting. I'm sure even the best cops get bored when they're working surveillance. It'd be hard to avoid. It must be an occupational hazard. All great detectives probably have to practice." I was trying reverse psychology with her—a Tom Sawyer approach. If she thought she could prove herself with a hard "assignment," maybe she'd stick with it, and I wouldn't have to worry about where she was and what she was doing.

"Practicing surveillance—it sounds sneaky and sleuth-like," she said. "Where shall I slither in and start?"

"Why don't you practice your super-sleuth techniques on the twi—" I stopped. I'd gotten too caught up in our "phone call." The students would be arriving, and there I was on the verge of suggesting questionable behavior without checking first to see if anyone other than Geneva might hear.

And clearly I'd made another tactical blunder. Geneva and I were not the only ones waiting to greet the students. Nadine was back in the lobby and Wes was there, too, looking at me with eyebrows raised. So was Clod Dunbar.

# Chapter 22

"Tell them staring is impolite and maybe they will stop," Geneva whispered. "Also, that it is impolite to listen in on private conversations, even if they are carried on in front of Clod and everybody. I am affronted on your behalf." Said she who planned to practice surveillance techniques.

"Thank you," I said quietly. I didn't usually speak *loudly* on my phone in public, and maybe I hadn't embarrassed myself this time, either, but the raised eyebrows made me wonder. I raised my own to the three of them, held up a just-one-minute finger, and tried to finish the conversation with Geneva without being too explicit. Or overheard. "I have to go now, but why don't you start with the quilting—practice, stick with it, and that should work out fine."

"I have no idea what message you tried to convey," Geneva said. "Try it again. Be less cryptic and do not mumble."

"If you want to *practice your technique*, watch Shirley and Mercy. You might learn something new or interesting if you *watch and listen*. If you do learn something, remember it so that you can tell me, because I'd love to hear all about it."

"Oh," she said, drawing the word out to show her comprehension. Then she gave me one of her hollow-eyed winks and flitted back to the education room.

I dropped my phone into my purse and went over to chat and be pleasant and try to appear normal to the others.

"Old friend," I said to Nadine, making the universal "phone" sign with my thumb and little finger. "She watches too much reality TV."

That remark didn't work to immediately lower her eyebrows, but then she must have decided I was joking, since she laughed. Wes didn't laugh, but his eyebrows came down anyway, and he offered me a quick "Nice to see you." He was dressed with his usual ready-for-a-board-meeting polish. Between the clothes, the cordial but less-than-warm greetings, and the way his eyes only ever made glancing contact with mine, he gave me the impression of always being on the lookout and ready for . . . what? The next idea or opportunity? I wasn't sure.

There were still times when I felt like a fish out of water in Blue Plum, and there probably would be for years. But Wes *looked* like a fish out of water. Was that enough reason to look at him with more suspicion than anyone else? No, it couldn't be. Equal-opportunity suspicion was the better approach. Although Fredda was looking more equal than others to me.

"Nice to see you again, too, Wes. Deputy." Smiling at Clod took some effort. Not asking him why he was standing there did, too. It took no effort at all to avoid babbling an explanation for last night's Quickie Mart misunderstanding; this wasn't the time or place, and the explanation would only have run downhill into something surly.

"Cole stopped by to let us know the students will be allowed to start excavating this afternoon."

"That's good news," I said. "Are the bones still at the site? Will that be a problem if some of the students are squeamish?"

"Hicks removed the bones," Clod said, "and the additional material."

"Is the sheriff releasing any details?" I asked.

"Not yet."

"Do you know any of the details that he isn't releasing yet?"

"No." His "no" was immediate and came firmly stamped with official snoot, but from the slightly calculating look he gave me, and the way his left eyebrow twitched . . .

Nadine interrupted my surveillance short course. "I meant to tell you, Kath—a gentleman interested in local history stopped by yesterday afternoon. He'd heard about the bones, and he has an interest right up your alley. He put together a proposal to research and attempt to identify them. He was quite thorough. I was impressed." She turned to Wes. "In fact, I told him if he doesn't watch out, we'll draft him the next time we have a board opening."

"Who is it?" Clod asked. "Who made the proposal?"

"There isn't a problem with approving the research, is there, Deputy?" Nadine asked. "I planned to inform the sheriff, but mainly as a courtesy. Do I need to get an official okay?"

"I'm sure there won't be a problem," Clod said. "But I'd like to know who made the proposal."

Nadine looked confused. "Does that matter?"

"I'm just curious. I wondered if it was anyone Ms. Rutledge knows."

"Does that matter?" I asked. The gentleman in question would be John, of course, who was down the hall with Ernestine, the Spiveys, and the quilt, and could answer any of Clod's unnecessary questions, but there was no reason I could see that Clod needed to know that.

Wes stepped into our moment of discomfort, proving that he was more than just a pretty suit. "Deputy, I'm sure you realize the bones present an interesting and special problem for the Homeplace. *Is* there a problem for your department if we go ahead with our own research?"

Clod held his hands up, as if to calm a rant of researchers. "There are no problems that I'm aware of. If your researcher comes to any conclusions, we'd appreciate being notified."

"Absolutely." Nadine was happy again. "I'll see that you receive copies of any reports or documents generated. You, too, Kath, if you'd like."

Sunlight glinting off a windshield alerted us to cars pulling into the parking lot.

"Here come the scholars," Nadine said. "Oh, and Kath, there's been a change in the schedule after all. Wes is going to follow up on the discussion he had with the students over lunch yesterday. He prepared another short program and we thought it would make a good starting point for this morning."

"It'll take about twenty minutes," Wes said. "Add time for questions, and you can tell your volunteers the students will join them in about half an hour."

"Sounds great." I hoped my smile was less wooden than my reaction. "What's the topic today?"

"The role of philanthropy in public history. You're welcome to sit in, if you like. You, too, Deputy."

It was a worthy topic. I knew that. But while Clod made his excuses, I made my escape.

The Plague Quilt had created peace in the education room. The former combatants had moved two tables side by side so the quilt could be spread out flat and seen whole. Each of them stood on one side of the square they'd created. Shirley and Mercy looked like an odd combination of prison guards supervising a visit and proud mothers watching their offspring entertaining guests. John's back was to me, with Ernestine opposite, magnifying glass in hand. She looked up when I came in, and her face said it all. She was thoroughly and genuinely enchanted. Geneva floated above everyone. It was hard to tell whether she was engrossed in the scene below or had simply fallen asleep. I hoped that if the twins had divulged any more information about the quilt, she had listened carefully and would remember what they said.

"Students on their way?" Mercy asked. "Time and quilting wait for no one."

"That makes no sense," said Shirley. "We're waiting, right now, for all of them. This is better—a diller, a dollar, our ten o'clock scholars, we only have them 'til noon."

"Unfortunately, there was a last-minute schedule change, and you're not getting them for another half hour." I told them about Wes' philanthropy talk. "You're all welcome to sit in if you want."

"We'll pass on that opportunity. Again," Shirley said.

"If Less-and-less Treadwell is taking precious time away from the kiddos," said Mercy, "then our time will be better spent pressing seams and stitching ahead for them."

"Better spent doing anything other than listening to Less-and less," Shirley said.

Mercy gave Shirley a quelling eye, maybe because she wasn't close enough to give her an elbow. Geneva was definitely awake. She watched the twins, looking from one to the other as they spoke, looking like a spectator at a tennis match.

"Why do you call him 'Less-and-less'?" I asked.

"It's his way of operating," Shirley said. "He starts out small. Treads with care."

"But with less and less care, as time goes by," said Mercy, "because he's predatory."

"Preying," said Shirley.

"A pirate."

"Listening at the cunning door," Geneva said.

The door between the education room and the auditorium was ajar. *Was* he listening? How would she know?

It didn't matter, I turned my back to the door and made mad hand signals for the others to be quiet. The twins and John caught on right away. Ernestine thought I was waving and waved back. While John whispered to Ernestine, the twins faced the door and made elaborate, dismissive, and alarming gestures.

"Ernestine and I think we'll attend Mr. Treadwell's talk," John said. "We'll see what sorts of insight we gain."

"Shirley, Mercy, thank you for letting us see the quilt," Ernestine said. "I'll be back to help with the students."

"What about you, John? Are you coming back or are you bailing?" Mercy asked. "That was a nautical term, by the way, to go with your boating background."

"Much appreciated, too," John said. "And I'm sorry, but I have other plans."

"That's no scrap off our quilt," Shirley muttered.

"Kath," John said, "I meant to spend the morning doing research. Now I think I'll change my schedule, too, and see if I can buy Mr. Treadwell a cup of coffee."

"Be careful," I said.

"Coffee in well-lit public places only," he said, and then he leaned close. "I'll start the research, too, and report on that and the coffee at Fast and Furious tomorrow."

"No need to be formal with Less-and-less," Mercy said, loudly enough to be heard through several closed doors. "What about you, Kath? Going to hear the squawk?"

I wanted to tell them they owed me *days* with the Plague Quilt, alone and unsupervised, for the way they were behaving. Instead I told them we needed to talk.

"I want to hear what you know about Wes Treadwell," I said quietly, "but not now and not here."

"Why don't we come to the shop," Shirley said, "later on this afternoon?"

"We'll come to your house tonight," said Mercy, "in time for dessert."

*Lord love a duck,* I said to myself. *What have I gotten myself into?*

Geneva swooped down and put her arm around my shoulders, making me shiver. "The darling twins are getting you down. I recognize the signs, which are like the neon lights on Broadway. I would like to see those lights someday. But you should take a walk and calm down. Do not worry. I will stay here and work on developing excellent surveillance skills."

Getting out into the Spivey-free air and sunshine felt wonderful, especially after Geneva's bone-chilling heart-to-heart embrace. I halfway toyed with the idea of wandering over to the retting pond to see if any of Clod's fellow deputies were still searching it for the weapon. I hadn't asked Clod how that was working out for them, and he hadn't told me. And if they didn't find anything, what did that mean? Would that make any difference to Grace?

I couldn't make myself go to the pond. The memory of Phillip lying there was too much—it had been only two days since I'd found him. His death was still raw. And his murderer was walking free; I was convinced of that. But how could any person kill another human being and not look raw and wounded, too? How could that person appear healthy and whole and unremarked on, as though nothing had happened or changed?

The thought of dealing with deputies and the rotten smell of retting was too much, too, and I went to find Jerry Hicks instead. Maybe he would tell me what artifacts he'd found associated with the bones and if he'd found anything to suggest a cause of death. In Geneva's memory, Mattie wore a dress of white lawn and Sam a frock coat. Sometimes she described the scene as though she'd been part of it, but at other times it sounded as though she'd stumbled across the horror. She had once mentioned a cameo at Mattie's throat. She hadn't said, then, that it was a locket. But her memories were so slippery.

"You can save yourself a walk." Clod's legs were as long as Joe's, but they never ambled. Clod's legs led a purposeful life. Their purpose now was to interrupt my free time and keep me from my goal. "You can save your breath and whatever questions you're planning to ask Hicks, too."

"You're presuming, Deputy. You don't know where I'm going."

"You're trying to make an end run for information," he said, "but it won't work."

"Again, you're presuming."

"Hicks isn't here." He got ahead of me, planting his legs and crossing his arms. Smug clod.

"Pig."

"Say what?"

"I said 'pig.' That's where I'm going, Deputy. To see Portia the Poland China. She's a heritage breed pig. Poland Chinas are known for slopping up anything you put in front of them. They aren't so good at going out and finding things on their own, but that's the way it is sometimes." *With pigs and some policemen,* I thought.

The way he looked down his long nose at me, Clod reminded me more of Fred the mule than of a Poland China. "Say what?" he said again.

"I said I came out here to see Portia and her piglets. Now that you've brought it up, though, I do have a few questions about the excavation. If I ask you, that won't be considered trying to make an end run, will it? I won't be committing some kind of foul?" My anti-sarcasm campaign was faltering. I stopped, breathed, and tried to dial it back. "Deputy, I really am asking this out of curiosity. Please don't think there's an implied comment. But why does it seem as though information about the excavation is being kept secret? Isn't it possible you'd come up with more answers by making what you do know public?"

"That's a fair question."

I was pretty sure there *was* an implied comment in *his* remark. I was big and let it slide.

"Now that the materials are secured, information will be made public," he said. "Obviously, we couldn't keep it entirely quiet."

"You had two dozen teenagers with phones here."

"Among others. But we didn't want scavengers, and we didn't want sensational or unpleasant stories or rumors floating around."

"Like what?"

"Are you kidding? Use your imagination. Oh, wait"—he snapped his fingers—"I forgot. You already *are* using your imagination. Conjuring cameo lockets."

"I explained why I asked about a locket. I could also have asked about shoe buttons or a particular style of eyeglasses."

"I don't think so. I think your locket goes back to your story."

"What story?"

"You know the one. Once upon a time, you heard a story about a sensational double murder that's completely unsupported by facts or local records. You're stuck on it. To say you're obsessed might be going too far, but you're dying to take these bones and cram them into your cameo locket fairy tale."

"That was uncalled for." And if that was the way he was going to play, then my sarcasm shield was coming down. "Tell me, Deputy, have you or your colleagues had any luck finding the weapon used to murder Phillip Bell? Have you had any luck figuring out what that weapon even is? And without those facts, are you still so sure that Grace Estes is guilty?"

"Let me tell you something, Kath. *Clue* you in, as it were. Most murders are fairly simple. They're nasty and brutal, and after the deed is done, people don't like owning up to it, but they aren't really all that puzzling. The simple truth about Phillip Bell's death is this: It was a crime of passion and Grace Estes is the only one in town who knew him well enough to be that passionate."

Darn the simple logic of his last statement. It's what kept going around in my mind, too. But I still didn't believe it. It was simple to the point of being simplistic and "true" only because the police had stopped asking questions. I hadn't and darned if I would. One question I couldn't ask was if he knew that Fredda had snuck into the cottage the night before. Asking that would open a whole bait shop of worms. But I had other questions.

"Then how do you account for the fact that you *haven't* found the weapon? And how do you account for the fact that Grace hasn't been able to tell you what that weapon is?"

"Again, it's simple. She's lying."

"Or maybe it's even simpler than a lie, Deputy. Try this—she's telling the truth."

When Clod had planted himself in front of me, he'd put his back to the barn, and he didn't see what I saw— Fredda standing at the edge of the big open doorway, arms crossed, head tipped, watching us.

# Chapter 23

Fredda stood in a shadow, making it impossible to see the expression on her face. I used the imagination Clod accused me of mishandling and pictured her eyes narrowed and assessing, her smile sardonic and amused. She lifted her hair off her neck and let it fall again. Then she crossed the open doorway and disappeared farther into the barn. I had questions for her, too, but I wasn't feeling brave or foolhardy enough to go after her. My imagination conjured pitchforks and scythes.

"Lost interest in pigs?" Clod called after me when I turned around and headed back to the visitors' center.

"Had enough."

Watching the students get caught up in creating their quilt blocks was soothing. Up to a point. Ernestine and I complimented them on color and pattern combinations and encouraged faltering stitches. We were the good-cop quilters. Shirley and Mercy stalked around the room, adamant about exact and unvarying seam allowances, clipped rather than dangling thread ends, and frequent use of the iron.

"Start as you mean to go on," Shirley told them.

"You don't just want to learn the *right* way," Mercy said. "You want to learn the *best* way."

"And that's *our* way," said Shirley.

I got the feeling that if Ernestine and I hadn't been there, there would have been some knuckle rapping and hand smacking to clarify that message and send it home. The students seemed to be enjoying themselves, accepting the warlord approach to quilting as easily as the good-cop approach. It was nice to see we hadn't lost any more of them overnight. Without more skeletons to exhume, Zach sat stitching a series of stylized coffins to each other. Even the tenderhearted girl, Carmen, was there. It must have been my deputy-certified overactive imagination that saw her cringe when Mercy stopped to inspect her needlework, because then Carmen proved her courage by asking Mercy a question.

"Ms. Spivey, if we can embroider as much as we want on our squares—"

"Quilters call that embellishment," Shirley said, closing in on Carmen from the other side.

"Ribbons, beads, lace . . ." Mercy ticked options off on her fingers. "They're all embellishments, and you can add what you like."

Carmen stayed strong. "If we can add as much embellishment as we want, then how will we know when we're finished?"

"Buttons and sequins, too," Shirley said.

"I'll tell you the secret," said Mercy. She paused and looked around the room, until our dozen avid, eager students looked back at her. "How do you know you're finished? You just do."

"And feathers," Shirley said.

"Or you don't," said Mercy.

Geneva, meanwhile . . . had started by following the twins around the room, peering over their shoulders, watching with fascination when they showed Ethan and Nash how to correctly press seams without pressing their fingertips, too. She floated by to tell me her sleuth practice was paying off because she already knew that Barb and Ethan were going separately but together to a party Saturday night. She studied Zach's coffin pattern. But eventually she floated over to the table where Shirley and Mercy had put the muslin bag holding the Plague Quilt. She settled on the table next to the bag, drew her knees up so she could rest her chin on them, and gazed at the bag. I don't know how long I stood looking at her look at it, but it was long enough that I'd tuned out the room, and I gave a start when Barb asked me a question.

"Ms. Rutledge, have you found out yet if Lillian Holston made her quilt?"

Geneva turned and looked at Barb, then hunched her shoulders and started rocking.

"The one she talked about in her scrapbook you showed us," Barb said.

Geneva answered. "No-oh," she said, in time to her rocking. "No-oh, no-oh, no-oh, no. Lillian, Lizzie, Ezra, and Flory, Sweet Uley, and Nan, it was the end of their story. No, Lillian did not finish her quilt. Lillian, Lizzie, Ezra, Uley, Nan, and Flory. Mattie and I were so very sorry. The plague came and they were all gone."

"Kath, dear?" Ernestine moved in front of me, her kind eyes peering into mine from behind her thick lenses. "Can I help?"

"It's okay, Ernestine. I'm fine." I turned to Barb. "I'm sorry, Barb. I don't think Lillian did make the quilt, and that's such a shame. Her scrapbook tells part of a story. Her quilt would have told more of it. That's one of the engaging characteristics of quilts. Quilts are folk art. Folk art is full of story. Engaging in story is a basic human endeavor."

"She's put on her professional hat," Mercy said.

"Which she was so recently obliged to take off," said Shirley.

"Hush," said Zach.

I smiled at him and at the other students, and then I zeroed in on the twins. They drew back, tucking their chins. "Shirley? Mercy? You haven't told the class the story behind your quilt yet. And I'd like to know why it's called the Plague Quilt." If they'd been turtles, their heads, arms, and legs would have disappeared inside their shells.

Carmen raised her hand. "Could it have anything to do with the cholera epidemic? We studied that in school."

"Eighteen seventy-nine," Zach said.

"Three-quarters of the population fled," said Barb. "Of those who stayed, two-thirds died."

Bless their avid, history-loving hearts.

"Bingo," said Shirley, followed by "Ow!" when Mercy's elbow caught her.

"Unfortunately," said Mercy, "Mr. Treadwell was given half an hour of our time this morning, and so we've run out. Your questions will have to wait."

"You could tell *me*," I said.

"Don't you have to be back at the shop?" Shirley asked.

Darn. She was right.

"And we have other places to be and things to do," said Mercy. They sighed identical, exaggerated sighs.

I didn't say anything more while the students put away their quilt blocks and materials. I held my tongue while the twins told the students how much they needed to get done on their blocks each day in order to have a quilt at the end of the program. I made pleasant small talk when Nadine came to take the students on to their next session. But before the Spiveys scooped up their muslin-wrapped treasure and escaped, I cornered them.

"We have an agreement, correct? You are here, doing a really fine job with the students. In exchange for letting you do that, I will get to spend an equal amount of time, alone, studying the Plague Quilt. Correct?" I didn't wait for answers. "I want you to know I do trust you. But I want to know when that's going to happen."

"At the end of the program," Mercy said. "Otherwise how would we know how much time to give you?"

"Shirley and Mercy Spivey," Ernestine said, coming up behind me. For a twinkling tiny mole of a woman, she could be extremely fierce. "I *don't* trust you and I want to hear you promise that's what *will* happen."

"Why don't you tell her about it now and let her see it?" Zach asked.

I hadn't realized he was still in the room, too. Or, judging by the door to the auditorium standing ajar, maybe he'd slipped back in.

"We have no problem sticking with the original agreement," Shirley said.

"Or trusting you to do the same," said Mercy. "See you later."

Geneva still sat next to the muslin bag on the table. The twins carefully lifted the bag, shivered, and left.

"I know why they won't tell you about it," Zach said, watching them go. "It's all about power. And theirs is the worst kind. It's old-people power and some of them flaunt it."

"Watch yourself," I told him.

"He's right, though, Kath. You are right, dear," Ernestine said to Zach. "A certain amount of power comes with old age. The thing is, we all have it, but some old she-devils abuse it. Now, that wasn't a kind thing for me to say. Not that it wasn't true, but I'm sorry you had to hear it." She patted his cheek.

Cool Zach's eyes went wide, and he blushed from the neck of his T-shirt up to his hairline. "I have another question," he said, with a bit of a squeak in his voice. "Do you think the skeletons in the dump were plague victims? We read about how they ran out of wood for coffins."

"That's a good question," I said. "I don't know the answer. I suppose, if things were so bad, with so many people leaving, so many sick or dead, if there wasn't any better choice, it might have happened. They weren't laid in the ground very respectfully, though. Did Jerry say anything that makes you think they might be plague victims?"

"He didn't say much about anything. I was just wondering. No big deal."

"Wondering is a fine thing to do, in my book. Here's what I'm wondering. Does either of you remember any of the names you saw on the Plague Quilt?"

Neither Ernestine nor Zach had paid attention to the names on the Plague Quilt. Like me, they'd been more absorbed by the colors, patterns, embroidery, and whimsical details of Rebecca's work. I didn't prompt them with the names Geneva had mentioned, but between them they came up with half a dozen—some first names, some last. I wasn't sure whether they were more access points for our search, or more pieces we'd be trying to fit together. I planned to take the names they remembered to Friday's Fast and Furious meeting the next afternoon, along with the names from Geneva's sad rhyme. But first I had to get through the evening—and dessert with the Spiveys.

What kind of dessert did one serve to enigmas such as the Spivey twins? Did they really expect dessert? I stopped at Mel's on the way home, ran in, asked for three slices of the honey nut cake, and dashed back out, happy that I hadn't run into Mel. She would have had the expected Spivey attack out of me in three seconds flat. Once home, I ate a virtuous green salad, then waited. While I waited, I nibbled around the edge of one slice of cake, reflecting on the appropriateness of my choice. Honey, to sweeten and soothe the unpredictable twins; nuts because I liked the symbolism. The clock ticked and I realized I could be knitting while dreading instead of picking at the cake.

I washed my hands and took up my knitting needles to work on a peony pink baby hat for Friday's Fast and Furious thousand-hat challenge. It was my third pink hat in as many weeks, and I was looking forward to the last of that color. Debbie never seemed to tire of knitting yellow hats, and Thea stuck with her mission to instill a love for reading and good literature early in a child's life by knitting red-and-white-striped beanies. She called them vestigial *Cat in the Hat* hats. Mel went with food colors. But I hadn't settled on a color or a theme or a mission. I also didn't knit as often or as fast as I should.

The Spiveys waited until full dark, parking down the street, away from the streetlight. They'd told me that after they crept up onto the porch, knocked softly, and scurried past me into the house. I was expecting them, of course, but I still had trouble making myself open the door wide enough for them to actually get in.

"In case he's onto us," Shirley said.

"Wes? What's he likely to do?"

"Let's go on into the kitchen," Mercy said, "away from prying picture windows."

"Cozier in the kitchen, too," said Shirley. "Oh, and look, you have cake for us."

They ate first and had seconds on sweet tea, then told me their story of Wes Treadwell. They didn't know details and they were fuzzy on dates, but they knew it had happened in California and involved taking advantage of bankrupt homeowners.

"Finding a weak spot and moving in is his forte," Mercy said.

"Exploiting the salt of the earth for personal gain," said Shirley.

"But you don't really know what happened or when. Just that it happened in California. How do you even know that much?"

"Shirley's ex keeps in touch with her," Mercy said. "He'd like her to move out there with him."

"Frank is a skunk," said Shirley. "That's why he knows another one when he smells him."

"And why Shirley left Frank," said Mercy.

"That and I don't like the idea of leaving everything I know and hold dear."

"Or moving to California and falling off into the ocean when the big one comes," Mercy added.

"Does Frank know the details?" I asked. "Could I call him?"

"Oh, I couldn't let you do that," Shirley said. "He suffers from high blood pressure."

"When Frank called last week and said he'd like to personally kill Wes Treadwell, Shirley had a terrible time calming him down again," Mercy said.

They left when I told them there wasn't any more cake. Mercy turned back before I got the door closed.

"Don't breathe a word of this when you see us at the Homeplace," she said. "We daren't rile him."

"You were trying to rile him loudly enough to get through to him on the other side of a closed door today."

"Sometimes we're too hotheaded for our own good. Thank you for the cake. Such dainty slices. The tea was a tad on the sweet side. See you tomorrow."

Bless my heart.

By Friday morning, the quilting session felt like a routine. The students made progress on their blocks and we'd fallen into an easy companionship of stitching. It was a quiet, unremarkable morning except for two things. One was that the twins avoided speaking to me about anything other than snipping threads and pressing seams. They even avoided making eye contact, and that was soothing. The other was an embellishment Zach added to his quilt block—two of the coffin-shaped pieces he'd stitched together turned out to be identical, and in those coffins he embroidered identical skeletons. All in all, it was a good morning.

"Do you realize," Ardis said that afternoon as we were setting up for Friday's Fast and Furious, "we have investigated enough crimes by now that we have our own organizational thing that organizations have. One of those things, if you know what I mean."

I wheeled the whiteboard into position so it could be

seen from any of the comfy chairs we'd pushed into a half circle in the TGIF workroom. The workroom—the same used by Joe and his fly tiers—was a flexible space whose odd assortment of chairs and worktables accommodated formal and informal meetings of needleworkers of all kinds as well as the posse's strategy meetings and information exchanges.

"If she does not know what she means, how does she expect you to know?" Geneva asked. She'd been floating near the ceiling but now came down and huddled in one of the chairs.

"Are you talking about the whiteboard?" I asked.

"Not the board itself," Ardis said, "but the idea of bringing the board in, and arranging the chairs just so, because that's how we work best. You know what I mean. It's an acronym. *S* something. Standard operating procedure. *That's* what it is and that's what we have. SOP."

"Stolen orange pencil?" Geneva asked. "Subterranean octogenarian panda?" The whiteboard always made her grumpy. She'd told me that the clean, white expanse of the board called to her. *It calls, but at the same time, it mocks me cruelly,* she'd said. *Because I can never answer.* Now she grumbled as she watched us. "Perhaps Ardis means we have stinky, odiferous peonies."

I flapped my peony pink baby hat at her.

"Is there a fly in here?" Ardis asked.

"Silly old poop," Geneva said.

"Use a newspaper or a swatter," Ardis said. "Don't risk ruining the only hat you finished in the past seven days."

"One of these days I'm going to blow everyone's mind and bring in . . ." I tried to come up with a fabulous number of sweet baby hats. "How about a dozen?"

"Four should be fine. With a reasonable goal, you'll feel good if you overshoot, and the rest of us will be surprised."

"I'll try my best." I'd read recently about several women who had each, personally, knitted a thousand baby hats in a year. I knew I didn't have that kind of knitting drive, but surely I could start pulling my weight in Fast and Furious. "Toss the marker over, will you? Yow!" Geneva had risen from her chair and the marker went right through her. It didn't hurt her, but I flinched anyway. I'd never got used to seeing objects or people pass through her. And of course it annoyed her.

"Stop oppressing phantasms," she muttered. "If you will excuse me, I am going upstairs to spend time with Argyle, a creature who is never snide, overbearing, or pedantic. On the contrary, he is always sweet, obedient, and purring." With that, she floated out of the room.

"What was that about?" Ardis asked. She stared at the doorway and rubbed her eyes.

"Nothing, I was thinking of a couple of questions to start us off," I said. "And oh boy, do you smell what's coming up the stairs?"

Mel came in with her knitting bag and an insulated carafe. John followed with his bag and the source of the spicy, herby aroma on a covered plate. If we ever lost Mel as a member of Friday's Fast and Furious, we'd be sadder and each of us several pounds lighter. She'd assigned herself the duty of bringing refreshments every Friday afternoon and had given herself the title Year-round Undersecretary of the Marvelous.

"Yum." Ardis leaned over the plate, eyes closed.

"That's my name, and you'll never wear it out," Mel said. "I brought something different today." She thumped

the carafe down on the Welsh dresser we used for refreshments, and took the plate from John. "It's savory,
not sweet like me. Yo, Ernestine, what's the holdup
there? You need me to come light a fire under you?"

Ernestine came in with a nearsighted smile for each
of us and one for the dress form standing in a corner. She
had a second carafe in her hand, but no knitting bag.

"Did you lose something downstairs?" Mel asked her.

"I might have put my bag on the kitchen table," Ernestine said. "Or the counter."

"I'll get it." If I ran down and back up, maybe the
calories in Mel's treats wouldn't be so noticeable.

"Any sign of stragglers?" Ardis asked when I dashed
back up.

"I'm not that late," Thea called from the kitchen.
"And I'm not deaf. Give me a minute." We heard her
puffing as she climbed the stairs. When she reached the
top, she sagged in the doorway. "I practically ran here,
and these shoes are not conducive." She dropped herself
into the nearest comfy chair and John brought two cups
over to her.

"A choice today," he said. "Cucumber lemonade or
unsweetened chai latte."

"Both." She took a sip of the latte and then a swig of
the lemonade. "That's better. Who's got hats?"

Starting our meetings with show-and-tell was SOP.
We took turns laying our contributions on the low table
at the center of our half circle, like so many poker play-
ers adding chips to a pot. Ardis kept count for us. She
went first, with a stack of sky blue hats.

"Six," she said, looking smug. "A little off my game
this week. Daddy was fractious."

Ernestine added the pale peach and the lilac hats

she'd knitted while waiting to see Grace, and three in orange tabby stripes with cat ears. "They're Argyle hats," she said.

John counted out four in aqua. Thea put in three of her red-and-white-striped hats.

"Sweet potatoes and cayenne," Mel said, laying out four hats in shades from deep orange to orangey red. "I've been working on a sweet potato biscuit recipe this week."

I put my one puny pink hat next to theirs.

"A bit of 'slow and tell'?" Mel asked. "That's okay, Red. We know your needles take a rest when we're on a case. What's our total, Ardis?"

"Debbie sent three," Ardis said. She laid three creamy yellow hats on the table, pulled a pencil from behind her ear, and totaled her running tally. "That makes six hundred forty-two, plus Joe's if he shows. We're ahead. But that's good, because I expect we'll slow down as the holidays approach."

"Well," I said with exaggerated exasperation, "some of us better not get any slower, or she'll be frogging what we already have, instead of adding to the pile. There—" I dropped my act. "I saved you the trouble and made the dig myself. Sorry I'm slow, guys. I'll make up for it by making the run to the hospital this month."

At the start of the challenge, the group had pictured taking their one thousand hats to the hospital in one impressive delivery at the end of the year. Ardis said she'd even toyed with the idea of dressing up as a stork for the delivery. But when hats started overflowing plastic bins in the workroom, we realized the hospital would have the same storage problem, and we'd started making deliveries once a month, sans beak and feathers.

"I'll run them over Sunday morning," I said.

"You are nothing if not generous, Red," Mel said. "Now we'll sit back and knit toward our personal goals, while you fall farther behind in yours by bringing us up to speed on the investigations."

"You're swell, Mel. Which case do you want first? Hot or cold?"

"Let's go with hot," Ardis said. "So it doesn't turn cold, too. Any objections?"

There were none.

"Good." Ardis settled back in her chair. "Tell them about the hackle. Unless someone knows who swung the blamed fool thing, finding the murder weapon is probably the biggest piece of news."

A floorboard creaked in the hall, immediately followed by the sound of light feet hitting about every third step on the way up, a muttered expletive, and then Joe's voice.

"Finding the blamed fool listening at the door might be news, too," he said. "Why don't you come on in, Cole? We'll teach you to knit."

# Chapter 24

Clod did his best to be in control of the situation in the TGIF workroom. It must have been hard for him, though, standing starched, stiff, and stern in front of people in comfy chairs knitting baby hats nonstop while he harangued.

"If you have information pertinent to the murder of Phillip Bell which you have not turned over to the sheriff's department, then be advised that you can and will be brought up on charges of obstruction of justice."

"Silly, outmaneuvered policeman," Geneva said. She'd heard the ruckus of the brothers' entrance and floated down from the study to enjoy it.

Ardis didn't make it easier for Clod. She was still knitting, but no longer sitting. She'd risen as soon as Joe prodded Clod into the room. She stood three feet from him, needles clicking, looking him straight in the eyes. Being his height, as well as his former third- and fourth-grade teacher, gave her an edge in any confrontation.

Joe slung off his backpack and sat in the chair next to mine. He took his knitting from a pouch in the pack, tossed three hats the color of water in a clear, mossy mountain creek on the table, and started clicking away on another.

"Glad you got here when you did and found him there," I whispered.

"Not an accident," Joe whispered back. "I've been following him."

"If you know the whereabouts of," Clod continued, "or if you are in possession of material evidence that pertains to the murder of Phillip Bell, which you have not turned over to the sheriff's department, then be advised that you can and will be brought up on charges of obstruction of justice. A weapon, for your information, is material evidence."

"Coleridge Blake Dunbar, explain yourself," Ardis said. Crossed arms and a tapping foot were implied; she kept knitting. "What in heaven's name do you think you were doing listening at our door?"

Clod didn't go down with the first punch. "Ms. Buchanan, please explain your statements *Tell them about the huckle*, and *Finding the murder weapon is probably the biggest piece of news*."

"Hackle," Ardis said, with moist, guttural emphasis on the first syllable. "If you're going to listen at doors, then listen accurately."

"He doesn't stand a chance against her," Geneva said. "She reminds me of my darling mama when she used to take my daddy down a peg or two." She floated over to stand proudly beside Ardis.

"Ms. Rutledge, did you find a weapon?" Clod's voice betrayed him. He was tiring. Or tiring of us.

"Sorry, no. Did you?"

"Then will someone please tell me what *finding the murder weapon* is supposed to mean?"

"Tell me why you were listening at our door, and I will," I said.

"This isn't a negotiation," Clod blustered. "The answer's simple enough, though. I knew you and your gumshoe group would be meeting this afternoon, because it's your standard operating procedure."

"Ignore him and his simply outrageous prattle," Geneva said.

It would have been so much fun to give her a high five for that remark. I settled for the universal A-OK sign. If Clod chose to interpret that as sarcasm for his answer, that was up to him. My conscience was clear.

"My answer's simple, too," I said. "I didn't *find* the weapon, any more than Grace told you where *you* could find it. She told you a likely place to *look*, which isn't the same as telling you where it is." I waited for him to agree. He didn't. He made an annoyed face. "I didn't find the weapon, but I found out what it probably is and where it came from." I waited for him to look interested or gratified. He didn't. He looked skeptical. "I think the weapon is a hackle, Deputy, and a hackle is missing from the storage collection at the Homeplace."

"God rest him," Thea said faintly, putting her hand to her neck.

Mel whistled.

"That sounds . . ." Joe stopped knitting and swallowed. "That sounds like it could be right." He laid his needles and wool on the table, and then he told Clod what a hackle was and what it looked like. "And if you swung it just right and hit the jugular?"

Clod made notes, some of the starch gone from his face. "Is that lemonade over there?" he asked. "May I have a glass?"

"No," Ardis and Geneva both said. Ardis blinked a few times and rubbed her ear with the heel of her hand.

"Fine," Clod said, "whatever. Ms. Rutledge, if you'll please come with me? I need to know where this hackle was."

"I'm staying right here. You can find out anything you want to know about the missing hackle and who had access to it from Nadine. I'm only a volunteer out there and I'm in the middle of a meeting here. Our SOP is knitting baby hats and I'm behind. So if you don't mind?"

"Sorry," Geneva said, "only posse. Step outside, pardner."

"We will notify you when there are new developments in the case, Coleridge," Ardis said.

Clod was too irritated, too professional, or too afraid of Ardis to grumble. He left, and soon afterward, Joe packed his knitting needles and followed.

Geneva left, too, but not before making me want to put my fingers in my ears. "I'll be at the bottom of the stairs," she said, "standing on patrol, surveilling our premises, and seeking out poltroons. Sayonara, old pal."

I waited until all footsteps and ghosts had receded, then I put my own knitting down and went to the white board.

"Back to our regularly scheduled murder investigation—take a look at these two questions."

Across the top of the board, I wrote: *What drives an ordinary person to kill? What drives an ordinary person to think killing will fix a problem?*

"Those questions keep running through my head," I said. "I have no idea if thinking about them will help us solve Phillip's murder, but I wanted to put them out there. Since we met Tuesday night, we've each pretty much worked on our own quilt block. Maybe these questions will help us bring the individual blocks together.

There don't appear to be any monsters loose in Blue Plum. An ordinary person killed Phillip."

"An ordinary person with a hackle," Thea said. "When were you going to tell us the small but interesting fact that you'd identified the weapon?"

"I was about to, and then we were interrupted. But let's get started now. Let's share the information we've uncovered and see who it points to."

"Grace," Thea said. "The most important piece of information we've uncovered about her is that the police think they've got a case. We can't discount that. They might actually be right. Even the horrible hackle doesn't disprove it. She volunteered at the Homeplace. She could have had access, right?"

"Unfortunately, yes." I drew a square on the board and wrote *Grace* in it.

"I like your question up there," Thea said, "about who would think killing someone would fix a problem. I want you to know I *have* been looking for someone besides Grace who might think killing Phillip could fix a problem. I didn't find anyone, and Grace had good reasons to think his death fixed a problem. Believe me, I read the police reports and the divorce decree. Phillip Bell?" She shook her head. "Not a good man."

"But they *were* divorced," Ernestine said. "Why would she kill him now?"

"Why did she follow him to Blue Plum?" Thea countered. "We know she did that. That doesn't imply clear thinking to me. Kath says she still loved him. That really doesn't imply clear thinking. I think we know enough. This time the police have it right. But—if you need more, Grace is still Phillip's beneficiary. And would you like to know if she has money problems?"

"She told me herself that she did." I wrote *Phillip*, *abuse*, *divorce*, and *money* in the "Grace" block.

"That's your quilt block, Thea. There's nothing wrong with the facts in it. But it's isolated. I want to see the other's blocks before drawing a conclusion."

"You don't think the police have already looked beyond Grace and come back to her?" she asked.

"So far I haven't seen or heard anything that makes me think they have." I drew another square on the board. "But we aren't getting in their way, so I don't see any problem with continuing. Here's another block. Who wants to go next?"

"Make that block *Wes Treadwell*," John said. "I'm interested in him. I'd like to know more about him."

"You were going to buy him a cup of coffee," I said.

"You can't learn enough about a man over a cup of coffee to hang him for murder," Thea said.

"He blew me off, anyway," John said. "But it's the way he blew me off that caught my attention. I got the feeling he'd looked me over, calculated how valuable I might be to him, and dismissed me. Three words came to my mind—'adroit,' 'practiced,' and 'slippery.' I have to confess, though. I had a hard time ignoring the Spiveys' opinions of Wes before forming my own. I don't know whether that's good, bad, or of no consequence."

John's brow furrowed and Mel handed him a cup of cucumber lemonade. While he revived himself, Ardis caught my eye.

"What are Shirley and Mercy doing mixed up in this?" she asked.

"Shirley's ex-husband knew Wes in California before Wes moved here. Her ex told her a story about Wes fleecing homeowners out there. The twins don't have any details, though, and the only thing I know for sure is that if *Wes* is ever murdered, Shirley's ex should be the number one suspect. I know all this because the twins dropped by my house last night."

That earned a chorus of sympathetic noises and served to deflect more Spivey-related questions from Ardis.

John drained his lemonade and looked restored. "I also made a start on our search for the victims in the dump. That's the cold case, I know, but we need to think about the possibility that Phillip's research touched on the victims and also touched a nerve that snapped. That's conjecture, but Kath said something Tuesday night about 'what ifs,' and that's mine."

"It's a good 'what if,' John." I twiddled the marker in my fingers. "What do you think I should I write in Wes' square?"

"I don't think we know enough yet," John said.

"At least Wes *does* drink coffee," Mel said. "I see him in the café two, three times a week. He likes to shake hands and talk. He comes across as somebody people should know. Except for the Limburger-cheese-and-liverwurst incident, I might've seen Bell in my place two or three other times total. Call me petty, but it made me not like him. Not enough to kill him, though. What we're still missing here is someone who *really* didn't like Phillip Bell. I've done a lot of listening over the past few days. Dropped into a lot of conversations. Asked people outright about Bell. I heard nothing. The man didn't mix. That's what makes me think it had to be someone associated with the Homeplace who killed him. No one else knew him well enough."

"I think you're right, Mel, and that goes back to the

second question I wrote up there. 'What problem did Phillip pose and who thought killing him would fix it?' "

"He was a problem for *Grace*," Thea said.

"He might have been the same kind of problem for Fredda Oliver." I told them what Joe had told me about why Fredda left Asheville.

"You think she fell into a similar relationship with Phillip?" Ernestine asked.

"Yeah, I do. I'm almost positive it was Fredda who answered Phillip's phone the night before he died."

"The other night you thought it might have been Grace," said Thea.

"That was before I met Fredda and heard her voice. I think she's a pretty tough woman, too, and strong from the type of work she does out there at the Homeplace. There's nothing wrong with that, but she's also sneaky. And remember, Cole says she's a good liar."

"This sounds like a promising lead," Ardis said. "The problem will be finding out what she was doing Tuesday morning. How do we do that?"

"Engage her in conversation," said Mel, "and bring it around to the murder, which shouldn't be too hard to do. It's on everyone's mind. Then say something like, 'Oh, it's so awful. I can't believe I was at home doing something inconsequential like drinking coffee while that was happening. What were you doing, Fredda?' Only try to make it less obvious. Probably not as easy as it sounds."

"It doesn't sound easy at all," Ardis said. "What we really need is another death, while Grace is in jail, so that she's obviously eliminated."

"And of course you don't really mean that," Ernestine said.

"I absolutely do not. Kath, whatever you do, be careful. I don't think you should get into a situation where you're alone with Fredda."

"I won't." I drew another square, and put Fredda's name in it. Below her name I wrote *Phillip*, *abuse*, and *liar*. Then I went ahead and made squares for Nadine and Jerry.

"Do we know enough about Nadine or Jerry to put anything in their squares?" John asked. "Thea, have you turned up anything on either of them?"

"Nadine earned her degree ten years ago, after raising a son and a daughter and then divorcing her husband. Jerry and Phillip knew each other in grad school. Different disciplines, but some of their classes overlapped. Grace and Jerry's sister were roommates."

"Do you know why Nadine got divorced?" I asked. "Or if Jerry and Phillip were friends?"

"Not yet."

"Have you found anything to back up the Spiveys' story about Wes?" I glanced over at her. "You had coffee with Wes yesterday, didn't you?"

"Yes, but give a girl a chance. It's only been a few days."

"It's not that you started with Grace and stopped there?" Mel asked.

"No, it's *not*. It's that I'm working on the library's budget and I'm spending most of my time trying to find ways I can avoid cutting money from the collection, cutting hours, or cutting staff. *Okay?*"

"Whoa, Thea, of course it's okay," Mel said. "Calm down." Then she turned to me and said, "Don't let her near a hackle anytime soon."

"Not funny," Thea snapped.

"Budgets are nasty things," said Ernestine. "Let's

have Mel's refreshments and then move on to our cold case."

"Because old bones aren't nearly as nasty as budgets," said Mel. "And I brought spicy flatbreads. See if you think they'll work well next to salads."

"Now you're talking sense," Thea said.

We put aside our needles and yarn to help ourselves from the plate on the Welsh dresser. The flatbreads were about four inches in diameter, a quarter of an inch thick, tender, buttery, salty, and spicy.

"What—," I started to ask.

Mel read my mind and went into hyper-recipe mode. "Cumin seeds, peppercorns, and fresh cilantro, besides the salt. You flatten a small ball of dough into a disk, spread the disk with melted butter and the seasonings, roll the disk into a cylinder like a jelly roll, coil the cylinder into another disk, flatten the disk, and cook it in a skillet, flipping it once to catch both sides for a couple of minutes each. What do you think? I'm experimenting with size. Traditional size would be like a tortilla."

"You should open a café or something," Thea said. "You're that good."

"Do you like the bread or not, Red?" Mel asked. "What are you thinking over there?"

I was thinking *mm-mm* and what a shame that Joe missed the bread, because it was delicious. Then I thought about Phillip and the interesting selection of spices on his kitchen counter, and how he might have liked Mel's breads. But the way I'd learned about his spices kept me from sharing that information. Then I thought about the pictures of the documents from his file, still on my phone. And then my thoughts skipped back to Joe and deliciousness.

"Hon, you carry the weight of your worries so plainly on your face. You want to be sure you never kill anyone."

"Good tip, Ardis. Thanks."

"And that is a perennial problem with these investigations," she said. "The villains don't make it easy for us. Not a one of our suspects is ever walking around out there plagued by guilt."

"What if we turned that thought around?" John said. "Who should be affected by Phillip's death but isn't? I think that goes back to Kath's second question on the whiteboard again: 'What drives an ordinary person to think killing will fix a problem?' What if, instead of looking for someone who looks guilty, we look for the person walking around Blue Plum who looks relieved?"

"I can tell you that person isn't Grace," Ernestine said. "She has very definitely been affected by Phillip's death. And I think that's another point in her favor."

"Prisoner's remorse," Thea said.

"I don't think so," said Ernestine. "I do not think so."

"Nadine seems to have bounced back," I said to distract them.

"How so?" Ardis asked.

"I hadn't really thought about it, but she was in shock to begin with. Visibly upset and short-tempered, as who wouldn't be? Now, not so many days later, she's on top of things and back in control."

"The way a professional should be," Thea said.

"You're right."

"But?" Ardis asked.

"No, she really is."

"But?"

I shrugged. "But she's got a lot to handle, considering that her workload has suddenly increased, and now she'll have to go through the process of searching, interviewing, and hiring again, in addition to finishing this major program and gearing up for her first fall at the Homeplace, and all the school visits. Under *ordinary* circumstances that's a lot. But she's got the added stress of extraordinary circumstances—a murder and the unexpected discovery of a couple of skeletons. Of course, she has her right-hand board member, Wes, helping out."

"You see competence and responsibility as suspicious?" Thea asked.

"I see Nadine's behavior as one of the many pieces we're trying to fit together. Wes is another piece."

"Piece of what?" Mel asked.

"We don't know." That was a chorus of at least three—John, Ardis, and Ernestine.

"The biggest piece of *mmhmm-whatever* in this whole thing is Phillip Bell," Thea said.

"And that's what makes me think this might have something to do with his research," John said. "He arrived at his new job. He read up on the history of the site. An aspect of the history caught his eye, and he started his own research. The skeletons were found in the dump. That discovery excited him further—that's right, isn't it, Kath?"

"Yes. That's why we were meeting the next morning. He knew the name Geneva. We were going to compare notes."

"Think of the money poured into the Holston Homeplace over the years," John said, "state funds and private funds. Think of all those Holstons and the foundation they created to support the site. Think of the pride invested, as well as the money. What if the discovery of the skeletons dropped a piece into place for Phillip, and what if the skeletons were going to help him prove a theory he'd hatched? Something that would rock the site and the benefactors?"

"It would rock the town, too," Ardis said. "Are you talking about something scandalous?"

"How about ruinous?" said John.

# Chapter 25

John took a moment to wipe butter from each of his fingers, and then picked up his knitting again. None of the rest of us moved. We might have stopped breathing as we waited for the rest of his "what if."

"Ruinous how?" Mel finally burst.

"Well, now," John said, "that's the question, isn't it? But as Thea said, it's only been a few days. It's going to take more time for all of this. But I'd say investors and passion, and especially unhappy investors and passion go together, and connecting that hackle with Phillip's neck was a passionate act of extreme unhappiness."

"Proof," Thea said, "is lacking."

"That's the sad truth," I said. "We don't have much proof of anything, for either case. But I do have some more names that might help us find out who our skeletons are. They're from the Spiveys' Plague Quilt."

"And the sad truth about that quilt is that it's exquisite," Ernestine said. "And a touch macabre, because of the coffins."

Thea snorted. "Ernestine, you kill me."

"But not literally, dear." Ernestine patted Thea on the knee. "You're too valuable to the community."

I told them about the coffins and the names on the

quilt. "Rebecca made the quilt at the time of the cholera epidemic of 1879. It's sort of a signature quilt, except all the names are in the same handwriting, which isn't typical. I think they're all friends or family who died in the epidemic."

"Are the skeletons cholera victims?" Ardis asked.

"I don't think so," I said, "but it's certainly possible."

"We've got the *Bugle* on microfiche from back then," Thea said. "If you've got names, it wouldn't be too hard to look for them. It was a chaotic time, though. People fleeing, people who stayed behind dying. People who fled probably died, too. The records are undoubtedly not complete."

"But worth looking at," I said.

"But, boy, wouldn't chaos be a great cover for murder?" Mel added. "There's no record of Kath's double murder. Maybe that's because no one knew they'd been killed. Kill them, dump them, and put out a story that they'd fled like so many others. How many people left and never came back to Blue Plum and were never heard from again? It must have happened at least a few times."

"That would explain it," I said. "Oh my gosh, that could explain the classified ads, and why none of them were reported missing. The perfect crime at the perfect, chaotic time."


Geneva wasn't at the bottom of the stairs or in the kitchen when the meeting was over. She'd probably lost interest when no one challenged her. Ardis was out of sorts herself, as we went through our end-of-business-day routine. Argyle tried to catch her attention by catching at her ankle as she walked past. She jumped but didn't say anything to him. When she and I stood next to each other balancing the cash register, she suddenly laid the stack of ones she'd been counting on the counter.

"Can you and Debbie handle the shop alone tomorrow?" she asked.

"I guess."

Argyle leapt up on the counter and sniffed at the ones. Ardis didn't say anything. I finished counting the fives and looked at her.

She stood with her head bowed and palms flat on the counter. Her eyes were closed.

"Ardis? What's the matter?"

"I don't know."

I grabbed the tall stool and tried to get her to sit. She wouldn't. She stayed where she was, hands still flat on the counter.

"Ardis, of course Debbie and I can handle it. No question. Come on now. Sit down."

"I'm fine. I feel fine." She opened her eyes. "I don't know what this is . . ." She trailed off, rubbing her ear. "A day off might do me good, though."

"By all means. Take more if you need to. Get some good naps in. That's what Argyle recommends."

Argyle pushed the pile of ones into less of a stack and lay down on them.

"No, I don't think a nap will do anything for me. I really do feel fine. Maybe some fresh air."

"You've been working too hard while I lollygag out there at the Homeplace."

"I don't know. I don't think so. But I'll run on home now. I'll see you Monday." She looked around the shop, squinting as though her eyes hurt. She turned to leave, turned back, looked around again, and shook her head.

"Ardis? Phone me when you get home, okay?"

"Good night."

I looked around after she left. "Geneva?"

No answer.

Ardis called me half an hour later, just as I was beginning to worry.

"The fresh air is already doing me good," she said. "I decided to take a walk when I got home. I put Daddy in his chair and the two of us are having a constitutional. It's doing us both good. Daddy's feeding the ducks in the park and I had a brainstorm. It's been years since I've been out to the Homeplace, and I don't know if Daddy's ever been. Do you think Nadine will be there tomorrow?"

"Most likely."

"Then I think I'll take Daddy tomorrow. Maybe we can sweet-talk Nadine into giving us a personal tour."

"Ask her to show you around while you talk about the herb festival she's planning for the spring. She wants us to do a natural-dye workshop."

"Perfect entrée. Thank you, hon. Good night."

I called Mel after hanging up with Ardis. "That flatbread was perfect. Thanks for bringing it. Really delicious."

"Yeah? What are you really calling about? You aren't one for idle chitchat on the phone."

"Fredda said something to me. It made me wonder."

"Well, I'm not going to sit here wondering for too long. I have to be up before you even want to know in the morning. What'd she say, and what's it to me?"

"That she'd heard I was dating the more delicious of the two Dunbars."

Mel was quiet.

I interrupted her quiet with apologies. "Forget it. Forget I said anything. I'm being insecure."

"I don't remember hearing anything about Fredda and Joe," Mel said.

"And it's not like he's seeing her now, so really, forget it. It's just the way she said 'delicious.'"

"I'll check around."

"Thanks."


After I talked to Mel, I called John and told him I had pictures of some documents I'd like to send him. "They're pictures of photocopies Phillip had. And I don't have pictures of all the documents, so you might not be able to tell anything from them. They might fit in or add to your 'what if,' though."

"Send them along. I'll see what I can make of them."

"And if you don't mind, I'd appreciate it if you don't say anything to anyone else about the pictures."

"Silence guaranteed."


"We'll need to be quiet as soon as we're near the creek," Joe said. "It'd be better if we didn't smell, either."

"I didn't know otters were so fussy. Would it help if I have the clam chowder and dab some behind my ears?"

"They're smart critters. Probably smart alecks, too."

It was Saturday evening, and we were waiting our turn to order at Mel's before taking off on our much-anticipated trek to look for the family of river otters Joe had seen. Mel's was hopping, but the line moved fast. Mel worked the counter, her spiked hair helping the overall impression of frenetic efficiency. The checks in her houndstooth apron matched the midnight blue and aqua in her hair.

"Evening, you two," Mel said when we reached the

counter. "Thank you for making the café part of your date-night experience. I hope you don't mind if I belabor the fact that you're dating, but you're darned cute when I do, because you both blush. What can I get you?"

"Popeye Salad with a side of the spicy flatbread," I said. "Glad to see you put that on the menu."

"I'll have the same," Joe said. "Sounds delicious."

Mel caught my wince. "Speaking of delicious sides," Mel said, "here's a little dish you might not have heard." She crooked a finger for us to lean closer and then lowered her voice. "For a short while after Fredda came to town, she and Cole were something of an item. A quiet item, as far as the general public is concerned, not unlike you two, but an item nonetheless. This is bona fide information from two independent reliable sources, names to be supplied on request." She stood up, voice back at normal volume. "Now move along, you two, and quit holding up the line."

"Did you know that?" I asked Joe as we went to find a table.

"No, but it's not surprising. Kind of hard to picture, though."

"Would he overlook a suspect if he'd been involved with her?"

"That's even harder to picture."

We took a booth being vacated by a touristy couple. Joe took a napkin and swept most of the crumbs and salt left behind to the end of the table.

"Makes you wonder, though." He balanced the octagonal salt shaker on some of the salt he'd missed. "The man does have a heart."

We drove past the Holston Homeplace and up a winding, narrowing road into the wooded foothills. When the

road turned to gravel, then to rutted dirt with the occasional spring-jouncing rock, and finally petered out into
a cleared area hardly big enough to turn around in, we
stopped and got out.

"Otters are more curious than cats, but shy, so we
might not see them," Joe said. "I'd been sitting a while
when I saw them." He grabbed our backpacks from the
bed of his truck and tossed mine to me. "The creek's
about a ten-minute walk from here."

"A loping Joe walk or a Kath walk?"

He adjusted his stride. "Fifteen minutes, then."

"How long were you sitting?"

"Two, three hours. We won't stay that long or it'll be
dark. Bacon Branch is a pretty creek. We'll find you a
rock above the bank to sit on. You'll like it."

"What'll you be doing?"

"I brought something along."

"If there's a Bacon Branch, is there an Egg Branch?"

"And a Tomato and a Lettuce and an On Rye Branch."
He helped me over a downed tree. "There are several
Bacon families in the area. My favorite creek names are
Dry Creek and Stinking Creek. No idea where the
'Stinking' comes from. Someone told me there was a sul-
fur spring along it somewhere, but I never found it, and
the creek smells good enough to me."

"Maybe the otters would disagree."

"We're getting close enough, let's hush."


I sat on a limestone boulder above the creek—the rock
dark gray and cool. The water, gliding past below, turned
golden where a few shafts of sunlight reached it; otherwise it ran a clear, cold, dark green. Birds called and answered through the trees. I heard insects, leaf rustlings,

the deep gurgle-splash of the creek, and not much else. Joe sat on another water-tumbled boulder, painting in a small sketchbook. The otters stayed away. Before we hiked back out, Joe showed me his watercolor sketch.

"It's beautiful. I don't know how you make the water look real like that. And the rocks and the trees. I'm pretty sure, though, that I'm wearing jeans and a T-shirt."

"You look good this way, too."

Sunday morning I remembered I'd promised to take the baby hats to the hospital over in Stonewall. What a shame. Laundry and cleaning the house would have to wait. As I pulled away from the last stop sign at the edge of town, a car came up behind me, closer than I liked. I looked in the rearview mirror to give the other driver the evil eye. The other driver was Fredda.

Fredda stayed with me. I slowed. She slowed. I resumed speed and so did she. She wasn't on my bumper. She wasn't hunched over the steering wheel, snarling and slavering after me. But she followed me on that winding road with too few houses or open businesses. Could it be called a car chase, I wondered, if we drove at the speed limit? I could have pulled off or turned down another road, but I didn't know the area between Blue Plum and Stonewall well enough, and I didn't want to end up cornered somewhere the sun didn't shine and my phone had no reception. Cornered in the ambulance zone at the ER would be okay. They knew how to treat victims of mayhem there. That was a comforting thought, because she stayed with me all the way to the hospital.

# Chapter 26

I lost Fredda when I turned in at the emergency entrance. It took no evasive skill—I stopped in front of the ER doors, and she drove on past. When someone came and knocked on my window, I apologized for being confused and upset. I proceeded, slowly, to visitors' parking, looking everywhere for Fredda or her car. After I parked, I called Ardis.

"Daddy and I had the best time at the Homeplace yesterday. I thought he was happy feeding the ducks in the park Friday night, but that was nothing compared to how happy scratching Portia's back made him. Portia's the pig out there. I think Daddy fell in love."

"Ardis, I'm at the hospital."

"*Oh my land.* What's happened?"

"Nothing yet. I'm here with the baby hats, but Fredda followed me here."

"Followed you how? With intent? *Hon!* This might be the break we need. Is she there now? Are you safe? Why are you calling me? Hang up and call 911. *I'll* hang up and call 911. What are your coordinates?"

"Ardis, it's okay. I'm in the parking lot. I think I lost her when I turned in at the emergency entrance."

"That was smart. What *do* you want me to do? Call Cole?"

"No—do you know what Mel found out yesterday? He dated Fredda for a while."

"Well, that's an example of his poor judgment, but I don't see—"

"I think that kept *him* from seeing. Here's what I'm going to do. I'm getting the hats, now I'm getting out of the car. Locking the car. Now I'm going to walk into the hospital, talking to you, ready to scream and throw a bag of baby hats at a murderer."

"I'll keep listening."

"I don't see her anywhere. I'm walking past a box hedge that's making me nervous."

"When you get inside, stop at the information desk and tell them it should be trimmed for safety's sake."

"I'm going through the door. I'm inside. I still don't see her. I think it's okay."

"You call me when you head back out to your car."

"I will."

When the volunteer came to meet me and collect the hats, I decided each TGIF member should take a turn making a delivery. Watching the woman look at each hat and exclaim, with her hand on her heart, how much nurses and families appreciated our time and effort made the trip and the year of knitting worth it.

"Would you like to see some of your hats in action?" she asked.

How could I resist?

She took me to the windowed hallway outside the Nursery Intensive Care Unit where we could look in at the babies in their incubators. Half a dozen fragile babies wore our soft knit hats. Thea's red and white stripes were immediately recognizable. Two babies wore hats that might have been from Mel during her celery and lettuce phase. A baby being held and rocked wore a yellow beanie that might have come from Debbie. The woman rocking and singing to the baby was Fredda.

"She's a baby cuddler, Ardis. She's there every morning from six until eight, except on Sundays, when she goes at ten. Like today. She does it because she lost her own baby. The volunteer told me she's the most faithful baby cuddler they have, that she cuddles the parents as much as the babies."

"Should the volunteer have told you all that? It seems like there's a privacy issue involved."

"I might have let on that I knew Fredda better and that I knew more of her story than I do."

"We could call that an ethical issue, but instead we'll call it necessary subterfuge."

"It means Fredda has an alibi."

"Only if she was there on Tuesday and only if Phillip was attacked during those hours."

"She was here Tuesday. They're very careful about volunteers signing in and out. And I'm no expert, but I don't think he died even an hour before I found him."

"We'll see if we can find out the time of death," Ardis said. "Then we'll knit ourselves a couple of thinking caps and put them on."

I e-mailed the rest of the posse and told them that if Phillip was attacked anytime after six Tuesday morning, Fredda had an alibi.

Thea e-mailed back, "Mm-hm."

Mel e-mailed back, "Time of death: post six. Source: Smiling Deputy Darla."

I e-mailed, "Cole's missing a good bet. He should hook up with Darla."

Thea sent, "E-mail is not sufficiently secure for transmission of sensitive information."

Mel shot back, "Cole's as sensitive as a disengaged transmission."

Monday morning, in the education room at the Homeplace, watching the twins in their unexpected niche as teachers of crazy quilting—thinking *who knew* and *good thing they came along* and *good thing they didn't get that phone call about not needing volunteers*—I realized how stupid I'd been. Of course *they'd* made those phone calls. Was I really that dense? I decided to blame it on the lure of the Plague Quilt. My subconscious must have known what they'd done, but it also knew that if I rumbled them, I might never see the quilt again. Knowing now, though, gave me an advantage about which they weren't aware.

I smiled and waved at Shirley across the room. She jumped. Maybe I wasn't being subtle enough. I didn't want to tip my hand.

"How's the detective business?" Zach asked when I stopped to admire the flame stitch he was adding to his quilt block beneath the coffins.

"Slow."

"Tortoise or hare slow?"

"Tortoise. I hope."

"Thought so."

"Anything new on the excavation front?"

"Jerry's doing the lunch lecture today. Talking about the artifacts we dug up with the skeletons."

"*Is* he? I think I'll have to stay after class today."

"Thought so."

Jerry Hicks disappointed some of us by not having the artifacts with him at his lunch lecture. What he did was probably better and smarter, though. He called the twenty-minute presentation a slide show symposium, and he showed photographs he'd taken of the excavation process, and of the bones and artifacts in situ, and then before, during, and after cleaning. Judging by the lack of fidgeting and the heads all tilted to look at the screen rather than electronic devices in laps, the entire audience thought the slides were cool.

Nadine, Wes, and I sat in a row behind the students. I didn't like the idea of sitting in a darkened room with either of them, but they'd joined me and it would have felt awkward to get up and move away. I took small comfort in Shirley and Mercy sitting in the row behind us. Clod stood alone in the back corner, for no good reason that I could see. I'd called Ardis to let her know I would be another half hour or so. I would have told her why, but she said she was in the middle of a sale and hung up.

Jerry narrated the slides as he flipped through them, telling a slight story of two young people who hadn't lived to be much older than the students in the room. He told the kids that his findings were preliminary.

"In the end, the bones and the artifacts, and the artifacts in the bones, will speak for themselves."

"What do you mean, *artifacts in the bones*?" Nash asked.

"Wait and see. Let's look at the bones first. We have two individuals interred in what we can call a nonstandard burial pattern. A male approximately five foot ten.

A female approximately five foot two." Jerry went through slide after slide, showing measurements of long bones, the difference between male and female pelvic bones. There was a surprising moment of humor when a set of red-gummed dentures came on the screen.

"The young man was fashionable and money-conscious," Jerry said. "You all might get your nose pierced to impress your best girl. Back in the day, you would have had your cavity-prone teeth pulled out and a set of dentures made. That way you came to a marriage with no more dentist bills in your future. These dentures will help us put a date to the bones. They're made of vulcanized rubber. That manufacturing process gives us one set of dates. They are also what you might call whistling dentures. Feel the roof of your mouth with your tongue, right behind your teeth. Feel the ridges? Those are called rugae. They serve a purpose. They're a sounding board. They help us talk. Our poor fellow's dentures were manufactured before the connection was made between rugae and clear speech. His dentures are smooth, and he probably whistled on the letter *S*."

"Do dental records go back that far?" a girl asked.

"It's certainly possible," Jerry said, "although I wouldn't say probable. We'll definitely be looking, though."

I would definitely ask Geneva if Sam had a new set of rubber dentures. And if the poor guy whistled when he said his name.

Jerry next showed photographs of buttons, shoe buttons, a belt buckle, miscellaneous metal clasps, and numerous small unidentifiable pieces of metal, and then what he'd tentatively identified as spiral steel corset stays. I was sure he was right about the stays. No textiles had survived, and I didn't see anything that looked like the remains of a bustle. The length of the steel stays might help date the bones. The absence of a bustle might or might not. Bustles were a changing fashion, and not every woman wore one every day.

When Jerry showed slides of an oval object that, when cleaned, turned out to be a locket with a cameo, I barely kept myself from gasping, or possibly crying. I turned to look at Clod. The lights were too low, though, and I could hardly see him. That didn't stop my mind's eye from imagining the look of irritated, surprised, confounded disbelief I longed to see on his face.

"These next slides show a silver pocket watch," Jerry said. "I wish I could tell you the watch is engraved with a name and a date. It isn't. But look at this." He flashed another slide, showing the watch and the locket turned over. "The script is ornate, but that's an *M* and an *S* on the back of the locket."

Mattie. Mattie Severs. Mattie and Sam.

"Mercy and Shirley," one of the twins whispered faintly behind me.

"Mercy Spivey," whispered the other more faintly.

"If Hicks had brought that watch or the cameo with him and passed them around," Wes said, "ten to one, one or the other or both would have disappeared in a kid's pocket."

"Baloney." Had I said that? I must have. It wasn't too dark in our row to see Wes look down his nose in my direction. Good for me.

Jerry's slide show ended with close-up pictures of the skulls. He'd told his story of the bones smoothly, and I hadn't noticed that we'd seen the skulls only from a distance in the full-skeleton shots, and he'd shown us the dentures only separate from their skull. If Geneva had been there with me, she could have told us about her friend Mattie's blond hair and her beautiful singing voice. But she wasn't, and I was glad, because the skulls spoke for themselves.

"These are . . . sad pictures," Jerry said quietly. "They're pictures of two murder victims. The black spots you see pocking the frontal bones are lead shot from a shotgun blast."

# Chapter 27

I didn't hang around after the slide show. I didn't speak to anyone. I needed to get back to the Weaver's Cat. I needed to think about what to tell Geneva. I needed to get away before Clod fought his way along the row of auditorium seats to reach me. I didn't want his questions or any discussion. An apology for doubting and mocking me would have been nice, but that probably wasn't coming and it wasn't worth waiting for, anyway.

Zach mumbled something as I zipped past, but when I turned back, he'd slouched off in the other direction.

Clod came out of the visitors' center as I pulled away. He might have tried to flag me. I glanced at him only long enough to see his ticked-off face. I didn't stop.

By the time I got to the Weaver's Cat, my emotions had run the gamut—from sorrow to excitement to worry to relief and back to excitement. We'd found Mattie and Sam. I was sure of it. Worry crept back when I wondered how the news would affect Geneva, but I was beginning to formulate a plan for telling her and for dealing with her reaction. Excitement rose to the top again when I pictured Ardis' reaction. But I hadn't counted on her looking every bit as ticked off as Clod.

"It's taken me a few days," she said when I walked

through the front door, "but I've finally figured out what you haven't been telling me."

She stood behind the counter, arms crossed, in the classic grade-school-teacher pose she used to good effect on former students. It had a pretty good effect on me, too, even though I wasn't one of her former students. But my excitement carried me forward with credible ease and a smile that I hoped would disarm her. I also had an idea what she'd finally figured out. Dealing with that meant the excavation news would have to wait.

"It took me a few days to figure something out, too, Ardis. And I'll bet there's a commonality between your something and mine, and if I'm right, I'll buy you lunch."

"That's not usually the way bets work."

"Doesn't matter. I'm reading Spivey irritation all over your face, and buying lunch is the least I can do to ease your burden. Let me run upstairs. I'll be right back and ready to listen."

I hadn't seen Geneva or Argyle when I came in. I ran up to the study and found them together in the window seat. Seeing Geneva backlit against the window, it was hard to tell, but she still looked "strong." She was less like rainwater or vapor. She also wasn't sitting in a dejected heap.

"We have been waiting patiently for you to remember us."

"I didn't forget you. I was out at the Homeplace longer than I expected to be."

"We like *this* place."

"I'm so glad you do, Geneva. Would you like to come downstairs? I'll be busy in the shop all afternoon."

"We're feeling like homebodies today."

"I'll come back up to see you later, then. There's

something I'd like to talk to you about. In the meantime, would you like to hear another chapter or two of *Murder, She Wrote*?"

"We would be delighted."

Ardis had to wait through several chatty customers before she could unburden herself to me, but a large bag of mohair going out the door served to knock the edges off her irritation. As I'd thought, she'd figured out that Shirley and Mercy were involved with the quilting for Hands on History. I apologized for not telling her and told her about the bargain I'd made.

"You sold out?"

"With everything else going on—*everything else*, Ardis—letting them help seemed like a small thing. I needed help; they were there. At the time it was the only thing to do. And they really are doing a fine job."

We shook our heads in unified wonder.

"Oh, and wait until you see the Plague Quilt. Ardis, if you can look at it and still judge me, I will buy you lunch for a year."

"But I'll only get to see the quilt if the twins live up to their end of the bargain."

"I know that's a big 'if.' But here's what *I* figured out this morning, when my brain finally had a lucid moment. They're the ones who called the other volunteers. They claimed to be Nadine and told the volunteers they weren't needed. The only way Shirley and Mercy could have done that was by getting into the volunteer file, in an office, where they didn't belong."

"You're going to hold that over their heads? Think it'll work?" she asked.

"I'll let you know."

"And I'll run pick up lunch at Mel's and put it on your tab."

Almost as soon as Ardis left through the back door, Ernestine came in through the front, decked out in her Aunt Bee outfit. She was a serious Aunt Bee, though. An Aunt Bee who needed to tell Andy or Opie she meant business.

"I'm going to go see Grace again," she said. "She's been in jail almost a week now, and she must be feeling quite anxious."

"That's a really nice idea, Ernestine."

"I'm going to apologize for misleading her last time."

"Um, yeah?"

"We need her help, Kath. I'd like your permission to tell her about the posse and ask her specific questions without beating around the bush. She might not be able to answer them. She might not know any more about Phillip's recent life than we do."

"But it's worth a try. You're right."

"Last time I went to see her, it felt more like fun and games. This time we need her, but I'm also much more certain that she needs us."

Ardis came back with two servings of Mel's black bean and yellow rice salad, extra jalapeños, and more of the spicy flatbread.

"Serious food for serious work," she said. "I feel like we're spinning our wheels on both investigations. I hope that's not an indication that we can't handle more than one at a time. I'd hate to think we're less competent than the sheriff's department."

"This morning we proved that we're *more* competent." I passed her my flatbread, because she'd eaten hers, and I told her about Jerry's slide show. "There's no real proof yet of who they are. But what Jerry and Zach found fits the story I heard, and it should be possible to date the remains from several of the artifacts—the length of the corset stays, the style of the dentures. Maybe we'll be unbelievably lucky and find the sales ledger from the store where the locket was bought and engraved. Sometimes they turn up in archives or historical society collections. I know it's them, Ardis, and if you'd seen the lead shot embedded in the skulls . . ."

"Mattie and Sam," Ardis said. "It gives me the shivers. I would say someone is walking over my grave, but think about it—people have been walking over their grave all these years." She shivered for real then, and I saw why.

Geneva hovered next to her. "I want to see their grave."

Ardis pulled a shawl from under the counter to wrap around her shoulders, then sat down on the stool.

Geneva floated over to hover in front of me. "Will you take me?"

"I don't know what's wrong with me," Ardis said, looking at me through Geneva. "Is there a bug going around?" She blinked, then rubbed her eyes.

Geneva looked at Ardis over her shoulder. She waved her arm up and down. Ardis put her hand over her eyes.

"This is very interesting," Geneva said. "We should talk about it after you take me to see dear Mattie and Sam."

Geneva peppered me with questions up both flights of stairs to the study in the attic. I didn't know any of the answers, so I didn't say anything. Her last question came with an impatient, though soundless, stamp of her foot.

"But what does it *mean*?" she asked.

"I don't know."

My answer and the silence of her foot stamping the attic floor frustrated her. She threw herself into the window seat. Argyle, roused from another nap, said, "Mrrph."

"I don't know why, Geneva. Ardis is more aware of you, and I'm not sure what to do about it."

"What do you mean 'do about it'? Is it such a terrible problem to see ghosts?"

"No-o."

"You're lying."

"No, no, I'm not. The problem isn't in *seeing* ghosts. The problem is in other people *not* seeing them while you *are* seeing them. You know that. We both know that. But the problem right now is that she doesn't *quite* see you and it's making her crazy." *Crazy.* I looked at the place in the wall where Granddaddy had made the clever hidden door and the cupboard behind it—the cupboard Geneva called her room, the cupboard where Granny had kept her private dye journals. What if I found something in those journals—a plant dye that helped someone see ghosts, or protected them from seeing ghosts? What were the ethics involved in making the decision to use something like that?

"Will you take me to see Mattie and Sam's grave?" Geneva asked quietly.

"Yes."

Ardis had recovered from her "bug" by the time I went back downstairs. She waved away my suggestion that she take another afternoon off. I didn't pester her about it. I knew she wouldn't have any more problems. Geneva had agreed to stay in the attic until I came to get her.

We stayed busy the rest of the afternoon. It was the steady kind of busy—three skeins here, an embroidery kit there, a lace shawl pattern and the cashmere to knit it—that didn't rush us off our feet, but made the register till happy.

"No time for our thinking caps, though," Ardis said. "And we have operatives who want to report in."

Ernestine had stopped by when she left the jail but hadn't stayed. John called and said he'd call back later. Late in the afternoon the back-door chime said "Baa" and Zach wandered in.

"Ardis, I'd like you to meet Zach Aikens, the man who discovered the elbow that led to Mattie and Sam. Zach, this is Ms. Buchanan. She's like me; she thinks she's a detective, too."

"Nice to meet you, Zach. Are you kin to Ezekiel Aikens?"

"Yeah. Why?"

"He's a fine man. He did me a kindness when my husband passed."

"Yeah? What?"

"That's between him and me. But the next time you see him, tell him Vernon Buchanan's wife says hey, and then go ahead and ask him. It was a pleasure to meet you, young man."

Ardis shook Zach's hand with both of hers, and then went to help a new knitter choose needles and yarn for her first scarf. Zach stuck his hands in his pockets and studied the mannequin and its quilted jacket.

"This is your first time here, isn't it? What do you think of the Weaver's Cat?"

He looked around, giving the bins of yarn and the racks of notions and patterns the same serious attention he'd given the mannequin. A display of hand-painted roving caught his eye.

"What's that for?"

"Spinning. It's carded wool. The different colors of dye were brushed on by hand."

He went to check it out, and a group of chattering, laughing women swarmed the counter. I rang them up and answered their questions. The camel bells jingled at the front door, and when I looked over, Zach had left the building.

"I know the posse met on Friday," Ardis said when we had a moment alone at the counter, "but I think we should call a special interim meeting. I'd say tonight, but it's Daddy's bath night and that's more than enough excitement for him or me. If you think tomorrow's time enough, I'll go ahead and call the others."

"Sure, that'll give us that much more time to learn something." Besides, I'd promised to take my ghost to visit a grave.

# Chapter 28

"**A**re you sure about this, Geneva?"

"I am feeling calm and confident. Do you see my hand? It is hardly shaking. Would you like me to drive? You look as though you might be having a case of the nerves."

"Thanks, anyway. I think I'll be all right driving."

I might be having a case of the nerves. More likely it was a case of early-onset lunacy. Driving didn't worry me, though. It was what we planned to do after we parked and got out that had my stomach dancing a jig. And not because we were going to sneak onto the grounds of the Homeplace after hours—been there, done that. But we were going to visit Mattie and Sam's grave after dark, because Geneva told me if Mattie and Sam were around, that would be the best time to find them.

"But you're around in daylight," I said as we left the friendly lights of downtown Blue Plum behind.

"I have been awake a long time. Mattie and Sam might be shy or frightened or unhappy. Like cats or dogs that have not had families caring for them."

"They're *feral* ghosts?"

"Please do not be like that around them."

"Sorry. How come all of a sudden you know so much about other ghosts?"

"Perhaps I am maturing."

"What if they aren't there?"

She didn't answer, and we drove the rest of the way in silence. This time I didn't make the mistake of parking at the Quickie Mart. I'd seen an old forest road beyond the Homeplace Saturday when Joe and I had gone to look for otters. I found it, turned in, and stopped.

"What are you waiting for?" Geneva asked when I didn't get out right away.

"For my eyes to get used to the dark."

"Trust me, they never do."

Walking down a country road in the dark with a ghost—not what I could have pictured myself doing six months earlier. What a sheltered life I'd led. Geneva started humming the dirge-like lullaby she loved, and together we made our way back to the Homeplace, around the security gate barring the drive, and toward the silhouette of the barn.

"Geneva? Are you really sure about this? Is there anything you want me to do?"

"Stay with me."

We skirted the barn, and I heard Portia and her brood snorting comfortably in their sleep. On the far side of the barn my feet slowed. A high moon shone down, but the slight breeze seemed to carry its light away before it reached us. I led Geneva to the excavation square and we stood at its edge looking down at the cold, black bottom of the pit.

And waited.

"Are they here?" I finally whispered.

"No."

"I'm sorry."

"They are in the field, and he is coming with his gun."

"You can see them? Where?"

She floated over the pit, leaving me behind. I picked my way around the black hole and stumbled, trying to catch up.

"Geneva? Where are we going?"

"To warn them."

I couldn't see what she saw, but we went toward the woods. The farther we went, the clearer she became, so that if it had been daylight, I knew I would see the details of her bodice and skirts, the heels of her shoes, and the coils of her hair. Her skirts tangled as she ran and kept her from going very fast. I was able to keep up, despite the dark. When we reached the trees, she didn't stop. I did for a second, but then I was afraid I'd lose her, and I went into the woods after her.

She'd found an old logging road—had she known it was there?—and we followed it, walking now. It hadn't been used as a road in years and hadn't ever been more than an unpaved cut through the trees. I picked my way along the uneven ground, and then I realized she was doing the same, and stumbling from time to time, no longer floating. We went downhill and crossed the creek, and there the road forked. One fork became a path, following the creek. We took the other, which ran out into an open field. As we reached the edge of the woods, Geneva cried out. She ran forward, caught hold of a tree for support, and stared at something in the field I couldn't see.

Then she screamed and ran back toward me.

"Geneva! Wait!"

She veered and ran down the path alongside the

creek, whimpering and stumbling, looking over her shoulder, and turning and running again. She ran until the path turned away from the creek and became lost in a rocky outcrop. She climbed over rocks the size of chairs and tables, and then tried to scramble up and over one the size of an elephant. Her long skirts made it almost impossible. She did make it, though, and crawled across the top. Then she turned around to let herself down the other side—but with a look of surprise and another scream, she fell from view.

"Geneva!"

My jeans and sneakers made climbing the rock easier, but I inched my way across the top, afraid of what I would see on the other side. What I saw was Geneva below me, looking up, reaching for help. She'd fallen into a space between rocks, a deep hole, and only her terrified face and reaching arms were visible. I fell to my stomach and reached down for her.

"Grab my hands, Geneva!"

She didn't see me. She wasn't looking at me. She was reaching for someone else. I looked over my shoulder and saw nothing. No one was there. She cried out again, and I turned in time to see her head drop back. Blood welled up on her forehead, her eyes closed, and her hands—her arms—fell limp, no longer reaching for the help that was denied them. Without another sound, she slipped away into the opening between the rocks, and was gone.

*"Geneva!"*

I stared at the dark place she'd fallen into, where no one would ever find her. All around me, the woods and the creek and the night murmured and gurgled and rustled—and she was gone. I'd watched her disappear and I hadn't been able to do anything about it. But what had I witnessed? *She* had been a witness. She saw who killed Mattie and Sam. She went to warn them he had a gun. She got there too late. He saw her and chased her. She escaped over a rock and fell into a hole—a cave opening? A sinkhole? She reached for help. He hit her on the head, and she fell to her death.

"I followed him." She was suddenly crouching next to me on the rock, and I thought my heart would stop from the shock of seeing her again. "He followed me. Then I followed him. Come on." She'd become watery and nearly transparent again.

"Wait! Wait. He saw you fall. He *hit* your head and made you fall. Who was he?"

"He had hair the color of corn silk. He was so pale in the moonlight above me, I remembered him as a ghost. He thought he loved Mattie, but if he had he wouldn't have killed her. He was Lemuel Umstead."

"Why didn't he bring Mattie's and Sam's bodies here and put them down—what is that, a sinkhole?" I looked back down at that awful opening. *"Oh."*

"I sat up here and watched him sweat to lever those rocks into place," she said. "There is still a space at the edge where people have been throwing beer cans. But he made sure no one could climb out."

"But I just *saw* the hole."

"You saw its ghost."

"But you haven't seen Mattie's or Sam's ghost. *Are* they ghosts?"

"I do not think so."

"Why not?"

"As I have said before, I am only dead. I am not an expert. I followed him. Come on. We will, too."

The outcrop of limestone boulders was difficult enough to negotiate alone. Why try to do it with two bodies—especially up and over the mammoth rock we were sitting on—when a convenient alternative lay not too far down the logging trail?

"Where are we going?" I asked.

"I think we already know."

She didn't say anything else. I slid down off the rock. She floated beside me all the way back to the barn at the Homeplace and then to the cottage where I'd met her.

"I followed him home."

"Did you watch him bury Mattie and Sam?"

"I couldn't bear to."

"Did you haunt him?"

"I meant to, but he died before he had time to feel much guilt. Cholera is a terrible plague. It robbed me of friends and it robbed me of retribution."

"I'm sorry, Geneva. I'm so sorry all of this happened."

"Are you sorry you met me?"

"No."

"Then there is a silver lining to the sinkhole."


Shirley and Mercy helped the students start piecing their quilt blocks together the next morning. They fussed when they realized Zach wasn't there and that he'd taken his block home with him. I told them not to worry, that I was sure he'd be back. They didn't seem to believe me. I wasn't so sure about it myself.

"You look peaky," Shirley said partway through the morning.

"Like you could use a nap," said Mercy.

"I'll step out for some fresh air."

I hadn't slept well. I'd been worried about Geneva

and about how reliving her death might affect her. She'd grown quiet on the drive back to the Weaver's Cat, and I'd stayed in the study until well after midnight, keeping an eye on her while I'd read Granny's private dye journals. I'd finally left when Geneva complained about the desk light keeping her up. It was keeping me up, too, so I'd gone home. But as soon as I'd closed my eyes, I'd been back in the woods following her.

I took a walk down the hall to wake myself up, and noticed Nadine's office door open a few inches. I hadn't seen her yet that morning and decided to say hello and find out what the plans were for the program's closing reception. I heard her moving around, and started to knock, but as I raised my hand, she pushed the door closed. *Good morning to you, too,* I thought, which was unkind, because she hadn't known I was there.

John came out of the storage room and waved when he saw me.

"I'm on my way to the courthouse and then the library," he said, "and I'll be at Ardis' tonight. I've made progress, though it's hard to say toward what."

He opened Phillip's office and ducked behind the door to put the storage room key in the box. I looked at the copier and wondered if I could ever get Clod to tell me what document he'd found there. Would it make any difference?

"You look tired, Kath. Don't let these investigations get you down."

"Not a chance."

"Good. The photographs you sent are quite interesting. They opened up the line of research I'm following this morning."

I put a finger to my lips. "That's great, John," I said at

normal volume. "I've made progress, too," I said more quietly. "See you tonight."

Geneva insisted on coming with me to Ardis' for the meeting.

"Do you feel how we bonded last night?" she asked as we went up Ardis' front steps. "Yesterday we were just best friends. Today we are a duo. No, we are better than a duo. Duos are too plain. We will be inseparable. An inseparable super-sleuthing duo like—"

Ardis opened the front door and the theme music for *Dragnet* blared out at us.

"—Joe Friday and Bill Gannon. See you later, Bill." She zipped ahead of me and disappeared into the den with Ardis' daddy and his TV.

"Was that a moth?" Ardis asked. "Come on in before we let them all in."

Ernestine and John were already sitting at the kitchen table. Mel came in behind me. Joe was in the den keeping Ardis' daddy company.

"Thea can't make it," Mel said. "And I didn't bring treats. We need to concentrate, cogitate, and get out of here at a reasonable hour."

"Good plan," I said. "Mind if I start? I heard the preliminary report on the skeletons." I told them what I'd told Ardis the day before. "I must say, I'm surprised we haven't had a visit from Deputy Dunbar congratulating us on our fine work. Or at least a phone call."

"Although he'd be the first to point out that we aren't more than ninety-nine-point-nine-nine-nine percent positive of the identifications," Mel said.

"Slackers that we are. But he'd be right, and I'd still

like to follow up on the other names we have. I have another one to add, too—Lemuel Umstead."

"Piecing together as much of their stories as we can," said Ernestine. "I'd say that's a kind thing to do for all of those who were lost in that dreadful time. Now, may I go next? I've heard some stories of perfectly dreadful behavior and unkind people."

"We'd be delighted," said Ardis.

Ernestine took a notebook from her handbag and adjusted her glasses. "I went to see Grace yesterday. I went again today. Although she seemed talked out yesterday, I thought she might like to talk more this morning, and I was right. We covered quite a wide range of topics, and returned to some this morning for additional details that percolated to the top overnight. I took notes. I also prepared a précis for each topic discussed."

"Bravo," Mel said.

"Thank you, dear. First topic, Grace Estes' opinion of Nadine Solberg. Nadine is not a serious historian. She lacks a sense of stewardship toward the artifacts and the documents supporting the artifacts at the Holston Homeplace Living History Farm. She is more interested in the visual impact of artifacts and buildings than in their historical or social significance. She is a fund-raiser, and as such will be good for the site, as long as there is a real historian on staff."

"Wow." I looked at the others. We were probably all hoping their conversations hadn't gotten around to us.

"Second topic, Grace Estes' opinion of Wes Treadwell. Wes is dangerous. Wes is out for Wes.

"Was that the précis?" I asked.

"The entire opinion. Topic three, Grace Estes' opinion

of Fredda Oliver. If Fredda would give herself time to heal, she would see that the world isn't such a hard place to live in. Topic four, Grace Estes' opinion of Jerry Hicks. Phillip was jealous of almost everything Jerry had. That's really an opinion of Phillip, but you need to hear that to understand what she means when she says that Jerry couldn't be bothered with Phillip's competitions. She knew Jerry's sister, Ellen, better than she knew Jerry, but had lost track of her when Ellen married and moved somewhere out West."

"What about her opinion of Phillip?" John asked. "It goes beyond reporting his jealousy of Jerry, doesn't it?"

"It consists almost entirely of jealousy. She says he was driven by jealousy and imagined slights. And entitlement and self-aggrandizement. She also said he saw himself as an investigative historian, looking for the truth the way investigative journalists do. She said 'he lived for ferreting out facts that would turn accepted history on end.' She also called him 'a breaker.' When I asked what she meant, she said he broke hearts, plates, marriages, friendships. He enjoyed proving people wrong, especially when they were repeating 'true stories.'"

"She loved this guy?" Mel asked. "She still loves him? Are we really going to value her opinions of anyone?"

"They're worth hearing, though," John said. "Taken individually they sound problematic. But she's there in the jail with plenty of time on her hands and a lot on her mind. Taken all together, they sound unvarnished, but well thought out. They're a piece of her story, at any rate."

"And that is a generous opinion, John," Ardis said. "What else do we know?"

"I've been trying to follow Phillip's line of research,"

John said. "To see if he might have been digging for information that ruffled feathers. Or, now that we've heard from Grace, maybe he was about to break something."

"Speaking plain would be good, John," said Mel.

"Specifics. You're right. Unfortunately I haven't come across enough of them yet. But Grace's opinions of Nadine, Wes, and Phillip all play into this. Phillip appeared to be tracing deeds and landowners for the area surrounding and encompassing what's now known as the Homeplace. I've seen some of the documents he was working with. I have some names and dates, and I've seen the casual way boundaries were described using impermanent markers such as trees and fencerows. I think Phillip was questioning Holston ownership of the Homeplace. What if, as an 'investigative historian', he was determined to dig, even if that meant undermining the legitimacy of the site? As I said before, ruinous."

"*Did* he find something?" Mel asked. "Have *you* found proof?"

"So far only irregularities that might mean nothing. But I haven't seen all of his research."

"But the deeds and other documentation still exist," I said. "Phillip's death doesn't change that."

"Unless you have someone in charge who lacks a sense of stewardship, as we've also just heard."

"But all those records are official. They're kept at the courthouse, aren't they?" Ardis asked.

"Many are," John said. "Others have gone missing over the years."

"Oh, hey, you know what else is missing?" I said. "I just realized it. John, when you were putting the storage room key back in Phillip's office this morning, his banjo wasn't there."

That was a conversation stopper, missing banjos being high on everyone's list of Dangerous Situations. And Geneva, hearing that sudden lull in conversation, chose that moment to pop in and start her own.

"The banjo might be lost, but your hackle now is found. That sounds like a hymn of joy, doesn't it?"

"What?" I asked. *"Where?"*

"In my silver-lined sinkhole."

# Chapter 29

"Here in the den," Joe said from the doorway. "He hasn't gone anywhere."

"Sorry—what?" I'd obviously missed something while listening to Geneva.

"Ardis' daddy is asking for her, and you asked where."

"Right, sorry. A little brain fritz going on." I wiggled my fingers next to my ear to show how that problem worked against clear thinking. *The hackle? Geneva saw it?* I dredged up a smile and attempted to make it look natural.

The others, except Ardis, smiled back. Ardis was busy darting glances into corners of the room. There was nothing for her to see, though. Geneva had said, "Oops," when I answered her and gone back into the den.

"Ardis?" Joe called. "Your daddy's trying to tell me about some cousins. He wonders if you remember the names."

"Ardy?" her daddy called from the den, beating out Joe Friday for volume. "Who are they? You know the ones. Live up there thataway. Beyond the pig farm, but not so far as the river. Had a mule fell in a ditch."

"Sarah and Charlie."

"Sarah and Charlie. I knew that."

"Well," Ardis said, with a clap of her hands and one last darting glance around the room, "We've done some good here tonight."

"And next time I'll bring double refreshments," Mel said. "Couldn't hurt. Might help."

"Before we go," I said, stopping them as they moved chairs back and stood up, "how much do any of you know about the woods around the Homeplace? Or the geology of that area?"

"You could ask Joe that," Mel said. "Why? What are you thinking now?"

"Still working it out. I'll let you know. I think we should all be careful from here on out, though. Be careful who you talk to about this, and be careful who hears you talking about it."

"I second that," Ardis said. "Meeting adjourned."

We said our good nights, and Ardis saw the others to the door. I hung back in the kitchen waiting to hear a commercial come on in the den before going in to get Geneva. *The hackle was in the sinkhole. Dropped in through the space at the edge of the rocks Lemuel Umstead had levered into place, imperfectly covering the hole. A hole used as a natural garbage chute for cans and who knew what else. A hackle, for starters.*

Joe came out of the den. "Walk you home?"

"Sure, I'll just go in and say good night to Ardis' daddy." And collect the ghost.

"Hey, now, where'd you go?" Ardis' daddy called from the den. He came shakily to the door. "There you are," he said when Joe went to steady him. "Thought you'd disappeared on me."

"Daddy, you watch your step in those slippers," Ardis said.

"He slipped away on me. Like those others we used to hear about. What were their names?"

"He's been on this reminiscence kick ever since we went out to the Homeplace," Ardis said. "Daddy, you'll have to give me a hint. What do I know about them?"

"You didn't know them, Ardy. You aren't old enough. *I* didn't know them and I'm older than dirt. But we used to hear about them. A cautionary tale for whippersnappers is what they were. Took off during the cholera epidemic and never came home. Gone and not forgiven because they never said good-bye. Brother and sister rascals is what we heard when *we* were young rascals. They were my mother's kin. Her mother's brother and sister. Jenny and Sam. No. Not Jenny and Sam. Sam and Geneva and Sam ran off with another feller's fiancée and Geneva went too. *Rascals.* And I ought to know, because I could out-rascal the best of them. Isn't that right, Viv?"

"He's talking to Mama again," Ardis said. "Daddy, let's get you to bed. Oh my land, I did not see this coming. Kath, I'll call you in the morning."

Geneva had missed the news that she suddenly had a great-nephew and a great-great-niece. She'd been engrossed in an episode of *Gilligan's Island*. She floated ahead of us singing about three-hour tours. Joe naturally said something about it on the way to the Weaver's Cat. I agreed it was an interesting development and admitted I hadn't considered the possibility of finding Sam's and Mattie's living relatives. Then I changed the subject before Geneva quit singing and heard us. It wasn't that I didn't want her to know she had a family. I just wanted to be prepared for when she did find out.

I also wanted time to think about this oddity. For reasons I still didn't understand—and maybe never would—I could see a ghost. See, hear, and talk to her. I suspected that Granny had seen a ghost or ghosts, too. Ardis didn't. Until recently. When Geneva had started feeling "stronger," Ardis started seeing and hearing things. And Geneva was her great-great-aunt. And I'd found a dye in Granny's journal that should help Ardis see Geneva more fully. One oddity after another to think about.

A nice thing about Joe Dunbar was his acceptance of another person's need for quiet and space. Also his acceptance of other people's oddities, such as unexplained detours. He walked with me to the Weaver's Cat, watched as I climbed the steps to the porch, stood for a minute looking at the door, and made a quick, quiet phone call.

"Hi, um, Ginger. Just calling to see how you're doing and to thank you for the silver-lining information you gave me. You actually saw it?"

"Along with bloodstained clothing," Geneva said.

"Wow."

"I did not mention it earlier, because I had other things on my mind."

"I know. Do you want me to come by your place so you can tell me more?"

"What? Tonight? Heavens no. I will be much too busy planning our trap to catch the Heinous Hackler. That is a good name for the villain, and a trap is a great idea. I will go get started immediately." She swirled through the door and was gone.

*Oh dear.*

I turned around, came down the steps, and resumed

the walk home. Joe, bless him, didn't make a single re-mark. I gave him an extra kiss good night in thanks.

I heard someone on my porch shortly after eleven. Joe had gone home. I'd been making the usual sort of racket brushing my teeth. When I'd rinsed and spit and bared their shining glory in the mirror, I heard the scrape of a shoe. Unless it was my imagination. Then something bumped against the front door. The porch swing creaked back, forth, and went quiet again.

Twitching a living room curtain to peek might alert the intruder. On the other hand, the porch light was on, so the intruder wasn't really in stealth mode. In fact . . . I risked twitching. Zach.

I didn't invite him in. I took a large glass of ice water out with me and joined him on the porch. I didn't offer the water to him or drink it myself. He spoke in a low mumble, saying he'd been trying to get up the nerve to tell me something for the past day, day and a half.

"I found this." He handed me the file I'd last seen in the cottage on Phillip's desk. "Actually, these." He turned and pointed toward the porch swing—at something lying on it. A banjo.

"You *found* them? Where did you find them?" From his reaction, I knew mine had been wrong. "Sorry, Zach. It's just that I know where I last saw this"—I tapped the file—"so where *did* you find it? But wait—if you don't want to tell me, you don't have to. If you do tell me, and you got it from somewhere you shouldn't have, I won't tell if I don't have to. Deal?"

"Okay. There's something else, though." He went over to the swing and bent to take something from under it. He straightened and turned with a hackle in his hands.

*"Freeze!* Right where you are, Aikens!"

A light flashed on, bathing Zach's terrified face in brilliant cop halogen.

"Coleridge Dunbar! What do you think you're doing?" I said, trying to imitate Ardis. It didn't work.

"Ms. Rutledge. Step away from the suspect."

"You *called* them?" Zach asked.

"No, I didn't call them, Zach. Deputy Dunbar, turn your light off and leave us alone."

"He threatened you with a huckle."

"Turn your light *off*. Do it *now*. This is *private* property. There is no such thing as a *huckle*. *Got* it?" I was breathing hard and feeling hoarse from channeling my inner drill sergeant. Lights came on at the neighbors' house, one of the beautiful features of living in a small town.

I heard Clod suck a tooth and say, "Yuh."

The light went off, and then I heard another Dunbar join the first one.

"Anything I can help with?" Joe asked.

Zach was slowly backing toward the railing at the end of the porch.

"Hey, Joe. I'd like you to meet a good friend of mine. This is Zach. Zach, this is Joe. He has a canoe and knows how to knap flint. He does not know how to play the banjo. Maybe you two should hook up and take lessons."

Zach sucked a tooth and said, "Yuh."

"Nah, the tooth-sucker is my brother," Joe said. "That stiff guy with the badge and the flashlight. I'm the cool brother."

Zach took some convincing, but Joe and I got him to come inside and tell us the rest of his story. I let Clod come in, too, on the condition he didn't interfere.

"I had things perfectly under control," I said after they'd trooped into the kitchen and were sitting at the table. "I had a large, heavy glass of ice water. I would have chucked it, glass and all, right in his face, if he'd come at me."

Clod rolled his eyes. Joe raised his eyebrows. Zach looked as though he wanted to say, "Cool," but was feeling too cool or too cowed to say it.

The hackle sat in the middle of the table. I felt sorry for it. I would never look at a hackle again and see it as anything but a weapon. Phillip's banjo and file were not on the table. Clod hadn't asked about the banjo on my porch swing, so I'd taken the chance that he'd arrived when Zach picked up the hackle, and missed seeing him hand me the file. I'd brought the file in and tucked it on a bookshelf in passing, slipping it between *Lady Cottington's Pressed Fairy Book* and *A Garden to Dye For*.

"Zach was about to tell me where he found the hackle," I said, "before we were interrupted. Where did you find it, Zach?" I gave him a gentle kick under the table, hoping he'd catch on that we weren't mentioning files or banjos. Besides being cool, Zach was quick.

"Backseat of my car."

"You're *kidding*. Sorry." My interview skills were lacking, but no wonder he'd been wondering what to do.

"Do you keep the car locked?" Joe asked.

"I will now."

"Why come here with it?" I asked.

"It freaked me out. I put it in the trunk, and I've been riding around with it since I found it. Since yesterday. I thought it was the one you said was missing. But why was it in my car, you know? But you're pretty cool, so I thought why not bring it over here? And then this dude"—he pointed at Clod—"he leaps out of the dark with a blinding light, acting like I'm going to hackle your flax stash or something. I mean, get a grip. It's a historic textile tool, not a—" The piece fell into place in front of our eyes. He moved his chair away from the table, looking pale and five years younger. "Crap."

"This hackle hasn't been used for decades at least," I said. "You'd agree with that, wouldn't you, Deputy?"

"We'll have to run tests—"

"No, you won't. I recognize this hackle. Zach and I saw it in the storage room at the Homeplace after Phillip's death. You can trace it by the accession number you'll find on it. And look at it. There's rust and dust and pieces of flax tow in it. No one needs any tests to see that this hackle hasn't been used for anything for years. It hasn't been taken care of properly, either. Zach, I'm glad you brought it here."

"Why would someone put it in my car?"

Clod must have had enough by then. He scraped his chair back. "Prank," he said, standing up. "Kids trying to scare other kids."

Zach didn't look like he was buying that.

"Or I could say it's an Aikens not falling far from the tree."

"I'll walk you to the door, Zach," I said. "And if I find out, I'll let you know."

After Zach left, I had one question for Clod. "Did the sheriff's department issue a statement identifying the murder weapon as a hackle?"

"No. But please don't think this incident exonerates Ms. Estes. It doesn't mean a murderer is still running loose in Blue Plum. Leaving a hackle in the kid's car would be a stupid move, if ever there was one."

Clod left and I asked Joe how he'd happened to appear at exactly the right time.

"I saw Cole when I was on my way home and I followed him again."

"How did *he* happen to be here at the right time? Has he been following Zach? Or did someone tip him off?"

"No idea."

"I need to show you what else Zach found in his car." I got the file and told him what it was. He almost made the tooth-sucking face, but stopped.

"I'm not comfortable keeping this from Cole," he said. "Just so you know. But I wouldn't have shown it to him, either."

"It doesn't feel right. But he would've thought Zach took it or that he was the one pulling the prank."

"Would you like me to be your watchdog tonight? I'm serious. Cole might not think there's a murderer running loose in Blue Plum, but you and I know there is."

"Thanks, but I think I'll feel better if you're keeping an eye on your brother. I'll make sure my doors and windows are locked."

I brought the banjo in and stayed up another hour, sifting through the copied documents in Phillip's file. My eyes blurred sometime past one. Before going to bed, I e-mailed the posse members, asking one question: Had they told anyone else that the murder weapon was a hackle?

Tired as I was, other questions kept me awake after my head hit the pillow. First, what was going through Ardis' head? How did she feel about being related to the

Sam and Geneva I'd been searching for? And then, why hadn't Geneva told me Sam was her brother? But the question that really didn't want to lie down and go to sleep was how would Geneva react when she found out Ardis was her great-great-niece?

Ardis called the next morning. When I answered, I was walking up the back steps of the Weaver's Cat, about to let myself in. I wanted to see Geneva before heading out to the Homeplace. Argyle came running when he heard the back door "baa." Geneva didn't come floating.

"*Hon!* Did you have any idea that *your* Sam was *my* great-great-uncle?"

"No—"

"I've been thinking about it all night, and I wonder— should we have a memorial service for Mattie and Sam? Daddy and I would be honored to bury them in the family plot. What if they've been restless spirits all these years? Then burying them in consecrated ground will give them peace."

"I hadn't thought of that." I scrubbed Argyle's ears and fed him.

"But we haven't found Geneva. You don't think that's because she's the one who shot Mattie and Sam, do you? Her own brother?"

"*No!* Ardis, no, I don't. She didn't."

"You're so sure?"

"I am, and if you'll trust me, I'll prove it. But later."

"All right. I do. Now, what prompted your midnight e-mail asking about the hackle? My answer is no, I did not tell anyone."

I told her about Zach's visit and Clod's dismissal of

the hackle in his car as a prank. I also told her about the banjo and the file.

"Cole might have taken the situation more seriously if you'd shown him those as well."

"I don't think so, or if he had, he would have accused Zach of taking them and lying about finding them in his car. I'll take the banjo back, and I'll give the file to John, if I see him at the Homeplace today. But, Ardis, do you see what it means if no one knew about the hackle except us and the police?"

"I do, but let's wait to hear from the others before we scare ourselves like that."

Geneva sat brooding in the window seat in the study. "You might as well take my badge away," she said. "I've failed."

"Failed at what?"

"Devising a trap to catch the Hackler. I had such hopes, only to see them dashed on their own petard."

"Hm. Well, I think coming up with the *idea* of a trap was super. *I* didn't come up with it. You did. And if someone else in the posse can come up with the actual trap, we'll still owe the inspiration for it to you. You played a key role."

"You are not just saying that?"

"No."

"Do you think the others will like the idea of a tiger pit with spikes?"

"They'll probably go for something more practical. Geneva, I've got some questions I'd like to ask you. I want you to take your time answering them, though, so I'll write them out and leave them here on the desk."

"Someone else might read them if you do. Leave them on the top of the bookcase. You never look up there to see the dust, and no one else will, either."

"Good idea. I'll be back around lunchtime. You can tell me your answers then, or later, or not at all. It's up to you. And if you find them upsetting, then forget them altogether, okay?"

"Can I look over your shoulder while you write?"

"If you want, but I don't want you to answer them right now."

"Then I will stay over here."

I took a piece of notepaper from a desk drawer and wrote my questions. *Did you ever think about the possibility that you have relatives living in Blue Plum today? How would you feel if Ardis could see and hear you? If we can get down to your bones, would you like them brought up and buried in the cemetery?* The last question, prompted by the conversation with Ardis, was hardest for me to write. *If we bury your bones, will I ever see you again?*

The closer I got to the Homeplace, the more on edge I felt. When I parked and got out of the car, I saw Jerry and Fredda laughing together near the barn and I wondered how well they knew each other. Nadine met me at the door and I second-guessed the sincerity of her smile. Wes was there, and I not only questioned his constant presence but caught myself assessing his tanned forearms for muscle tone and weapon-swinging ability. Shirley and Mercy seemed edgy, too. They might have picked it up from me. Or they might have been anticipating the end of Hands on History and the stress of leaving me alone with the Plague Quilt. Zach hadn't shown up, again. That worried me.

Checking my phone every few minutes for answers to the hackle question didn't help my nerves. Over the course of the morning, all the answers came back negative—none of the posse members had told anyone the murder weapon was a hackle. I looked up from reading the last response, and saw Nadine watching me from the door to the auditorium. She probably saw me jump. I used the excuse of helping Carmen with a French knot to break eye contact with Nadine. But in turning to Carmen, I saw Wes passing the other doorway. He paused, lifted his chin toward Nadine, and moved on.

When John arrived to continue his research, he stopped in the education room to say hi, and I had a moment of panic. Why hadn't it occurred to us that if Phillip had been killed because of something he'd found, then John was in danger for trying to follow Phillip's trail? I motioned him over to a corner of the room and asked him.

"It did cross my mind," he said.

I cast uneasy glances around us, feeling like a cheap actor playing a badly trained spy. "Let me show you something." I'd brought Phillip's file in a messenger bag. I held the bag open and let John see inside while I scanned the room for prying eyes.

John gave a low whistle. "Is this the rest of the documents? As the young people say, this is huge."

"I know. And at first I was thrilled. Then I began to wonder." I told him about seeing the file in Phillip's cottage, then about getting it from Zach and about the file and the hackle in Zach's car.

"What was the point of leaving them in the boy's car?" John stroked his clipped white moustache. His eyes, the color of the ocean he'd left when he came home to the mountains, moved from one possibility to another as he thought. If I'd worried about adding to the wrinkles around those eyes, I needn't have bothered. He was puzzling, and anyone could see the energy that gave him.

"May I give you another piece to consider?"

His eyes snapped to mine. "Please do."

"I shouldn't have been in Phillip's cottage to see this file. That's a fact, plain and simple. Here's another fact— Fredda was there that night, too. I don't know what she did while she was there or *why* she was there. I don't know if she saw the file. If she did, she might have gone back and taken it, or she might have told someone else about it. That's totally conjecture."

"A flourish of embroidery that's more of a distraction. There's a word that springs to mind, though. 'Cahoots.'"

A question from one of the students about the Plague Quilt gave me the idea for how to set Geneva's trap.

# Chapter 30

"Ms. Spivey and Ms. Spivey, *are* the names on your Plague Quilt people who died in the cholera epidemic?" Carmen asked. "Because wouldn't it make a cool research project to go find their graves?"

"Do you know how many church cemeteries there are in the county?" Nash asked. "And family cemeteries?"

"Hard work is its own reward," Carmen said.

"Some of them are labeled," Shirley said, reflexively bringing her arms in to protect her sides. She was safe, though. A table stood between her and Mercy's elbow.

"You might've missed the significance," said Mercy, "of the stitched paths leading from some of the coffins."

"You can follow them with your finger," Shirley said, "and recognize the churches. Rebecca was an artist with thread."

"Like us," said Mercy.

I called Ardis before I left the Homeplace and asked her to set up an emergency meeting of the posse. When I got back to the Cat, Debbie was behind the counter and told me the others were already waiting in the TGIF workroom.

"You don't mind staying another hour?"

"My budget is happy to do it and so am I."

I dashed up to the workroom. Thea, Ernestine, John, Ardis, and Joe were there. Mel couldn't make it, for obvious reasons. I stopped at the door before running up to the study.

"Joe, do you mind telling Ernestine and Thea about the stuff in Zach's car? I'll be right back."

"Lunch hour ticking away," Thea called after me.

Geneva and Argyle were in the window seat, feet and paws tucked under them. It was a scene I'd grown used to and would miss terribly if . . .

"The posse's having a quick meeting," I said. "I figured out how we can set the trap. Do you want to come hear about it?"

"You can report to me later," she said. "Right now, Argyle and I are discussing metaphysics. We are thinking, therefore we do not wish to be disturbed."

I crept quietly back down to the workroom.

"I want you to know I get it," Thea said as soon as she saw me. "I get it that if no else but us and the police know about the hackle, then you think the murderer has to be the one who left the hackle in the kid's car. But why would the murderer do that? To frame him? That's the clumsiest frame job I've ever heard of." She sat back and crossed her arms.

"You're right. Absolutely." I joined them in the half circle of comfy chairs. "That's why I think we need to look at it another way. Remember the question I wrote on the whiteboard Friday—*What kind of person thinks killing someone fixes a problem?* All right, then what problem did leaving the file and hackle in Zach's car fix? Because Thea's right, it makes no sense as a frame job. Grace is already in jail and the police aren't looking for anyone else."

Thea opened her mouth and pointed her finger at me. Nothing came out of her mouth until she'd closed it and opened it again. "That's the first thing you've said that might make me think Grace is innocent." She crossed her arms again. "Unless Grace is working with someone on the outside."

"You don't believe that."

"Instead I'm supposed to believe the murderer has a vestigial conscience?"

"What conscience?" Ardis asked.

"Kath thinks the murderer feels bad about Grace being in jail, but instead of confessing and going to jail in Grace's place, the murderer left a 'message' for the police—a message that only the murderer could have left—so the police will know they have the wrong person."

"Except the police didn't interpret the message right," Ardis said.

"That's because the murderer doesn't know how Cole thinks," said Joe.

"But why leave the file as well as the hackle?" John asked.

"To tie the hackle to Phillip and the case," I said. "Otherwise the hackle's just a hackle."

"But Cole didn't see the file," Ardis said.

"I know. And that might have been a mistake on my part, but I think Cole still wouldn't have read the message right if he'd known about the file, and he would have caused trouble for Zach."

"So, what's this meeting about, then?" Thea asked. "We haven't learned anything new, except that I'm willing to believe Grace is innocent. That's major, I admit, but except for eliminating Fredda, we aren't any nearer to figuring out who *is* guilty."

"And what if Fredda is working with someone else?" I asked.

"Oh swell."

"But we *have* learned something about the murderer," Ernestine said. "He or she has a conscience, however tiny, and also isn't familiar with the thickness of our local police skulls. Begging your pardon, Joe."

"Much good that does us," Ardis said. "None of the suspects are local. What now?"

"A trap."

"Beg pardon?" Ardis spoke, but judging from the others' expressions, she spoke for all of them. At least I knew I had their attention.

"I've got it all worked out. A plan, a map, a trap, voilà!—we catch a murderer."

"Just like that," Thea said. "Voilà! And what could possibly go wrong?"

"It involves the Plague Quilt," I said, ignoring her. "Of course, we could turn this information over to Cole instead."

"Let's hear the plan." Again, Ardis spoke for all of them.

"Quilts tell stories—"

"Rev it up," Thea said. "Lunch hour is still ticking away."

"Rebecca, who made the Plague Quilt, turned it into a record of the cholera deaths of her friends and family. In addition to the pretty and fanciful embroidery on it, she stitched maps showing where some of the victims are buried. They aren't precise maps, but the places are recognizable. It gave me an idea—"

"Nutshell it," Thea said.

I held up my left index finger, being careful not to use

it aggressively. "Fact: The hackle is in a sinkhole, along with bloodstained clothing." I held up my right index finger. "Plan: We tell the suspects we're researching the quilt and the epidemic, and we found a story about a young woman falling into that sinkhole and dying because no one could get her out. We tell them we're going to send down a video camera to see if we can see anything. We hide and wait. The murderer comes and either tries to retrieve the hackle and clothing, or more likely, to put more stuff down the hole to cover them. Voilà, we trap a murderer. That's the nutshell edition. The full-sized cedar-chest version comes with details on timing, gives tips on lying in wait, and tells how I know where the hackle is."

Thea called her coworker at the library to say she was going to be unavoidably delayed.

The full-sized cedar-chest version of finding the sinkhole and hackle was edited and revised, but near enough to the truth. I rationalized any embellishments by telling myself that all good stories and quilts have them. I told the posse I'd overheard some of the students talking about a place they liked to go in the woods, to drink, mostly. They claimed the spot came complete with nature's own garbage chute so they didn't have to carry out empties. I'd asked them to show me what they meant, because I was interested in garbology.

"They showed you, a grown-up, where they go hide in the woods and drink?" Thea asked.

"They said I'm cool. Anyway, the opening isn't big, but it is big enough for a hackle. Actually, it looks like the opening *is* bigger, but at some point someone shoved a rock over it and piled a few more on top, probably for safety reasons. But still, right along the edge, is enough space to dump your bottles. When I saw it, I realized it was the perfect place to get rid of a hackle, better even than a retting pond. So I took a look."

I told them I'd attached my camera and a flashlight to a rope, put the camera in video mode, and lowered it into the hole.

"You had rope with you?" Ardis asked.

"I went back. It's creepy there when you're alone. And the hole is deep. I'd hate to see anyone fall in it." My shoulders had drawn together as I talked about the hole and pictured Geneva disappearing into it.

"And you found the hackle and the bloody clothes," Ernestine said. "What a terrible sight."

"Can you show us your video, Kath?" John asked quietly.

"That's the bad news. The footage isn't there. It's not on my camera. I must have deleted it." This was such a tremendous lie, but my shoulders, still drawn, spoke of such misery that they believed me, and forgave me, and Ernestine blessed my heart.

"The good news is, we don't need to depend on a camera tied to a rope for the trap. Tomorrow afternoon we tell Nadine, Wes, Jerry, and Fredda the story about the young woman and the hole. We tell them we've got someone coming at seven tomorrow evening with a professional camera and lighting so that everything in the hole will show up. We make it sound as though it's really going to happen and there's no way for anything down that hole to hide. We need to give the murderer a window of opportunity to cover his or her tracks, but not too much time, because we can't sit out in the woods waiting all day. What do you think? Give them an hour? Two?"

"Two ought to do it," Joe said. "Tell them at five that it's happening at seven. That gives the murderer time to make a plan without too much panic."

"And a murderer who isn't in a total panic is probably a plus." I looked around at them. "Does this really seem doable?"

"Where do we hide?" John asked.

"There are plenty of trees and car-sized rocks," I said. "But we don't all have to be out there hiding."

"The hiders can be in place before the suspects are told," Ardis said. "That way the trap is set in case the murderer hares off immediately."

I asked them again. "Doable?"

"Doable, definitely," Thea said. "And if no one shows up, no big deal. There's no expense involved and only some of us get bug- or snake-bitten. I love it. And let me be the first one to volunteer to sit in the comfort of my library and make phone calls to suspects. I mean, really, what could possibly go wrong?"

In the end, we decided several things could go wrong. But as Ernestine said, we might also set something right.

# Chapter 31

"**S**hall I tell you why the posse works so well together?" Ardis asked during a lull in business later in the afternoon. "I've been giving this some thought. It's because, to a greater or lesser degree, each of us has a quixotic streak."

"You're sure it's not just a love for harebrained adventures?"

"It's what Ernestine said. We like to set things right."

"I can see that."

"And in this case, a tiger pit is going to do the trick for us," she said.

"What?"

"That's the kind of trap we're setting—sharp spikes at the bottom of a hole—a tiger pit."

"She is quite brilliant," a voice said in my ear.

I felt a chill around my neck and Geneva shimmered into view, her arm around my shoulders.

"I wonder which of her relatives she gets her brilliance from?"

Ardis wasn't easy to hide in those woods. John's knees and hips had a dozen years on hers, but they folded without complaint, and he fit neatly behind one of the large rounded boulders. Mel wore a dark knit cap over her spikes and sat behind a huge poplar. Joe leaned his back against a hemlock and became one with the trunk. Ardis moved from tree to rock to rhododendron thicket and finally found a rock behind a tree and was happy after Joe arranged cut hemlock boughs to cushion it.

"There. I'm good," she said, and she took out her knitting.

I went around to check on the others. They were hidden, but alert and ready. And knitting.

"Does a wild Mel knit in the woods?" Mel asked. "Idle hands, Red. Idle hands."

And that, I reflected, was why I would never produce baby hats at the primo posse pace. I went to my own hiding place behind a rock, took out my phone, and put my idle hands to work another way. It was five o'clock. I called Thea, and then Ernestine, and told them we were in position. Then I pictured them each making their two scripted phone calls. Nadine and Wes would hear from Thea that research undertaken at the Homeplace was about to bear fruit. Fredda might be surprised to get a call from Ernestine, but Ernestine would be sweet and charming and tell her why she could expect to see vehicles in the parking lot after hours, in case she was working late. Jerry wouldn't know who Ernestine was, but she would tell him that she'd heard of *him* and knew he'd be interested in the search for the sinkhole skeleton.

If I'd taken my knitting, I could have finished the last of the peony pink hats. It would have ended up with embellishments of leaves and twigs, though, so I felt virtuous for leaving it at home. I'd invited Geneva to come see her trap sprung, but she said she was afraid to.

"I do not want to become one of those ghosts who is

caught in an endless loop, reliving one sad moment over and over again," she'd said.

I didn't blame her, so, knitless and ghostless, I waited in the woods. Insects droned. A pileated woodpecker hammered. Ardis' phone rang. She silenced it, but that was the first thing that went wrong. It was five twenty.

At five thirty-five John developed a cramp in his left calf. He whispered an oath, walked it off, and whispered an apology.

At five forty-seven we heard someone coming.

We'd chosen our hiding places with care. Each of us, moving with stealth, was able to get into position so we could see the area around the sinkhole. I held my breath, imagining the others each holding theirs, as we all waited for . . .

Jerry Hicks came whistling down the path. He whistled his way unerringly through the rocks to the sinkhole, stopped midwhistle, and sighed. Then he did what I hadn't quite expected. He started shoving aside the rocks covering the hole. He had the muscle for it, from his years of digging, and it didn't take long for him to uncover enough of the hole that a person might climb—or fall—into it. Geneva had told me that Lemuel put the rocks there, so it didn't surprise me that Jerry could move them away. But after he moved them, he climbed up onto the large rock Geneva and I had scrambled over, the rock she'd fallen from. And he stood at the edge, looking into the hole. Looking like someone gauging the water's depth before a dive—or someone who'd stepped out onto a window ledge.

This wasn't what we'd planned, and I didn't wait for our prearranged signal to come out and confront the murderer. I moved into the open so Jerry could see me, and called to him.

"Hey, Jerry. That's kind of dangerous, don't you think?"

He didn't answer. Mel and Joe came out, still knitting. Jerry looked at them, then looked again. He didn't move, but his forehead furrowed.

"Blast," Ardis said from her rock. "I dropped the whole dang row." She waved when Jerry looked at her, but she stayed seated, trying to recover her stitches.

While Jerry's attention was on Ardis, John moved closer to the sinkhole. When Jerry noticed him, John saluted with his knitting needles and began dancing a jig, moving around the edge of the hole, his face perfectly serious, not saying a word.

"Hey," Jerry said, watching John. "Hey, back away from there. What is this? Why's everyone knitting?"

John kept dancing, moving forward and back.

"That's crazy," Jerry said. "Who is that guy? Tell him to back away and stay back."

"Both of you back away," I said. "I mean it. John, stop it. Jerry, please. Get away from the edge. I've already lost one person down there."

"What are you talking about?" Jerry asked.

"The hole. I don't care about the hackle. I don't care why you killed Phillip. Get away from the hole."

"Who fell in the hole?" Jerry asked.

John stopped dancing, but neither of them moved back.

"Who fell in the hole?" Jerry asked again. "It's impossible. No one's moved those rocks in years."

The edge was like a magnet, and it was going to draw both of them in—the thought made my breathing hurt.

"Geneva fell in the hole," I said. "It's her skeleton down there. She slipped, and Lemuel could have helped her, but he hit her and let her fall. And I saw her fall again. And if she were here now, she would fall *again*. And again and again and again in a horrible endless loop. So get away from the hole. Stop standing there, and get away from it. *Stop* it!"

"I am. I am. I did," Jerry said. But he didn't move away from the edge fast enough for my hysteria.

"Stop it or it's going to happen again!"

"It's not happening again. It's okay." Hands out, trying to calm me, he backed away from the edge. "It's all right. It's stopped. Okay? I fixed it. No one's hitting anyone again. We don't need things happening again." He sat down and pressed the heels of his hands to his temples. "I stopped it."

And then one more thing went wrong. John slipped into the hole.

# Chapter 32

"**Y**ou terrible old man." I leaned over John and kissed his forehead. "What were you thinking?"

"That I'd give him a fright and make him confess. Gave myself one, too. I didn't realize that ledge was quite so far down. I won't lie, Kath. My life flashed before my eyes, and I am heartily sorry for scaring you so badly."

"Goofy old man." I burst into tears, and Ardis wrapped me in her arms while I sobbed for Geneva, who hadn't had anyone to save her.

"Shh, now, shh. Don't talk any more now. You have a good cry. We'll talk later. But did you really see her fall?"

I nodded against her shoulder, and she rocked me like a baby.

"Is she going to be okay?" I heard Zach ask.

"Red? She's cool. She'll be fine," Mel said. "*You've* got nerves of steel. I think you've got a free lunch at my place anytime you want it. And that's fine — a shrug is all I need to see."

Our plan had gone into improv mode as soon as Jerry uncovered the hole. John's jig was his addition to the plan, and in dancing close to the edge of the hole, he saw the narrow ledge partway down. It must have been the ledge Geneva initially landed on when she fell. Where she was, reaching for help, when Lemuel hit her and sent her to her death.

John's next embellishment to the plan, in his bid to scare Jerry into confessing, was to let himself slip down onto the ledge. But he misjudged the depth and everyone else's reaction too. The interesting part, for me, beyond the sheer panic on top of my hysteria, was realizing how tall Geneva must have been. Her head was still visible in the hole; John—all of five three or four—disappeared entirely.

And that was where Zach entered. Without hesitating, he hopped down onto the ledge and held on to John until Joe and Jerry pulled them both out.

Clod, who had been following Zach, for no good reason any of us could determine, shone his halogen light down the hole.

"It's down there," Jerry said. "Shirt, too."

"We'll send a light down," Clod said. "Maybe a camera."

"Good idea," said Joe.

"See if you find my knitting, while you're at it," John said. "I dropped it."

Clod cautioned Jerry, told him he should wait for a lawyer, but Jerry said he needed us to understand.

"I want you to see why," he said. "This was . . . I didn't plan it, okay? He bullied. Phillip Bell bullied. He broke. He hurt people. He hit women." Jerry's hand came up, rigid as a karate chop, the veins in his neck standing out. "I knew him. I knew him in grad school. He'd do anything to get ahead. He'd do anything to put the other guy down. He did whatever he wanted. I heard about him after grad school, too, from my sister. He hit Grace."

He pressed the heels of his hands to his temples again, then continued more quietly. "You can't be powerless to stop what's happening around you. When it happens again and again. It's an obligation. You have an obligation to make people understand that it has to stop. I didn't save my sister from her husband."

He held his hands out, looking at us as though waiting. But for what? For more words? For us to fill in his blanks from dark spaces we might have in our own lives? No one helped him.

"Phillip hit Fredda," he said. "I saw the bruises. She told me. I went over there that morning to make him see that he had to stop or—that's all. I went to talk. To fix it for her. To stop it. When I found him, he was taking pictures of that thing—the hackle. Of that and the pond for the Web site or a newsletter, and he didn't care why I was there. He laughed and said he might use the thing like a hairbrush on her the next time Fredda misbehaved. I didn't know what that thing was. But it was effective. The camera's in the hole, too. Tell Fredda—it's hers, and she's been looking for it. That's all. But I didn't mean for Grace to go to jail."

"You didn't mean for yourself to go, either," Zach said. "You put that stuff in my car?"

"I didn't know whose car it was," Jerry said.

"Pffft."

Nadine made the decision to cancel the rest of the Hands on History program. From what I heard, the students were disappointed. Their parents were grateful. Shirley and Mercy felt thwarted. I did, too. They tried to back out of their end of the bargain. They had the nerve to come into the Weaver's Cat and tell me. But only enough nerve to come tell me when I was alone in the shop.

"Oh no you don't," I said. "You owe me. In fact, you owe me more than we originally bargained for, because I know you two impersonated Nadine. You called the other quilting volunteers and told them you were Nadine. And I will tell Nadine you did that, if you don't honor your end of the bargain. And I will tell Wes Tread-well that you're spreading stories about him. I think you owe me a one-week unsupervised visit with the Plague Quilt, don't you?"

They agreed and said they would deliver the quilt that afternoon, but if looks could kill, I'd have cholera by nightfall.

When they brought it, I surprised myself by asking them if they'd be interested in teaching a quilting class for the shop. They were surprised, too, and possibly sus-picious. They said they'd have to think about it. I won-dered how I'd tell Ardis, if they said yes.

I shared the Plague Quilt only with Geneva for the first few days. We sat up in the study during the evenings, por-ing over it. She told me what she remembered of the people whose names Rebecca had embroidered on it. She told me about Rebecca, my great-great-grandmother, and about Mattie and Sam.

"Why didn't you tell me that Sam was your brother?" I asked one evening.

"It was my fault they were in that field. I encouraged them to run away. I told Sam to take Mattie away from Uley."

"I thought it was Lemuel."

"We called him Uley. He was meaner than snakes. Al-ways was."

"Their deaths weren't your fault, Geneva." I wasn't sure she believed me.

I took pictures of every inch of the quilt and wrote a full description of the fabrics and stitches, and wrote down Geneva's stories, too. Ghost oral history was a new field for me.

"Do you like the way I deduced you were talking about Ardis when you asked if I had thought about the possibility of having relatives?"

"It was very clever of you."

"I have thought about the other questions you left me. Have they found my bones in the sinkhole?"

"They were able to bring up the hackle and the clothes Jerry threw down. And John's knitting. But for now, to dig down farther would be difficult."

She floated over to the window seat and sat with her feet tucked under her. "I have a home, a cat, friends, and a family. My bones do not need to be disturbed."

Two loose ends were tied up in one afternoon's mail. The first was a letter from Grace, thanking me for sending Ernestine to see her and give her hope. She was recovering from her ordeal with a friend back in West Virginia. She planned to go back to school full-time. She no longer had to worry about money. Phillip had never changed his insurance policy, and she was his sole beneficiary. The second loose end was an article in the *Blue Plum Bugle* about the library receiving a generous grant for materials and programming from the Holston Family Foundation. Thea and Wes both smiled in the accompanying photo. Ardis and Mel were of the opinion that Thea's objectivity, where Wes and the Holstons were concerned, had been compromised while her grant application had been under review.

Joe and I stopped at Mel's for an early supper that same evening, before setting out to look for otters again. Clod was there at a corner table. With Fredda. Clod turned a gentle shade of pink above his collar when we went over to say hello. Fredda winked at me. Clod handed me a folded piece of paper.

"You saw it on the machine in Bell's office," he said. "It's a copy."

I opened it, looked at it, and then looked at him.

"Actually a copy of a copy," he said. "Nothing valuable."

I refolded it and put it in my pocket.

Clod was wrong, as he so often was. It was a treasure. That it was a copy of a copy didn't matter. It was a double image—two small, delicate drawings—a sketch of a young woman's head and shoulders and a close-up of the cameo locket she wore. The artist had signed her name— *Geneva*.

John decided to continue his—and Phillip's—research. I still wasn't sure it was a good idea, but he was hooked.

"It's riveting," he said. "Between the indecipherable antique handwriting and incomplete, misplaced, and missing records, I've got enough to keep me busy for years with no idea what the conclusion will be. It's my own crazy quilt, and it just might make me crazy."

The Plague Quilt was too extraordinary to keep to myself for long. I asked Geneva if she thought we should throw a small party and invite the posse to come see the quilt.

"After all, the quilt played a role in wrapping up the investigation," I said. "Fictionalized, but still, I'm sure they'll love to see it."

"A viewing party!" she said, clapping her hands. "Like a gala gallery opening!"

We set the date for Saturday night, and I sent out invitations. But I sent a special invitation to Ardis, inviting her an hour early, for her own viewing ahead of the others. She accepted, and I spent the next few days with Granny's dye journal getting ready.

"You did not exaggerate," Ardis said when she saw the quilt laid out in the TGIF workroom. "I want to fall into it. I want to walk through it. Your great-great-grandmother was an artist. It's so obvious where Ivy's talents came from. And I haven't asked you about your Geneva—*my* Geneva. I didn't want you to relive that terrible experience again. But do you think my Geneva knew Rebecca?"

"I do."

"I'm so glad. Isn't this extraordinary? Wouldn't it be phenomenal to have a connection to those two women? A letter, a diary, something in their own words to tell us about the quilt?"

"Ardis, close your eyes for a minute, will you? And hold out your hand."

"If you say so."

I tied the green bracelet I'd braided onto her wrist. It was a lovely grayish green and made of cotton with a recipe Granny called "Juniper for Long Lasting and Friendships."

"Open your eyes, Ardis. I want you to meet someone."

She did. And then she opened them wider. Geneva floated in front of her.

"Hon," Ardis said, reaching blindly for my arm. She couldn't take her eyes off Geneva. "Does she . . . does she *speak*?"

Slowly, Geneva floated closer. She opened her mouth.

"Oh my word," Ardis said. "Yes? Do you have a message for me?"

"Y-e-e-e-e-s-s-s-s," Geneva said, swaying back and forth.

"What?" Ardis asked, leaning close.

"Boo!"

# Double Dark Chocolate Devastators

Yield: 30–60 cookies, depending how big you make them

  2 cups all-purpose flour
  ½ cup cocoa powder
  2 teaspoons baking powder
  ¾ teaspoon salt
  4 large eggs
  2 teaspoons vanilla extract
  2 teaspoons instant coffee
  10 tablespoons unsalted butter, softened
  1½ cups packed dark brown sugar
  ½ cup granulated sugar
  16 ounces bittersweet chocolate, melted
  2 cups semisweet chocolate chips

Preheat oven to 350° F.

Whisk flour, cocoa, baking powder, and salt together in a large bowl. In a separate bowl whisk eggs, vanilla, and instant coffee together until coffee is dissolved.

Beat butter and sugars together in a large bowl until light and fluffy, approximately 3–6 minutes. Stir in egg mixture. Beat in melted chocolate, scraping sides of bowl as necessary. Stir in flour mixture until combined. Stir in chips.

Scoop dough into balls, 1–3 inches in diameter, and place on a parchment-lined baking sheet, spaced about 1½–2 inches apart. Bake until edges are set and tops are cracked but centers are still soft and underdone, approximately 10–12 minutes. Let cookies stand on the baking sheet for 10 minutes, then transfer to a wire rack.

# Spicy Flatbreads

2 cups unbleached bread flour
¾ cup water
2 teaspoons cumin seeds
1½ teaspoons peppercorns
1 teaspoon salt
¾ cup fresh cilantro, chopped
2 tablespoons unsalted butter, softened

Put flour in a medium bowl, making a well in the center. Mix in water to form a soft but not sticky dough. Turn out onto a lightly floured board and knead until smooth, about 5 minutes. Rinse out the bowl, set dough back in the bowl, cover with plastic wrap, and let sit for 30 minutes.

While the dough is resting, dry-roast the cumin seeds in a small skillet over medium heat, stirring constantly until they start to change color. Transfer to a spice grinder or mortar and grind to a powder. Set aside in a small dish. Dry-roast peppercorns in the same way, grind, and set aside. Put the salt in another bowl and the cilantro in another.

Divide the dough into 8 pieces. On a lightly floured board, roll one piece of the dough into a 5- to 6-inch circle. Spread ½ teaspoon butter onto the dough, then sprinkle ¼ teaspoon cumin, ¼ teaspoon pepper, ⅛ teaspoon salt, and 1 teaspoon cilantro onto the dough.

Roll up the dough fairly tightly, as you would a jelly roll, to make a cigar shape. Coil the roll into a flat circle.

Flatten gently with your hand, then roll out to a circle 5–6 inches across and less than ¼ inch thick.

Heat a lightly oiled cast-iron skillet over medium heat. Cook the bread for 1½–2 minutes on the first side, until lightly golden. Turn and cook for 1 minute on the other side. Assemble and shape another bread while the first is cooking. Serve breads warm or at room temperature.

# Crazy Mug Rug or Hot Pad

Designed by Kate Winkler, Designs from Dove Cottage, 2014

Designed for Molly MacRae's *Plagued by Quilt*

**MATERIALS:**

*Assorted scraps of felt—bits of felted sweaters work best, but craft felt will also work*

*Embroidery floss, perle cotton, or needlepoint wool in colors to coordinate with felt*

*Sewing thread in a neutral color*

**TOOLS:**

*Crewel or embroidery needle with eye large enough for your thickest embroidery fiber*

*Scissors*

*Pinking shears (optional, but recommended)*

*Pins*

**INSTRUCTIONS:**

1. Cut a circle from one piece of felt: 4½–5" for a mug rug, 8–9" for a hot pad. This will be the base.
2. Arrange random scraps of felt on top of the base to cover it—don't worry if they extend beyond the edges of the base. Do not overlap edges of scraps; rather, butt the edges together like the pieces of a jigsaw puzzle. Trimming edges of scraps with pinking shears will facilitate butting them together smoothly.

3. It's helpful to take a digital photo of your final arrangement to refer to during sewing.

4. With sewing thread, whipstitch scraps together, skimming your needle through the felt—you don't want the sewing thread to show on the other side of the patchwork.

5. Using the base as a template, trim patchwork to same size and shape.

6. Turn patchwork over to unstitched side. With embroidery fiber, embellish joins between scraps with whatever color and stitch strikes your fancy, e.g. feather stitch, fly stitch, herringbone, etc. Chain stitch "vines" with lazy-daisy "leaves" and flowers; French knots are nice, too. You may add flowers or other figures in the centers of some patches.

7. When patchwork is embellished to your satisfaction, pin it to the base and stitch through both layers ¼" from the edge—a simple running stitch will do, but you could work around it in blanket stitch if you prefer (again, trimming the edge with pinking shears can help you evenly space your stitches).

8. If your finished mug rug or hot pad is wavy, press it with an iron set to "steam" and the appropriate heat setting for your felt.

Read on for a sneak peek at
the next Haunted Yarn Shop Mystery,

# KNIT THE USUAL SUSPECTS

Coming in fall 2015 from Obsidian

Waiting for twilight would have been a good idea. Waiting for full dark, even better. I would've been less conspicuous, anyway. A sunny weekday morning was hardly the best time for scuttling up the courthouse steps and sliding behind one of the massive columns—not if I wanted to call myself "sneaky."

I hesitated at the bottom of the steps. My friends and former colleagues back in Springfield, Illinois, might not think so, but from where I stood, Blue Plum, Tennessee, bustled. Crowds didn't jostle me, but in the way of small towns, as long as *anyone* was around, there was a chance that someone would see something and mention it to two or three others. The problem was my own fault, though. If I'd completed my one measly measuring assignment for TGIF sooner, I wouldn't have had to worry now about being surreptitious in broad daylight. The occasional criminal investigation aside, TGIF—Thank Goodness It's Fiber—was not a group ordinarily dedicated to furtive operations, so I didn't want to let them down as we prepared for our first ever clandestine yarn bombing.

The way to sneak successfully, I decided, was to act normal. Eyes open, not casting shifty glances left and right. Shoulders square, not hunched as though ready to creep. Air of confidence. Relaxed smile.

I walked up the dozen worn limestone steps, looking for all the world like anyone else on her way to renew car tags, attend a trial, or probate a will. But at the top, rather than follow an older couple across the portico and through the doors, I stopped, turned around, and pretended to enjoy my elevated view of Main Street.

I didn't really have to pretend. The streetscape, a mix of mostly Federal and Victorian architecture, looked and felt exactly right to me. Pink and purple petunias spilled from half-barrel planters along the brick sidewalks. Window boxes with scarlet geraniums and sweet-potato vines brightened storefronts. Looking right, I saw the bank and a half dozen office buildings and shops and, down at the end of the next block, the sign for the public library. To the left, along past Mel's café, my own shop, the Weaver's Cat, basked in the morning sun. This view, this town, had been part of my life through all my childhood summers when I'd come to visit my grandmother in her hometown. Now, thanks to her generosity in leaving me her house and the Weaver's Cat, Blue Plum was my hometown, too.

I watched Rachel Meeks, the banker, deadhead a couple of geraniums in the planters at the bank's door. Somewhere in her mid-to-late fifties, Rachel's business suit mirrored her straightforward business sense. Apparently, so did her sense of gardening decorum. She carried the withered flowers inside with her. I strolled to the end of the portico, still looking out over the street and assuming I still looked casual; then I sidled around behind the last column, where I'd be in its shadow and couldn't be seen from the steps or the door.

There I took a coil of string from a pocket in my shoulder bag.

A second pair of hands to hold one end of the string would have helped. Unfortunately, my favorite second pair of hands had other business that morning. Joe—the Renaissance odd-job man-about-town who'd worked his way into my heart—had gone over the mountains early to deliver a half dozen fly rods he'd built for an outfitter in Asheville. That was just as well; two of us fiddling around a column would have drawn more attention. I took a roll of painter's tape from my bag, tore off an inch-long piece, and pressed it over the end of the string, sticking it to the column at about waist height.

The plan was to circle the column with the string and mark the string where it met itself again, then remove the tape, recoil the string, return string and tape to my bag, and retreat to the Weaver's Cat. I'd barely started around the column, though, when a familiar voice made me pull back out of sight.

"Ms. Weems, ma'am—*oof*—now, that was uncalled for."

"You're a quack, and I'll tell anyone who asks."

"Let's step on inside, then, ma'am, and you can tell the sheriff."

I inched around the column in time to see Joe's uniformed and starched brother, Deputy Cole Dunbar, ushering a tiny elderly woman through the courthouse doors. The woman, Mayor Palmer "Pokey" Weems' mother, wore tennis shoes, and it was a good thing. As she passed Joe's brother, she hauled off and kicked his shin. He winced, but there was no second "oof." That led me to believe the first "oof" had been a reaction to a different kind of assault—maybe a swift connection between Ms. Weems' pocketbook and his midsection.

Snickering at someone else's pain isn't nice, even if that person is a clod. And even though Cole Dunbar would always be "Clod" to me, I was fairly sure I *hadn't* snickered. But, just before the door closed on him, something made Clod turn toward me and my column. I immediately knelt and retied my shoe, pretending not to notice him noticing me.

"I'm not sure he fell for that," a voice from a little farther around the column said.

At one time in my life an unknown and unexpected voice addressing me out of the blue might have startled me. Not anymore. Now I practically yawned to show how blasé I was about such surprises. I also flicked an inconsequential speck of dust from the toe of my shoe to show I wasn't worried about whether Clod fell for my retying pretense. Then I stood up to see who seemed to think I might be worried. That I *could* see a living, breathing human standing there was a plus, even if I hadn't ever seen him before and had no idea who he was. Judging by the light gray overtaking the dark gray in his beard, I guessed he was in his fifties—older than Clod by at least ten years and Joe by more than a dozen.

"That was one of the Dunbar brothers, wasn't it?" he asked. "Weren't they named after composers?" The camera around the stranger's neck made him look like a tourist. The soft twang in his question sounded local.

"Poets. That was Coleridge," I said.

"And the other one's name . . ." He tried to tease it from his memory by tipping his head and waving his hand by his ear.

"Tennyson."

"That's it."

"Coleridge Blake Dunbar and Tennyson Yeats Dunbar," I said, "except the deputy there goes by Cole and his brother is Joe."

"Smart move." The stranger nodded. "Better than Cold Fridge and Tennis Shoe, both of which I remember hearing when the boys would have been at a tender age. Huh. I haven't thought about them in years. But even back then I wondered how they'd turn out, weighed down with those names." His tone was mild rather than judgmental. It had a reminiscent, storytelling sound to it.

"You're from Blue Plum?"

"Not for a few years, anyway," he said.

Not for a few decades, if he hadn't known Clod was a sheriff's deputy and that Joe was, well, Joe.

"Can I give you a hand with your string there?" he asked.

"Oh." I'd let go of the string when I'd pretended to tie my shoe. The end was still stuck to the column with the painter's tape.

"Measuring it for a school project, right? You hold it there and I'll just—" He picked up the dangling end and walked around the column to meet me. "One of my proudest moments in the fourth grade was when I made my cardboard model of the courthouse. Of course, a flexible metal tape measure would be the best way to do this, but your string works, too."

I took a felt tip pen out of my shoulder bag and marked the string. He pulled the tape off the column, coiled the string, and handed it to me. I tucked it and the pen back into my bag.

"Thanks. It was nice of you to help," I said, turning to go.

And I saw Clod. He'd come back out of the courthouse and stood beside the door in his police-issue posture, arms crossed, watching me and whoever the guy was who'd just helped me with my string-and-column project.

"Hey, Cole," I called, with a wave as wide and insincere as my smile. "Here's an old friend of yours." I pointed over my shoulder, then turned back to my new friend to reintroduce him to his old acquaintance. But no one was there.